Death of a Teacher

Death of a Teacher

Lis Howell

JDON

© Lis Howell 2010
First published in Great Britain 2010

ISBN 978-0-7090-9160-8

Robert Hale Limited
Clerkenwell House
Clerkenwell Green
London EC1R 0HT

www.halebooks.com

2 4 6 8 10 9 7 5 3 1

Typeset in 10/13pt Janson
Printed in the UK by the MPG Books Group

Chapter One

Lo, children are an heritage of the Lord, and the fruit of the womb is his reward.

Psalm 127:3. Folio 31e. **Les Très Riches Heures du Duc de Berry**

The young man stumbled towards the school gates.

One, two, three…

He needed to step really carefully. Outside the car it was much brighter than he'd expected. The glare of the sun made it worse, despite his dark glasses. He had been sitting in the taxi from the airport for so long, he felt disorientated. After this, he would ask the driver to take him and his luggage to his brother's house. But on a whim, he had wanted to visit the school first.

He could see nothing, now, from the corner of his eyes. He stood trying to get his balance and his bearings. Then he slowly shook his head. He was too late. The playground was empty.

Ahead of him, in the school, he could hear a child droning a rhyme in a flat monotone. But the child he wanted to see, really *see*, had already gone.

> *Mr Findley long and spindly*
> *Takes his pills to keep him friendly*
> *Mrs Rudder, what an udder*
> *When she screams it makes you shudder*
> *Fat Miss Hodgy pasty podgy*
> *Cut her up and make her splodgy*

The rhyme was being chanted rapper-style in the school toilets. Alison MacDonald, the new teacher for Year Six, hurried to see which child was still hanging around. But then she heard a little giggle, and the slam of the door. From the corridor window, she saw that the sunlit playground was empty. She shivered, though it was warm. The rhyme went round in her head.

Of course it was just a joke. Kids loved them. One of the younger ones had told her another as he ran out of school that afternoon.

'Miss, what's the scariest number?'

'I don't know, what is the scariest number?'

'Seven.'

'Why's that?'

''Cos seven ate nine.'

She had laughed to please him. But now she had nothing to laugh about. She was alone; it was nearly four o'clock on a Friday. She was waiting to talk to a parent, and her fellow teachers had stampeded off for the first warm weekend of the year. The battered blinds swayed at the staff-room window like broken birds in the April sunshine, exposing the coffee and grease stains.

'I hate it here!' Alison MacDonald shouted, uninhibited, her words bouncing back from the dingy breezeblock walls. She was twenty-five, bright, enthusiastic and confident, and she had never made a mistake like this before. She'd been teaching in Manchester when she'd heard about the job at St Mungo's in Pelliter. It meant taking on the top class in mid-year because their teacher had suddenly suffered a breakdown.

'Go for it,' her own head teacher had said. 'You might not get it, but the interview would be great experience. And you're good, Alison.'

Why not? she'd thought. She knew Pelliter. It was a village with a big council housing estate, on the West Cumbrian coast near her home town. The post would mean promotion; it was a challenge; she could teach more art, her speciality. And she could live with her parents, which was cheaper.

To her surprise she'd got the job. She'd been thrilled. It was a tough school with a great reputation. But now, she had been at St Mungo's three and half months, and it was three and a half months too long. She stood alone in the staff-room and acknowledged it out loud; the realization caused a pain in her gut.

'I've been a fool,' she whispered to the walls. But how could she tell Mark? Her fiancé had been delighted about her coming north to take the job. It wasn't as if they'd lived together in Manchester. She'd had the expense of her own flat, but now living at home would be much more economical while they saved up for a house. She had promised to drive down to Manchester every weekend to be with him and once they were married she would go back permanently. But in the meantime Pelliter looked like a great move.

That was another joke....

She went to the window and yanked the blinds fully open.

A man was standing in the playground, in a suit, with no bag or overcoat. That's odd, Alison thought. Was he a dad? It was unlikely, after all the children had gone home. As Alison watched he turned away from the school, but paused to talk on his mobile phone. Should she go after him? Had he come to see her?

But that was unlikely. Alison had been waiting to talk to a parent because she was worried about one of her class, Molly Spencer. But she had been watching for Molly's mother, not her father. Molly Spencer's dad had decamped long ago, according to the new deputy head, the formidable Liz Rudder. Mrs Rudder was virtually running St Mungo's now, and that was the problem. Mr Findley, the head teacher, was completely distracted. It had been his wife who had taught the top class, and had the breakdown. The upheaval, and the head teacher's anxiety over his wife's illness, had led to the school becoming a jungle which Mrs Rudder couldn't really control. Eleven-year-old Molly Spencer and her friend Becky Dixon were the sort of kids who suffered. They were the odd ones out, in an aggressive environment where the kids fought for attention and advantage in the stress of Year Six. Alison suspected that with Molly her alienation was just a phase. But Becky was different. There was definitely something unusual about her, something that couldn't just be put down to being brought up by her grandparents.

As Alison watched, still wondering if she should go out and speak to him, the young man swayed slightly. He had his back to her and his thick dark hair was blowing in the breeze coming up from the sea. But by the time Alison reached the door to go out and speak to him, he had gone. Maybe he was just lost, Alison thought, although there had been something strange about the way he looked....

She mooched back to the staff-room. Then the visitors' bell rang and Alison hurried to the main entrance. A friendly-looking, fair, spiky-haired woman was struggling with two bags, a bunch of keys, and a couple of books. The woman smiled cheerfully at Alison, and made exaggerated signals through the window. Alison opened the door.

'Hello, you must be Mrs Spencer. Are you with that man who was here a minute ago?' But even as she asked, she knew the man was too young to be Molly's father and that Mrs Spencer was here by herself.

'The chap in the black cab who was just leaving?' Suzy Spencer answered. 'No, he wasn't with me.'

Even odder, Alison thought. There weren't many black cabs in Pelliter. But she put the mystery of the young man out of her mind and said, 'It's good of you to come, Mrs Spencer. Actually, I'm rather worried about Molly.'

A few hours later, Suzy Spencer was back at home, making the supper. She and her partner Robert Clark lived in The Briars, a large double-fronted Victorian house in Tarnfield, a pretty village just east of Norbridge and fifteen miles from Pelliter. When Suzy had moved to the area seven years earlier, the local schools were full and she had happily sent Molly to St Mungo's. Now, though, she regretted it. Rumours were rife about the

Findleys, the head teacher and his wife who had run the school. Ray Findley was a respected headmaster and had married his Year Six teacher after a discreet romance. They were a great team until Sheila Findley's breakdown. It was Mrs Findley's replacement, Alison McDonald, whom Suzy had been to see that afternoon, and she seemed very young, with a lot on her plate. Year Six was always a difficult class, and the breakdown of an experienced teacher had been disruptive. As if that wasn't enough of a crisis, the school atmosphere had been made far worse. The recession-hit local private school was planning to offer last-minute discounted scholarships to local children. The top class at St Mungo's was a seething mass of raging hormones and cut-throat competition.

But Molly Spencer's problems weren't only to do with the mess at school.

Suzy's partner, Robert Clark, was supposed to be scraping the first of the year's new potatoes, but instead he left them in the sink, poured two glasses of wine, and sat down and waited for Suzy to talk. He had known for a while that Suzy was worried about her daughter, but he had tried to be tactful. Puberty was pretty personal and it wasn't something they had really discussed. He suspected Suzy wanted to ignore the changes in Molly until it was all over and she was a beautiful swan. But it wasn't going to be that easy. In the space of a few months Molly had become lumpy, spotty, morose and alienated. And although Tarnfield was a beautiful village there weren't many pre-teens living there. Becky Dixon was the first friend Molly had talked about in weeks.

'Becky Dixon's mother was a drug addict who died. She overdosed when Becky was a baby,' Suzy said, chopping spring onions with concentration. 'Becky's being brought up by her grandparents.'

'And Becky Dixon is Molly's new best friend?'

'Her *only* friend,' Suzy said fiercely, chopping the last onion with such force it bounced on the breadboard. Less than a year ago, Molly had been one of the brightest and most popular girls in the class. Not any more, thanks to the spots and an ungainly growth spurt. Not to mention her recent lack of interest in pop and celebrities, unlike her cool classmates.

'So how did you find out about Becky's background?' Robert asked.

'The new teacher Miss MacDonald told me. It's common knowledge in Pelliter. The Dixons are originally from this area, and they moved back here from Cheshire a few months ago. The grandparents have been very open about the death. Apparently Becky knows everything. They think that's preferable to secrets and lies.'

'And presumably the Dixons took Becky on when she was small?'

'Yes. Becky was only a few months old. Living with her grandparents makes her a little bit old-fashioned, Miss MacDonald says. That's probably why she and Molly get on so well. Neither of them are exactly catwalk material.' Suzy finished mixing the salad and plonked it on the table.

'But Molly's teacher didn't just want to discuss Becky Dixon, did she?' Robert asked gently. He knew Suzy was avoiding the real topic. She sat down opposite her partner and he saw her blink fiercely. It was a release, at last, for her to talk to Robert about all this, but it was also upsetting to face it. The changes in Molly had been so dramatic that she had hardly known what to say to herself, never mind to him. A few nights before, Suzy had dreamt that Molly had been abducted. The perennial parental nightmare. She had woken up flooded with relief. But the child who had returned in Suzy's waking moments had been the old Molly – the pretty, happy one, not this new lump with greasy hair and bad manners. Molly really had been abducted, Suzy thought, abducted by adolescence. It had made Suzy cry, sitting up in bed, hoping Robert wouldn't hear because it was such an awful thing for a mum to think. And Robert wasn't even Molly's dad.

But she had scolded herself for thinking like that. Robert really cared for Molly and her brother Jake, even though he had been a childless widower when they met. Suzy wondered how she would have discovered Robert on a website, the only way to meet a new partner these days – wanted, a childless churchwarden with GSOH willing to take on a crazy agnostic freelance TV producer and her two kids. They'd fallen for each other when she drove into his garden fence – hardly internet dating, but the low-tech way had worked for her. They weren't an obvious couple but they were really very happy and she knew she could trust his judgement, even about something as embarrassing and unexpected as Molly's sudden change.

Robert said, 'You shouldn't worry so much, Suzy.' He hated to see her agonizing. 'At least Molly has this new friend now. It was lucky that Becky joined the class. Even if her background is a bit difficult.'

'But it isn't just a case of her needing friends! Molly's school work has gone downhill even though we know she's pretty bright. And her father phoned yesterday to ask if she had lost any weight. Last time he met her from the train she was wearing those hideous shorts and leggings, and he said he didn't want a daughter who looked like a pregnant page-boy.'

'That was a bit harsh.' But Robert knew where Molly's dad was coming from. Nigel Spencer wasn't the only one to have noticed that Molly wore some odd outfits. 'You do your best, Suzy, but it's really hard. What did Miss MacDonald say? It wasn't all negative, was it?'

'Well, she does think Molly might be good at art. I think that might explain her weird taste in clothes. Miss MacDonald has suggested that Molly paints something as a backdrop for an end-of-term show. It would mean she and Becky could be part of the gang.'

'Art? That sounds promising.'

'I hope so. I've offered to video the art project. It's a big commitment but I'd like to try and help.'

'So Molly's got something you can get involved with, which she can do well and enjoy. And at least she has someone in the class she gets on with. It will get better Suzy, really.'

'I hope so. I feel better for talking to you about it.' Suzy sipped at her wine. 'And Miss MacDonald was perceptive, though she did seem very young to be in that job. You're right, Rob. It's good that Molly has a new best friend.' She paused, thoughtful. 'Although it's not just her background that's unusual. I do get the impression that Becky Dixon is a rather odd little girl.'

A few miles away, Philip Dixon sat on the bench at the top of the rise, where the edge of his land suddenly dropped to the Solway Firth. It was one of his granddaughter Becky's favourite spots. It was warm enough for him to have his sleeves rolled up.

He was surprised to see how young and tanned his own arms looked contrasted with his grey hair. His wrists were only lightly wrinkled, like the pearly shore below him where the soft mud melted into the sea. Behind him, the gorse-covered headland slowly settled inland, to the farms on the outskirts of Pelliter. In the far distance towards the east, the edge of the Northern Pennines made a smudge on the horizon. The place felt good and, as always, he relaxed when he looked out over the Solway.

Two walkers passed him. 'How do,' said the man, trying the Cumbrian greeting.

''Ow do,' said Phil, and smiled. I look like the local bumpkin, sitting here in my cords and check shirt, he thought to himself. But this is all my land, and I'm really the local lad made good. He roused himself from the bench, and felt the comfortable weight of the iron keys in his pocket. Then he scrambled down the path and inserted the keys into the door of St Trallen's Chapel. Phil loved the chapel. No one knew whether it was a folly or had once been a real shrine. But it had been one of the reasons Phil had bought the farmhouse, and the land, when he decided to come back to Pelliter.

Perhaps it had been a mad idea, with all the place's associations, but he had to confess that he had been drawn here. His parents had lived in Pelliter all their lives, starting in one of the smallest terraced houses where Phil had been born, before graduating to a bungalow near the shore. Phil had left home at seventeen to work in the south, like a lot of ambitious young working-class lads did in those days. He had never expected to come back. Then his youngest child, his only daughter, had gone to Cumbria to study art at Norbridge College and the area had started to resonate with Phil again. His daughter had chosen to live with her grandparents – until she had moved to the squat on the Pelliter Estate.

Becky's mother had been creative, innovative, and unconventional. Inside the chapel Phil sat down and bowed his head. He thought of his two sons who had both inherited their mother's practicality. One was an accountant in London, and the other was a teacher in the Midlands. But as always in the chapel – and everywhere else – he remembered his favourite child.

'Oh, Samantha,' he whispered into his cupped hands. 'How could you?'

He asked her regularly when he was alone. How could you? How could you? To die and leave a child, a tiny baby. To take your own life through stupidity and indulgence, expecting everyone else to cope with the mess you left behind. He had always felt an affinity with Samantha and he had been shocked to the core by her death. But his wife Judith's common sense and pragmatism had pulled him through the tragedy, and he was grateful to her for that. And, above all, they had Becky to care for.

The silence of the chapel gave him time to think, unlike the hive of domestic activity at home. He sometimes thought that Judith's way of coming to terms with things was by dashing round in never-ending activity, but she had always been a busy housekeeper, dedicated to the family – to the boys, anyway. It was an ugly truth he rarely dwelt on, but Judith and Samantha had never really got on.

But that wasn't true of Becky. She was a great kid, bright and talented, who loved her grandad and grandma. Her adoption had been almost trouble-free.

Phil stood up and straightened the big picture board on the stone wall of the chapel. It was a copy of a page of the medieval *Book of St Trallen*, showing the young St Trallen weeping in the famous scene where she rejected the pagan prince. The *Book* was the chapel's only claim to fame, once housed here and now safely in the Norbridge Abbey crypt. Phil opened the chapel every morning and locked it at teatime. There was one simple window at the north-east end, and a rusty bell over the door to the south-west. It was very plain. Few people bothered to go inside, besides himself and Becky.

But Phil noticed that the little pewter dish had tumbled off the altar table again. That was very odd, he thought. It was the second time he had found it on the floor. It reminded him that his wife had found a stainless-steel pan lid in the garage early that morning.

'How did that get there?' Judith had said, irritated. She liked everything to be shipshape. She'd be expecting Phil home soon. Becky would be waiting for him too, busy on the computer. She would shake her head irritably when he patted her dark curls and say, 'Grandad, I've told you not to do that. It's childish.' And he would laugh at her and do it again. Becky was a clever girl and that brought problems too. Now to add to his worries, the local private school would be announcing the date of the new special scholarships with temptingly reduced fees. Judith was desperate for Becky to enter. But it would still be a financial struggle and what would be right for his granddaughter?

Phil stood up slowly from the pew, suddenly feeling his age. The calm of the chapel was a rare oasis in his life. He locked the door on the peace, and started the ten-minute walk over the coastal path to his family in the old farmhouse.

That evening at dusk, when the pretty shoreline south of Pelliter was quiet, one of the walkers who had passed Phil Dixon earlier, discovered that she had lost her compass. A few minutes later, she and her husband left their B&B and were striding back along the silent road, looking for it. They panted as they clambered up the softly rounded cliff head. Her husband stopped. St Trallen's Chapel snuggled into the bracken on his left. On his right, there was a sudden dip down to the sea.

'Watch out,' her husband said. 'You could have a nasty fall.'

Then he yelled out. Someone else already had. A life-size puppet in a business suit was sprawled just a few feet below them, its neck at an angle. A mop of dark curly hair was ruffled softly by the breeze. At the sound of the walkers, a foraging animal lurched reluctantly away, darting almost silently through the gorse.

The woman's shrieks went on and on. Her husband had tried to shield her from it, but she pushed his arm aside. She couldn't help screaming at what she saw. The dead man's face had been slashed and he had no eyes.

Chapter Two

Mine eye is consumed because of grief

Psalm 6:7. Folio 65r. **Les Très Riches Heures du Duc de Berry**

The next day, at Norbridge police station, the sergeant from community policing was on the phone to the pathologist at the hospital. It was Saturday morning and Sergeant Liddle had come to work specially. Fatalities were rare when it wasn't a car wreck or domestic violence, and he wanted the information from the horse's mouth.

'So what do you make of it?'

'Well, don't quote me, Sergeant, but the bloke died from a nasty fall. Broke his neck. The face was probably slashed afterwards with one of those cat-skinner knives. That's the only sign of an attack.'

'Why would they do that?'

'Well, if he was being chased and fell, maybe the attacker didn't realize he was dead and went on slashing around the face.'

'Sounds nasty. What are the crime investigators thinking?' Sergeant Liddle had transferred to community policing a few years earlier, but he had kept up his contacts. He disliked going cap-in-hand to the CID for information. The pathologist could supply him with plenty of useful inside gen.

'The man was obviously robbed. There was nothing left on the body of value. In fact, I hear that there were no personal details at all.'

'So it was a violent mugging? In the middle of nowhere? Some wandering thief got lucky, did he?'

'Very funny, but what else do you make of it? Perhaps the chap was walking on the headland and this was his look-out.' The pathologist grunted. 'Or not, when you see what's happened to his eyes. That's the sort of nasty touch these gay-bashers go for. Knife crime is everywhere.'

You don't say, the sergeant thought. As far as the community team was concerned, their job would be to revive anti-knife talks in schools and church halls. And in the meantime the mystery man would stay in the morgue.

Police Community Support Officer Ro Watson had found the body at the chapel hard to cope with. PCSOs didn't usually do death, and it had been her first time at a fatality. She had been sent to the chapel the night before to make sure bystanders didn't gather at the scene, but it had been late and the place had been deserted. When she got there, the body had been roughly covered up, thank goodness. PC Jed Jackson, one of the constables in the community team, had been given the job of taking the walkers back to their accommodation and, while he was away, Ro managed not to look too closely at the slack figure under the piece of tarpaulin borrowed from the farm.

'So who do you think he was?' Jed had said when he got back. They were waiting outside the chapel for the paramedics. The ambulance was having trouble negotiating the sandy track.

'I don't get involved in solving crime, you know,' Ro intoned in imitation of Sergeant Liddle. 'That's not the role of a PCSO.'

Her imitation made Jed laugh. 'That sounds just like him. But seriously, Ro, I'm interested in what you think.'

Ro had rolled her eyes, but she had been secretly flattered. She hadn't expected a younger person to care about her views, never mind a man with deep-brown eyes and a face like a junior George Clooney. However confident you seemed, it was never easy going back to work as a middle-aged woman, and at first she and Jed had merely exchanged platitudes while they waited for the ambulance. But then, the isolation and silence had given them an odd sense of comradeship. Jed was a bit of a loner at the station. He was reputedly a churchgoer with strict views on drink and drugs. But he seemed to enjoy talking to Ro about the local legend of St Trallen. Ro was originally from Liverpool and all this was new to her. As they waited, he told her about the history of the chapel and the medieval frontispiece of the *Book of St Trallen*, which he had seen in Norbridge Abbey. He liked art, he said, and so did she. But inevitably their conversation came back to the covered bump of the body, out of place on the cliff side.

'Is there really no identification on him?' Ro had asked, aware of how strange it felt to be standing in the growing darkness, talking to one young man she hardly knew, about another.

'So they say,' Jed answered. 'But he's not a vagrant. If he was, we'd probably know him round here anyway. He was wearing decent clothes, and a good quality jacket. But apparently there was no wallet or cards or anything.'

'Any sign of a car parked?' Ro asked.

'Not yet. They'll check the bus service, but it's only twice a day along the coast. His shoes were in good nick and smartly polished so he can't have walked far.'

'Then someone must have dropped him off here, don't you think?'

Jed said 'Maybe,' and looked at her with more respect.

It had taken quite a while for the paramedics to get the body on to its stretcher, and down the track to the road. When they eventually said good-night, Jed promised to let her know what the crime scene guys figured out.

The chapel had haunted Ro's sketchy dreams. On Saturday morning, after a virtually sleepless night, she was shattered. She needed to get her twelve-year-old son Ben up, and over to his grandparents in the morning. It was her routine to go to the big supermarket for the weekly shop every Saturday. Her eyes felt hot and scratchy, and while Ben was dilly-dallying around getting dressed in his painfully slow way, she made herself a scalding hot black coffee.

Ro's cottage was an old weaver's house and workshop, one of a cluster in Burnside valley, with three floors built into the river-bank. She had bought it when she moved from Liverpool to Cumbria, and she loved it. Her sitting room led straight from the front door, and in the recess, on the right-hand side of the huge fireplace, was Ro's pride and joy – an original painting in a heavy gilt frame. The rest of the walls were bare, and the room had only a three-piece suite, a TV and Ben's computer. Ben needed more space to get around than other kids. But it looked cosy and the huge basket of spring flowers in the fireplace lit up the plain room. The kitchen was in the base-ment, with one wall taken up by two big windows looking into the valley. The back door led from there to a patio beside the river.

Before going outside, Ro caught herself in the reflection from the back-door window. She was in her mid-forties but she knew she looked older. The product of a hard life, she thought, and laughed at herself, but there was some truth in it. The scar on her left cheekbone was an ugly pink colour compared with the rest of her skin tone; there were deep worry lines on her forehead and a constant crease across the bridge of her nose.

But things are getting better, she told the harassed woman gazing back at her. You have a great home. Ben is improving. And you have a really inter-esting new job, even if half the people you meet think PCSOs are a waste of time. Watch this space, she thought. Getting the job was thanks to a tip-off from her next-door neighbour, who had suggested she apply to be a Police Community Support Officer.

'Don't be daft!' Ro had said. 'Me, a woman with a fatal attraction to double yellow lines?'

Mrs Carruthers had laughed. 'You do make me smile, Mrs Watson. You'd be really good 'cos you make mistakes like everyone else.'

'Thanks a bunch!'

But Ro had decided to take this as a compliment. Her elderly neighbour was pretty shrewd; Ro had a lot of time for her. She even let Mrs Carruthers look after Ben sometimes. Ro's son had been born prematurely with cerebral palsy and Ro had cared for him ever since, doing freelance work from home when she could. But her neighbour was right. Now Ben was settled at

Norbridge High School, it was time for Ro to move on, and being a PCSO sounded interesting.

And maybe Ben needed a break from constant maternal monitoring.

'It's a really worthwhile job,' Mrs C went on. 'I could stay with Ben when you work shifts. And you've said yourself you want to do something useful. You used to be in public relations, didn't you? And you're a good listener.'

I'm not really, Ro thought. It's just that these days I don't say much, and her neighbour could talk for Britain. Mrs C had been a godsend, but Ro hated the idea of being dependent on anyone. One of the reasons she had moved to Cumbria was that Ben's paternal grandparents lived in Norbridge and they were anxious to help. They compensated for Ben's father, who was now married to someone else and living in Sydney. But it meant she could keep Ben's care largely in the family, with no need for a wider social network.

So now she thought of herself as a loner, a Scouser in exile like most of the others! But the idea of being a PCSO had stuck in her head. She had been outgoing, once. A job like Police Community Support Officer would be a different sort of public relations, one which was much more important. It would give her a role in a community where she still felt a bit of a stranger. And if Ben needed more independence, the best way forward was to be more independent herself.

A few months later she had seen an advertisement for PCSOs in the library, and she'd applied. The fact that PCSOs were underestimated appealed to her. What were they sometimes called? Plastic police. Their role was community liaison, patrolling streets and making relationships. Hardly the stuff of TV dramas. That suited Ro. The punitive side of policing wasn't for her. She knew what it was like to have people pointing the finger and making accusations – 'She must have drunk while she was pregnant' or 'What did she do wrong to have a baby with all those problems?' Perhaps that was why she rarely talked to anyone at work about her home life. The last thing she wanted was to be labelled as the single parent with the disabled son, like some sort of case study. Sometimes she feared that she had got the job as part of some secret diversity policy, which didn't bear thinking about.

She took her coffee outside, sat at the garden table and tried not to think about the dead young man, either. She made a rough shopping list on her notepad, but her mind wandered. Pelliter was just a few miles away from the valley where she lived, but it was completely different, and a place she had hardly visited. The sprawling coastal area was an interesting mix: some wealthy farms and some light industry which was just about surviving; the notorious Pelliter Valley council estate; the funny little chapel on the headland looking over the Solway; and a big shiny supermarket on the outskirts, with a massive car-park, which was where she should be going rather than sitting drinking coffee in the fresh early sunshine.

'Come on, Ben,' she called from the kitchen, and heard him bump down the stairs. In some ways it was a crazy house for a boy like him, but he treated it as one big climbing frame. He clattered into the kitchen, and walked towards the counter. He could get around well now. Adolescence for Ben meant increasing strength in his muscles, and increasing confidence too.

But there was one remaining problem. Ben had developed cataracts as the result of a bad fall when he was a toddler. Ro hated thinking about that. But soon he would be old enough for an operation, a relatively safe one, though all surgery had its risks. Ro knew that her son, normally so brave and capable, was worried about it. Stop thinking about it, Ro told herself, as the idea of the dead man at the chapel with his injured eyes flashed on her own inward retina.

'I'm dropping you at Grandma's while I do a big shop,' she told her son. 'Make sure you've got your Xbox.' Ordinary family life, she thought. Great. What she wanted now, most of all, was for her and Ben to be an ordinary family. And tentatively, she thought they might be getting there.

Suzy Spencer and Robert Clark hardly constituted an ordinary family, but Saturday shopping was a great leveller. Life at The Briars in Tarnfield usually followed a pattern at the weekends. Suzy hated the supermarket, so she would give Robert a list and he would go into Norbridge or the new superstore at Pelliter. In return, she would do the housework, which she hated only slightly less than the shopping, and Robert would call in at the library on his way home. Robert was a lecturer at the local college, but he really wanted to be a writer. He'd tried several genres, from literary novel, through Gothic melo-drama, to a recent attempt at chick-lit which had made even the grumpy Molly laugh at how useless it was. Saturday morning after the shopping session was his time for research, which usually meant sitting reading in the corner of the big comfy kitchen while Suzy made a late lunch.

But this Saturday the kitchen table was occupied. Suzy made signs at him to follow her into the living-room.

'Becky Dixon's here.'

'So I see.'

Robert ruffled Suzy's spiky blonde hair. She seemed tense, but smiled back and grabbed his hand, putting it on her shoulder and squeezing it.

'Becky's grandma called me and asked if they could drop her off. Of course, I said yes. There's been a fatal accident on their land. A young bloke fell down the cliff, Judith Dixon said. He'd been slashed with a knife, too.'

'That sounds grim. Was he someone local?'

'That's the weird thing. Judith Dixon says there wasn't any identification on him. He was found near this old chapel.' Suzy shuddered. She and Robert had come across violent death before. The idea that country life was placid and pastoral was a myth. 'Nature red in tooth and claw' meant human nature too. Robert put his arm around her, and to distract her he said, 'Oh, you mean St Trallen's Chapel. Fascinating place ...'

'Saint who?'

'Trallen. She helped bring the relics of St Andrew to Scotland. She's supposed to have plucked out her beautiful eyes to stop a local pagan fancying her. She's a patron saint for ophthalmologists now.'

'You're kidding me!'

'I'm not. Google her yourself. The chapel is named after her. Her other name is St Tribuna. There's the fragment of a book about her in Norbridge Abbey. It's supposed to be a scrap of a medieval illuminated manuscript, like the *Duc de Berry's Book of Hours* – you know, all those fantastic miniature paintings.'

'Talking of books,' Suzy asked, equally keen to change the subject, 'did you get the one you wanted?'

Robert nodded. His latest fiction attempt was historical, tracing the branch of the Clark family which had emigrated to Canada. Now he could look forward to a few blissful hours of good old-fashioned research, reading his massive tome on the history of Ontario. He smiled at Suzy. They both knew that he enjoyed reading more than writing.

'You've had an upsetting morning. Shall I do lunch?' he asked.

'No, it's OK. I'll make it, except I can't find the casserole dish. It's too heavy to be mislaid but it's not in the cupboard.'

Suzy went back into the kitchen and started banging pans around. Robert left her to it, and popped his head round the door. Molly, lank hair tucked behind a garish pink headband, wearing wellies with black tights and football shorts, was discussing a big drawing with a small dark girl in small dark clothes. The girl looked up and flashed Robert a look of surprising intensity.

So that was Becky Dixon. She looks all right despite this accident, Robert thought. In fact, both girls seemed happy and absorbed. Maybe Molly would really turn out to be gifted at art, as Miss MacDonald had said. He hoped so. Something had to explain her dress sense.

Alison MacDonald trudged irritably behind her mother around the Pelliter superstore. Teaching wasn't a job you could leave behind at the weekend. She was thinking about her meeting with Molly's mum the afternoon before. Liz Rudder, the deputy head at St Mungo's, knew everyone in the area. So how come she had got Suzy Spencer so wrong? Mrs Rudder had certainly given the impression that Mrs Spencer was an irresponsible parent with a dysfunctional lifestyle. She'd been keen to explain that Molly was the child of a broken marriage, likely to turn out badly – and Mrs Rudder was absolutely certain there was no hope for Becky Dixon with her dead druggie mother, despite the Dixons' love and money, and Becky's own brains.

But Liz Rudder had been wrong, about Molly at least. Mrs Spencer had been desperate to do anything she could to help, and was well aware that Molly was having a difficult time.

'But it isn't just Molly,' Alison had reassured Mrs Spencer. 'They were all unsettled when Mrs Findley was ill at the start of the year. Now there's all this panic about the Dodsworth House private school scholarships, and the end of year tests too.'

'I know, it's a really difficult time. Everyone is so competitive.'

'Exactly. The children need to focus on something else, otherwise the pressure will reach boiling point. I think a concert planned for the end of term might give everyone a chance to shine. Molly has certainly become more withdrawn, and her work isn't as good as it used to be, or so I've heard. But she's very good at art, Mrs Spencer.'

'Is she? But how could that help?'

'Molly and Becky Dixon could paint the scenery for the concert. We could start them off on it now. It would boost Molly's confidence and give her a new role in the group. But it would mean some extra work, coming in on Saturday mornings and things like that. I'd really need your support.'

'Well, of course, I'd do anything I could. My background's in TV production. Maybe I could make a little film of the project? How would Mr Findley feel about that?'

'Mr Findley wouldn't be the one to ask. It would be probably be Liz Rudder. She's really at the helm at the moment.'

'Oh.' For a second Suzy Spencer's face had fallen. When Mrs Rudder had been Molly's teacher in Year Five, Suzy had been put off by the deputy head's smug manner. And the older teacher had been dismissive when Suzy had first noticed the changes in her daughter. But Miss MacDonald was different.

And as Alison outlined her plan, Suzy Spencer had brightened up. The idea was that Molly and her new friend could paint a mural to be used as a backdrop for an end-of-term talent show, which would feature the rock stars and catwalk models of Year Six. 'The Six Factor' or something. Everyone in the class would be involved at a level which was right for them. A DVD of their efforts would make a great leaving token. It could actually turn the tide for Year Six, and make them all friends again.

It was a great idea. Enough to make you daydream by the frozen foods. But Alison was suddenly brought back to reality.

'Hey, Miss MacDonald, over here!'

A cackling voice cut through the supermarket aisle like a fire alarm. It was Callie McFadden, a teaching assistant at St Mungo's, beckoning Alison over, with an air of giving an order. There was never any escape from a summons from Callie, even on a Saturday morning. The teaching assistant was, as usual, dressed like a hippy, but she certainly wasn't laid back and relaxed. Her little eyes watched everything, with a view to the main chance for herself or her family. Her eleven-year-old son Jonty was the most aggressive boy in Alison's class, spoilt by his mother and feared by his peers.

'Well, Miss MacDonald! Fancy meeting you here. I thought you were more of a delicatessen type,' Callie sneered loudly.

The two other women in Callie's orbit both watched Ali's reaction with interest. Surprisingly, one was Faye Armistead, wife of a wealthy local landowner, who also had a son in Ali's class. Faye Armistead had a superior manner, and she stood slightly to one side, watching Callie McFadden as if she were a useful but smelly gundog who might just snap.

Even more surprisingly, the other woman with Callie was veteran teacher Brenda Hodgson, Liz Rudder's best friend. *Fat Miss Hodgy, pasty podgy* in the rhyme that had been chanted the evening before in the school toilets.

The three of them stared at Ali.

'We called you over to see if you'd heard the news. It was on Radio Cumbria.' Callie McFadden paused for effect, looking at Alison like a choco-holic saving a soft centre. 'A man's been found dead. Head smashed in and face knifed. He was on the Dixons' land.' She added the last remark with relish.

The two other women seemed to be holding their breath, waiting for Alison to say something. They had the same hungry look. Alison shivered in the aisle, not just because of the fridges. The accident really did sound terrible. But the way Callie savoured it was worse.

Alison said, 'It'll be a matter for the police, I suppose. You'll have to excuse me. I need to catch up with my mother …' She looked round madly for an escape route. Her mother had disappeared.

But luckily Callie was suddenly distracted. 'Hey, there's that local community policewoman,' she said to Faye and Brenda. 'The poor man's bobby. Let's see what she can tell us. See you on Monday, then, Alison.'

Looking at Callie's trolley, laden with frozen chips and instant sauces, Alison made her escape towards the fresh fruit-and-veg aisle. Not Callie's food of choice. Alison would be safe behind the grapes and apples for a while at least.

Chapter Three

Their heart is as fat as grease

Psalm 119:70. Folio 48v. **Les Très Riches Heures du Duc de Berry**

PCSO Ro Watson stood in the supermarket wondering how long she could deliberate over buying wholemeal pasta or organic long grain rice. Ben was at his grandparents' and she should have been enjoying a few moments to herself, even in the grocery aisle, but she was tired and still distracted by thinking about the body at the chapel. And since when had shopping become a moral maze? She almost longed for the days when it was either instant mash or spaghetti hoops and you didn't have to worry about the planet. Her thoughts were interrupted by a frowsy woman in a floppy skirt. Callie McFadden. Ro vaguely recognized her from an incident in Norbridge, where Callie's son had been involved in some mayhem in a local park. His mother had arrived on the scene breathing fire, and accusing people of picking on the boy, who had stood there smirking.

This time, it was Callie McFadden herself who smirked. She grinned at Ro in a fake friendly manner as she went on asking questions about the death at St Trallen's Chapel, but Ro didn't respond to the insistent tone. She could cope with Callie McFadden. There were times when coming from Liverpool was an advantage, she thought with amusement.

'I really can't tell you anything,' Ro replied, refusing to be bullied. Ro tuned out of the other woman's badgering, and remembered a joke she'd heard from one of her colleagues on the Norbridge Force.

'Hear about the coach crash on the M62?
Loada Scousers dead and queuing for the pearly gates.
God sent St Peter to sort them out and he came running back.
"They've gone, Lord."
"What, the Scousers?"
"No, the pearly gates."'

You had to laugh, even when it made you mad. But there was some truth in it. Liverpool could be a tough place, and that meant Callie's hectoring manner cut no ice with Ro.

'I'm sorry,' Ro said to Callie finally. 'I can't tell you anything more. I think you'll hear all the details about the accident on Radio Cumbria.'

'Accident, was it?' Callie pounced.

'Excuse me. I really need to go.' Ro smiled in a final sort of way, and left Callie and her two acolytes behind. So much for the wholemeal pasta, but there was no way Ro was going to wait to be interrogated by this woman and her coven.

Callie made a face and watched Ro disappear towards the check-out. Then she marshalled Faye Armistead and Brenda Hodgson towards the patio outside the coffee shop. Callie needed a fag. Her New Age image was spoilt by the cigarette she had dangling from her mouth whenever possible. It made her maroon lipstick creep further into the wrinkles running upward to her nostrils like little rips. Callie's face was sunburnt and her small eyes were untouched by mascara, but she always wore lipstick in reddish-brown colours. Her fair hair was greying now but there was lots of it, gathered into a floppy bun on the back of her head. She wore scooped necklines with plenty of cleavage, and long flowing skirts.

Callie had been a meals supervisor at St Mungo's, serving school dinners. When the teaching assistant jobs had been introduced, she had applied and been appointed straight away. Since then she'd insinuated herself into the centre of school life. When Mr Findley had been at the top of his game, Callie had been under control. But now he was distracted, she was becoming more and more key to everything that happened at St Mungo's. She had cosied up to deputy head Liz Rudder. And she was loving the power.

'Well,' Callie said with satisfaction to the other two women with her, as she sucked at her cappuccino, 'we got nothing out of Juliet Bravo, but we've certainly given Miss Alison MacDonald, queen of Year Six, something to think about. She thinks the Dixons are the dog's bollocks around here.'

Brenda Hodgson, the teacher, tittered. She was a stocky woman, with pale-brown hair and a shiny clean, smooth face. Until recently she had spent most of her free time with her best friend, the new deputy head, but since Mrs Rudder's husband had had a stroke, Brenda had found herself at a loose end. Liz was so taken up with the invalid that Brenda had been rather sidelined. Now, she smoothed her short hands with scrubbed fingernails over her pastel-coloured tracksuit trousers, her standard Saturday wear. She was really rather thrilled to have been taken up by Callie McFadden, such a driving force at the school. It almost made up for Liz Rudder's neglect. But not quite. Brenda flicked a tiny speck of fluff away.

'Oh, the wretched Dixons at St Trallen's!' Faye Armistead sighed. 'We all sympathize, but really, one has to ask about the daughter who topped herself. Becky Dixon's mother.' Her two friends knew what she was thinking. Just because Philip Dixon had been born in Pelliter didn't mean he could suddenly return to join the gentry on account of buying a bit of land. And the way his brainy granddaughter thought she was above the others was outrageous! Fay's son Toby was not the brightest lightbulb, but he was part of the landed gentry. The real landed gentry. A place at the local public school, Dodsworth House, was Toby's by right, and should not be even dreamt of by someone like Becky Dixon.

Brenda Hodgson sympathized perfectly. Like Faye, she felt that people who left Pelliter and expected to come back trailing clouds of glory should be brought down a peg or two. Brenda Hodgson had gone away to university herself, but things hadn't worked out. She had come home with her tail between her legs, and gone to a local teacher training college instead. She and Liz Rudder had both got jobs at St Mungo's, and settled in for life. Pelliter was Brenda's world and that was quite enough, thank you.

'Well,' Faye Armistead drawled in her upper-class way, 'one wonders if all these sad things are just a coincidence. Perhaps this poor dead man at the chapel was on drugs too, like the Dixons' daughter. You don't really think Becky Dixon will get one of these Dodsworth House scholarship places, do you?'

'Maybe this tragedy will affect her work,' Brenda Hodgson suggested.

'Yes.' Faye raised an immaculate eyebrow. 'Maybe it will.' She sipped her cappuccino.

At the same time, in the Norbridge suburb of High Pelliter, in the breakfast-room of her large Edwardian villa, Liz Rudder was enjoying an espresso alone. For years she had spent Saturday mornings with Brenda Hodgson, but lately she had really enjoyed the peace of being by herself. These days, she no longer needed someone to listen while she moaned about her husband's roving eye. His stroke had left him harmless as a baby, though just as much trouble, from what she'd heard of motherhood. She listened to the squeak of John's wheelchair as he came through the hall. But she could also hear the crumbling sound of earth flaking from dirty shoes. Her brother Kevin was pushing John in from the garden where the carers had parked him – and Kevin would be scattering muck, no doubt.

Liz called, 'Just leave your shoes at the door. Kevin, are the boys with you?'

'Nope – a dad's work is never done, but I've left them playing footie at the school pitch. Under supervision. Is the coffee on?'

'Of course it is!' Liz couldn't help smiling, though she shook her head at the lacy brown dried mud disintegrating from the tread of Kevin's trainers. She was always pleased to see her brother although he had the friendly messiness of a large golden Labrador. 'I'll just get you both a cuppa. Do you want some, John?'

But she didn't wait for an answer, because it cost her husband too much effort to speak. And everyone knew she anticipated John's every need. She paused to stroke her husband's dark curly hair. Kevin smiled at her in approval. His big sister had had a lot to cope with since John's terrible stroke. John Rudder had been a big handsome fellow, a real hunk. Now he was a heavy burden. Liz Rudder, on the contrary, was a small, pale woman with small, delicate hands and feet – and a surprisingly luscious figure, which provoked lewd comments from the kids at St Mungo's. Kevin had heard the chant. *Mrs Rudder, what an udder.* His own sons were at Dodsworth House, but they still hung out with the local lads, and they'd brought the rhyme home. *When she screams it makes you shudder.*

'Have they identified the man who died?' Liz Rudder asked.

'No, not according to the radio,' her brother said, 'which means he probably wasn't local, which is one good thing.'

'Absolutely,' Liz said. 'That's a relief.'

And she smiled at her husband. John Rudder grunted back at her from his wheelchair, but it was impossible to understand anything he tried to say. Tragic, Kevin thought.

The week ahead brought no new information about the dead man, but at work Ro Watson felt more and more as if she was really settling in to life as a PCSO. Having been sent to the scene of a fatality seemed to give her some status. On occasions she spoke to Constable Jed Jackson, and their time spent at the chapel seemed to have made a bond between them. Stupid, Ro told herself. There's no way a young bloke like Jed would really want to discuss things with her. But there was no doubt he deliberately stopped to speak to her more than once.

The following Friday was a night off for Ro before she went on weekend shift at the police station. Ben would stay with his grandparents over Saturday, but their Fridays alone before her weekend shift had already become a sort of ritual. Ben insisted on trying his hand at cooking, a procedure which usually had Ro on the edge of her seat in terror as he manoeuvred boiling water and slippery pans of pasta. At this point, his good right arm was slicing maniacally at the tomatoes while his bad hand held them in place. I know he's going to cut his hand off, Ro thought, forcing herself to sit calmly at the kitchen counter, but she gulped her red wine rather than sipping it. A fat lot of use she'd be if Ben did stab his hand. How would she get him to A&E? – pissed Police Support Officer and bleedin' kid … ha ha….

But Ben wasn't a child any more, and the tomatoes slipped into neat rings. He was laughing, knowing she was nervous.

'Hey, Mum, what did the man say when he walked into the bar?'

'I don't know, what did the man say when he walked into the bar?'

'Ouch!' Ben gurgled with laughter. It wasn't that the joke was funny; it was that he could tell it and cut tomatoes at the same time. 'Hey, Mum, what's the difference between a bad marksman and a constipated owl? The bad marksman shoots but can't hit, and the owl hoots but can't ...'

'Enough!' Ro said, and Ben snorted with laughter again. It was a joy and a blessing that he had such an easygoing nature. It was as if he saw his life as one long triumph over adversity. Where did he get it from? His father had been a dour young man reading history at university, where they had met. Their relationship had been a lukewarm sort of thing, on and off for a few years, and she had been four months pregnant before she had realized. They had married in haste. It was as if there had always been something odd about Ben from the start – his conception unnoticed, his development in the womb slightly out of step. But she knew there was no real explanation for his sudden dramatic arrival at thirty weeks, and the panic that followed. Except that, from the start, the fear and misery had been hers, not his. Ben had smiled the day he came home from hospital and he'd been smiling ever since. Not like his mother.

But she had tried. At one stage, she'd even gone back to work, hired nannies and babysitters, gone to bars and parties. But that had gone wrong too, and Ro had gone back to her mother's smart little semi in the posher part of Liverpool – yes, there were posh parts. She and her mum had supported each other, and Ben, until he was seven. That year Mrs Lloyd suddenly announced that she had fallen in love with her next-door neighbour, and now she wanted to move away. Ro had been devastated and it had taken her at least a week to see the funny side. Her mother and new boyfriend, aged seventy-six, had wanted to sell up and move to a seaside flat in Llandudno, and Ro had given them her blessing. The proceeds from the family house sale had funded her move to Cumbria at precisely the time when Ben was ready to change schools. And it was Ro's in-laws' turn to help, something they'd done gladly, to Ro's relief. Ben had survived the move with a mixture of sunny fortitude and a sensitivity which more mature people might have envied.

We've managed all right, Ro thought. Even though we're pretty much on our own now. Her PCSO's uniform was hanging on the back of the kitchen door. It looked sort of comforting. Protecting. But whether it was to protect the community or to protect Ro herself, she wasn't quite sure. She wondered what this weekend would bring. Not as much drama as the last one, she hoped.

*

Friday night meant family night in for a lot of people. A few miles away, the phone rang at The Briars in Tarnfield. Suzy Spencer recognized her estranged husband's number on the display again. Nigel Spencer had called fifteen minutes earlier and they had argued about Molly. Suzy had slammed the phone down on him in anger. She regretted it now, and was glad Nigel had rung back, but she couldn't resist poking fun.

'Patronizing old gits' helpline. How may I help you?'

Nigel sighed noisily at the other end of the phone. 'I don't know why you say these things, Suzy. I was only trying to offer some advice.'

'And I was only trying to be funny.'

'It didn't work. I just called back to suggest that maybe Molly come and visit again.' It was an olive branch which he immediately used to beat her with – 'But I don't want her looking like something from a pantomime.'

Nigel and Suzy Spencer had been apart for six years, but Suzy still felt herself bristling at his criticism. Nigel had been the one to leave, but somehow he had regained the moral high ground. Perhaps that was because his affair with his PA in Newcastle had ended up in the out-tray, while she had found herself a lover.

'Well, it will be nice for Molly to stay over with you,' Suzy said neutrally, thinking about how she could make a rebellious Molly look presentable for her father.

'Yes. I'll pop over in two weeks' time and pick her up. It's a pity Jake will be playing in his band, but it will give us the chance for quality time with Molly. I'm afraid I'll have to bring her back before the May Bank Holiday. We've got a prior engagement.'

'That's OK.' Suzy had learned that her husband's *noblesse oblige* rarely stretched to having the kids on a public holiday. And who was this 'we'? Nigel must have a new girlfriend.

Nigel was still droning on, but one phrase cut through the platitudes. 'My solicitor says …'

It took Suzy a moment to catch up. 'What?'

'It's not as if we have any real issues to discuss, is it?' Nigel said. 'As regards divorce, I mean?'

'No. That's right.' Suzy sat down heavily on one of the kitchen chairs. 'Of course. If that's what you want.'

When he rang off she poured herself a large glass of red wine. A divorce at last. She felt ninety per cent relief, but there was a sense of sadness too. She and Nigel had met at university and she had thought they would be partners for life. She had found herself thinking about her undergraduate days more and more in recent weeks. It was odd, the way she and Nigel had clung to each other, scared eighteen-year-olds thrown together away from home. But she had made some good friends – Rachel Cohen, Paul Watson, Nigel Spencer of course, Sandra and Rosemary whom she'd met in the third year. She was still in touch with Rachel but she'd lost touch with Sandra and Rosemary. Perhaps it was because Jake was going into his final year at school in September that she had been thinking of her past so much recently. After wanting it for so long, Suzy felt suddenly shaky at the idea of divorce. Jake got on well with Robert, and Robert was great with both the kids – but he wasn't their real dad. How would the kids feel about the final split? How did she feel herself, now it was happening?

In a minute, she would go and tell Robert the good news. It *was* good news, wasn't it? Then the phone rang again. It was Judith Dixon.

'Mrs Spencer? Could Becky come and stay with you again this weekend? We've got such a lot of bother over here with folk coming to rubberneck at St Trallen's since the accident. Phil could bring Becky over.'

'Of course,' Suzy said. At this rate Becky Dixon's visits would become a weekend fixture. But it was no bad thing. Suzy would have welcomed Becky eight days a week in order to ensure that Molly had a friend.

So the news on the divorce would have to wait. Suzy put it to the back of her mind while she set about sorting out evening meals, bedding, and their extended family night in.

Friday night at Callie McFadden's was also a family night in. She lived in a council house on the Pelliter Valley Estate. Her eldest son was lying on the tatty sofa, with his feet in huge trainers lolling over the end. He wore his baseball cap back to front in all weathers, indoors and out, and he was never without a can of drink. He was on his fifth or sixth, after coming home from his job on a building site in Norbridge. To celebrate the fact that he probably wouldn't be working much longer in the current economic slowdown, he'd decided to get pissed at home. He'd go out later to hang about with his mates on Pelliter High Street, but for now he was watching telly and waiting for his mam to serve his tea.

Callie was in the kitchen talking to her daughter, a heavy girl with a pregnant stomach bulging out of her sweat pants.

'You shouldn't be drinking that stuff now you're expecting.'

'Ooo says?'

'Everyone says. And I suppose you're going to hang about till I feed you?'

The girl shrugged and plonked herself and her can down at the kitchen table. 'This stuff's crap. Got any wine?'

Callie ignored her. She liked having her family all around her and she needed to know what they were all doing. She was making a real dinner – pasta with mince and instant sauce. She knew that once they'd eaten it, they would be off to the various Pelliter outlets for their doses of fatty kebab or deep fried faggots. But this was still their Friday night gathering. She put her cigarette into the ashtray and went to the door between the kitchen and the living-room.

'You, get your boots off that sofa now! Yes, I mean now. And put that can in the bin or back in the fridge if you haven't drunk it all.' Her son lurched upright and staggered towards the kitchen.

Good, Callie thought with satisfaction. They all needed a boot up the bum. Except her youngest, Jonty. He had come along when Callie thought she was past it, and she had saved the best till last. He was the cleverest of her kids and her pet. Jonty would go far. He had his mum's forcefulness. And forceful she certainly was! Callie thought with satisfaction that it was her drive and Liz Rudder's experience which were keeping things going at St Mungo's, where soppy Ray Findley had his eye off the ball just because his wife was cracking up. That afternoon, for example, Callie had been irritated to find that a schoolroom was in use without her say-so.

'What's going on here? Have you got permission to do that?'

A harassed mother injecting a diabetic child in Year Four jumped back. 'Mr Findley said we could use this room.'

'I don't think so.' Everyone knew that Callie was in charge of room organization, and no one had told her about this. Kids with health problems like that should be in special schools. Callie had stared down the mother who looked as if she was about to cry. Stupid cow.

But when Callie turned to leave she saw Becky Dixon staring at her, with that funny look of hers. The child should have been off the premises by now, but Miss MacDonald let the kids hang about till all hours on their so-called 'art work'. Becky Dixon looked questioningly at Callie and then turned away, showing no fear. Becky gave Callie the creeps. She gave lots of people the creeps. Jonty had hated Becky Dixon ever since Miss MacDonald had put her in charge of the classroom printer instead of him.

Thinking about Becky's little white face made Callie shudder, so now she jabbed her grown-up daughter between the shoulder blades.

'Hey, take this garlic bread.'

Then Jonty came sidling around the door. 'Mam?' he asked in a wheedling voice.

'What is it, lad?'

'Can we do the ouija board after tea?'

Callie smiled. The ouija board! That was always good fun.

'Good idea, son.' And Callie laughed out loud, assured of some sport.

Chapter Four

But some of them said, He casteth out devils through Beelzebub, the chief of the devils

Luke 11:15. Folio 166r. **Les Très Riches Heures du Duc de Berry**

A n hour later, Callie McFadden turned the lights out in the cluttered living room, except for a reddish lamp in the corner. She'd given the usual lecture on how the ouija board was just a bit of fun and not really messages from the spirits of the dead, and how they shouldn't take it too seriously – all delivered in a very serious voice.

'Have any of them been murdered?' Jonty asked. 'Or tortured?'

Callie's daughter popped her headphones from out of her ears and rolled them up into her pocket.

'Loada rubbish,' she said. But she stayed by the board.

Callie had made the board herself years ago. It was a big cardboard square covered with shiny cellophane, and she had made the letters of the alphabet on twenty-six separate cards which she laid down around the square. In the middle was an upturned drinking glass.

'We've all got to be quiet now, and sit with just our fingertips touching and our eyes closed.'

After the noise which incessantly filled the house, the sudden silence was dramatic. 'Now,' said Callie, making her voice as deep and sonorous as she could. 'Don't open your eyes but, at a count of three, put your forefinger lightly – I mean lightly – on the glass. One, two … *Three.*'

Jonty stuck his hand out, fingers hovering. Callie guided it into place over the tumbler. She had put the glass in the freezer earlier. The atmosphere was working.

'Now *without moving a muscle*, open your eyes and look at nothing but the board.'

Two pairs of eyes snapped open.

'Are you there?' droned Callie. 'Is anyone there? Send us a sign.'

It was important that nothing happened at once in order to let the tension build, but Callie could usually bank on something – a curtain fluttering or a car horn. If not, she would nudge the coffee table herself. A dog barked.

'Spirit, are you there?' Callie asked. She had to press quite hard for the message to read 'G.E.T …

'Get!' shouted Jonty.

'B.'

'E.'

The glass really seemed to struggle under their fingers, and then suddenly hurtled itself around the letters to make 'CKY.'

'Get Becky!' whooped Jonty, delighted. That will cheer him up, thought Callie. 'Maybe you should take the board's advice, son,' she said. She took another gulp of lager. No harm in building the boy up a bit. Everyone said boys were doing worse at school than girls these days. No wonder, if silly teachers like Alison MacDonald favoured creepy sexless creatures like Becky Dixon. Her Jonty wasn't going to suffer 'cos some teacher made a pet out of a druggie's daughter. Jonty was a real lad, and she'd see to it he lacked no confidence at all.

She was about to take her hand away from the board, when Jonty said, 'Worrabout you, Mam?'

This was a surprise. Callie never organized messages for herself. 'Oh, go on then….'

'I'll ask this time,' said Jonty. 'Spirit, is there a message for me mam?'

The glass seemed to jump under their hands. The letters came so quickly that Callie couldn't follow. Jonty said, 'It spells something, Mam. It spells DONT RUST.'

'What?' Callie snapped. 'Don't rust?'

'Don't trust,' said Jonty. 'Gerrit? But don't trust 'oo?'

The glass spun away. Jonty shrieked each letter out. 'B.R.E.N.D.A.'

'I don't know no Brendas.' Jonty was already bored and looking at his Xbox.

But I do, thought Callie. Though it was all just bloody rubbish and she should know!

Miss Hodgson knew the children called her 'pasty podgy' but her vanity wasn't her looks. It was her personal cleanliness. By Friday afternoon she was itching to get away from the creeping sticky grime of school. For Brenda, Friday was the second best evening of the week. Wednesday was best, but that was top secret of course. Brenda loved secrets. She had nurtured them all her life.

She had parked her little car and walked from the lock-up garage at the end of the road to the small terraced house that she had inherited from her grandmother. It was a pleasant evening, if cloudy, but the sky was clearing and there was a pinkish glow over to the west. In the past she had usually visited the Rudders for Saturday supper. But since John's stroke, that had slowly changed. Liz didn't seem to want to know any more. Of course, Brenda told herself, her friend was under awful pressure.

Still, Brenda enjoyed her new mateyness with Callie and Faye. What a surprising and interesting friendship! Brenda loved it when Callie said confidingly, 'Don't tell anyone, but ...' Or when Faye said, 'Of course no one else knows ...' It was so satisfying to be in the know!

The only other feature of Brenda's weekend was the regular Sunday lunch with her brother, Peter.

She hung up her jacket, scrubbed her hands and face with an antibacterial lotion in the tiny downstairs cloakroom, and checked phone messages. There was one routine call from her brother about a pudding he fancied. And there was another message which made Brenda dizzy with excitement. She should ring back. But she didn't redial straight away. She wanted to savour the anticipation.

She went upstairs and changed into her tracksuit trousers and a T-shirt. It was warm in the bedroom, and a trapped fly, precocious for late April, buzzed against the window pane. Brenda swatted it with the *Pelliter Tribune* and put the little black body down the toilet, flushing with bleach. Then she went downstairs, through the hall to the cramped but shining kitchen at the back of the house and opened the door. Standing outside surveying the concreted yard, she could hear children shouting in the field behind the house, where the soggy marshes of the River Pell were a dump for the people of the Pelliter Valley estate, where her new friend Callie McFadden lived.

Brenda went back indoors into the spotless kitchen and took the bottle of gin out of the shiny clean unit under the sink, pouring a large measure into a glass which had been washed, polished and set ready on the counter the night before. Then she added a small measure of tonic, and some sliced lemon which was waiting in a bowl in the sparkling clean fridge. The clink of the ice cubes from the neat and sorted freezer was the trigger sound and made her tummy rumble. She lifted the drink to her lips. Delicious. There was something pure about gin and tonic. It went down without touching the sides. She mixed herself another, careful to put the bottle away after wiping the top for drips.

She took her drink into the sitting-room behind the kitchen, sat on the sofa, and leafed through the *Pelliter Tribune*, the free local paper which had been delivered the night before. There was a big front-page story about the body found at Dixons' chapel the previous Friday. The man was still unidentified. The police were trying their best to jog local memories. Someone must have seen something. Once again, she read the quote which had caught her eye yesterday, and caused her to leave that all-important message. Her breath came faster and her heart palpitated.

'We have searched through the man's clothing and belongings. He had a paper with a sort of diagram on it slipped into an inside pocket. His fingers had some darkish marks. His jacket pocket was ripped and in the lining we discovered a Canadian dollar coin. There was nothing else.'

Brenda picked up the phone and speed-dialled her brother. His answering machine said importantly: 'Father Peter Hodgson is not available. Please leave a message after the tone.' It sounded a little like Gregorian chant.

'It's Brenda,' she breathed. 'I need to speak to you.'

Then she replayed the other message, the one she had been savouring, before dialling back with clumsy fingers. She was still unfamiliar with the mobile phone number. As she waited to be connected, she found she was breathless with nervous excitement. Goodness me! To have one big secret was exciting, and to have two was a little overwhelming. And now, it seemed, she had three!

Alison MacDonald drove into the school car-park the following day, Saturday. This part of Pelliter was quiet on a weekend morning. But Suzy Spencer's car was already parked outside, and Alison saw Molly and Becky in the back, collecting bags and belongings.

'Hi!' she called as Suzy emerged. 'Eleven o'clock. You're right on time.'

'How's the mural going?' Suzy asked.

'It's going well, isn't it, Molly?' Alison MacDonald looked down at her pupil and realized with a shock that Molly seemed to have grown again overnight. Becky was much smaller, the top of her dark curls coming up to the lank brown locks on Molly's shoulder. Molly was wearing a school blazer which was two sizes too small and a vermilion silk scarf over harem pants.

'It's OK,' said Molly carefully. She'd learnt to curb her enthusiasm. Year Six at St Mungo's thrived on knocking anything which didn't involve sport, modelling or pop music.

'It's great, Molly,' said Becky. Her voice was unusually deep for such a small body. She had a thin, pixie-like face and huge eyes. She wore an outsize navy-blue pea jacket. If anything, Becky was getting thinner and slighter while Molly grew bigger and more shapeless.

Alison felt a frisson when she looked at the mural, which was tacked along the back of the classroom wall. She'd asked Molly to choose the theme. It was already looking like a medieval fantasy and the detail really impressed her. Molly had outlined a winding road leading to the top of a low hill with a squat building which she hadn't yet completed. There was the beginning of a parade which would eventually show men-at-arms, peasants with livestock and goods, jugglers and tumblers, noblemen on horseback and ladies in pale fluted hats with gauze veils. The path broadened out at the bottom of the huge sheet of paper, and the plan was to extend it on to the stage, where the performing artists of Year Six would pout and mince their way through a series of X-Factor-type turns. The only constraint would be that the costumes had to echo the theme of the Middle Ages – but it was hardly a problem, Alison thought, given the pre-occupation with princesses, body building, sports heroes, bullying and hierarchy which obsessed the kids in St Mungo's top class. Twenty-first or twelfth century, what was new?

'It's lovely, Molly. And Becky.' Suzy Spencer was behind them, taking her camcorder out of its case. 'Let's get some footage of you working on it.'

Suzy studied the viewfinder, but Alison caught a movement in the playground. Perhaps other kids were coming. She'd mentioned to the class that Mrs Spencer would be videoing the mural work today. She'd hoped a few of the others might offer to help on Saturday morning, but there had been an orchestrated lack of interest.

'I'm not doin' it. I think it's feckin' stupid,' Jonty McFadden had mumbled at the back of the classroom. Two or three of his mates had sniggered. Alison had come to terms with the fact that getting group-wide participation was going to take time.

But at least Mrs Spencer was here with the two girls, and once word got around that the filming was really happening, more children might turn up. Molly was already drawing at the bottom of the picture. Obeying her instructions, Becky was standing up working at the top. She concentrated, tongue gripped between her teeth. Alison found it slightly mesmerizing to watch her, so that when the crash came she sensed it, rather than saw it.

'Watch out!' she screamed.

There was the sound of feet pounding in the playground and the light changed as the window shattered into opaque shards. Alison leapt back involuntarily as the splinters cascaded through the classroom. Suzy grabbed the camcorder and tripod just before it lurched. Molly had fallen to the floor and was screaming.

Alison ran to the smashed window, hearing the crunching underfoot. A group of kids were running away from the school. But one boy turned round, and she saw him in the instant before he turned away again, and ran, arms and legs wheeling, to the gate.

'Jonty McFadden!' she shouted. 'Jonty McFadden! I saw you.'

Then she turned back. Suzy was hugging Molly. Becky had been in the direct line of fire. She could have been seriously hurt. But she was still drawing, face white and eyes shining.

'Did you see what they threw?' Suzy asked.

33

'I think it was a hammer; it slid over by the desk. Don't walk through the glass. If it had hit us we could have been injured. Let's get out of here. Stop working, Becky. I'll phone the police and Mr Findley.'

Molly was shaking. 'We'll still do this, won't we? It won't stop us, will it?'

'Not likely.' It was the first thing Becky Dixon had said since the breakage, in her strange deep adult voice.

'No. It won't stop us. It's just stupid vandalism.' Alison held the door open. 'We'll get this lot cleared up and we'll carry on in the staff room.'

In Norbridge police station, PCSO Ro Watson was called over to Constable Jed Jackson's desk. They were to go out to an incident. Saturday morning shifts were usually quiet but there had been trouble at St Mungo's School in Pelliter. A teacher had called to report a window being smashed by a gang of kids. It could have been serious, but no one was hurt, luckily. It was a matter for the community team.

Ro got into the passenger seat next to Jed and fastened her seatbelt. Jed had stopped her in the corridor only that morning. He had told her about being asked to give a quote to the *Pelliter Tribune* about the mystery of the dead man at the chapel and what had been in his pockets.

'Nothing,' Jed had said. 'That's what was so weird. A Canadian coin and a funny diagram on really thin paper. And we haven't told the Press but he had dark stains on his fingers. Like nicotine only blackish. That was all.'

'So was he robbed?'

Jed had shrugged. 'Who knows?' He put his foot on the accelerator and the car shot forward. Despite their new camaraderie Ro didn't want to push. There was something reserved about Jed nevertheless. He was certainly charming and self-assured, being the graduate on the team, but occasionally she had noticed a hardness in his features, and she had overheard some of his more draconian views on drugs and drunkenness.

'I used to go to St Mungo's Church of England School,' Jed said, as he drove overconfidently towards Pelliter.

'So you're a Pelliter boy?'

'Absolutely. Though I must say,' Jed said, frowning, 'there was never any vandalism in my day.'

Ro laughed out loud. 'For goodness' sake! Your day! Jed, how old are you? Twenty-six at most? You sound like a middle-aged man!'

'Well, maybe there's nothing wrong with that,' Jed said cheerfully. It had been a risk, joshing with him. Ro got the impression that if Jed Jackson took something the wrong way, he could be pretty awkward to deal with. But for some reason he had taken an unexpected liking to her. She leant back in her seat and tried not to panic at his driving as he put his foot down, left the roundabouts of Norbridge behind and sped down the dual carriageway towards the coast.

Vandalism. Ray Findley, the head teacher, put the phone down and sat at his kitchen table. Opposite him his wife stared into space, her fingers curled round a cooling mug of coffee.

'I'm going to have to go up to the school,' he said. 'Someone's broken a window.'

Sheila Findley shrugged. He got up and left his crumb-filled plate in front of her. She didn't react. He climbed the stairs and went into the spare room, where he now slept. They had grabbed a long weekend the week before, with Ray taking a day's compassionate leave. But that was a technicality. He hadn't really been into St Mungo's in spirit for a few weeks now.

The weekend away had been promising at first. Not relaxed; he wouldn't have expected that. But Sheila had smiled once or twice, and they had walked around the island of Lindisfarne, visited the monastery, and been to a talk on Celtic Christianity.

'Do you remember going to see the St Trallen *Book*?' he had asked her afterwards.

'Yes, I do.' She had smiled softly.

He had tried to get her to talk, reminding her of the time, a few years ago, when they had started seeing each other discreetly. They had visited the abbey at Norbridge together. Sheila had told him that she was hopeless at art, but that in the classroom she could be Botticelli or Damien Hirst, given a swag of upholstery fabric or a few old kitchen-roll tubes. Ray recalled the conversation with affection, because they had found themselves confiding their weaknesses rather than their strengths, the beginning of their affair. He had been a forty-five-year-old head teacher whose longstanding relationship had ended a few years earlier. From the moment Sheila had come to work at St Mungo's, he had admired her. Working together, they had gone from being friends, to lovers, and very quickly to being a popular married couple. How everything had changed.

'Why don't we leave St Mungo's? Get out of Pelliter? I suppose you still see that stupid woman?' Sheila had asked Ray in a flat voice over dinner at their hotel.

'I can't do otherwise, can I?' he had answered, equally flatly. 'I can't just walk away.'

'You have already. You're not there now.'

'But this is a special holiday. I have to go back.'

'Why?'

He had shut up, then, and pushed his dessert to one side. They had walked back to the car and driven back in silence. Now this wretched vandalism incident, a week after arriving home, meant he would have to go to St Mungo's on a Saturday morning. Sheila will see it as another sign of disloyalty, he thought. He couldn't face her cold, silent accusations. He took his mobile out of his jacket pocket and, hating himself, he dialled Liz Rudder's number.

'I know this is an imposition,' he said, 'but could you go over to school? I'm afraid there's been rather a silly incident.'

He tried not to hear the restrained satisfaction in his deputy's voice as she stepped up to the plate yet again.

Chapter Five

I beheld the transgressors, and was grieved:

Psalm 119:158. Folio 59v. **Les Très Riches Heures du Duc de Berry**

Alison and Suzy sat in the staff room, waiting for the police. Alison had walked over the broken glass and unpinned the mural. Now it was Blu-Tacked to the staff-room wall.

'Get the paints, girls, and we'll go on working.'

The kettle bubbled, hissed and subsided. Alison poured the boiling water on to the little clusters of coffee from the sticky half-used jar on the staff-room table.

'Will black coffee do?'

'Thanks.' Suzy smiled. 'It will probably be more bracing. I need it. When the window smashed you called out a name—'

'She said Jonty McFadden,' Becky said in her deep voice. 'Mrs McFadden's son.'

Suzy raised her eyebrows and sipped her coffee. She remembered having a bit of a run-in with Callie McFadden a year earlier when she had gone back into school after Molly had forgotten her lunchbox. There had been a faint smell of cigarette smoke, and the teaching assistant had been bad-tempered and unhelpful. Not a likeable woman, Suzy thought.

There was the sound of a car drawing up. 'Oh,' said Alison, surprised, and Suzy followed her eyes. 'It's not Mr Findley; it's Mrs Rudder.'

Oh dear, Suzy thought. The deputy head wasn't exactly a sympathetic type either. It hadn't mattered while Mr and Mrs Findley were in control. But now …

She watched the deputy head open the school door and heard her trotting down the corridor. Then there was the crunching of glass as Mrs Rudder went into the damaged classroom to have a look. She called out, 'Are you all right, girls?'

'It was Jonty McFadden who did it,' Becky shouted.

'Good heavens! Jonty McFadden? Why on earth would he do this?' Mrs Rudder had wheeled into the staff-room.

'I have no idea,' Alison said. 'But he's been hostile since we started this project.'

'Really? That sounds rather extreme.' The deputy head tutted and fussed about, pouring coffee for herself. She seemed to be thinking. Then she looked at Alison speculatively. 'Alison, I need to speak to you in the corridor.' The senior teacher pulled at Ali's sleeve and guided her out of the staff-room. 'Look, dear, I think you really should be careful about what you say. Do you really want to make these sorts of allegations? Especially if you're not sure?'

'But it was Jonty's anorak. And I saw his face.'

'But you could easily have been mistaken. A lot of boys wear that style of jacket.'

'It was Jonty McFadden, Mrs Rudder. I saw him.'

'But what are you doing here anyway? Who gave you the authority to come into school this morning? I certainly didn't. The person in charge of non-teaching activity out of hours is Callie McFadden. Did you ask her permission?'

'No. She's only a teaching assistant.'

'But you should have OK'd it with her. Especially with Mr Findley being away and so very distracted. You really need to be careful before you drag the McFaddens into this. It might look as if you're trying to offload the blame for your own irresponsibility.'

'That's crazy!'

'Listen to me. You're relatively inexperienced and I just want to help you. You were here without permission and that puts you in a weak position. The most likely explanation is that this was just a silly prank – stupid vandalism, probably by boys at Norbridge Secondary School. Don't make an unnecessary fuss.'

Then there was the sound of another car, and doors slamming. 'That's the police arriving. There really was no need to call them. But I'll deal with them.' Liz Rudder went back into the staff-room and added in a louder, more authoritative voice, 'Mrs Spencer, I suggest you take the children home right now. They've been disturbed enough. There's no need to upset them by speaking to the officers.'

She trotted away. Alison heard her open the main door and say briskly, 'Of course, PC Jackson. I remember you from when you were in my Year Five. I'm dealing with this. I'm sure it won't take long. I rather think my younger colleague might have overreacted. You'd better come into the head teacher's office.'

At the same time, a meeting was going on at St Trallen's Place, Phil Dixon's house. So far Phil had sat quietly, listening and saying nothing. His visitor was Peter Hodgson, a retired priest who had come back to the area where he had been brought up, rather like Phil himself. Peter's sister was Brenda Hodgson, the teacher at St Mungo's.

'So, as my sister Brenda reported, we certainly do have an issue about this,' Father Hodgson was saying prissily. He had a pale-pink puffy face and the old-fashioned look of a man who had chosen his own clothes for forty years. Phil sighed. He was a churchgoer himself, but he had never really understood why an Anglican priest would want to make such a point of celibacy. It was a private issue, surely? But Peter Hodgson seemed to feel it had sacerdotal significance, along with his general air of being superior to the rest of the human race.

'I suggest that we speak to the bishop at once,' Father Peter went on. He was leaning forward in the most comfortable armchair, dangerously nudging the plate balanced on the arm. It had held four of Judith's homemade chocolate biscuits until a few minutes earlier.

'Why should we do that?' Phil Dixon asked.

'The bishop needs to act,' Father Peter snorted. 'With all due respect, Mr Dixon, we cannot have your family using St Trallen's as your own private chapel, especially now there has been this horrible death. The subject of reconsecration must arise.' Fussily, he produced a tissue and rubbed at his mouth until all traces of the biscuits had gone. There was something slightly compulsive about the way he scrubbed at his chin.

'But it *is* our own private chapel,' Phil added in a conciliatory way, 'If it's a chapel at all, really. It could have been a folly, or just an old byre. The family who owned the land in the nineteenth century did the place up, just to house the fragment of the *Book of St Trallen*.'

'And the *Book of St Trallen* is a fascinating, late medieval piece of art with unique Cumbrian connections!' Peter Hodgson snapped.

'Not necessarily. It's not local for a start,' Phil said gently. 'The Victorian landowner was very devout and tremendously lucky to find a piece of the *Book*. It was probably something he picked up somewhere in Europe on the Grand Tour.'

Father Hodgson said tetchily, 'Excuse me, but I was born and brought up here. I'm completely familiar with the history of the *Book*. In my view St Trallen's Chapel is a vital local religious shrine and it should be treated as such. But now my sister tells me that people are crawling all over the place. Apparently children from the school have been hanging round there re-enacting a violent crime. It must be stopped!'

'Well, maybe I can put a barrier of some sort around the place, for now,' said Phil helpfully. 'I agree that sightseers are a nuisance, even though the police have finished there.'

Father Peter was sweating. 'But we must go further. The chapel should be officially consecrated. What's more, we should campaign to have the *Book* brought back to its real home!'

Oh dear, Phil thought. This was going way too far. He murmured something noncommittal, collected up the plates and coffee cups, and nudged the retired priest to the door.

'I will speak to the bishop as soon as possible,' Father Peter trilled.

'But the chapel is private property and it would take something dramatic, I think, for the Church to step in officially.'

'We'll see about that,' the retired priest almost shouted.

Phil Dixon sighed. If Peter Hodgson got his way and the medieval *Book of St Trallen* was brought back to the chapel, there would be more hikers tramping over Dixon land. His and Becky's private place would be ruined. He might have to make a car-park and employ staff to watch over the place. He would have all the expense and none of the value.

Phil Dixon tried not to react as Peter Hodgson went ranting on, but he did look when the retired priest suddenly brought out of his pocket an old, slightly curled picture postcard of the fragment of *St Trallen's Book*. It struck him how simple it was, though beautiful in its own way. Not really like other medieval artworks at all. Perhaps it had only ever been a draft, though he had no idea how medieval artists worked, and it hardly seemed likely they would waste vellum on a trial run. Was it vellum? He hardly knew anything about the actual artefact. But one thing he did know was that the *Book of St Trallen* was no longer a major Norbridge tourist attraction. The postcard was very dated. Maybe the powers-that-be at the abbey might be tempted to relinquish it and send it back to Pelliter. Especially if there was a noisy local campaign led by a troublesome priest and his sister, a well known local teacher. Phil shook his head. What could stop them?

He was able to get rid of Father Hodgson and see him off down the path, when the farmhouse phone started ringing. Whoever was at the other end wasn't going to let up. When Phil finally managed to hurry in and answer it was Robert Clark on the other end.

'Hello, Phil. Suzy's just been on the mobile to me,' Robert said. 'There's been an incident at the school. A smashed window. Local vandals. Becky's OK, but Suzy thinks you or Judith ought to get over there.'

Phil didn't ask for any more details.

'I'll get there straight away. Thanks.'

Judith was shopping at the Pelliter superstore. Phil didn't wait. He slammed the door behind him, leapt into his car and gunned the engine. As he rounded the corner, where the farm track met the main road, he was dimly aware that Father Peter Hodgson had to leap smartly out of the way and was staring at the departing car with a look of fury and disgust.

PCSO Ro Watson was on her own now, outside St Mungo's School waiting for Jed to come back with the school caretaker. She wondered fleetingly if dealing with Liz Rudder, his old teacher, intimidated him. He seemed to have gone quiet, and to have left Ro to pick up the pieces, literally. In the unlikely event of a member of the public turning up, it would be Ro's job to keep them away from the icicles of glass still hanging from the window frame, and the crumbly bits littering the playground. Ro thought that the deputy head had been a little too keen to dismiss the matter and get away. The vandalism looked nasty to her. There was still glass everywhere.

A car squealed to a halt in the playground.

'Hello,' Phil Dixon was saying, as he slammed the driver's door. 'I think my granddaughter was here.' He was aware that he had driven a little too fast towards St Mungo's.

'I don't think you've got anything to worry about,' Ro said, hearing the anxiety in his voice and coming forward quickly. 'No one was hurt and the children had gone before we arrived. The deputy head teacher insisted that they leave. She was here almost immediately.'

'Well, that's a relief. I'm Philip Dixon.' The man nodded at her. 'You must be a Police Community Support Officer.'

'Well, that's what it says on the tin,' Ro said, pointing to her badge.

Phil grinned, suddenly relaxed now he knew Becky was fine and on her way back to Tarnfield. He would call over there and check whether or not she wanted to come home. Ro smiled back at him and he felt reassured. He had looked at the PCSO with misgivings when he had drawn up in the car. She had been hunkering down, staring at the window, and when she had straightened up and peered at him in the sunlight, his impression had been of a grim-faced woman in her late forties. But when she smiled, she changed. Her face had a mixture of confidence and warmth, and the strange scar under her left eye made her look both tough and vulnerable.

'Any idea what did the damage?' Phil asked. 'Have they found a brick or anything?'

Ro shrugged. 'We'll have a look when the community constable gets back with the caretaker. We've seen the damage. I suppose there's not much more we can do.'

'And will you be all right here on your own?' As soon as he said it, Phil realized how silly the words sounded. Ro Watson laughed, but it was warm rather than dismissive.

'I should think so. If the vandals come back I'll throw my hat at them. It's got the dynamics of a Frisbee and is about as fetching.'

Why did I suddenly feel protective towards her? Phil thought. She was a tallish, slim-looking woman with an air of being fit enough to look after herself. Maybe it was the scar, he thought. Or the fact that she didn't talk like a professional. His own dealings with the police after his daughter's death had left him feeling like an hysterical idiot most of the time.

They said their goodbyes and Phil felt Ro's warm, confident handshake. She was a funny mixture, it seemed to him. But likeable. Very different from the police officers he had met when Samantha died. The thought concentrated his mind on Becky as he got into his car and turned sharply towards Tarnfield.

Back home at The Briars, after being so briskly dismissed from the school by Mrs Rudder, Suzy served Molly and Becky with fish fingers and chips for lunch. Comfort food. It had been a tough morning and she didn't feel like serving up salad. But the girls were animated as much as upset, and seemed to feel that breaking the window was just another Jonty McFadden outrage.

'Jonty's a real bully,' Molly said. 'He's got it in for us.'

'What do you mean?' Suzy asked her.

'He doesn't like me,' Becky Dixon said. 'He hated it when I joined St Mungo's. Miss MacDonald said I was best at computers. Jonty said that was boys' work. And he's always talking about sex.'

'He says he's done it,' Molly stated in a matter-of-fact voice. 'Yuk, imagine doing it with Jonty!'

'Really?' Suzy was alarmed. She was shocked to hear Molly talking about 'doing it' with anyone. She and her daughter had had all the usual chats about biology, loving relationships and having babies, but so far she had thought it was all theoretical. This was a bit of a shocker.

Phil Dixon called in at The Briars in the middle of lunch, but he didn't stay. He satisfied himself that his granddaughter was perfectly happy. That evening, as planned, Suzy called the Dixons with an update.

'It's very kind of you, Mrs Spencer,' Judith Dixon said. 'And I'm really glad Phil didn't drag Becky home because of this. To be frank, this is giving me a chance to talk to him about these Dodsworth House scholarships. Is your daughter going to do it?'

'I'm not in a position to pay fees, Mrs Dixon. Not even reduced scholarship fees.'

'Won't her father divvy up?' Judith Dixon had asked sharply. People like Judith prided themselves on saying what they thought. 'Or her stepfather? Robert Clark? He's a college lecturer, isn't he? That's a good job. You should get him to pay.'

Mind your own business, Suzy should have said, but she was too taken aback. 'We've never discussed it. I'm sure Molly will do perfectly well at Norbridge High.'

The idea that Robert might be inveigled into paying school fees for Molly left Suzy feeling uncomfortable. When it came to the children's schooling, Suzy was happy with the state sector. Jake had sailed through, but then he was a bright, easy-going lad. Maybe with Molly it would be different. Perhaps she, too, should be thinking of paying for her daughter's education. It would be a strain, though.

Judith Dixon's blunt words made Suzy worry. So far, Nigel had supported his children, but where exactly should Robert come in? He wasn't technically their stepfather, but if Molly was really having problems, could she ask Robert for help? A loan perhaps? Nigel talked a good act but she knew he spent his money on his new smart lifestyle whenever he could. He maintained that he disapproved of private education and his children should make it on their own merits like he had. And he was pretty unsympathetic to Molly as it was.

Perhaps it wasn't so simple after all. The longed-for divorce seemed to bring unanticipated and embarrassing problems in its wake. Somehow, as the weekend went on, Suzy found it hard to find a moment when she could talk to Robert. And the longer she left it, the harder it got.

Mrs Rudder had arrived home at her villa in High Pelliter after sorting out the police and putting them right about the broken window. So much fuss! Alison MacDonald and those children shouldn't have been in school anyway. She parked her car neatly in the garage. It was a hatchback, just too small to get her husband John's wheelchair in the boot. There had been some talk at the hospital about trading up to a vehicle which could pack the chair and a Zimmer frame into the back, so that John could be taken out.

'Let's give it a try!' her brother Kevin had said when the neurologist first suggested that John was well enough to come home.

'If you can get him back on his feet it will really help,' the consultant had said. 'It could even increase his life expectancy.'

The physiotherapist had given them a sheet with a list of exercises for John to do. There had been some talk of a private physio coming to the house, but Liz had been worried about the cost.

'But we can try taking John out ourselves,' Kevin had insisted, and had loaded John into his SUV.

The trip had been a disaster. The barmaid at the Crossed Foxes had said, 'Ah, bless him', in a voice which had made Liz mad. John made a disgusting mess and Kevin had to feed him, which was downright humiliating. She didn't want to be seen with an old man in a wheelchair, rather than the charming and attractive person she had married. John was getting all the help he needed from the National Health Service at home, and that was where he would stay. Liz didn't really feel caring was her bag. She hired an agency for getting John up and putting him to bed. Her brother Kevin was such a godsend, sitting with John a lot, especially on Wednesday evenings when Liz had her Spanish lessons. Kevin had been John's business partner in the past and he certainly owed the Rudders a lot. But even so, what he did now was above and beyond the call of duty.

'Hi, Kevin, hello, John,' Liz ruffled her husband's dark hair and bent to kiss him, missing his face by an unnoticed half-inch.

Kevin watched her approvingly and said cheerily, 'Was it bad? The attack at the school?'

'It wasn't an attack, Kevin. Just a broken window. We had rather an inexperienced teacher in there, doing extra-curriculum art without the proper procedure. Asking for trouble.'

Liz saw her brother out, and then went back inside and made herself some fresh coffee. Just before the agency workers were due to arrive that evening, she would put out a microwave shepherd's pie from the freezer with a glass of juice. Till then John would be all right. He was grunting at her as she passed the sitting-room door, but she ignored him. How was she supposed to know what on earth he was mumbling about?

She went up to her own bedroom, redecorated in the Easter holidays. It was her favourite room. John now slept on the ground floor in what had been his office. The little dim room was quite adequate for his needs. John had been bothered with night blindness before the stroke, and he still had a bright Anglepoise lamp. Liz was glad to be rid of it. She'd hated having the light on in the night, and now she had the prettiest of pale-pink bedrooms, with soft cherry lamps.

She pressed a button on her cerise landline phone.

'Hello, Callie,' she said in her brightest teacher's voice. 'Have you got a minute? I think I may have something of yours. Are you missing a hammer?'

Chapter Six

For he hath regarded the lowliness of his handmaiden.

Magnificat. Luke 1:48. Folio 59v. **Les Très Riches Heures du Duc de Berry**

At half past twelve on Saturday morning, after the police had gone, Alison MacDonald set off to drive to her fiancé's flat in South Manchester. Mrs Rudder had dealt with the police constable, while Alison waited in the staff-room. But the PCSO woman had come to chat to her. Alison had said, 'At first I thought it was a boy from my class. But now I can't be sure.' As Mrs Rudder had said, she couldn't be really sure, could she? But she felt vaguely ashamed. She had been convinced it was Jonty McFadden running away from the smashed window. So why had she been persuaded by Mrs Rudder that she might have made a mistake, or even have *wanted* it to be Jonty?

Alison picked up speed once she reached the M6 and turned south. It was a fine spring day, the blue sky and sage green hills momentarily lifting her spirits. But she couldn't stop thinking about the 'minor vandalism incident', as Mrs Rudder had called it. If mere vandalism had been the aim, why hadn't the vandals smashed the staff-room window or the big glass doors? Alison had experienced working with disruptive children in Manchester, but this was different. She felt personally victimized. Not for the first time in the last few weeks, she thought about handing in her notice at St Mungo's.

But the Police Community Support Officer had put a different point of view. Alison felt the woman had been older, friendly, non-judgemental; and she had been the only person to ask how Alison felt.

'You shouldn't let these people affect your behaviour,' Ro had said. 'They've won if you change things. Make sure the school takes security measures. We can help you on that. But get back to normal and don't let it stop you.'

Get back to normal, Alison thought. Right … That meant putting the incident out of her mind and looking forward to seeing Mark. He needed to relax at the weekends and had a very determined idea of how to do it. Sometimes she resented being jumped on as soon as she went in the front door, but in another way it was flattering. As always, she called him from her last pit stop on the motorway, and when she arrived she put her key in the door as if it were home.

'Hi, honey,' he called out.

Mark lived on the top floor of a beautiful Victorian house. His tiny flat was costing him an arm and a leg, but, as he told Alison, the high mortgage meant that when they were married he could transfer it to a house and they could get a really good start. And Mark liked style. It was one of the things Alison found attractive about him. The flat was an oasis. He had white wine chilling in the fridge, and there were flowers on the table. Alison started to cry. It wasn't a dramatic bursting into tears, or a romantic weeping. She was snorting and snuffling, stuck in the doorway with her luggage and her coat over her arm, making a fool of herself. 'Oh Mark, I'm sorry. It's so good to be here after the school, and the kids. And the other teachers....'

Alison shuffled across the room and collapsed on the sofa, feeling the mascara smearing down her cheeks. 'Sweetheart, I can't stand it any more. Couldn't we get married this summer on the cheap? I could junk the job and come down to live here with you. We could manage.'

Mark put a roll of kitchen towel into her lap. 'Baby, pull yourself together. You know that wouldn't work. This place is far too small for both of us and our stuff. If you jacked it in and came here you might not get another job for months. Then where would we be?'

'But I hate it in Pelliter.'

'Oh Ali, get over it. Have a good cry and then we'll curl up in bed and talk about it.'

But talking, Alison knew, was what they wouldn't do.

Brenda Hodgson was pottering at home. Saturday afternoons could be very dull these days. She had washing to do. As usual she'd had coffee with Faye and Callie in the morning, and arrived back from Norbridge too late for lunch. The rich sticky cake Callie had pressed on her at the coffee shop was giving her wind. She sniggered at the sort of expressions Callie might use. Brenda had been brought up to be polite. Her parents, slightly older than average, would refer to 'spending a penny' or 'paying a visit' in an arch sort of way. No bodily functions were spoken of. When Brenda had started her periods she had thought she was going to die.

'What on earth...?' her mother had said in her usual cross voice. 'Well, I suppose it had to happen sometime. I thought you'd know all about it. Didn't anyone tell you?' Somehow Brenda was to blame, as usual. No friends or teachers cared enough to keep her informed. Her mother had rolled her eyes to heaven. 'And you'd better get used to it because it comes every month. And another thing ... you don't ever talk about this, especially not to men. It's secret. Do you understand? A secret.'

Brenda nodded. She understood about secrets. But she couldn't possibly imagine having a secret from Peter. Her brother was the only person she could talk to. That night she had confided to him about what had happened, but he sprang away from her as if she were contaminated. The next day at school, desperate for reassurance, she told the girl she sat next to.

'Oh, you've started! But you shouldn't talk about it.' Liz had looked at her with round eyes. She and Liz had spent the whole of break-time discussing it in the corner of the yard. And so a friendship had begun which had lasted over forty years.

Forty years. One of the oddest things about getting old was that time suddenly seemed to have passed so quickly. Where had the years gone? The inevitable cycle of the year seemed to get faster and faster. First there was the start of the autumn term with the new children, all keen, clean and shiny, eager to please. Then came practices for the Christmas concert and nativity play. Then there was the dull routine of the winter, as the children somehow grew greyer and duller like the weather outside. Then in the first warmth of a spitefully unreliable spring, they suddenly became overconfident, rude and brutish, with pointy arms and legs, and flabby spare tyres of tummy. By April they were all overheated and flapping with grimy layers of clothing: cardigans, fleeces, anoraks, scarves and gloves for every occasion, so that teaching became overlaid with a constant search for missing coats, bags, books, and nowadays even mobile phones! St Mungo's had never really had a uniform, though the children were encouraged to wear bottle-green tracksuits and the school shirt with the logo on. Brenda hated bottle green. The children looked like overcooked vegetables sitting there in their spinach-coloured sweatshirts.

Brenda had taught Year Four now for over ten years. It was a role she thought she found entirely satisfactory. Liz Rudder had always taken Year Five, which was of course the best year. The children were aged eight to nine, cute and enthusiastic, old enough to be responsible, but not burdened with SATs tests or puberty like Year Six. But it was only right that Liz Rudder should teach the easiest year. Liz was deputy head, and she had always had more responsibility, especially since the Findleys had gone to pieces.

Admiring Liz Rudder had been part of Brenda's psyche for so long that she felt disturbed and dislocated now the need had gone. There was only one word to describe the way Liz had behaved to Brenda. It was such a horrid cruel word that Brenda hesitated to use it, but it was a word that came flying into her brain like a demented bat when she wanted to shoo it away. Dumped. That was the term the children used, too. She had been dumped by Liz. It was almost inconceivable and it was a total mortification.

Brenda poured herself a gin and tonic, and sat in her spotless little sitting room. She had tried not to brood about it, and to find new friends, but it was hard to accept that since John had had his stroke Liz had cut her out. She just couldn't understand why. For years she had been Liz's confidante and support, her bridesmaid when she had married, her handmaiden really. But now, she was ditched. These Spanish lessons on Wednesday nights, for example. Liz had hardly ever done things without Brenda before, but she hadn't even suggested that Brenda take lessons too.

Had Liz dropped her because she was embarrassed about John's awful stroke, his lolling head and dribbling mouth? Was it because Brenda had known John when he was young and handsome, though now he had become a burden? A burden with his own secrets. Secrets were Brenda's thing, and my goodness, now she had secrets galore!

Brenda thought about what she had recently discovered. It was astonishing, and if Liz knew she would be horrified. More than horrified. The satisfaction of being 'in the know' sometimes made Brenda feel triumphant. She had been genuinely fond of Liz and there wasn't a day went by when she didn't feel shocked and hurt that their friendship was in decline. And humiliated and vengeful too, she had to admit. But the whole business had left Brenda smarting to show Liz a thing or two, and there was no doubt that she'd found a way to do just that. The knowledge should have buoyed her up and made her feel better because now she, Brenda Hodgson, was the one in the picture, and clever old Liz, repository of all grown-up knowledge, was out of the loop, as they said on the TV.

Brenda sniggered, but the laughter didn't console her. There was her new friendship with Callie and Faye too, but it wasn't really enough either. Sometimes she felt bad about what she'd done, but *any* way she could find to get her own back was justified, wasn't it? It wasn't disloyal when you had been so badly treated. She had told her brother all about it, and he had agreed. And he was a priest, so that must be all right.

It had been a wearying day all round, Liz Rudder thought as she went to check that John was tucked out of sight in the little room where he slept. The carers had been, and he was in bed at eight o'clock. Back in the living room, Liz relaxed in her favourite armchair with a glass of Rioja at her side. She picked up the headphones connected to the laptop on the sideboard. Putting them on, she heard the relaxing voice, full of promise, saying '*Bu-en-os di-as.*' The Spanish lessons had started partly as a way of getting out of the house, away from John and his squeaks and smells. But a few months ago, like an epiphany, Liz had suddenly envisaged herself living in Spain as soon as she could. Why not?

If John died, this would be easy-peasy. Even if he stayed alive, he could eventually be put in a cheaper type of nursing home. No one would blame her. That way, she could afford something very attractive near Marbella when she retired. Of course she would need her full pension from St Mungo's and the money from the sale of the house. She'd hoped at first that her oldest friend Brenda might come with her and purchase a neighbouring apartment, but practicality ruled that out. Now that Brenda's brother had come back to Pelliter to live in their parents' house, Brenda only had the little terraced house near the council estate. Property prices at that end of the market had tumbled far more than for the big villas in High Pelliter. There was no way Brenda could afford the sort of place in Spain Liz had in mind.

And recently Liz had realized that Brenda was so tedious. All those silly little secrets she made so much of! Who cared? Liz recognized that she and Brenda had been friends for forty years, but increasingly she felt that Brenda hadn't been a confidante so much as a parasite, feeding from Liz and John's precarious relationship.

But it wasn't precarious any more. With John in his wheelchair, unable to move, it was just about as settled as any relationship could be. John's roving eye couldn't rove any further than the ceiling.

And there was a satisfactory element about being able to ditch boring Brenda. The Hodgsons had always been so snooty, with their son the vicar and their posh house. But now Peter Hodgson was back in Pelliter under some sort of cloud, and it was Brenda who had the mean little terraced house near the Pelliter Valley estate while Liz was contemplating an off-plan apartment in Andalusia. How things had changed!

Liz clamped the headphones securely over both ears so she could hear nothing but the sound of Spain. She could almost feel the sun, and hear the gentle waves on the shore under her balcony.

Chapter Seven

Save me, O God: ... I sink in deep mire where there is no standing.

Psalm 69:1-2. Folio 153r. **Les Très Riches Heures du Duc de Berry**

'Hello, home,' PCSO Ro Watson said on Saturday evening, as her car lurched on to the track which led down to the Burnside cottages. Although her weekend shift meant Ben was with his grandparents overnight, she never felt alone here. It was always a real delight to come back to Burnside. She wasn't concerned about the fall in house prices, because she was never going to sell. There was recession here too, of course, but the rugged countryside and the matching doggedness of the locals offered her the security she badly needed. She had no illusions, either. Pretty scenery didn't necessarily make for pretty behaviour – as you could see any Saturday night in Norbridge. But the area was still beautiful and she loved it.

Ro dumped her bag on the sofa and clattered downstairs to the kitchen. She filled the kettle and sat down at the table; then she looked out of the window and let the scenery do its work. It never failed to calm her. The sun was dropping over the other side of the valley, so the peachy colours of evening were already tinting the fells to the east, though it was barely six o'clock. It would be light until eight. The back of the house was sheltered, staying warm until late.

Peace. She needed time to think.

For a start, she had to face something embarrassing. She knew she was in danger of making a fool of herself over Jed Jackson. Her face reddened thinking about it, and the tight skin round her half-moon scar prickled. Why was she overreacting to him? Was it because respect for older women seemed in short supply at Norbridge Police Station? Was it the novelty? A form of maternalism? The fact he laughed at her jokes? Or was it the last kick of her ageing hormones? Her reaction was physical as well as emotional, as her pink face testified. Rose felt like a teenager when Jed spoke to her, and she hated herself at the same time as longing for his attention.

'So who do *you* think vandalized the school?' Jed had said that morning in the coffee shop.

50

'I don't know,' Ro had answered slowly. 'There's something odd about it. I thought the deputy head was too calm about it.'

Jed was quiet for a moment. 'Mrs Rudder and Miss Hodgson both taught me at St Mungo's. They've been there for years.'

'Mrs Rudder was very composed. In control.'

'Yes, she was. Just like her. Doesn't like things to be out of place.'

'But things *were* out of place. There was a great big hole in the window! And why break a window at the school, when you are so likely to be seen? Vandals don't usually operate on a Saturday morning in broad daylight. I don't want to let this go, Jed.'

'So what do you want to do?'

'I'd like to talk to the other teacher, the one in the background, the younger woman. She was there when it actually happened. I took her name and address. Miss Alison MacDonald. Will you come and see her with me? She's away for the weekend but she said she'd be back on Sunday evening.'

And what did I really want? Ro asked herself, looking back at the morning's meeting. To go and interview a teacher on a Sunday, my day off? To pretend to be a real cop? Or was it an excuse to be with Jed Jackson again?

Ro ran her fingers over the ridges of her scar. Much as she loved having her son racketing around, Mrs Carruthers had been right: it was good to be on her own and able to think. She would have to get a grip. Blushing every time Jed Jackson spoke to her was downright stupid, and there would have been no point even if he had been twenty years older. Since going back to Liverpool to live with her mother when Ben was a toddler, Ro had decided there was no room for men in her life; moving to Cumbria hadn't changed that. For the last five years the only men she had met were doctors, Ben's teachers and Mrs C's husband, who was dentally challenged and enough to put you off the opposite sex for life. Maybe that was why Jed was having such an effect.

You're an idiot, she told herself. You're a wrinkled, middle-aged woman. There was only one cure. She opened a bottle of wine and decided to do the ironing. At least she could get the creases out of something!

At about the same time, Brenda Hodgson opened the gin bottle. Then, after thinking for a few minutes, she went into the sitting-room of her cluttered but shiny clean house and pressed the 'quick call' button for her brother.

'Hello, Peter. Did you get anywhere with Phil Dixon on the chapel?' she asked him.

Peter said, 'I certainly hope so. I made the point most firmly. He must have understood my point of view.'

'You know,' Brenda said quietly, 'I really think it might be better if the chapel were closed altogether. It has such nasty associations now. And there have been doubts cast on its validity, and the validity of the *Book*.'

'Don't be ridiculous!' her brother snapped. 'It's a vital piece of local history. Just because one silly rambler goes walking and falls and gets killed, it's no reason to talk abut closing the place completely. You must never say such a thing again.'

He put the phone down. It was the nearest they had come to a quarrel in a long time, but Brenda knew how touchy her brother could be. She sighed. She had said the wrong thing, so she would have to work on him a little harder. But he would come round to her way of thinking. He always did.

She flicked the pages of the novel she was reading but she felt lonely. Callie would be surrounded by her kids and no doubt Faye Armistead would be having an elegant dinner party in her beautiful Georgian farmhouse. In the past Brenda had often spent Saturday evening with Liz and John Rudder. Why not try again? After all, Liz used to talk to Brenda about everything, especially her marriage.

Brenda was totally trustworthy with secrets. Liz and John had had married quickly, just three months after meeting. Liz had told Brenda all about it – being seduced in John's Ford Capri, then the worry about being 'late'. To get pregnant was a disaster in those days!

'In sickness and in health' – what a commitment. And Liz said she had to do everything for John now. How awful and repellent, Brenda thought. No wonder Liz was touchy. When Brenda met John these days, he was all clean and tidied up – and Brenda wasn't on her own.

'Hello, Liz?' she said breathlessly into the phone when Liz answered. She tried to ignore the irritated note in Liz's voice.

'Oh, hello, Brenda.'

'I know we haven't met for a while,' Brenda said, sounding wheedling but unable to stop herself. 'I'd like to see you. Just for a chat. I've had cross words with Peter and you know how much that upsets me.'

'Really? What about?' Liz sounded as if she couldn't care less.

'That silly chapel on Dixons' land. I said I thought it ought to be closed permanently since that poor man was attacked there. But Peter got all upset. He's very keen on the place, you know. He thinks it ought to be some sort of proper shrine.'

'Oh, well, come over if you like,' Liz's voice was grudging. 'I can tell you about the vandalism today at school. Teenagers have broken a window. Give me half an hour before you set out. Kevin's just popped in; he'll help me tidy John up. You know how messy John can be.'

Vandalism at the school? That was new. This time last year, Liz would have been on the phone about it to Brenda straight away. But Liz's reluctant manner made Brenda cross. Once, she would have been Liz's right-hand woman.

It was too warm for a mackintosh and too breezy for a cardigan, so when Brenda went out she put on her anorak as usual. She had her bag over her shoulder and sensible shoes for the walk. It was such a nice evening that she decided to walk down through Pell Marshes instead of round by the road. She would have avoided the marshes if they had been full of screaming kids, but they were mostly at home now, for their tea, computer games and Saturday night television.

She walked briskly along, aware that a cool breeze was blowing up from the sea. Two men who had been dumping a mattress saw her coming, and hared off back to their white van. A chap walking his dog whistled. 'Here, Bonzo!' he called.

Suddenly the marshes were quiet. The sun still shone, but there was a metallic edge to it. The wind blew up over the lip of the valley and down towards the river which ruffled as if a hundred knives had flicked over the surface.

Brenda strolled along the path, faster now, deep in thought, the gin making her angrier.

At The Briars in Tarnfield, Becky Dixon and Molly Spencer sat on Molly's bed watching *High School Musical Three*.

'This is rubbish,' Becky scowled.

'Yeah. I used to like it though,' Molly said. 'When I used to be mates with the others.'

'And now you've only got me. You feel rejected and you've lost self respect. I've had counselling. I know about all that.'

'Have you? Had counselling? Was it 'cos of your mother?' Molly was curious. It was one of the many fascinating things about Becky.

'Yeah, you know why. Everyone does. My mum took an overdose by mistake and died. *"She was a lovely looking girl, and got in with a bad crowd"*. That's what Grandma says. But I think she must have been a bit weak. They never say that, but you don't have to win the Nobel Prize to work it out.'

'And what happened to your dad?'

'Don't know anything about him. He could be anyone. I'd really like to know, but I don't suppose I ever will. And there's another thing I'd be interested to know – like, when did my mum start her periods? That's hereditary. I bet you'll start soon Molly, 'cos you're big. Tall is good.'

'And my chest hurts, and I feel sick a lot. And my hair has gone all ratty. But it needn't be hereditary from your mum. You could take after your granny, or an aunty or someone. And it's nothing to do with size.'

'You might be right there. Lily Smith's got bigger boobs than anyone, but she hasn't started.'

'How do you know?'

'I asked her!'

'Becks! How could you? You're amazing!'

The two girls started to giggle and rolled about on the bed until the fit passed. Then suddenly Becky sat bolt upright.

'Why do you think Jonty's hammer missed me?'

'Who says he was throwing it at you? It could have been me.'

'It was me.' Becky scowled. 'And that old Rudderless bitch knew that. She hates me. So does Cow McFadden. I hate her too. And Jonty. He's a creep. He's got an evil face. I think Mrs Findley was going to have a baby and it died inside her. Maybe Jonty McFadden looked at it,' Becky growled.

Molly started to laugh again, the rising wave of hysteria collecting in her throat.

'No, Molly, I mean it,' Becky said leaning forward and staring into Molly's eyes. 'It's not funny. Jonty McFadden is evil. I can tell these things.'

The two girls stared at each other until the rest of the room went into a blur. Then Molly said, 'Let's watch *The Dark Knight* again, Becky. It's a classic now. We can see it before supper. It's ages yet. Or we could go out for a walk. It's the first really nice evening of the year.'

'Walking's boring. Why don't we take a couple of bikes? I bet you haven't been out on your bike for weeks.'

'I'm too big for my bike now. I've outgrown it.'

'Well then, I can go on yours and you can go on your brother's. Come on, you need to get fit, Molly.'

In the kitchen, Suzy Spencer heard Molly and Becky crashing down the stairs. Why can't they just place one foot at a time? she thought irritably.

'We're taking the bikes out for a ride,' Molly called. 'I'm going to ride Jake's. I don't mind the crossbar. We won't be long. Promise.'

'Molly, wait…' Suzy was sorting out potatoes and carrots for a casserole. Having Becky to stay meant Suzy felt compelled to make a bit more effort with the family meals in a sort of fruitless competition with fiercely domesticated Judith Dixon.

'You must be back in half an hour,' she called. 'Wear your helmets. And don't speak to anyone you don't know. And don't go on the main road, OK?'

'All right,' Molly yelled back. She and Becky were already making for the garage where the bikes were kept.

'And put your jackets on …' Suzy shouted.

'Let them be, Mum,' said Jake in his deep voice. 'You always say people are tougher on girls.'

Suzy carried the vegetables to the sink. 'OK, OK. So how about peeling these?'

Jake shrugged and slammed the microwave shut on his popcorn. 'Where's the potato peeler?' he asked.

'I don't know. I've just been looking for it.' Suzy rummaged in the drawer. 'Robert!' she called. 'Have you any idea where it is?'

'Where what is?' Robert pulled himself away from reading his book on Canada. Suzy glanced at him guiltily. They had hardly talked this weekend, what with the window incident and having Becky to stay.

'Robert, look at me. Read my lips. Where is *the potato peeler*? I can't find it anywhere. I've been losing a lot of things lately.'

'Is it your age?' Robert asked mildly, and then had to duck to miss a plastic plate that went flying past his ear.

'Now you've lost that too,' he said.

Brenda Hodgson looked at her watch as she walked. It was only 6.30, but the marshes were deserted. Behind her was Pelliter village, and then the spread of the Pelliter Valley estate. From a distance it looked neat – rows of red-brick semis with patches of garden, flat windows and sloping roofs. It was only close up that you could see the junk – broken bikes, old TVs, furniture with the stuffing coming out. Brenda tutted as she passed the mattress which had been abandoned only a few minutes earlier.

Suddenly she felt something career into her back and the shock took her breath away. Her first reaction was that kids had run into her and she had to stop herself falling. She stumbled forwards and the heels of her hands hit the damp ground, making a ridge in the earth.

At the same time the first kick hit her in the small of her back. Then there was an almost businesslike silence. I'm being attacked, she thought, and for the first few seconds she felt no pain, only outrage.

She tried to cry out in anger, but another kick landed on the back of her head and forced her face into the mud. She felt the pressure on her nose and the dirt ramming into her left eyeball. Her right eye was shut but she opened it for the last time as her head was jerked backwards.

She was pulled by what seemed like a hundred little claws and then thrown forward. She knew immediately she had landed face down on the mattress.

Suddenly she writhed, raising her head half an inch. Through her battered and stinging left eye she saw the little hand and the flash of the knife. Then she lost consciousness.

Chapter Eight

Unto the upright there ariseth light in the darkness

Psalm 112:4. Folio 61r. **Les Très Riches Heures du Duc de Berry**

O n Sunday morning at six o'clock the phone rang in Ro's cottage. 'There's been a murder, Ro.' Suddenly she was wide awake.

'Sergeant? Where? Who was it?'

'A woman called Brenda Hodgson. Teaches at St Mungo's. Body's in a heck of a state. Knife wounds. You need to get into work. There could be panic about this. You were there at St Mungo's yesterday morning, weren't you? Some vandalism thing? Well, forget about that now. We're going to need you to visit the head teacher and some of the key staff. This is one occasion when a PCSO could actually be useful.'

Shock had a funny effect on people, Ro thought. Sergeant Liddle had betrayed his feelings about the role of the PCSOs, but this wasn't the moment for her to react.

'Anyway,' the sergeant went on, 'Jed Jackson's been here since the early hours when some revellers found the body. He suggested I call you. He seems to think you could be some help. Let's see if you can do anything. Get over to the station now.'

Suzy Spencer and Robert Clark had gone to church early that morning without hearing the news. At the end of the service the vicar came up to Suzy.

'Molly goes to St Mungo's in Pelliter, doesn't she? Something dreadful has happened to one of the teachers there. The rector in Uplands has been there most of the night and called me this morning. You'll want to check it out and speak to Molly.'

Suzy and Robert hurried home and put on Radio Cumbria. Brenda Hodgson's body had been found at two o'clock in the morning and reporters were already at the scene. It was a big story already making national news. The usual crimes of a Saturday night were nothing compared with the brutal knifing and mutilation of a blameless middle-aged schoolteacher.

Upstairs, where the girls were sharing a bedroom, all was suspiciously quiet. There was a TV there too. Suzy raced up but it was too late. Molly and Becky were sitting on the bed, pale-faced, hunched over Molly's mobile phone, the TV news in the background.

'So you've heard about Miss Hodgson?' Suzy asked.

'Oh, Mummy!' Molly began to cry uncontrollably and Suzy threw herself on the bed between the two girls. Molly plunged her head on to Suzy's shoulder and grabbed her arm.

'I didn't like Podgy Hodgson,' Molly sobbed. 'No one did. But getting murdered is horrible.'

'We got a text about half an hour ago while you were at church,' Becky explained. 'Since then everybody's been texting everyone else.'

Suzy hugged them both to her. 'I'll go and make some hot chocolate for you. Don't watch any more TV or read any more texts. Come downstairs.'

Left behind on the bed, Molly started to shake. Becky held her arm in a fierce grip. 'No one knows about us. We mustn't say anything....'

The two girls stared at each other. Becky's eyes looked huge and Molly felt as if she was falling into them.

Philip and Judith Dixon were enjoying breakfast in bed. Becky's friendship with Molly Spencer was a real boon, Judith thought. It gave them a well-earned break when they could talk about things like the Dodsworth House scholarship. She knew it was on Phil's mind – he had gone out for a long walk the night before to think about it. Judith was desperate for Becky to go to a nice private school. She had always worried that Becky might make unsuitable friends, like her mother had done. Judith had never had any illusions about Samantha's attraction to a wild lifestyle. But she'd be damned if Becky went the same way. But then Samantha had always been a handful – spoilt by her soft-hearted father from an early age because he thought she was so 'creative'.

Judith had seen to it that Becky was never spoilt like Samantha. And in any case, Becky was stronger and smarter than Sam had been. Becky had inherited Sam's artiness, but also Judith's common sense. And whoever Becky's father had been, Judith recognized that he had given her granddaughter a sharp, practical intelligence, as well as her thick dark hair and sparkling eyes. Becky wasn't arty-farty and pretentious like Samantha. Judith had loved her daughter in her way, of course. But Sam had always irritated the heck out of her, and since their first argument, Judith had always suspected and feared the worst for her.

Phil was putting the tea tray on the dressing-table. 'Shall we put the radio on?' he asked. It was such a treat not to be woken by the alarm at 6.30 in the morning that the radio seemed intrusive. This was one of the few Sundays when Phil had decided not to go to church and, after all, they were supposed to be having a lie-in.

'Oh, let's hear the nine o'clock news,' Judith said. 'We might as well.'

The first headline was Brenda Hodgson's brutal murder.

At the same time, in one of the new detached houses in Minster Mews, head teacher Ray Findley was drinking tea with PCSO Ro Watson. He looked tired. He often couldn't sleep these days, he told Ro. He had spent a large part of the previous night outside, watering the borders. The garden had been Sheila's hobby before her breakdown. The police team had called round at the house to talk to him at the crack of dawn about Brenda Hodgson's death. At the sergeant's request Ro had followed up the police's questioning with a visit to talk about how the school should respond.

Ro knew all the details. Miss Hodgson's body had been easy to identify. Her purse with all her personal details was still intact, along with fifty pounds in the inside pocket. So robbery wasn't the motive, and in that case why would a thief have mutilated the body with a knife? Brenda's brother, the retired priest Father Peter Hodgson, lived in a decayed but grand Victorian house on Pelliter's main street.

'He kept wringing his hands and talking about the dirt,' Jed Jackson had said. 'It's odd how it takes people, the sergeant says.'

But Ray Findley had been surprisingly calm when Ro arrived at his home, though she reminded herself that he'd had a few hours already to absorb the news. Like most people in Pelliter that morning, he had both the TV and radio on, but in the Findleys' house they were at very low volume.

'My wife had a breakdown earlier this year,' the head teacher said. 'I need to keep anything that could be upsetting away from her. She worked with Brenda Hodgson for quite a few years.'

'And you did, too. You must both be very upset.'

'Yes, of course.' Ray Findley looked surprised that anyone should consider his feelings. 'But I must admit that I wasn't close to Brenda. She was a very capable teacher and there were very few problems with her classes. She just got on with it. Do you have any idea yet who could have done this terrible thing?'

'It's early days, Mr Findley. And I'm a PCSO so I'm not involved with solving crime. I'm here to ask what you want to do about your school.'

Sometimes people could bridle when PCSOs tried to help, but Ray Findley just looked at her blankly. Ro went on, 'Our advice is not to do anything dramatic yet. Maybe you could close for a half day or something like that, in her memory, later on.'

Ray Findley nodded. He still stared a little glassily at Ro, but she could see that he was beginning to think beyond the walls of his own home and his own problems.

'Maybe you could get the children together and tell them about Miss Hodgson first thing in the morning. We have a form of words you may like to use. Her own class might need counselling. We can help you with that. And you'll need someone to teach them.'

'I'll speak to Mrs Rudder about all this. I might have to stay at home with my wife.'

'But it's your school, Mr Findley. You need to be in control. Look, this is a massive press story too. Journalists will be sniffing around everywhere. There are already TV and radio reporters at the Marshes. I used to work in public relations. I know they'll be all over you like a rash. You need think about what you want to do.'

Ray Findley nodded slowly.

'They'll want you to say something about Miss Hodgson. I'm sure you have protocols about talking to the press, but I doubt the Local Education Authority will be up to speed on this one on a Sunday morning. You need to make sure your staff members aren't talking to all and sundry, too. There needs to be some leadership. You're the head teacher.'

'Yes, that's quite true.' A woman's voice came from behind her. Ro turned to see Sheila Findley standing in the doorway. She was a tall, thin, dark-haired woman. She might once have been slender, but now she was haggard, with a long pale face and heavy shadows under her eyes. She said, 'Ray, you can't leave this to Liz Rudder. And you need to contact the Education Authority. The policewoman's right.'

I'm not a policewoman, Ro thought, but I am right. She turned back to look at the head teacher. He was staring at his wife. 'Sheila … are you all right?'

'Yes, I am. Which is more than you can say for poor Brenda Hodgson. It sounds truly awful.' Sheila Findley pulled up another chair and joined them at the kitchen table. 'You need to take charge, Ray. As the lady pointed out, it's your school.'

Callie McFadden was usually woken on Sundays by the kids screaming or someone banging on her bedroom door wanting something. But this time the house was silent when she finally drifted out of sleep. Her mouth was dry and her head ached.

Then she heard the rumble that meant the telly was on in the front room downstairs. But instead of the usual shouts and arguments, there was quiet.

Callie padded down the stairs. Unusually, the living-room door was shut. She pushed it open. She could tell at once that something had happened. Her daughter was in her nightdress, with a can of lager in her hand, and her boyfriend was there too. They were both transfixed by the screen. There were no kids around.

'Hey, Mam, look, Pelliter's on the telly.'

'Yeah,' said the boyfriend, taking a swig from his can. 'There's been a murder. In the Marshes. Frigging unbelievable. We're on the map now.'

'There's a TV crew at the bottom of the road, Mam. Jonty's down there now. You must have heard it on the radio.'

'No. I haven't heard it on the radio.'

'Has no one rung or texted you, Mam?'

'No, no one has rung or texted me neither.' Callie sat down heavily, pushing some dirty washing and *Heat* magazines off the only armchair in the room.

Her daughter's head jerked towards the screen. A snap of Brenda Hodgson on a school trip, with the faces of the children marbled out, stared at them. Brenda looked at them with the sort of forced smile she used on school occasions.

'Miss Hodgson. It's just been confirmed. Relatives have been informed.' Callie's daughter loved TV cop shows and knew all the jargon. 'Awful, innit? She was your mate, wasn't she? Fat Miss Hodgson. Brenda Hodgson. I didn't know her name was Brenda.'

'We'll get the details from the net,' said the boyfriend with relish. 'The reporter talked about a knife though. My mate texted me about it. He said it were a cat skinner.'

'Where's Jonty?' Callie suddenly jumped up. 'Where's he gone?'

'I told you, Mam: he's down at the Marshes.'

'So get off your fat bottom, and go and bring him back here. I don't want him hanging around down there. It's not nice. Go on, pronto. Get Jonty.'

Ro's session with the Findleys had been exhausting, but Jed Jackson had briefed her well. He remembered Miss Hodgson as a teacher and he certainly knew her as one of Pelliter's fixtures. He'd kept up with the school gossip and knew all about the Findleys and Sheila's breakdown.

What he didn't know was that Sheila Findley had lost a baby and that had catapulted her into depression. While her husband was phoning his staff, Sheila Findley had walked Ro around the garden and told her all about it. 'It started with a miscarriage. I'm on medication for depression. And astonishingly it's working.'

'Well, it does, you know!'

Mrs Findley had smiled. 'Until recently I thought I would never come out of it. There was nothing to live for. I thought that expression was a stock phrase until I felt it myself. But now, I hope to be teaching again in September. I haven't told Ray yet. He's very protective of me. He's really a very nice man.'

Her eyes met Ro's. 'OK, maybe he's too nice. He'll tell everyone what a wonderful teacher Brenda Hodgson was. But she was never very good.' Sheila Findley laughed at Ro's raised eyebrows. 'What's the point of lying? The only good thing about depression is that you don't give a toss what you say. Poor Brenda was all right – she never caused any trouble. That was the best you could say for her. Liz Rudder is far more subversive. Liz would use Brenda from time to time to make trouble. They were so-called best friends, but Liz has dropped Brenda like a stone lately, or so I hear. Poor Brenda. She idolized Liz. Tell me what really happened to her. I can take it.'

Ro had told her. Already an exaggerated version was going round the pubs and social clubs of Norbridge to whet the appetite for Sunday lunch, dwelling on the knife wounds to the teacher. Why did people enjoy all this so much? Ro wondered. Was it the change to routine and the excitement of it all? Or the joy at still being alive? Or some sort of voyeurism? But there was also a glee which she found hard to understand. It made millions of people relish the gruesome details in books about serial killers. Did big, macho, scary evil take your mind off the real thing in its nasty, petty, most insidious and frequent form?

'We all need to sing from the same hymn sheet at school,' Ray Findley said, coming out to join them, suddenly decisive after his phone calls.

'Yes,' Sheila Findley said. 'You should invite someone from the Education Department to come here to discuss what to do. I can make a cold lunch.'

If Ray Findley felt he was in control, that had to be good, Ro thought, and if Sheila was helping him that was even better. She felt she could leave them now.

When she got back to Norbridge, Ro wondered what she should do now. Sergeant Liddle had gone home and the CID were in control. But there was no point her leaving before the end of what would have been her normal shift. Ben was safe with his grandparents and it was pointless disrupting his routine. Of course, there was always her plan to go and speak to the younger teacher from St Mungo's about the broken window. The vandalism seemed trivial and irrelevant now.

Ro's mobile phone rang. Thinking of Ben as always, she fumbled for it in panic. She didn't recognize the number on the display.

'Ro, it's Gerard Jackson.'

'Oh. Hi, Jed.'

'I've been home after working all night, and grabbed about two hours' sleep, but I can't relax. You wanted to talk to that other teacher about the vandalism at St Mungo's. You've got her address, haven't you? She might be able to tell us something relevant to the murder. We can take a car. I'll be back at the station to pick you up in half an hour.'

'Great.' Ro felt a tingle of pleasure and then told herself to stop being an idiot.

Chapter Nine

The wicked walk on every side.

Psalm 12:8. Folio 61r. **Les Très Riches Heures du Duc de Berry**

Alison MacDonald had woken really late on Sunday and stayed under the duvet with Mark. When they eventually got out of bed, they didn't watch the television or listen to the radio, and for once Mark didn't log on to his laptop as soon as he got dressed.

The night before they'd had a Chinese meal, and then gone to one of Mark's favourite clubs, staying till about four in the morning. Alison hated these late night sessions, but she felt she owed him the time, as she had been such a misery the day before. At about midday on Sunday, they had dressed dopily before leaving the flat to wander in the summer sunshine to a bistro for brunch.

Ali felt much better in the morning sunshine. St Mungo's seemed manageable at a distance. And Mark was right: they did need the money. Leaving school wasn't an option. She felt new enthusiasm talking about the future, discussing the house they wanted if they could possibly afford it in Timperley or Sale. There would always be a need for primary-school teachers, Mark said, and she had experience in two schools now.

Mark was good with figures, and as they sat outside sipping cappuccinos and waiting for the food, he made calculations on the paper napkin with a biro. If Alison went on earning – and, he hinted, if she didn't walk away in hysterics from a perfectly good job – a mortgage for a terraced house was definitely within their reach.

He said, 'So next year we should be able to afford to buy. It will be brilliant not to be in a flat. I'll be the first one in the sales team to have my own house!'

One of Mark's five-a-side football pals had recently got married and bought a house in Urmston. He and his wife had a cream leather sofa and laminated wooden floors with a plain cream square rug. It all toned in mushroom and magnolia, like something out of a catalogue, and Mark had mentioned more than once how it was all do-able for him too.

And meeting at weekends had its advantages, Mark thought. It was exciting. And it gave him a bit of space for doing his own thing in the week.

Once he was married he'd give all that up, but you were only young once. And it meant he was always ready for a bit of real bedroom action by Friday. That was the most annoying thing – if Alison would only get her act together and arrive on Friday night, they could have much more nookie. He said as much over his Full English Breakfast.

'Next Friday?' Alison said. 'But I have to be at school again on Saturday morning. This mural is huge and we didn't get much done yesterday. And I'm not going to let little thugs like Jonty McFadden stop me working when I want.'

'You've changed your tune. Yesterday you wanted to jack it in.'

'It's amazing what a good night's sleep can do.' Alison looked at him with a raised eyebrow. Mark hadn't let her sleep much. But in the early hours when he dozed, she had lain there thinking. He was right: living together in the tiny studio flat would be hell. And this mural was the best thing she had done since coming to St Mungo's. It was possibly one of the best things of her career. She wasn't going to give up on it, or give up on the children who were relying on her. Like the PCSO woman had said, it should be business as usual, despite the broken window.

Mark's face darkened. 'But, Ali, you said that you'd be here every weekend.'

'But not till Saturday afternoon. You know I have to help Mum with the shopping. And other times I can't face the long drive. And then there are school things. Like the mural.'

Mark felt the acid of irritation interfering with his scrambled egg. 'That's not fair, Ali. It wasn't the deal.' He coloured slightly. He looked pink and shiny in the sunshine. 'It's tough enough having no sex Monday to Thursday. Three times a week is the average for old married couples, not people like us. I'm missing out. You should get here on Friday night.'

'Is that all you care about?' Lately, Alison had felt that some of Mark's bedroom demands were going a little too far, and the result had been to put her off, not turn her on. It would be different when they were together all the time, she thought. Their desire would be mutual and properly paced, without this pressure for a weekend marathon.

She glanced at the short fuzz of Mark's blond hair and the breadth of his shoulders. He had put on weight since she had gone back to Norbridge. His muscular stockiness had always attracted her in the past, but today in the bright sun he looked slightly greasy and tough. Perhaps she was prejudiced by overexposure to the bulky beta males of Pelliter with their tattoos. Most dads in Pelliter looked like football hooligans. Except that smart young man she had seen in the playground, a week ago. The one in the black cab. She had never found out who he was. There had been that confused expression on his face which she couldn't place.

She'd read in the free paper about that dead man at the chapel being unidentified, with no bag or coat, but dressed like the young man at the school. How many unknown smart types were there in Pelliter on a Friday night? Maybe it was the same guy. Perhaps she should tell someone, although it really seemed too trivial to mention to the police.

But there was always that Police Community Support Officer. Alison had told her that she would be home by five o'clock on Sunday night if they needed to talk further about the vandalism. Maybe she should mention the young man in the school playground at the same time.

'If you want to go to back to bed after we've been to the pub, we need to think about eating up,' she said in a conciliatory tone to Mark. 'Even if I just have one glass of red, I'll need a chance to sleep it off before driving.'

'And I'll need a chance to tire you out,' Mark said, more cheerfully now. 'Let's go back to the flat straight away.' They left the bistro and wandered back. But this time they didn't hold hands, and Alison pulled her jacket tight around her even in the pools of thin spring sunshine.

Further north, the not-so-chic greasy spoon café on Pelliter High Street had made a brave attempt to re-invent itself for the police and press who had gathered at the west side of the Marshes. They were serving cappuccinos and lattes; the creaky old espresso machine had been forced into action. The proprietor's wife had made trays of 'millionaire's shortbread' and they were doing a roaring trade; usually on Sunday they stayed closed.

Jed and Ro sat together at a rocky, plastic-topped table. They nodded to a few blokes from CID, and avoided a reporter who was trying to get information out of a flirtatious waitress.

'So what are we going to ask Miss MacDonald?' Jed said.

'Well, she'll already know about Brenda Hodgson, I suppose. Someone will have told her. She'll probably think we're unbelievably misguided, wanting to talk about a broken window at a time like this.'

'But vandalism is still an offence. Remember zero tolerance?' Jed asked.

'Not really. I think it was a buzz phrase before I came into policing.'

Jed stirred his coffee. 'So why did you do it? Come into policing? Well, community support anyway. You know what they call you lot? CHIMPS: Completely Hopeless in Most Policing Situations.'

'I didn't do it to be popular. I really do want to support the community. Even if they don't think they need it.'

'Seriously?'

'Yes, seriously. The vulnerable people anyway. My son Ben has cerebral palsy,' Ro said. It sounded very matter-of-fact. She thought, if Jed Jackson uses the word 'spastic', I will kill him, big brown eyes or not.

Jed stirred his coffee more vigorously. Ro waited for his response. Ben's condition was both absolutely vital to her life and peripheral to her job at the same time.

'I suppose it's very interesting,' Jed said suddenly.

'What?'

'Interesting. Dealing with cerebral palsy. I don't know much about it. Ben obviously gets out and about though. You said he was away this weekend? That must be quite an achievement.'

Interesting? Well, that was one way of putting it. When most people heard about Ben, they either gushed with embarrassed sympathy, or rabbited on about their own children's minor ailments. And often, people wanted to be able to blame her, to make Ben's cerebral palsy to be someone's fault, so they could enjoy their own good fortune as if they deserved it. But Jed wasn't going down that road. He had impressed Ro by remembering Ben's name and she found his curiosity much easier to deal with than the usual fake sympathy covering shock and blame. And Jed was right. Dealing with cerebral palsy was interesting. As well as awful.

'Yes, we're actually quite lucky. Ben's made massive progress. He goes to Norbridge High and has a teaching assistant for support. They've been brilliant. He's getting more independent all the time. He's at his grandparents' this weekend.'

'How limited is his movement?'

'He has what we call his wobbly walk. And his left hand isn't good. But these days the worst thing is his sight. Ben had a bad fall when he was three and the trauma led to cataracts developing.'

'I thought it was old people who had cataracts?'

'Not always. Ben's cataracts started affecting his sight when he was about seven. They have to wait for them to grow to a certain stage before anything can be done.' And we've reached that stage now, she thought with a shudder. It was a simple procedure, but it meant a general anaesthetic for a kid of his age. Without it, Ben would go blind.

She said, 'There's an operation they can do. We're pretty nervous about it, but we're hoping to go ahead with it this summer.'

'That must be tough, but it still doesn't explain why you wanted to be a PCSO.'

'Yes it does. I didn't have much of a career after Ben was born. At least, not after his fall. And as he grew up I thought – I want my son to be able to go out in the High Street and have a couple of pints and lark about and be protected. I think we're all weak in some ways, and need protection. What about you?'

'Oh, I take the opposite view. I think weakness is the problem. I think we should make people face up to their responsibilities.' Jed's face took on a set sort of look, as if he was used to having to defend his position, but was sticking to it. He was less attractive when he was on his high horse, she had noticed. But being less attractive was better as far as she was concerned. Blushing every time he spoke to her was deeply embarrassing.

'That's sounds a bit uncompromising.'

'Maybe.' Jed bridled slightly. 'Anyway, what time are we seeing Miss MacDonald?'

'Five o'clock. And I need to be away at six at the latest. I need to pick up my son.'

'And you don't feel happy until he's home? Until you're both home? With the drawbridge up?'

Ro looked at him in surprise. For such a self-righteous young man he could still be perceptive. I must come across as defensive myself, she thought. Ro Watson, chatelaine of her own little castle. The remark about the drawbridge rankled a little bit but she had to admit he was right.

Alison listened to music as she drove up the motorway back towards Pelliter. The traffic wasn't too bad, but it would be brilliant when she didn't have to do this any more. Then she remembered something Mark had said....

'If you're feeling so much better about your job, it wouldn't do any harm for you to stay on there after we're married, till we could get a really decent house. Your mum doesn't charge you any rent and your car's in good nick. As long as you're here from Friday to Monday morning it might be silly to give up a secure job these days.'

At the time Alison hadn't really been listening. But now, in the car, singing along with Jamie Cullum, a nasty little worm of thought wriggled in her brain. For all his fuss about having her there for the whole weekend, why did Mark actually want his weekday evenings to himself? Was it because he really liked clubbing and socializing and she wasn't so keen?

She had met Mark in Manchester on a night out with her colleagues. It wasn't really Alison's scene and she had been hanging back. He had come over to buy her a drink. It had been serious from the first night and she had been swept off her feet by his determination. People said men were scared of commitment, but that had not been true of Mark. He'd wanted a partner and a conventional family life, and he'd been honest from the start about wanting to get promotion too. She had always liked his drive and practicality, and she had appreciated the luxuries he took for granted on his wage as a sales manager. Foreign holidays, the way he dressed, the clothes he bought her, the meals out, and their mutual fantasies about fitted kitchens and soft furnishing all suited her. Mark had modern taste, in contrast to her parents' clutter-filled terraced cottage.

But despite all the insecurity and preoccupation with money, he wasn't scrimping and saving as she was. She suddenly felt frustrated with the dreamy music she was playing: she snapped on the radio for the news.

It had been a quiet news day – except in Pelliter. The national bulletin still led with Brenda Hodgson's murder. Alison drove for another five miles on autopilot. Then she started taking deep, rasping breaths and pulled over on to the hard shoulder. She sat there in silence for a few minutes. She called Mark, but got his irritating voice message system. It struck her with physical force that there was no one at St Mungo's she could talk to. Liz Rudder was out of the question. Ray Findley was out of the frame. She had no colleague she could call, to share some of her shock.

She rang her mother who said yes, everyone in Norbridge was talking about Brenda Hodgson's death, and that a killer was on the loose. Her mum always enjoyed a bit of drama. She added that the police had telephoned, and wanted to interview Alison about a broken window.

'You'd think they'd have better things to do,' her mother said. 'But that's what they wanted.'

Ro Watson and PC Jed Jackson were waiting in the car outside the MacDonalds' house in Norbridge. They had been talking for half an hour, mostly about Ben.

'All his support systems are in place now,' Ro said. 'He's made huge strides, literally. When he was small we thought he wouldn't walk at all. The Norbridge schools and Cumbria Scope society have been great. I like it here, though I would never have described myself as a country lover before.'

'Oh, Cumbria gets to most people in the end.'

Ro thought, Jed has so little real experience of life, yet he sounds so self assured. 'But what about you, Jed, have you never been tempted by the bright lights? Sex and drugs and rock and roll?'

'Absolutely not.'

He sounded horrified. OK, I'll shut up then, Ro thought.

Jed talked a little himself too, about his own background. His father was a manager at a local factory and his mother worked part-time for an insurance company. He was from an extended Pelliter clan, but there had been a rift in the family, and his immediate relations were his parents and a younger brother who was currently at college. Jed had been to Norbridge High, done a gap year in Belize and Guatemala, and then read theology at Durham University, not too far away. But he loved West Cumbria and was glad to be back. He'd had a few girlfriends, but nothing special for a while. Ro wondered if he would ever have talked much about his family if they hadn't been stuck in the car together waiting for Alison MacDonald to come home.

Then her car drew up and she parked neatly outside the row of cottages.

Alison emerged, her long copper hair loose unlike the neat pony-tail she wore at school. She grabbed an overnight case from the back seat.

'That's her,' Ro said.

'Let's give her a minute to get her breath back and then we'll knock on the door.'

When they strolled over and rang the doorbell, Alison's mother answered and asked them to step into the front room. She offered them tea or coffee. Jed accepted a coffee, but Ro thought that if she had any more caffeine she would bounce off the walls.

Alison came to join them. The young teacher looked tired, and paler than Ro remembered from the day before. She had almost translucent white skin. She was wearing jeans and a drooping turquoise smock top which showed her bra straps, and her long red hair swung over her shoulders. At the school she had been wearing a black zipper jacket over a crisp cotton blouse. There were also three or four silver loops in her ears which had not been there the day before. And there was the faintest outline of a love-bite on her white neck. She's younger than I thought, Ro realized.

'You'll have to forgive me if I'm a bit out of it,' Alison said. 'I'm so shocked about Miss Hodgson. And I've been away for the weekend with my boyfriend. We had a late night last night.'

'Clubbing, were you?' Jed asked sharply.

'Yes. It's not really my thing, but my boyfriend likes the club scene.'

'Can you tell us more about this window business?' Jed snapped. He sounded brisker and more abrasive than usual, Ro thought.

'But I want to know about Miss Hodgson first,' Alison said. 'I've really been knocked sideways by this terrible news. I only heard about it an hour ago, on the radio, and I've literally just walked in. What exactly happened?'

'We're not here to discuss that,' Jed said. 'We made it clear we want to talk about the window breakage, in the context of community policing and vandalism. We need to know exactly what you think occurred.'

Alison suddenly blinked and withdrew into her armchair. She looked as if she was under interrogation, rather than having a helpful talk with fellow professionals. She said formally, 'I see. We were painting a mural in the art room. I heard a noise; then a hammer came through the window. The glass was shattered, but no one was hurt.'

There was a long, tense silence. Alison felt Ro looking at her, and she stared down at the carpet.

'Is that all you can remember?' Jed asked loudly.

'Pretty much.'

'Oh come on! I thought you were supposed to teach art. You know – visual stuff. Didn't you *see* anything?'

'I'm not always looking for bad things,' Alison said. 'Unlike you. Anyway, shouldn't you be thinking about poor Miss Hodgson at the moment? I've got to deal with my class on that too.'

Ro leant forward, embarrassed by Jed's rudeness. 'But we want you to know that the vandalism matters. I'm sure the children will ask about the window tomorrow, and you need to think about what you are going to say. The two things will seem mixed up to the children, and it will be as if their whole world is upside down.'

Alison looked at Ro, and nodded. 'That's true,' she said slowly, as if she didn't wish to admit that someone in a uniform could be sensitive. 'That's how the children think.'

'Look,' Ro said, 'why don't I try and help? I could come and do a question-and-answer session with your class? Perhaps on Tuesday when the shock over Miss Hodgson has calmed down a bit? Here's my business card with my number and email address on.'

Alison nodded, relaxing slightly. 'OK. That sounds like a good idea. I'll ask Mr Findley. The children will be quite shaken up by everything and it could be good for them to speak to you, as you're a police officer.'

'She's a Police Community Support Officer, not a police officer,' Jed barked.

'But I can explain what is happening,' Ro added gently.

'That would be useful.' Alison nodded, suddenly more authoritative. 'Thank you. I'll go with that. In the meantime if you don't mind, I need to get myself together, so perhaps I've said everything I can?' She stood up.

Jed looked as if he was about to contradict her but Ro said, 'OK, we'll go. You must phone Mr Findley, Alison. I think you'll find that he's back on top, organizing things at school after this terrible incident. Thank you for seeing us.'

Ro stood up too, and Jed followed her out slowly. Alison walked them to the front door, but she closed it behind them the moment they were outside, without saying anything. Then she went back into the front room and stood at the window, watching as the tall young policeman and the older woman marched silently to the car.

As the door slammed and Jed reached angrily for his seat belt, Ro said, 'What on earth were you thinking of in there?'

'What do you mean?'

'You were so aggressive with that young woman.'

'She wasn't telling us the truth.'

'Of course she wasn't. You stride in there in a uniform and act as if we're bad cop, good cop. For goodness' sake, Jed, we're the community team, not something out of Lynda La Plante. The whole point was just for us to have a chat.'

'I'm the police officer. You're just support. I say what we're supposed to do.'

'Why? She was my contact. You wanted to come with me.'

Jed started the car and drove aggressively towards the main road. Ro put her hand on his arm.

'Stop, Jed. Tell me why Alison MacDonald annoyed you so much?'

Jed ignored her and put his foot on the accelerator. Finally he said, 'You think you're so liberal and understanding, don't you? But people like that disgust me, the sort that wear ironmongery in their ears. Who go out "clubbing". She looked shattered didn't she? She's probably a recreational substance abuser and then turns up to teach people's kids on a Monday.'

'Jed! You have no idea whether or not that's true.'

'Oh come on! Don't be naïve. She looked like a drowned cat, white as a sheet, hair all over the place, and neckline down to her navel.'

Ro turned and looked at him. 'I think you behaved insensitively.'

'Well, perhaps you're too sensitive by half.'

'Sorry? What do you mean?'

'Well, being soft-hearted is all that matters these days, isn't it? Maybe that's why having a disabled child could be an advantage when it comes to getting a job as police support officer. You had no other qualifications, did you? I suppose you thought a bleeding heart would be enough. But don't expect me to be soft on crime too.'

Ro clenched the door handle. Don't react, she told herself. Jed drove in angry silence, but she was aware of the sharpness of his movements. He's deeply upset about something, she thought; that's why he's been so appallingly rude to me. But that doesn't make it excusable. No one should ever talk like that about my relationship with Ben.

Jed was still working himself up. He said, 'And thanks to your softie approach, that interview didn't tell us anything new.'

'Really? Is that what you think? Alison MacDonald actually told us something quite crucial, but you were too full of your own self-righteousness to hear her.'

'What?'

'The hammer. That's the first we've heard of a hammer being used to break the window. So much for your interrogation technique. If you hadn't snapped at her we might have been able to ask the crucial question.'

'Oh yeah? What's that?'

'Where's the hammer now? You were the investigating officer at the school. You didn't investigate very much, did you?'

Jed drove silently into the police station car park. Ro opened the car door, got out, and slammed it behind her.

Chapter Ten

April, as if summed up by a French medieval 'chanson' "Et s'est vestu de broderie, De soleil rayant, cler et beau."

Folio 4v. **Les Très Riches Heures du Duc de Berry**

After the brutal murder, Pelliter remained frozen in shock. But on the last Monday morning in April there was also the drip, drip, drip of a mental thaw. Gossip started to flow like spring water. Maybe Miss Hodgson had been on a secret assignation with an internet date, or was into drugs, or had confronted bad characters dumping the mattress?

One by one the suggestions evaporated. It soon became known that she didn't even own a computer. The drug dealers in the town swore it was nothing to do with them, and the men who dumped the mattress came forward and were exposed as fly tippers, terrified of being implicated.

Everyone knew the details, which were reported in the papers. Inevitably more gossip had emerged via the hospital and police-station chat. Pelliter had never received so much media attention and all sorts of people thought themselves privy to special knowledge, which they immediately passed on. In offices and factories all over Norbridge, people huddled over the newspapers, initially to find out more, and increasingly to see if anyone they knew had been quoted. A teacher was public property.

But no one really remembered anything much about Miss Hodgson as a private person.

Ro Watson was off shift on Monday. She got up to see Ben off in his taxi as usual. Watching his lurching walk made her heart turn over with love and a painful, visceral sympathy. Whenever she thought about Jed Jackson and his horrible remarks – which was too often – she felt rigid with anger. Why had he suddenly turned on her like that? What was it about the young teacher that had infuriated him so much, to the extent that he'd lost his professionalism?

Later, Alison MacDonald left a voicemail message on Ro's mobile asking her to come and talk to Year Six the following day, Tuesday. Although the young teacher sounded formal, there was no hint of hostility from the evening before. But Alison had made it quite clear the invitation was a personal one, to Ro. She said she would be delighted if Ro came into school, and that Mr Findley also thought it was a great idea; Year Six were even more unsettled now, and needed something to differentiate them as older and more grown up than the rest of the children. A session with a PCSO might help.

Ro went back to doing her usual day-off chores – washing, and thinking. Occasionally she put on the news to keep up with the coverage of what everyone was calling the Marsh Murder.

The same morning, Suzy Spencer dropped Molly off at St Mungo's at 8.45. She was relieved that her daughter showed no sign of wanting to talk about the murder. Molly had chatted about her artwork all the way to school. When they got there, there were two film crews interviewing groups of parents outside the building. Judith Dixon came straight over to Suzy to say how good the girls' sleepover had been, despite everything, and remarked what a relief it was that they were so preoccupied with their mural now there had been this terrible crime.

Then Mrs Rudder suddenly appeared at the school gates. The TV crews literally sprang into action.

'Mrs Rudder, can you tell us something about your friend?'

'Was Brenda Hodgson seeing anyone, Mrs Rudder?'

But the crowd parted silently and the white-faced but dignified deputy head came through, with Callie McFadden immediately behind her. The two women passed into the school and there was something like a sigh from the waiting mums. With a sense that the show was over, they melted from around the gates.

That morning, Ray Findley took a special assembly at St Mungo's, and was clearly back in charge. Questions from the pupils included asking if Miss Hodgson's throat was cut, and if the Dodsworth House exams would still go ahead. There was an undercurrent of panic, made worse by the sinister shade of the boarded-up window. As Ro had predicted, the children confused the two events. Before long, one theory was that Miss Hodgson had been dragged out through the window by the killer, who was coming back for the children.

Alison MacDonald found she was looking forward to the talk from the PCSO, which would help settle them down. And to her surprise Mark was suddenly interested in St Mungo's, constantly texting her. She found his fascination with the lurid details in the tabloids slightly disturbing. But, he said laughing at her, men were like that.

That evening at The Briars, Robert could hardly hear himself speak for a row that was going on at the top of the stairs.

'Mummy, I've told you, I've got a summer cold. I don't want to go to school tomorrow. I want to take some Night Nurse and sleep it off.'

'Molly, you're just doing this to be difficult. I know it's horrid at school because of Miss Hodgson, but you can't stay off just because you feel like it.'

'That's not fair! I'm sick. It's unethical of you to expect me to go to school when I'm not well.'

'Unethical? Where do you get these words from? It's more unethical to pretend you're ill, hanging about in your pyjamas with no slippers and no dressing gown.'

Suzy came thumping downstairs and into the kitchen where she poured red wine into her glass and slumped at the table.

'What's up?' Robert asked.

'Molly doesn't want to go to school tomorrow, but I can't see anything wrong with her. She ought to go. They're having a talk from the community police. Miss MacDonald thinks it will be a useful session. She's sent a note round.'

'Sounds like a good idea.'

'And I want things to get back to normal. I've spent half of today ferrying Molly backwards and forwards because I was feeling protective. Tomorrow she should be back on the bus, murder or no murder.'

Robert agreed. The sooner Norbridge calmed down the better. He mused for a while on what Suzy had said.

'And she really hasn't got a summer cold?' he asked thoughtfully.

'It's April, Robert. And no, she hasn't got a cold.' Suzy sat frowning, and then said, 'Do you think she wants to avoid the talk with the police? It's a bit like she's in denial about this murder. She hasn't mentioned it, although everyone else is talking about it.'

'Maybe,' Robert shrugged. 'It could be her way of dealing with it. But it doesn't seem very realistic. Better to cope with it now, I think.'

Suzy drank her wine, thought about what he'd said, and then pounded up the stairs. Molly was reading in bed, but the set of her face, ignoring her mother at the door, showed that she wasn't really concentrating on the page.

'Molly, is there anything you want to tell me?' asked her mother, more gently. Molly put her book down and her face crumpled. Suzy sat on the mattress and put her arms around her. Molly's sobs made the bed shake. Holding her daughter in her arms, Suzy felt for the first time the soft but firm bounciness of breasts. It was such a surprise, she almost let go. Molly was still a shapeless lump, but it seemed the puppy fat might be about to redistribute itself.

'What's wrong, Molly? Is this about what happened to Miss Hodgson?' Molly was crying and snivelling now. There were no histrionics, just a runny nose and increasingly puffy eyes.

'Yes,' she snuffled.

'Molly, it's a horrible thing but the police will find who did it. The Police Community Support Officer will tell you all about how they'll be caught and punished.' But her reassuring words made Molly sob louder.

'Calm down, Molly. Look, I'll take you to school in the car tomorrow so you can lie in bed a bit longer in the morning.'

Molly's crying quietened. She snuggled down into bed, turned on her side and, while Suzy watched, she fell startlingly into an exhausted and deep sleep.

Suzy overslept the next morning. She and Robert had been talking for hours into the night.

'Robert, I haven't mentioned it before, but Nigel said on Friday that he wants to push on with a divorce.' She stretched her feet down to the end of the bed, and tensed, wondering what Robert would say.

'Then we can get married,' Robert had said. 'Let's have Molly as a bridesmaid. And Becky. Stripy tights and pink shorts all round.'

Suzy laughed. 'I know we've talked about getting married in the past, but it's not that simple, is it? It's not just you and me. It's the children too. There was something Judith Dixon said that annoyed me …'

'She can be quite blunt, can't she? Not a sensitive woman.'

Suzy had taken a deep breath. 'It was about the Dodsworth House scholarships. She suggested that Molly should enter. I said I couldn't really commit to paying the fees. My job has always been a bit up and down. And she said I should ask you for the money.'

'Well she's right. If that's what you want. I've got savings, you know that. And Molly is my stepdaughter now.'

It was a subject that had cropped up before, but Suzy had always asserted her family's independence, financially and emotionally. If they married, it would be different.

'Rob, a new family at your age is a big change.'

'I've still got a year or two before I get my bus pass. Anyway Suzy, it's hardly sudden. And I like having stepkids. Stepfathers get a bad press, but if you think about it, bringing up children who aren't yours by birth is a massive tradition. It's natural, in its way. I've been reading more stuff about medieval times lately. I'm thinking of writing about it.'

Suzy had laughed. 'Not another project?'

'When I've finished my definitive work on Canada? No, seriously, Suzy, bringing up children has always been done by people other than natural parents. Think of those squires sent away as little boys to be brought up in another noble family. Or apprentices sent off as teenagers to be indentured. Or the kids brought up by grandparents today, like Becky Dixon.'

'And it's often a horror story, isn't it?'

'But that's why the horror stories are horrible! It's hard to explain to the natural parents, but you can love them with real intensity even when they aren't yours. What's that old saying about babies, they bring their love with them? It's true about all children, Suzy: when you live with them you love them. Molly's my stepdaughter now and, if she wants to go to Dodsworth, I'll do as much as you to find the money. There is one thing though ...'

'What?' Suzy had asked anxiously.

'Have you asked *her* if she wants to go?'

She hadn't, of course. Somehow, this conversation left Suzy feeling more disturbed than reassured. Robert clearly loved the children; she had no doubt of that. But what about Nigel? He was Molly's real father. How would he feel about Robert having a formal role in the children's lives? And how would the children feel in turn? For a few years now, she and Robert had assumed they would get married. But when it came down to it, it wasn't that easy. He seemed happy about marrying the whole family. But how did she feel about being part of a package?

It was all a can of worms. As soon as you got one issue sorted, another bubbled up. Suzy rolled over in bed and slept heavily when she eventually dropped off.

That was why she had found it hard to wake up on Tuesday morning. Molly was pale but quiet. She ate her breakfast, grabbed her school coat and bag, and waited patiently to be taken to Pelliter, while Suzy flew round eating toast and getting dressed at the same time.

In the car, Suzy grasped the nettle and said suddenly, 'Molly, would you like to go to Dodsworth House?'

Molly turned and looked at her mother as if she was mad. 'Nah,' she said. ''course not.'

'What about if Becky goes?'

'Becky doesn't want to go either. She says she won't do the exam.'

'Even if her grandma insists?'

'Becky says she won't do it. She wants to go to Norbridge High, like me and Jake.'

Suzy said no more. She felt relieved, but the conversation with Robert had awakened other worries. She drove distractedly, and when they arrived at St Mungo's the playground was empty and everyone was already inside.

'I'm sorry, Molly. It's my fault we're late. I don't want you to miss this talk from the PCSO. I'll come with you into school and apologize. Come on, get out of the car.'

Her daughter ambled in an ungainly way across the yard, bag and coat flapping. Suzy followed her, but Molly ignored her mother and didn't even stop to say goodbye. She plodded on down the corridor to her classroom.

The Police Community Support Officer was waiting outside the head's office. Suzy took in the shape of her back, the heavy jacket, dark trousers and flat shoes. Then the PCSO turned round.

Despite all the changes, Suzy recognized her at once.

'Rosemary? Is it you?'

'It can't be … Susan Smith! Are you a parent here?'

'Sure am. My daughter's come to listen to your talk.' Suzy grinned excitedly. 'Look, I'll hang on till you've finished. We must grab a coffee and catch up!'

Chapter Eleven

Mine eye is consumed because of grief: it waxeth old because of all mine enemies.

Psalm 6:7. Folio 65r. **Les Très Riches Heures du Duc de Berry**

An hour later in the café on Pelliter High Street Suzy said, 'I suppose we're the last generation not to be inevitably stalked by Facebook. So we can be genuinely surprised to meet!'

Ro smiled, but there was wariness there. The idea of being stalked in any form horrified her. She was surprised that Suzy had waited so long outside the school for her. And she was unsure about 'catching up'. In her experience, old friends made a quick getaway once they found out about Ben. It was easier to talk about the Marsh Murder and the broken window.

'Well, I'm exhausted!' Ro said, sipping her coffee. 'Those children were hard work. With that age group they don't really discuss things, or debate. You need loads of material, because they just want answers.'

'Which I imagine you can't give in the circumstances,' said Suzy.

'Yes. It's a truly horrible business. Quite honestly, no one has a clue. It seems astonishing that an elderly woman could be attacked like that in daylight and no one saw anything.'

'So what are the police doing now?'

'Well, it's only day three of the investigation. They're still doing house-to-house enquiries and they've started to take Brenda's own house apart inch by inch. Next step will be to round up all the local people with form, and quiz them.'

Suzy shuddered. 'Awful. Anyway, never mind gruesome murders, what about this amazing coincidence! Where do you live, are you married, did you ever make it with that history student? He was rather gorgeous.'

'I married him in the end. But it didn't last. And, yes, I do live near here, in a hamlet of cottages called Burnside. We've been there about five years.'

'So close! We're in Tarnfield. Nigel and I are separated too. Remember Nigel Spencer?'

Ro could vaguely recall a gangly boy who combed his hair a lot. Suzy giggled. 'Now I'm actually living with a man who's a pillar of All Saints Church.'

'Susan Smith, arch critic of the establishment?'

'And what about you? You were hardly fuzz material.'

'Ah, well, that was then and this is now. It isn't the Sweeney any more. Are you still a TV journalist?'

'I'm more into production these days, when I can get it. So why don't you give me the headlines on your life? Kids?'

'I have a twelve-year-old son with cerebral palsy. No, don't screw your face up in sympathy Suzy. It's all right. He's pretty good at mobility now. But he's also got an eye problem. He's having surgery for it this summer and that should make a big difference. He's at Norbridge High and gets really good support from a teaching assistant.'

'I'm glad to hear it. I'm not keen on teaching assistants if they're anything like the cow they've got over there.' Suzy jerked her head in the direction of St Mungo's. 'Callie McFadden. Have you come across her yet?'

'Oh yes. She collared me in the supermarket. Not a happy place, is it, St Mungo's? Mind you, I think the head teacher might be getting back into his stride.'

'Mr Findley? I hope so. He's a good bloke and his wife was great before she had this nervous breakdown. Robert my partner says ...'

Ro sipped her coffee, and tuned out a bit. Suddenly meeting Suzy again after all these years was disconcerting. Her old friend seemed so together, with her new partner and her two kids, and her career in TV. And chummy chats over a cappuccino weren't what Ro did anymore. She couldn't take the risk that Suzy would drop her once she knew what a mess Ro had made of her life until now.

'Look, Suzy, I need to be going.'

'But we've only just met! We must get together again. I don't suppose you and Ben would like to come over one weekend? Sunday lunch maybe? Ben and Jake might know people in common from school. Does he use a wheel-chair?'

'On no, he can walk, though he's a bit wobbly. I'll give you my mobile number and, if you like, you can call me.' But I won't, Ro thought. She never approached people, however keen they seemed. Look how Jed Jackson had turned out. It would be awful if anyone thought that she was foisting herself and her disabled kid on them. Even Suzy Smith. The thought prompted her to get up and grab her jacket.

'I must get back to the police station.'

'Hey, you haven't given me your number. Write it down here. And your email.'

Ro reluctantly scrawled down the information on a serviette, in a flurry of police paraphernalia. She was late now. She had to dash back to the school playground and pick up her car to get back for the rest of her shift.

Suzy watched Ro Watson hurry away. Do I look as old as that? Suzy thought. Ro was very different after two decades. She had been a pretty girl, healthy looking, taller than Suzy, with brown hair and a good figure. Now, she looked drawn and old. But it wasn't just age, surely? There was a strained, deeply lined aspect to Ro's face which shocked Suzy and made her glance at her own reflection in the glass door of the cafe. In contrast to Ro, Suzy was flushed and animated, with a trace of make-up and far fewer lines.

Time had certainly taken its toll on her friend, Suzy thought. And there was another thing: the scar on the left side of her face made Ro look older too.

As she drove towards the centre of Norbridge, and before she thought more about the chance meeting with Suzy, Ro disciplined herself to go over the St Mungo's session. The children seemed to have relegated the murder to the fantasy land of a TV cop series, publicly at least, but Ro knew that in the middle of the night it would come back to haunt them.

Funnily enough, she had found that the window issue was tougher to cope with than the murder. The boarded-up pane was far more visible than Miss Hodgson's death. And Ro sensed that suddenly there was more tension in the class when she spoke about it.

'Do you know who did it, miss?'

'No. But we probably will,' Ro had said.

A boy at the back had asked sneeringly if the police would use DNA to find the window breaker. Unlikely, Ro replied. But they would be working hard to find whoever had done it. It was still a crime. Hurting someone was hurting someone, whether it was in a high-profile murder case or a vicious act of vandalism.

'If any of you know who did this then you must tell the police. Vandalism which nearly injures people is not a bit of fun. No one needs to know, if you contact us. You can phone or text the police station.' She hadn't planned her next move but she felt that a pivotal moment had come. She turned to the whiteboard, and gestured to Ray Findley to pass her a marker pen.

'This is especially for you. It's my private email address and my phone number. I'll ask Mr Findley to put them on a piece of paper to print out and give to each one of you too. If there's anything you want to tell me, email me. Or text me.' Standing by the board with her email on it in giant black letters, she seemed to make an impression on the class. There was silence. Then the children all began to talk at once, fussing with folders and bags.

'We're grateful for that,' Mr Findley said as he saw her out. 'I'm not sure how many of the children have access to email, but lots of them have mobiles and text each other. If they feel they know you, it makes all the difference. It's important that we mustn't forget the window, in all this awful business about the murder.'

'Yes, thank you for coming in.' Alison MacDonald looked terribly pale again. Today she was wearing a black trouser suit. It was formal even by Jed Jackson's standards. There was a small single silver stud in each ear, and her shiny auburn hair was tied back in a tight bun. 'I'm sure the parents will appreciate your efforts,' she said, with a rueful look which made Ro smile.

The parents. As she drove, Ro turned her thoughts to the extraordinary meeting with Suzy. It had been a coincidence, but these things happened. She wondered if her former college friend really would make contact again. Maybe she would, maybe she wouldn't. So many people had good intentions where Ben was concerned.

Yet Suzy had always been a 'can do' person. She had been secretary of the Junior Common Room at one stage, which was why they'd been so friendly. They'd both read English Lit and Ro remembered talking with her about Graham Greene. Suzy had started to laugh and called Ro 'The Quiet Scouser'. It had appealed to Ro. She knew she could be funny, but she hated the 'life and soul' Liverpudlian stereotype. She was sick of being expected to be either a comedienne or a trade union leader just because she was a Scouser, and those were the expectations back in the 1980s. But now, all that seemed aeons ago and meant nothing to anyone under forty.

Still, it brought back to her how young people could be very rigid in their views. As if on cue Ro pulled up at the police station in time to see Jed Jackson going up the steps two at a time. To her disgust, her heart flipped involuntarily and her mouth went dry. She felt that she could never speak to him again without anger and distaste – but she still had this stupid physical reaction. She paused for a moment to let him get ahead of her, and looked at her hands on the steering wheel. What a mess her fingers were. They were stained with the marker pen. I hope that washes off, she thought. At the back of her mind, the dark marks rang a bell.

I'm going crazy, she thought. What can stains from a marker pen have to do with anything?

At St Mungo's, Callie McFadden had watched the Police Community Support Officer leave the premises. Stupid woman, Callie had thought, all dolled up like a police officer with the words 'police staff' on her jacket – who did she think she was? Cagney, or Lacey?

Year Six were making a real racket, left alone in the classroom. Callie put her head round the door. Her son Jonty was spitting at Becky Dixon's back, at the same time as cuffing another lad round the face.

'You at the back, stop that!' she said. Usually one word from Mrs McFadden was enough to silence the whole school, including her own son. But Jonty went on hitting the other boy, and gathering saliva in his mouth in a disgusting chewing motion, ready to spit.

'I said stop it!' Callie shrieked, her voice rising.

'Thanks, Mrs McFadden.' Miss MacDonald had come back into the room. 'Sit down, Jonty.' The unusual forcefulness in his teacher's voice made him stop, startled.

Callie sidled out of the classroom into the corridor, just in time to block Ray Findley's progress back to his office. She shut the door to Year Six's room behind her, and folded her arms.

'Ray, I want to speak to you.'

'Yes. But I'm busy at the moment. I need to get back to Year Four. They're with someone from the Education Department at the moment. Can we catch up at lunchtime?'

'Sooner than that.'

'Of course. Brenda was a friend of yours. You must be especially upset.'

'Bollocks. I want to talk to you about something else. You know what.'

'I'm sorry, Callie. I need to be with Miss Hodgson's class. Now excuse me.'

Callie's eyes narrowed. Then the classroom door behind her opened and Year Six poured out on their way to the playground. She and Ray Findley formed an island, and the children streamed around them. The head teacher took the opportunity to detach himself and flow with them, leaving Callie behind.

At lunchtime, Alison stationed herself at the shared school computer in the corner of the staff-room. It was usually the focus of territorial rows arbitrated by Callie McFadden, but no one was interested today. Once the BBC and Sky News websites had been checked, they drifted towards the kettle.

'The police are coming this afternoon to impound that computer,' the caretaker said importantly. 'If you want to use it, now's your chance.'

The respectful quiet of yesterday had now become a buzz, as the handful of staff vied with each other to describe how they were coping. Mrs Rudder was alone in her classroom, rather than presiding over the teachers. Callie McFadden wasn't patrolling around giving out administrative diktats to the support staff. Alison wondered if their absence was the reason the few people left in the staff-room were talking to each other, for a change.

She needed to act quickly. She logged on, and then entered Ro Watson's email address. Alison could have phoned Ro – she had called the PCSO's mobile the day before. But emailing was more formal, more of a commitment.

Alison wrote: '*Mrs Watson – You asked the children to email you if they knew anything about the broken window. I do, and I would like to take the chance to talk to you further about it. And about something else too. Please call me back.*' She gave her own mobile number and hit 'send'. Involuntarily she looked for Callie. It would not have surprised her if the woman had magically appeared at her elbow, but she was still in the corridor, with her arms folded, rocking slightly on the heels of her creased suede boots. Her long patchwork-style skirt swayed with her.

Out of Alison's view, Callie leant forward, confident no one could see her and uncaring if they did. She had ambushed the head teacher again and she hissed at Ray Findley.

'I thought you were going to speak to me at lunchtime.'

'I didn't expect a local councillor to turn up on a flying visit. What did you expect me to do, send her away while I talked to you?'

'There's no need to be funny. This is serious.'

Ray Findley shut his eyes for a moment. 'Callie, we've discussed all that. This isn't the time or the place for discussing it again.'

'Oh yes it is. You may be so far up the arse of the councillor that you can see her tonsils, but your whole career will be in ruins if you don't find time for me.'

Ray Findley recoiled. And then Callie gave her big beaming smile, leaning forward to touch him on the arm. There was something proprietorial about the gesture. The head teacher flinched, but he failed to shake her off so he moved to side-step her. Callie let him go and watched as he walked down the corridor.

That afternoon, Tuesday, day three of the investigation into the Marsh Murder, there was a strange atmosphere in Pelliter. Business was quieter than ever and the streets were silent.

Liz Rudder's brother Kevin let himself into her big detached house. He had a key, because he liked to help out whenever he could. In his job as an independent financial adviser he had the occasional free moment when he could pop over and see poor old John.

Actually, free moments were not so occasional these days. But really, it was a bit of good luck that he didn't have so many clients currently. It meant he could do so much more for his brother-in-law. Kevin was grateful to John. John had left their business very well set up and Kevin managed to toddle along happily. He was just as good with figures as his brother-in-law, but he didn't consider himself to be a 'people person'. He had never built up much of a client base. Still, John had had enough personality and charm for two and, under his guidance, they had done very well. And just enough money was still coming in despite John's illness. Thank goodness John had had the foresight to take out self-employed health insurance years earlier. Stroke or no stroke, Kevin really liked and admired his brother-in-law. He felt it was his personal mission to keep John alive and well for poor old Liz.

But he was dreading today's visit. Liz had had no idea what a loss Brenda would be to the Rudder family. Kevin and Brenda had been working together on a surprise for his sister. It was tragic, really. Brenda had originally just been Kevin's sidekick in the 'Great Surprise Plan', as they called it, but she had developed into a mainstay.

He had hatched the 'GSP' for Liz as a secret, and Brenda had been all for it. Each week, when Liz was at her Spanish class, they sneaked in and put John through extra physiotherapy exercises. Once they had even taken him out in Kevin's car. The aim was to try and get John back on his feet. If Liz had known she would have been dead against it. She was already so demoralized. But unknown to her, they had made great progress – and without Brenda's help Kevin wouldn't have got nearly so far. It had been a brainwave of Kevin's to ask Brenda to help. He had seen her one Saturday morning on her own outside the coffee shop at the superstore. She'd looked rather forlorn.

'Hello, Brenda,' he had said cheerily. He wasn't a ladies' man like John had been, but Kevin was attractive in a puppyish sort of way. He was built like his sister, with a small but solid, strong body, good features, and delicate hands and feet which gave him the impression of being a light mover. Kevin knew that, when he wanted, he had a winning manner.

'Kevin!' Brenda's face had softened. She had always had a soft spot for Liz's little brother, ever since they had been kids. Kevin had noted her squat but muscular figure, strong arms, and the fact she seemed at a loose end. All useful indications.

'Can I join you for a minute?' Kevin had said. 'The old tootsies are killing me.'

'Of course. My friends have just gone and I'm having a little rest.'

Kevin had chatted to her, testing the water a little bit, and had soon gauged that Brenda could keep a secret too. She was strong, she had time, and her loyalty to Liz was wavering a little, so it didn't preclude her being part of the GSP. Perfect! They had soon hatched a little plot. Kevin would call for her each Wednesday, and they would go over to High Pelliter together. Brenda volunteered to get all the physiotherapy exercise plans, plus a Zimmer frame, and keep them at her house because obviously Kevin didn't want Liz or his wife to stumble on them. The Great Surprise Plan had been going great guns with John making real progress.

But now Brenda was dead it would be much more work. Still, Kevin would persevere.

'Hello, old chap,' Kevin said to John, as soon as he entered the house. John's voice, distorted to the point of being unrecognizable, boomed back incoherently.

'You know about poor Brenda, don't you, John?'

John made a gurgling noise.

'Poor, poor Brenda. Everyone's saying that some crazy person walking through the Marshes attacked her. And she's dead. But I know she'd want us to go on with the Plan. We're going to keep trying, John. I still want this to be a fantastic surprise for Liz. I can try lifting you by myself.'

He went up to John's wheelchair and hooked his arms under John's shoulders.

'We must stick to the schedule, John old son. Come on, let's try again. We want you to be walking by the summer! And think how thrilled Liz will be!'

Chapter Twelve

*The Procession of Saint Gregory was known as 'The Great Litany' or 'The Great Supplication.' The scene is based on **The Golden Legend** by Jacobus de Varagine, a famous history of saints and martyrs.*

Folio 71v. **Les Très Riches Heures du Duc de Berry**

The next day, Liz Rudder decided that it might be fruitful to be absent from school after the horrors earlier in the week. She deserved it. She had lost her best friend in a hideous way. Everyone knew she had been heroic, going to work on Monday and Tuesday. To her annoyance Ray Findley seemed to be coping, shepherding politicians, clergymen and reporters around the school. Of course, he'd had the full network of social and educational services looking after him. Today was the first day he wouldn't have full-on support. So she would stay at home and see how he managed without her!

She called the office. 'I've got a terrible migraine,' she murmured down the phone. 'It must be the stress. I'll try and get in tomorrow.'

Then she snuggled down under the bedclothes. John's carers had let themselves in early to get him dressed and breakfasted, so she didn't have to deal with her husband.

Liz tried to think about Brenda and to squeeze out a few tears. But, when she revisited the past, the person she felt most sorry for was herself, the girl from the wrong side of the tracks. Brenda's mother had been a terrible snob. Liz thought of the Hodgsons' house, where Father Peter now lived, with its garden full of dark shrubs and a paved path to the stained-glass front door. It had smelt of carbolic and polish; Brenda's mother was frantically house-proud and had treated Liz like a bad smell. No wonder Brenda had been obsessed with domestic cleanliness. It had been no surprise when her attempt to leave home for university had ended in tears.

'It was horrible,' Brenda had wailed. 'The other students were nasty and common and it was dirty and cold.' Brenda's head had been full of Oxford, where Peter had studied. She had gone to Manchester, then a Northern city in decay. No wonder she had been disappointed.

In contrast, Liz had gone to a nice, organized, local teacher training college. But then, Liz had always wanted to have a secure job and a boyfriend, and to get married to someone well off.

Liz remembered an incident when they had been teenagers. She and Brenda had found one of those old-fashioned post-war manuals about sex and marriage, disguised as a medical textbook, in a glass-fronted bookcase in the Hodgsons' chilly dining-room. The detail was rather clinical, with strange black-and-white diagrams. It made them giggle, but it was also mildly arousing. It was the only information on sex which they had ever seen, apart from problem pages in *Woman's Own*. They had had their heads bent over it when Peter Hodgson came in. He was dumpy and pale-complexioned, but he was a boy. And Liz was interested in boys.

'Look at this!' she had said to her friend's brother. 'It's about marital relations.'

She had pushed the book towards him, while Brenda went 'Oooh' and put her hand over her mouth. Liz had looked up at Peter Hodgson slyly from under her eyelashes. It was the first time she had tried flirtation. He sent the book spinning back across the polished table top. 'That's disgusting!' he had snapped. 'If you ever look at that again I'll tell Mother.'

'Peter, I'm sorry, really ...' Brenda had held her hand out to him.

'You should be. If you promise not to look at this sort of filth again, it can be our secret. Do you understand?'

'Oh yes, Peter, I do.' Silently, Brenda had picked up the book, replaced it in the case, shut the glass doors and turned the key.

Liz wondered if the police knew about Peter Hodgson's attitude to women. Was the church so full of priests that they could spare a good one? Liz thought not. There had to be something odd about his early retirement. She had heard that in murder cases it was usually someone close to the victim who was the perpetrator. Surely the police should want to know more about Brenda's brother. She parked that thought for future reference and snuggled down deeper into bed.

Jake Spencer, too, was absent from school. He was supposed to be revising for his summer exams. His mum was working, and his sister was at St Mungo's. Robert was at Norbridge College. Jake had a whole wonderful day to himself. There would be nothing wrong in watching a film. He had hours left to study the effect of the Repeal of the Corn Laws. He went into the sitting-room where the big family TV was mounted on the wall. He had a clutch of DVDs in a little pile on his own rack.

The one he was looking for was *Screaming Zombies Three*. He liked horror movies. He wasn't allowed to watch anything much when Molly was around, and using his laptop in his bedroom was a long way from the full home cinema experience. So access to his chosen genre was pretty limited. Jake was an easy-going lad who was fond of his sister. He saw his mother's point about restricting his viewing in the family zone.

But today he could have the big screen to himself. Except that his DVDs weren't there on his rack. Who had moved them? Edgily, Jake started to look around. If Molly had hidden them for a laugh, she would have milked it by telling him. But the films were definitely gone. All he could do was mooch round the room in the hope they would turn up. Jake looked under the chairs and in the drawers, in case the thin discs had slipped below the furniture, or been put away. On a whim, expecting nothing, he pushed the sofa forward.

The DVDs were there, scattered down the back. Weird or what?

Jake collected them up, but instead of deciding which one to play, he put them back where they belonged on the DVD rack and started to think.

The Le Creuset pan. The DVDs. What else had gone missing? His mother had been ranting only the day before about losing the potato peeler. The bread knife had disappeared. His old-fashioned bicycle clips which hung on a nail in the shed had been gone since Becky and Molly had been out with his bike. In fact, all these things had gone missing since Becky Dixon had started to visit. They were such trivial things, but they had started to mount up.

Jake wondered if there was a sort of Childline equivalent he could ring, to do with weird crimes. But was it a crime? Should he tell his mum? But that would jeopardize his sister's only friendship.

There were five years between Jake and Molly. The age gap meant that they didn't really *talk*, but he was fond of her. In the past she had been a sort of nuisance, full of herself, and showy-offy. He had found her a pain in the bum and frequently told her so; but now he felt sorry that she had become such a miserable lonely lump. At least, until Becky came along....

Jake pulled his laptop out of his schoolbag. He logged on, and sat there feeling a bit silly. He really didn't know what to do next, but he thought he should do something. Feeling a little bit treacherous, which was unlike him, he went into Google and started tapping in – 'pol …' The site he wanted came up straight away.

He paused. Was this the right thing to do? He had a horrible feeling he was grassing on his sister's best friend. But he pressed 'enter'.

By Thursday, day five of the investigation into the Marsh Murder, Ro Watson had slipped back into the normal timetable of day shifts at Norbridge Police Station.

She had a routine with Ben. After school, he let himself in. He had to get changed, feed and brush the cat, lay the table for supper, complete at least one homework task and turn on the cooker. When Ro got back they would have a chat together, and more often than not she poured herself a drink. Then they would eat supper, plan the evening's shared TV or DVD viewing and relax. There was no doubt community support was tiring work. On Thursday evening she felt particularly down after the drama of the murder.

'Supper will be ready at seven,' she called to Ben.

'OK,' he said. 'I'll come down to the kitchen when I've finished doing this.'

His speech was really great, which was a bonus. But his eyesight was worsening. Trauma cataracts, the specialists called it. The cataract operation could cure him. It was like a miracle, people said. Ro was going along with it. There were always risks. The hospital hadn't yet confirmed that they would do the operation during Ben's summer holidays, and the year before they had been all geared up for it but it hadn't gone ahead. She knew it was the one thing Ben was worried about. He had always been sensitive about his eyes. Perhaps this year it would be cancelled again. Part of Ro's approach to everything with Ben was to live one week at a time. The call would come from the hospital at some point, but until it did she wasn't thinking about it.

She chopped up the vegetables, letting her mind wander. Her talk at St Mungo's seemed very distant now. Since Tuesday, she and the other female PCSO had visited a youth centre, patrolled a couple of after-school groups and walked the beat. It had been a normal working experience. She had seen Jed Jackson once in the canteen and he had seemed about to come towards her, but she had turned away from him. The warmth she had felt for him seemed ridiculous, and the memory of how she had craved his attention was just humiliating.

Ro walked upstairs from the kitchen. For once, Ben wasn't on the computer. He had a system which gave really large print on the screen and meant he could use the internet as well as anyone else. But today he was lying on the sitting room floor, reading with the help of a big magnifying glass. Ro hoped that by the autumn he would be able just to use ordinary glasses like loads of other kids. His walking was improving all the time because he was growing stronger. Puberty seemed to be an advantage because as he grew bigger he became more agile and more confident. He was in that 'in-between' stage now, where he hadn't put on the final growth spurt – though his voice had started to drop and there were tell-tale spots on his chin.

Ro knew she was biased, but she thought her son was actually quite handsome. She had dreaded his adolescence, but instead of finding a sex-obsessed alien in her home she discovered that Ben had actually become even more likeable. They still seemed able to discuss things. Perhaps because Ben had always been so physically dependent on her, it was actually easy to talk about bodily functions. For the past few months, since she had started as a PCSO, they seemed to have reached some sort of calm. Their lives were limited, but contented. As always these days, she felt that settling for just settling was the best option.

She sat in front of the computer. There were a few new messages. The most recent was from Suzy Spencer.

Hi Rosemary
So great to find you again!!! I didn't think about it when we spoke but
Monday is the May Day Bank Holiday. I'd like you and Ben to come over for
a barbecue in our garden. We're at The Briars in Tarnfield, on the left down
the lane on the road out of the village to the east. How about one o'clock? Let
me know?
Suzy

Ro's instinct was to decline, but Ben had struggled up and was looking over her shoulder.

'What does that say?'

'We've been invited to someone's house.'

'Us? Wow. What does it say?'

Reluctantly she read it out to him.

'Hey, Mum, a barbecue! Sweet!' For someone with vision problems he always managed to identify issues she wanted to hide. What excuse could she give Ben this time for saying no?

Thanks. That would be very nice. We'll be there if we can, she wrote for Ben's benefit. We'll see, she thought. We don't have to go if we can't cope. So we probably won't. Then she looked along the list to a second unexpected email. It was from Alison MacDonald.

Ro read it, and thought about it for a minute. She looked at the Victorian clock mounted on the sitting room wall. It was 6.30. Probably just the right time to catch the teacher after school. She took a sip of her wine, and then grabbed the phone and dialled Alison's mobile.

Chapter Thirteen

Why art thou cast down O my soul? and why art thou disquieted within me?

Psalm 43:5. Folio 61v. **Les Très Riches Heures du Duc de Berry**

On Thursday evening when the phone rang, Alison MacDonald was at her parents' home in Norbridge. It had been a shattering week. But she had kept things going as smoothly as possible at school.

Until yesterday.

At two o'clock the school secretary had come bustling into the classroom. She had told Alison in a loud voice that Dodsworth House had been on the phone. They had announced that the scholarship exams would be taken on the second Saturday in May, the week after the Bank Holiday. Chaos had broken out. Faye Armistead's son had leapt up and punched the air. Then he punched the boy next to him who was Jonty McFadden's best mate, so a brawl had threatened to begin. Several of the girls had begun to scream and whimper and generally fuss. It had taken Alison a while to calm them all down.

On Thursday morning, there had been a queue of grim-faced parents at the school office by 8.45, demanding to know how Miss MacDonald was going to tutor their children for the Dodsworth exams.

Alison had been backed into the corner of the foyer by sour-faced people with questions, marshalled by Faye Armistead. How many scholarships were there? How was St Mungo's planning to cram the children in time?

Faye had yapped, 'You must be prepared to hold special classes. I know this murder is dreadful, but Miss Hodgson would want us to get the children into Dodsworth House. We must put it behind us. We've got just over a week. Dodsworth will be putting out mock exams and an examination schedule. Now *anyone* can apply it will be much more competitive.'

Alison had looked at the aggressive, jabbering faces in front of her. She said nothing until the questioning died down.

'First,' she'd said slowly and clearly, 'Dodsworth House is a private school. What they do is up to them. Secondly, St Mungo's is a Church of England state school. It is not my role to tutor your children for the private Dodsworth scholarships. If you wish to pay private tutors you will find a list on the Internet.'

'That's outrageous!'

'Mrs Armistead, your children have all been educated to Year Six level and St Mungo's passed its last Ofsted inspection with flying colours.'

'Yes,' Faye Armistead had snapped, 'but that was when Mrs Findley was taking Year Six.'

'And now I'm taking Year Six, and we still meet those standards. If you want your children to sit for private scholarships with extra tuition, then it's up to you to pay for it. I will do everything I can to make sure the children are equipped and not unduly stressed by this. I suggest you do the same.'

Faye Armistead stared at her, her rose pink shiny mouth opening and closing.

Alison turned away and began walking towards her classroom when someone plucked at her shoulder. It was Judith Dixon.

'What sort of chance do you think Becky has?'

'Mrs Dixon, I can't really say. Your granddaughter is very bright in class, but I don't know what the competition will be like. For all the children's sakes, don't make a big deal of it.'

At break time, Mr Findley had asked to see Alison. 'Mrs Rudder is ill today so I'm very pushed. We're expecting another supply teacher next week. But that isn't what I wanted to say. I heard how you dealt with the Dodsworth scholarship people. That must have been very difficult. I know Sheila always found that type of parent very trying. Well done.'

Alison had smiled, relieved. Now, by Thursday night, she was exhausted, but she couldn't relax. Her mobile rang in her handbag. It will be Mark, she thought. I must tell him I'm definitely going to be in Pelliter, painting a mural, on Saturday morning.

But instead of Mark, it was a return call from Ro Watson. Alison swallowed her surprise and said, 'Thanks so much for calling back, Mrs Watson. But I'd rather not discuss this on the phone.' She was in a restless mood and wanted to escape from her mother's constant fussing and ill-disguised attempts to gossip about the murder. 'Can I meet you, to talk about this? Tonight? Where do you live? I could come to you.'

Ro Watson paused. She and Ben rarely had visitors.

'I'm a long way from you. I'm at Burnside near Tarnfield....'

'That's fine. I know where it is. I can be over there in half an hour.'

It suited Alison's mood to be up and doing. She went out to her car and set off in the direction of Burnside.

Liz Rudder was still in bed at Thursday lunchtime. Another day off school would do her good and show just how much she was needed! She had made herself a nice boiled egg, popped it on a tray, taken it upstairs, and eaten it. She was about to snuggle down again and watch a weepy film on TV when Callie McFadden called her.

Callie reported that Alison MacDonald had coped well with the angry parents wanting to know about the Dodsworth exams, and it seemed that she had Ray Findley's backing.

Liz felt distinctly cross. Alison McDonald coping had never been in her plan. Liz had definitely wanted a Year Six teacher who would be under her thumb, and who would go to pieces without Liz Rudder's guiding hand. Perhaps the young woman hadn't been a very good choice for the new teaching post after all. But at the time she had seemed the best candidate. She was available, she was local, and her experience was limited so she would be malleable. Liz's luck had been in on the day of the interview. Mr Findley had been dealing with some domestic crisis as usual, so Liz had stood in for him. Alison MacDonald had certainly been keen and presentable so she had been given the job without too much discussion about the other more experienced candidates. Once the decision was made, Liz had made it clear to everyone that Alison was really an also-ran.

'We had such weak applicants. I don't think she'll cope, poor girl. And we have to keep an eye on all this painting paraphernalia. It's going to be a real nuisance.'

Liz had expected that within months Alison would be begging for support, in Liz's pocket like the rest of the staff, but the younger woman was showing more resilience.

But, Liz hoped, not for long. This was turning out to be a tough week for teachers at St Mungo's, and the news about the Dodsworth scholarships meant Alison would be under more pressure than ever. Liz had only been doing her duty by suggesting that Faye Armistead go up to school, on the rampage. If Miss MacDonald was rattled as a result, well, that was what happened with younger staff who overreached themselves, wasn't it? They had to learn from experience.

Liz had taught Year Five for the last fifteen years, and it suited her very well. She knew that before Sheila's timely breakdown, the head had been thinking of a shake-up. The last thing Liz wanted was change. All she needed was to tread water until she reached that final full pension in a few years' time. Fortunately Sheila's collapse had derailed him. But now, Liz worried that Ray Findley might be back on form. Say he started having bright ideas again? Like giving his stalwart deputy head the top class next year? Liz Rudder shuddered under the bedclothes. She had to pick her way along a delicate path. She needed a Year Six teacher who was just capable enough, so that Liz herself didn't have to take the troublesome eleven-year-olds. But at the same time, that teacher mustn't get above herself and threaten Liz's new status. A keen but inexperienced teacher like Alison had seemed perfect. Until now.

And if Ray Findley was getting back on his feet, it didn't bode well. Say he and Alison MacDonald joined forces?

But maybe something else could take Mr Findley's mind off reorganizing St Mungo's. Liz smiled. Callie was just the person to help with that. She had a hold over Ray Findley, and Liz knew all about it. Of course, Callie might need a little encouragement to use that hold to Liz's advantage, but that shouldn't be difficult. Liz opened the drawer of her bedside table and smiled. In it was a rather ugly-looking hammer. Callie might need to be reminded that Liz had found it under the smashed classroom window. Despite what Liz Rudder had said to anyone else, she was convinced that Jonty had broken the window. And no one was more aware than Liz Rudder that Jonty McFadden was a very nasty piece of work indeed, and that his mother would go to any lengths to protect him.

Ro Watson stood in the porch of her cottage in Burnside and looked up the hill towards the main road. The lane wound down towards her, lined by silver birch and elder. She saw the car bounce slowly down the bumpy track. Alison came to a halt and parked.

'Thanks for this,' she said as she approached. 'It's good for me to get out. My mum is lovely, but she's hovering over me all the time at the moment.' She was wearing jeans, a T-shirt and a hooded jacket. But her hair was loose, rippling over her shoulders. She's really very pretty, Ro thought.

'Come in. I can't offer you a drink if you're driving, but how about a coffee? This is my son Ben, on the computer, but we can go downstairs.'

Alison smiled at the faired-haired boy looking closely at his computer screen, and followed Ro down the stairs to the kitchen, with its big windows and a view over the river.

'What a beautiful house!' she said.

'One of the benefits of living in Cumbria.'

'You must get loads of visitors. This would be a great room for a party.'

'We don't actually.'

'That's a shame. It's fantastic. My boyfriend and I want to get a house in Manchester. It's a great city, but I'll miss all this.' Alison looked out at the valley, where the darkness was dusting the opposite fell.

Ro handed Alison a mug of coffee and a piece of home-made cake. She said, 'It's not that I want to be a domestic goddess or anything. I just don't get out much.'

Alison laughed, with a warmth that encouraged Ro to go on. 'I want to apologize for my colleague on Sunday. I don't know why Jed was so aggressive. That's not community police tactics.'

'That's OK. I don't have to deal with him again. Look, Mrs Watson, you asked us to email you if we had anything to say about the broken window.' Alison stopped, awkwardly.

'It was done by a hammer, wasn't it?'

'Yes! How did you know?'

'You told us on Sunday. I don't think you realized what you said. We didn't find the hammer, so no one knew. There were some children there, weren't there. And a parent?'

'Yes, Mrs Spencer and Molly and Becky. But they didn't see what came through the window.'

Ah, Suzy Spencer! That was interesting, Ro thought. So her old friend could corroborate anything Alison said.

'So what happened to the hammer, Alison?'

The young teacher sat there, trying not to face the obvious facts. Ro could see the confusion in her face.

'I think,' Alison said painfully, 'that it's been removed. I've looked and I can't find it anywhere, not under the desks or in with the art stuff.' She swallowed. 'I think Mrs Rudder has taken it away. That's the conclusion I've come to.'

'Yes,' said Ro. 'So have I.'

Alison seemed to breathe a sigh of relief. At last, here was someone who understood what she was up against. 'And I'm sure I recognized the boy responsible for the vandalism,' Alison said. 'He's in my class. I didn't tell the police because Mrs Rudder was adamant. When she started to quiz me I lost my nerve. She can be very forceful, in a quiet way.'

'So what made you decide to tell me now?'

'You were good with the children and I felt I could trust you. If it had been that other policeman, the man, I wouldn't have said anything.'

'Why do you think this boy did it?'

'I think it must have been premeditated; there was something odd about it. I felt that he was aiming at the girl who was drawing – Becky Dixon.'

'Why?'

'Because the boy really resents her. It's taken me a while to work it out, but he's been aggressive and unpleasant about everything to do with Becky Dixon. She's an unusual child, very clever, being brought up by her grandparents.'

Ro thought straight away of the man with the grey hair and suntanned arms who had been at the school.

'Is that Phil Dixon? Late fifties or early sixties? Thick grey hair. Tall?'

Alison nodded. 'The boy who threw the hammer is called Jonty McFadden. What complicates things is that Jonty's mother is a TA – a teaching assistant – and she … well …'

'Well what?'

'I think she encourages him. And Mrs Rudder knows and lets them get away with it. There's a horrible atmosphere at St Mungo's now. Mr Findley's the only teacher who cares about all the children. The other staff just suck up to the ones who are tough, or rich.'

'Is that Mrs Rudder's approach?'

'Absolutely. And there's something else I want to tell you, Ro. Something quite different.'

'Go ahead.' Ro was aware that Alison was suddenly opening up after weeks of confusion. Her eyes were bright and there were two red spots on her pale cheeks.

'The day the man died at St Trallen's, I was working late. I was at the school, on my own. A youngish chap in smart clothes came to the school play-ground at about four thirty. I wonder if it could have been the same man who was found dead at the chapel. But to be honest I couldn't identify him. I only saw him for a moment.'

'What did he look like?'

'He was tall with very thick dark hair and tinted glasses. He reminded me of someone. There was something odd about the way he moved. I don't know …'

'Well, the dead man had dark hair,' Ro said, 'but there were no glasses. And, as you probably heard, he'd been stabbed around the eyes.'

'Yes, I know. Horrible.' Alison drained the last drop of coffee from her mug. She glanced at her watch. It was nearly nine o'clock. She should go home. But it seemed easier to sit in Ro's kitchen and carry on talking now the floodgates were open.

'Maybe you should talk to the crime squad about it …' Ro said, but Alison shook her head. 'No way.' Ro knew she was thinking about Jed and his boor-ishness at the weekend.

'OK, if you don't want to, that's that. And the smart young man you saw may just have been a coincidence. Frankly we're completely tied up with Miss Hodgson's murder at the moment.'

'Maybe I should stop worrying about it,' Alison said thoughtfully. 'We've got assessments in a few weeks, and all that has been controversial and confusing enough over the last few years. You only have to say SATs for a lot of people to get hysterical. And on top of that, there's the nightmare of an extra late entrance exam for Dodsworth House. It's a tough job teaching Year

Six, and Liz Rudder really isn't supportive. She listens to people like Callie McFadden more than she listens to me. It would be good if both the Findleys got back in control. St Mungo's used to have a really good reputation. Just because it's Pelliter doesn't mean it should be awful.'

Alison said it with conviction. She's a really keen teacher, Ro thought. How could Jed Jackson have got her so wrong? But then, she thought, he got me wrong too.

'Let's sit upstairs,' she said, 'now that the sun has gone down across the valley.'

She led the way up the stone staircase to the big living-room, and switched on a lamp in the corner. The light flared up in the niche next to the fireplace and caught the gilded edge of the picture.

'Oh, that's beautiful!' Alison gasped. 'Art is my thing! How unusual. I've never seen anything quite like it.'

The boy on the computer started to laugh. 'That's Mum's prized possession,' he said. 'But I can't see what she's on about. Literally!' He seemed to think this was hilarious, and got up to face the light and peer at the golden frame. Alison watched his short-sighted play-acting until he lurched out of the room. She moved backwards, and sat suddenly into the armchair opposite the fireplace.

'Ro, your son can't see properly, can he?'

'Please don't be upset. He's kidding a little bit. He can cope. And anyway, he's hoping to have an operation in the summer.'

'No, you don't understand. Ben didn't upset me. It's just that ...'

'What?'

'That was the way he looked. The man in the playground two weeks ago. He stood just like that. As if he couldn't see.'

Phil and Judith Dixon were arguing in hushed voices in the living-room of the old farmhouse, both acutely aware that Becky was on the computer in the kitchen just past the open door. Judith was absolutely determined that Becky should sit for the Dodsworth House scholarship. Phil had finally said he was against it. They just couldn't really afford it at their age, on a pension. But Judith had argued that if Becky got the scholarship, it would mean a huge discount on the Dodsworth fees.

'We can manage, Philip. We owe it to her.'

Phil was unsure. Molly Spencer was going to Norbridge High. There was nothing to stop Becky getting into a good university from the local state secondary school, and that seemed to be what she wanted. He had suggested gently to Judith that they just let it be.

'So you want Becky to turn out like her mother?' Judith hissed.

Phil had said mildly, 'But you can't blame the school for what happened to Sam.'

'Who can you blame then? You, for spoiling her? You were soft. You let her go to that awful comprehensive and it was the beginning of everything.'

Stung, Phil had withdrawn from the battle. Then he had done something quite uncharacteristic. He had gone for a solitary pint at the Crossed Foxes in Pelliter, where he had bumped into Robert Clark. The two men had chatted for quite a while, enjoying each other's company.

When Robert got home, he too was catapulted into a full-scale row.

'You invited who to the barbecue?' Suzy yelled at Robert ungrammatically. He had taken a cab from the Crossed Foxes and had rather a golden glow. 'Phil and Judith Dixon? Judith is a bit too free with her advice, *and* she makes her own bread. I can't handle her as well as Ro and her son. Say Judith Dixon starts giving Ro the benefit of her opinions about disability? And Becky's so … Robert Clark, how could you? How can I cope?'

But in the early hours, with a sudden sense of impending summer that made it too hot to sleep, Suzy got up and went to the window. She opened it and felt the rush of cool air from the eastern fells.

Of course the barbecue would be good. It would be exciting to have all these people come over. There would be lots of kids: Jake, Ben, Molly. And now Becky, which was fine, of course … But what was it about Becky Dixon that was so disturbing? Feeling an uncomfortable draught, Suzy left the window, hurried over to the bed and snuggled into Robert's back.

Chapter Fourteen

On the first of May, one had to wear green. The expression 'Je vous prends sans vert' ('I've caught you out') comes from this tradition.

Folio 5v. Les Très Riches Heures du Duc de Berry

The Bank Holiday weekend was a fraught one for Norbridge Police. The CID were ignoring the holiday, still examining every scrap of paper and clothing in Brenda Hodgson's house. The only item which seemed odd was a Zimmer frame, along with some articles and books on physiotherapy, but it suggested that maybe Brenda was thinking of a change in career. Her brother Father Peter Hodgson had become increasingly standoffish and touchy about police questions, but it seemed he had neither listened to nor known his sister very well.

The police had also started going through the hard drive of the school computer. With the help of the uniformed force, they were bringing in anyone local with a history of violence towards women. A profiler from Manchester was reputed to have said the attacker could have been female, because the knife assault on the victim's flesh was light and not sexual.

'Just like the bloke at the chapel,' Jed Jackson mentioned to Sergeant Liddle. 'Mutilated after death.' But it was hard to see any other connection between the two bodies. Unlike the CID, George Liddle gave the community team Sunday and Monday off.

On Sunday, Ray and Sheila Findley lay together in bed. They were holding hands after making love.

'That was nice,' Sheila said.

'Yes.' Ray was frightened to break the spell. 'Thank you.'

'Nonsense! I should thank you. I hardly look like Kate Winslet at the moment, do I?' Sheila giggled.

Ray could hardly believe the sound. He looked at the ceiling where the lampshade became fuzzy because his eyes were moist. Would it last? Against all the odds in a week that followed a ghastly murder and had most people still reeling, Sheila had been better. On Monday she had got up to wave him off. And in the evening, though she was still in her dressing-gown, she had asked him what had happened at the school. On Tuesday, she had been wearing jeans and a jumper when he came home and she had wanted to know all about Year Four and the PCSO's talk to Year Six. On Wednesday she had made him some breakfast.

And on Saturday they had gone to the garden centre. She hadn't shied away from babies in buggies, or children in the play area.

I mustn't expect it to go on like this, Ray told himself. It will be one step forward and two steps back. But at least it was one step forward. It's a reward, he thought, because I've been tougher. For a moment he thought about Callie McFadden. He wondered what revenge she would take, because he had ignored her demand for a meeting. She would want some petty advancement, or endorsement of her power. She fed on attention. She would try something, he thought. But he would face that when he had to.

He and Sheila had a Sunday morning breakfast of toast and tea in the bright sunny kitchen. Sheila said, 'I think I'll do some gardening. I can put those bedding plants around the lawn. You stay and read the paper.'

'Fine.'

Ray stationed himself by the French windows and watched her to see if she would really do it, or relapse into a sort of depressed stupor. For weeks in the early spring she had sat on the bench in the garden, swaddled in fleeces and a big anorak, lost in depression.

But this time she was serious about the gardening. He saw her walk down to the shed, get out the trug and the trowel, and put on the gardening gloves. The bright bedding plants, sweet william and busy lizzies, were the sort of thing at which she would have turned her nose up in the past. But this year the sharp colours had amused her, and he had bought trays of them for the pleasure of hearing her laugh.

'You should get a gnome, while you're at it.' It was the first joke she had made for months.

'I'll buy you one with a golden fishing rod if it makes you laugh like that....'

'Don't push me, Ray,' she had said, but with a rueful smile of acknowledgement which made him want to hug her. He had looked at her as she stacked the plants in the trolley and seen the old Sheila – thinner, with dark shadows under her eyes and longer, untidier hair. But different from the jaded angry woman he had been living with for the past six months.

He and Sheila had been ready to leave the garden centre when the Rudders' car had driven into the car-park. Ray could smell fresh plants and potting compost, and the sun had come out from behind greyish clouds.

Sheila was beside him in the passenger seat. He had been allowing himself to feel happy. But the sign of Liz Rudder's little red Volkswagen had turned his mouth instantly dry; he had glanced at his wife.

Please God, don't let them see each other, he thought. There had always been silent enmity between the two senior teachers and Ray knew that Liz had been part of what had pushed Sheila over the edge. But it was too late. Liz and her brother Kevin had jumped out of the Volkswagen. They appeared to be discussing the plants on sale in a rack by the entrance.

Without waiting, Ray had started the engine. But to his astonishment, Sheila had raised her hand and waved cheerily at Liz. As he manoeuvred the turn on to the main road, he could see Liz Rudder's amazed face in the rear-view mirror as she stood holding a begonia.

Kevin had spent Saturday morning with Liz at the garden centre while his wife took their children to the swimming pool in Norbridge. Liz had surprised him by suggesting they could leave John on his own for a few hours and use the time to go out to buy more bedding plants.

'You never know when we might have to sell the house,' Liz said. 'And most sales around here are to local people wanting to trade up. If they're used to seeing the house looking smart it will help maintain the value, these days.'

But Liz had been in a foul mood when they got back from the garden centre. She had driven home irritably and parked the car without speaking. Then she had silently unloaded the plants, putting the begonias and alyssum on to pages of newspaper spread out at the side of the garage in the shade.

'I'll do those later,' she had said crossly. 'I want to make a phone call now.'

She had been crabby with Kevin because his trainers were dirty and she had made him take them off before he went into the house like she always did.

And poor John was actually standing up when they came into the lounge. Kevin guessed that he hadn't heard them because they were walking around on the carpets in their stockinged feet. Liz leapt forward. 'John, sit down,' she shouted, and she had run over and pushed him back into the wheelchair. She was right: John could have fallen and caused himself such damage!

Oops ... Kevin had to admit that John walking by himself so soon had not been in the Great Surprise Plan. Of course, he had been getting stronger every week, and in their last session, even without Brenda, he had managed to walk. He had always needed lifting up, though. Or at least he had, until today. But there he was, standing by himself.

If he had fallen, where would they be? He couldn't even call for help. Oh dear, oh dear, Kevin thought. The cat was very nearly out of the bag!

Liz had been even crosser after that. Not that she suspected anything.

Tentatively, Kevin had said, 'It looks like John might be getting his strength back, Liz. Wouldn't that be wonderful?'

'Wonderful? It would be a miracle,' Liz said. 'Victims of strokes this severe don't tend to live for longer than a further three years. John had his stroke a year ago. He's got two years left and I can't see what could change that.'

Ah, thought Kevin, but you don't know about the Great Surprise Plan! Not only will it improve John's life expectancy, it will be wonderful for Liz to see him on his feet again. It was Liz's birthday in June. Kevin had wondered whether on that day John might be able to stand and walk to Liz with a bunch of flowers. Wouldn't that be marvellous?

The following day, over a routine family Sunday lunch at the Rudders', Liz announced to Kevin and his wife that she wanted to go out that afternoon. But she didn't want John to try to stand again, and risk falling, with all the fuss and blame that would go with an accident.

'If the boys are happy to play in the garden, would you look after John if I popped out, Kevin?'

Kevin was surprised. 'Of course,' he said.

'Thank you. I need to go and speak to someone from school. These exams for Dodsworth are taking place next Saturday and we're having a meeting about it. You've all had a lovely lunch, haven't you?'

Kevin said, 'Super. Of course we'll stay with John. He'll be very happy with the boys.' His eldest son grimaced and did Quasimodo-style actions behind John's wheelchair, out of Liz's eye-line.

'Be careful!' Liz said 'I don't want John trying to get out of that chair again. Kevin, make sure John stays sitting down. Don't let him move. It's not safe.'

'OK,' Kevin said. 'You just leave him with us, Sis. He'll be fine.'

Liz Rudder got into her little red car and drove out of the drive. If Kevin had watched her go, he would have been surprised to see her turn towards the Pelliter council estate.

Liz drove efficiently but angrily. She had been horrified, the day before, to see Sheila Findley at the garden centre. It had almost looked like the old Sheila waving jauntily to her from the car. She had written off the possibility of Sheila ever coming back to St Mungo's, but now she wondered. If Sheila Findley was back in the saddle it might make Liz Rudder's new-found powers hard to wield. And there was that that awful business of seeing John standing up by himself! Liz had been highly perturbed. If John was on the mend, and the Findleys back on top, her cosy little world would be upside down after all she had done to secure it.

She had phoned the one person she knew she could trust to help.

Callie didn't have a car. She had obeyed Liz's instructions and was waiting in the car-park of the Crossed Foxes. Liz swept around and parked, opened the door, and Callie climbed in. What could be more natural than two colleagues getting together for a chat and a sentimental walk after the awful murder of a mutual friend? Liz drove to the Marshes in a silence which Callie did not break. Liz was the only person who knew Pelliter and its people better than Callie, and the only person at St Mungo's never fazed by Callie's loud-mouthed bullying.

Liz pulled up near to Brenda's house. She and Callie got out of the car and walked to the point on the road where they could look over the river. To any passer-by they appeared as if they were standing respectfully in memory of their friend, within sight of where she had died only a week earlier.

'Now then, Callie,' Liz Rudder said, in her light, brisk, rather prissy voice. 'It really is time to put some real pressure on Mr Findley.'

'Maybe having this wretched barbecue tomorrow is just too much pressure,' Suzy Spencer said on the Sunday of the Bank Holiday weekend. Robert did not remind her that it had been her idea. They were in the superstore in Pelliter. Suzy had to manoeuvre the trolley, much to her annoyance, while Robert darted round, chucking in the sorts of things he thought would be fun.

Suzy hated the supermarket and she particularly hated it on Sundays. Though she was hardly a traditionalist, she still felt she was entitled to one day of rest a week. She heard Robert greeting someone behind the wine bottles. It was both a joy and a huge irritant to her that Robert seemed so popular and knew everyone in the area. She trundled behind him, nearly slicing his ankles with the trolley. Robert was talking to a plump, pretty girl with glossy brown hair sporting a few blonde stripes, and a variety of odd droopy earrings.

'Suzy, this is Poppy Robinson. You remember. Poppy and Tom. What are you up to now, Poppy?'

'Great to see you, Poppy,' Suzy said. 'Sorry I haven't got time to chat, I've got to get over to the bread counter before all the buns go.' She backed the trolley away, hearing Robert encourage Poppy to talk about her career to date.

'I'm going to be a journalist,' Poppy said enthusiastically. 'I'm doing a post-graduate MA and I'm back here doing work experience. I'm at the *Tribune* group. The free papers.'

'And what story are you working on? Brenda Hodgson's death, I suppose?'

'No such luck,' Poppy said, making Robert wince. 'But I did the stuff on the mystery man. You know, the death at the chapel.'

Poppy was beginning to talk in headlines, Robert thought rather sadly.

'Actually,' Poppy leant forward conspiratorially, 'I wrote the piece last week. I got the quote from this cute policeman. You know, about the Canadian coin, and the picture.'

'Picture?'

'Yes. Well, tracing really. The one the mystery man had. On tracing paper. It was so thin it was tucked in his inside pocket and the mugger missed it. It just looked like a doodle. But it must have meant something to him.'

'And what was it like?'

'It was quite rough. Like this. I tried to get a pic on my phone, but it was too faint.' Poppy had a pencil in her bag, and a reporter's notebook, Robert saw. He was amused to see she still had the old tools of the trade.

Poppy drew a square on the page. Then on one side she drew what looked like a cherub, and replicated it on the other side. In the middle she drew a letter S with a big flourish and then spiralled from it various swirls. 'It was like one of those Victorian sampler things,' she said reflectively.

'Interesting,' Robert said. The drawing reminded him of illuminated art, like the *Book of St Trallen*.

'You can have this drawing, if you like,' she said. 'They've spiked any follow-up 'cos of the murder, and I go back to college next week. Anyway, I don't really see the significance. I mean, why on earth would the mystery man have a tracing like that? What could it mean?'

'Well,' Robert said thoughtfully, 'I suppose it could mean he was interested in art.' He put the drawing in his jeans pocket.

Then he said goodbye and hurried to find Suzy in the bakery aisle.

Father Peter Hodgson had rarely been out of the house since Brenda's death. It was eight days after his sister's murder, and the police had finally let him alone. He had been disgusted by some of their questions and grateful when they had gone away. He had avoided other people. At some point there would be a funeral for his sister. It would be an ordeal, mobbed by sensation seekers and those who gained attention from claiming friendship with her.

But he knew that Brenda had had few real friends. Only Liz Rudder. She was an unusually sensuous-looking woman whose egg-timer body still held the shape which he had watch develop with strange fascination in his teens. Yet there had been a neatness about Liz Rudder too. She had beautiful tiny white hands, he remembered, like an innocent child, and tiny feet. All totally out of proportion to her bulging body.

His sister Brenda on the other hand had been rather shapeless, with small breasts as if two cakes had been flattened on to her chest and strong hips which had become tubular in middle age. He had watched her change over the years, flattering himself that, although he was plump, his face was unlined as she became faded and aged. Throughout their adulthood, until moving back, he had dutifully telephoned Brenda once a fortnight and had visited her and his parents three times a year. The routine had started shortly after Brenda had come home from university.

What a disaster that had been! Brenda had passed her A levels with flying colours and had announced that she was taking up a place at university. It had almost cost their mother her health and been so selfish of Brenda when their parents had already scrimped and saved to get Peter to Oxford! That was different, of course – he was a boy, and everyone had said that Peter was brilliant, not just 'above average' like Brenda. Peter remembered the huge effort his state grammar school had made to get one or two really bright pupils to Oxbridge. It might have been at the expense of the others, but it was a sensible use of resources in his view. In some ways, that had been the happiest time of his life, when he had been the undisputed star in a small solar system, all lesser stars reflecting his glory.

The year Brenda went to university, Peter had been at home until October. He had told her that at Oxbridge that they didn't need the same longer term times as other places. He had visited his sister on her first weekend away, and expressed his disgust at the redbrick facilities, so different from his own college. He had certainly opened her eyes to how sordid her shared flat in Ardwick was! A week later, he had still been in Pelliter when she had made her hysterical phone call, demanding to be brought home. She had lasted a fortnight.

Thankfully Liz Rudder had come to visit, and sung the praises of a local teacher training college. Slowly Brenda had come to terms with her failure and had applied there. She had rarely gone out of the county since, except on coach holidays to Bournemouth and Torquay with their parents.

Brenda gave him all the local gossip when he called each fortnight, including news of John Rudder's stroke, but he hadn't really had time to think about it. At much the same time, his own local difficulties had developed. He had had to face the bishop over tedious complaints from his parishioners. He had scolded a silly woman parishioner for leaving disgusting rubbish in the waste bin in the church kitchen, and this had escalated into a full-blown feud. Apparently his flock found him obsessive, unsympathetic and lazy! Peter would never forgive the bishop for siding with his congregation. He shuddered. Dealing with bourgeois values was really not his forte.

He looked at the peeling wallpaper in the dark corner of his parents' master bedroom and the growing tea-coloured damp stain on the cracked beige ceiling. He heard the ancient pipes groan and creak with the pressure of hot water for his bath. The faint smell of drains lurked on the landing where the shabby carpet was starting to lift. He had discovered that maintaining a big old house, which had been neglected for years, cost far more than he wished to spend.

But in the meantime, Brenda's death would help. Although her house was worth very little in the current climate, selling it would bring him in enough to tide him over. Poor Brenda, he thought. In some ways she had been rather a liability. That outrageous suggestion that the chapel be closed for good! What a crazy idea! The product of a mind with too little to do. Peter Hodgson thought that most intelligent people would agree with him that poor Brenda had got the chapel issue wrong. Very wrong indeed. Rather than being closed, the place should be opened up. With a proper priest in charge. Someone like himself.

Chapter Fifteen

And they had no child, because that Elisabeth was barren, and they were now both well stricken in years.

Luke 1:7. Folio 43v. **Les Très Riches Heures du Duc de Berry**

B ecky Dixon was missing Molly Spencer this weekend. Molly was staying at her dad's, but she was coming back for the barbecue at The Briars on Monday. That would be great.

Becky did some work on the mural with Miss MacDonald on Saturday morning, but it wasn't the same. They chatted, and Becky explained to Miss MacDonald that the building Molly featured in the mural was St Trallen's Chapel.

'How interesting,' Alison said. 'I come from Norbridge but I've never seen it.'

'It's a very, very special place,' Becky said. 'It always makes you feel calm and peaceful. I think it's my favourite place on earth.'

Miss MacDonald laughed when Becky added, 'Second favourite is Burger King.'

Becky spent the rest of Saturday hanging round at home, going on the computer and getting under her grandma's feet. Sunday was even worse. By the afternoon she was fretful with boredom and frustration.

'You should be revising for the Dodsworth exam,' Judith said. 'Phil, can you find her some more online programmes?'

'I've done them all!' Becky wailed. 'I want to play Intergalactic Warriors.' But the game wasn't that much fun either. Becky itched to get her hands on the mural again, but it was no good without Molly.

It was looking fantastic now, she thought. She was still amazed at Molly's basic idea. Miss MacDonald had talked to them one day about the Renaissance, and they had Googled 'Renaissance Art' that evening when Molly had come for tea. They'd been most impressed by what Molly called the 'travel paintings': journeys of the magi, and soldiers coming home from battle, or the huge procession pictures by Bellini with hundreds of finely drawn characters.

'Better than computer games,' Molly had said, and Becky was inclined to agree with her.

She found it fascinating that it was history, too – not cartoon characters or graphics but real people who had actually worn those costumes and done those things. It gave her a funny feeling to think that something similar might have happened here, on Grandad's land. If the Chapel of St Trallen had really been a medieval church, had it been host to processions like that? Not as grand as the people in Sassetta's or Gozzoli's pictures, but scenes of devotion nevertheless. That was the sort of thing Molly was trying to paint, a bit like the Duc de Berry's fantastic *Book of Hours*. They had spent ages poring over that. Molly was leaving painting St Trallen's to the very end. At the moment it was just a picture of a block on the top of a low hill, but when it was finished it would have the solid oblong shape of the chapel with the stained-glass window at one end and the bell tower on top, with yellow and bottle-green gorse bushes and a pale-blue sea shimmering in the far background. It would be unmistakable, Becky thought excitedly.

'Where's the vegetable knife?' Grandma was saying in a loud exasperated voice. 'Things keeping going missing round here. The grater has gone, and the kitchen scissors.' Oh, not again, Becky thought, and crept down from the big chair in the living-room where the computer was kept. Judith didn't see her as she sneaked away to the front room, yards from the kitchen, and sat curled up on the sofa under the window.

Becky's phone bleeped in her jeans pocket. She had been hoping to hear from Molly, but the number that came up wasn't hers.

'Hey, Becks, let's meet,' the text message said.

'Who u?' Becky messaged back.

'Lily. Got new fone. Want to tlk about M.'

This was interesting, Becky thought. She had never been texted by Lily Smith, the most mature girl in the class, and gang leader, before. Even the text about Miss Hodgson's murder had gone to Molly, not Becky. Becky felt flattered but annoyed with herself. The flattery won out.

'OK,' she texted back.

'C u at Briggs.'

Briggs' shop was down the road from St Trallen's Hill on the shore. It was a favourite place in the summer for kids on bikes, horse riders, and trippers going to the beach. In winter it did a meagre trade in cigarettes, newspapers, and the odd packet of frozen food, but now it was a cornucopia of fabulous wares ranging from fluorescent green fishing nets to rude postcards. Becky had been allowed to walk there alone in the summer for the last two or three years. She had forgotten that Briggs would be opening their famous ice-cream stall for the May Bank Holiday. Suddenly the idea of bright plastic buckets and spades seemed compelling. These days her grandma wouldn't let her go anywhere, because there was supposed to be a murderer on the loose, but that had been a week ago now and no one else had been attacked. Grandma was busy chopping mint for her delicious mint sauce, with the radio on. She wouldn't hear if Becky slipped out, just for a walk.

Becky grabbed her jacket and set off in the warm soft spring sunshine towards Briggs. As the path dropped from the house towards the main road, hardly a major thoroughfare even on the hottest day, she thought: why did Lily Smith tell me in that text that she had a new phone?

It's not as if I knew the number for her old one.

In the Rudders' house, Kevin had been dozing for most of Sunday afternoon after that heavy lunch. John had been tucked up in his wheelchair by the window for his afternoon nap. Liz had been away a long time, he thought. Still, a meeting about the Dodsworth exams was bound to be a fraught affair.

John started grunting.

'What is it, old son?' Kevin said in a kindly voice.

John heaved himself in his wheelchair; then he shut his eyes and slumped backwards.

'Ah,' Kevin said. 'Time for your painkillers. Sorry, old mate, should've remembered. Now, no acrobatics. Don't want to panic the horses, do we? We'll save that for Wednesday night, even if it's just the two of us now.'

Kevin heaved John upright in his wheelchair, pulled up the footrests and started to wheel it towards John's bedroom. The wheelchair was a sticky mess, he thought, with food caught in the creases of the seat and the armrests. He wondered whose responsibility it was, because Liz was usually so particular. In the bedroom, Kevin lifted John up, and into a tall-backed armchair.

'There we are. Here are your pills. Can you reach the glass of water? Jolly good. Shall I pull the curtains shut?'

John grunted again; then he lay back and shut his eyes.

'Poor old boy,' Kevin murmured sympathetically. 'Have a good nap. I bet Liz will be back soon.' He walked backwards out of the room, waving at John in a rather silly way.

John Rudder watched him go. He had really tried to speak, but it was too much for him. His brain distilled the words perfectly but his mouth wouldn't work. Why do people treat me as if I'm a helpless child amused by silly antics? he thought. Is it because I fall in and out of sleep with vivid dreams which I think are real? Or because I can't do more than grunt? Not that he blamed Kevin. At least in his cheery way, Kevin was trying. And he had given him his painkillers, which was more than Liz would have done.

I am helpless, John thought bitterly. Some days he hardly surfaced to reality. Other days, arbitrarily, like today, he knew exactly what was going on. The stroke had been serious and had deprived him of his speech and the movement down his left side. He suspected his body was getting weaker. But on a good day, his brain still worked.

He had often wondered what had been the reason for his stroke. He knew all about the physical causes. In his case, there had been a blockage caused by a loose bit of fat – cholesterol perhaps – or other detritus in the veins. But why had it happened to him? Yet if what they said was true and stress was really anything to do with it, then he had the answer himself.

A few weeks before his stroke, he had told Liz that their marriage was over.

John Rudder thought, as he always did nowadays, about the past. His marriage to Liz had been over for a long time. He'd been trapped into marrying her in the first place, but that had never really worried him.

He'd actually been pleased when she had said she might be pregnant. He was getting ready to settle down and have kids – he was five years older than Liz, after all. He'd been a magnet for the Norbridge totty since being trans-ferred there from the building society in Newcastle, but womanizing got tiring after a while. By the age of thirty he had given up on the idea of romantic love and Liz was as nice as any of the others. Her parents were working class like him, although Liz was clever and educated. Her father was keen, and her affectionate younger brother, Kevin, was a bit of a divvy, but he hero-worshipped John. Marrying Liz wouldn't be too bad.

'I can't believe it,' Liz had said after they had been together a few months. 'I'm late. It's never happened before. I don't know what to do.'

I do, John thought. I'll do the right thing. John had never been in this situ-ation before, but it didn't feel as catastrophic as he'd expected. In fact he was rather proud of himself. He could imagine himself as a family man and he thought he loved Liz in his own way. And the time had also come for him to think about being self-employed. Liz's father had agreed to advance him a very small loan and in return he'd offered to take on young Kevin, who wasn't doing very well in the office at Pelliter Mill.

When Liz's pregnancy hadn't materialized, he'd thought, well, there's next time. But there hadn't been a next time. At first they'd used precautions anyway, but after two years he'd suggested they tried for a baby. Nothing happened. Liz had been working at St Mungo's and had seemed happy to stay there.

The next ten years had been taken up with buying their first house in Pelliter village, and then with the big move to High Pelliter. He'd been sad but fatalistic about not having children, and he had agreed with Liz that the last thing they wanted was any sort of treatment. Who needed doctors messing around with them finding out who was 'to blame'? Without anything being said, he had assumed the sterility was his. Perhaps, he had thought guiltily, the fact that he had no illegitimate children despite his misspent youth was not the luck he had thought it was.

Then over a decade ago, things had changed. It had been so simple that, looking back, John wondered if perhaps all along he had suspected, and chosen not to see the truth.

He had come home early on a hot summer's afternoon. He'd had a good lunch and a bottle of wine with a client at the Crossed Foxes. He was over the limit for driving and so he had walked down the empty High Street and up the hill to High Pelliter. The heat was so intense that everything seemed muted, and the back door of his house had been open into the garage. He had taken off his shoes, as Liz always insisted, and crept, just as she had done yesterday, through the hot silent house.

'I think I'm starting with it early,' he had heard Brenda say. 'I've been flushing and feeling really panicky. It's awful really. But of course that won't happen to you, will it? I suppose you'll just go on taking the mini-pill until the doctor puts you on HRT.'

Liz had laughed. Neither woman had a clue he was there. John had slipped back into the shadows. Then he turned and walked back to the garage. He sat on the step for a minute and thought about what he had heard.

Had Liz been on the mini-pill for years? He knew at once that he couldn't ask her. If her answer was an outraged negative, she would be appalled that he had even asked the question. His life would be made a misery. If her answer was yes, what could he do? But, if he had heard correctly, it meant that for twenty years she had deceived him. She had deliberately denied him the chance to father children. He found that unbelievable. It was a fundamental refusal of his human rights.

For the next few days he had gone on behaving towards Liz in exactly the same way. He was tortured by indecision. While Liz slept, he tossed and turned, telling himself he was wrong, that she could never do such a terrible thing.

He should have had it out with her and found out the truth. But instead he left his marriage in limbo, and set about seducing female clients with a sort of calm fury. He took no precautions if they didn't insist. If they got pregnant, so be it. They would at least have the chance to have the children. Unlike him. And at the end of this crazed spree he had fallen in love. It had been a disaster, of course. He hadn't had the bottle to leave Liz at the time. But at least he had known what real love was like. And years later when he'd finally had the incentive to go, the stress had led to the stroke.

What an irony. You had to laugh, really, and John did, in a dry, cracked sort of gurgle. The effort exhausted him, or maybe it was all the memories. Anger played hell with his blood pressure. Even on a good day, whole tranches of time slipped out of his mind, or elided blurrily with other mental slide-shows of the past. He worried that he would not live too much longer, although Kevin and Brenda's cack-handed attempts to keep him alive had actually done some real good. After all, with some help, John had managed to get up and even to use his old PC, still sitting in the corner of what had once been his office. He had to make sure Liz still thought he was a vegetable. But that wasn't hard. It was so much what she wanted to hear that convincing her wasn't difficult. And she hardly ever came close enough to him to look at him and see the new light in his eye.

In the distance he heard Liz's car pull up, and then Kevin's slightly pissed voice welcoming her home. So John wouldn't be able to use the computer today.

But there was always tomorrow, if he survived that long.

Ro had taken Ben out for a Sunday afternoon drive. The sunshine was fierce. But there was the sense of possible treachery lurking behind it. Spring was always volatile, and grey clouds and rain could come in from the west at any time. Still, the weather had attracted them out. Ben had been fractious stuck at home. He had gone on and on about going to Suzy's barbecue the next day.

'So Jake Spencer will definitely be there?' he had asked Ro five times. In the end she had stopped trying to persuade him the barbecue might be a bad idea. It looked as though they would have to lower the drawbridge again, this time to go out.

She parked at Briggs' shop on the coast. Before she had taken off her seat belt, Ben was out of the car. The speed at which he could move sometimes astonished her, and she watched him lurch forward, peering through his thick glasses and groping his way along the edge of the car-park wall.

'Ben, wait!' she shouted. He always thought he could do more than he actually could. If he went barrelling along like that he would fall. 'Ben, not so fast, I'm coming …'

But Ben didn't listen. He knew the place. They had been to Briggs a few times. He could see the shop ahead, the blur of colour and the open door with the other kids hanging outside. He had no idea if the boys were from his school or not – he could see nothing but the bunch of indeterminate bodies and bikes. But he recognized they were around his age. With the optimism that made Ro terrified for him, she could see that he was making for the group in the belief that at least some of them would be kids he knew.

'Are they doing chocolate crunch this year?' he called to them.

She knew at once by the other boys' reactions that Ben had read it wrong. She was standing ten yards behind him, slowed down by locking the car and a natural tendency not to shepherd him like an over-anxious mother. But she could see what he couldn't. These weren't kids from Norbridge High who would know and welcome him. Ben was protected by his school community, and he faced everyone with the bright assurance confirmed by their kindness. But there was no kindness here.

Suddenly Ro knew what to answer when anyone, ever again, asked her why she was a PCSO. I want every kid to be safe, she would say. I want everyone to behave decently to the disadvantaged and the needy on our streets, whether it's in the middle of the city, or here in one of the most beautiful parts of Britain. But she couldn't intervene this time. It was her own son and she had to watch him fight his own battles and lose. She had to strain every nerve in her body to stop herself rushing forward.

'Whadya talking to us for, spaz?' said the biggest boy in the group. Ro knew who he was. It was Jonty McFadden, recognizable from that incident in Norbridge where he'd been part of the gang in the park. Here on his home turf he looked bigger and more threatening. She could see that the rest of the kids were younger than Ben, but Jonty, already big and dominant, with thick, curly black hair and a mocking grin, was in that strange, half-boy half-youth stage, where they could turn from sweetness to sadism at the flash of a knife.

Ben stopped stock still. 'Is Briggs open?' he asked, more to make contact than to get an answer.

''Course it is, yer effin' cripple,' said Jonty in a more threatening voice. His mates were circling around Ben on their bikes, like scavenging gulls.

Ro thought, this is it. I'm moving in here.

But she didn't have to. A small, dark-haired girl in jeans and a navy pea-jacket came hurtling down from the path behind them.

'Who's a cripple, Jonty?' she called out. 'You're morally crippled. This boy was just asking you a civil question. You should answer it.' She turned to Ben. 'Yes, Briggs' famous ice-cream shop is open for the season. Please go in.'

Ben said 'Thanks,' and wobbled unsteadily to the shop. Ro could tell by his walk that he was all right, that he was used to this in a way she had never realized. She made herself lean back against the car, as if it didn't matter to her. She wanted the little thug on his bike to realize that Ben's mother was here, but he wouldn't see her cowering or outraged, or needing to interfere. She would sneer at his crassness with the same insouciance he had displayed himself.

The wait was unbearable, but she didn't follow Ben into the shop. It was a while before he came out, and the world was normal again. He walked jerkily but jauntily to the car, then turned and waved at the girl in the jacket with his ice-cream cone.

'Guess what, Mum? That's Becky Dixon,' he said. 'She's a friend of Jake and Molly Spencer. We had a chat. She's going to their barbecue tomorrow as well. That'll be good. Anyway, shall we walk along now like we usually do?'

He laughed. Ro followed him as he walked confidently towards the shore. Her eyes were full of watery relief, but, of course, it was just the sun.

Becky Dixon came out of the shop and she knew what would be waiting for her. Jonty McFadden had skewed his bike across the shop doorway.

'Saint Becky Dixon,' he said contemptuously. Toby Armistead, who had a much smarter bike and iPod earphones, laughed sycophantically.

'You're the devil, then,' Becky spat.

'Ooh, spoilin' for a fight, are you?' Jonty spat back.

'Where's Lily Smith?' Becky asked. But as soon as she said it, she knew that would be just an excuse for more hilarity from the boys gathering around Jonty.

'She's not here,' one of them said, and whooped with laughter. 'She wouldn't want to be arsed with you.'

Of course. There had been no message from Lily. It must have been Jonty who had texted her. He had put in that line about Lily having a new phone in case she knew Lily's mobile number. But I should have known, Becky told herself. Even if Lily had had a new phone she would have had the same SIM card. Stupid, stupid me.

But nothing could happen to her outside Briggs in the warm sunlight. At some point her grandad would come looking for her anyway. And even if he didn't, she would stay and fight back. Everyone said bullies had to be stood up to. The way Jonty had behaved was disgusting. In fact everything about Jonty was horrible. She stared back at his turnip head with the thick dark hair and little piggy eyes like his mother's.

'You're ugly,' she said coldly. He didn't scare her. Becky had seen Jonty in action. He tormented the little boy with diabetes in Year Four. He kept Toby in his gang by a mixture of physical and emotional bullying. He mocked everyone else in the class.

Becky was aware that, as if by arrangement, Toby was nudging her ankles with his bike, strategically placed alongside her. But like an invitation to run, Jonty moved his bike aside. Involuntarily, Becky moved forward. Toby moved in to prod her again. Then she realized what was happening. They were herding her. Behind her, Toby's wheel kept nudging her on. Jonty was at her side, still on his bike, his feet tapping at either side to keep him upright, but pushing her with his thick, brawny arms. The big fists on the end looked like a man's. Fearful of making a scene, Becky kept walking towards the path to St Trallen's Hill. It was the way home. What could they do to her there?

The path started to wind uphill. Toby was behind her on his bike. Jonty was beside her, slightly to the front, pushing her with his thick arms. There were two other boys whom she hardly noticed alongside. They were in Year Six too, but they were nobodies – just Jonty's gang members. As she trudged in the middle of the little ring of bikes, she thought for a moment of Molly's mural. Was this what it felt like to be a prisoner in the square in Florence? Or a medieval virgin being taken for execution? Was this what St Trallen must have felt like when they took her into a forced marriage with the pagan prince and she plucked out her own eyes?

The boys had obviously agreed previously where to stop. Jonty rode his bike in a 'wheelie' on the back wheel over the brow of the hill as if it were a living horse pawing the air. Where the path forked, the little procession turned into the dip. Phil had cleared a track to the left for legitimate walkers. The route to the chapel was cordoned off with wire, and a sign Phil had printed out.

Jonty picked up the wire and held it while his retinue dodged underneath and spread out in front of the chapel. The old police tape trailed over the gorse. In the dip by the chapel door, Toby's bike bumped Becky's calves forward. Jonty pulled his bike up. To Becky, he seemed like one of the haughty mounted soldiers on Molly's mural. Knights did what they liked with maidens, didn't they? Feeble maidens anyway. Not ones like St Trallen. Becky looked at him levelly.

Jonty dismounted and parked his bike against the chapel wall.

'Saint Becky,' he said again in his mocking voice. She knew exactly what Jonty wanted. She knew he was worried. She thought about the evening she and Molly had gone out on the bikes and seen him down by the Marshes. The evening poor Miss Hodgson had been murdered. Jonty wouldn't want anyone to know he was there and the police were asking every day for witnesses to come forward. He leant towards her, and Becky saw the glint of his knife.

'You know what happened to St Trallen, don't you?' said Jonty. Every primary school child in Pelliter knew the myth. 'You've got to do what I tell you Becky Dixon. You must never talk.' He was leering right in her face now, so the others couldn't hear him. 'Do you understand? Never ever say anything about me being down the Marshes that night, or I'll kill you and do something worse to your big-bummed friend Molly Spencer.'

Then for the benefit of the other boys he shouted, 'You've got to stop painting your stupid mural, and you've got to back out of the Dodsworth scholarship. Otherwise …'

Jonty twisted the thin knife so its blade caught the pink glow from the sun in the west. Becky glanced over his shoulder at Toby Armistead, who looked momentarily shamefaced. So that was the deal. Toby had agreed to do this to her, as long as Jonty frightened her out of taking the exam. But Toby didn't know that Dodsworth wasn't really what it was about. I don't even want to go there anyway, Becky thought. And whatever you say I'll protect Molly. I'm strong enough to do that. The realization made her smile. It infuriated Jonty, who began to prance in front of her.

'Do as we tell you! Fuck up the mural,' he said. 'Fuck up the Dodsworth exam. And fuck up Miss MacDonald, your hero!'

'What have you got against Miss MacDonald, Jonty?' she said. 'Who's pulling your strings? Your horrible mother?'

It had been a shot in the dark but Becky saw that she was on target. 'Who got you that knife, Jonty? Tell me. Was it your mam?'

'No! It's not me mam. Keep me mam out of this, you witch.' As if on cue, the others began to chant: 'Witch, witch, witch, witch.'

Becky saw the knife in his hand but she wondered if Jonty would have the nerve actually to do anything. She felt comforted by the calm little chapel, and she knew any minute now Grandad would come over the ridge, his check shirt with the sleeves rolled up, showing his arms which were three times bigger even than Jonty's. She could almost see him in her mind's eye. What could Jonty do in the next few minutes?

He could cut her, or worse, he could assault her in some way. Jonty was in silhouette now with the sun in the west behind him. He was eleven years old, almost a man. She had heard stories about girls being raped by big overgrown boys at school. Is that what he was threatening to do to Molly? How long did rape take? She had no idea. It had nearly happened to St Trallen. She had been a girl at the time. How old had the pagan prince been? What was so different these days?

Behind her, Becky felt the warm comfort of the chapel door in the sun. She touched the wood with the flat of her hands. She thought, they can try and hurt me but they won't succeed. St Trallen plucked out her own eyes rather than have them used against her. She hadn't been anyone's victim.

Jonty advanced on her with the knife. He waved it in front of her face. She looked back at him. She noticed for the first time that he had dark curly hair like she did, and though he was tall he had a muscular body. He was big and she was small, but they weren't so different, except that he had murder in his eyes. The knife swished through the air. It really did make a swishing noise, just like it said in books, and it was coming nearer....

Becky screamed, 'Save me, St Trallen!' And then she shut her eyes and waited for the agony.

She was aware suddenly that the brightness had gone, but it was only the sun behind the clouds. She opened her eyes. Jonty was standing there, looking down at the sandy track. His knife was on the ground and still spinning in the dust. It was no longer shiny and bright in the sunlight. It was a mucky, grey-looking thing. Jonty was holding his wrist and yelping in pain.

Becky took a deep breath and walked between him and Toby, away from the cluster of boys on their bikes. The knife had whipped out of Jonty's hand. She didn't know how or why it happened, but she didn't look back. As she walked towards St Trallen's Place, her body was shaking, but her mind was clear. She had beaten Jonty McFadden this time, but he would be after her again. If it was just Jonty she would have laughed in his face and stood up to him for ever. Even Callie was just a fat old cow.

But when she had asked him who was pulling his strings he had denied it was his mother. So if it wasn't Callie McFadden, who was it?

Chapter Sixteen

For I am become like a bottle in the smoke; yet do I not forget thy statutes.

Psalm 119:83. Folio 48v. **Les Très Riches Heures du Duc de Berry**

Sheila Findley had been thinking about Callie McFadden too. But for the first time in ages, she was able to put Callie's mocking face out of her mind at will. Sheila spent most of Sunday in the garden.

Towards the end of the afternoon, Ray went upstairs into what had been his office in the spare bedroom. The window looked over the back garden. From the corner of his eye he was aware of Sheila's tall figure bending to tend the plants, but as time went on he stopped looking and checking. It was the first time for months he had been at home without being aware of what she was doing every minute.

The room contained his PC, his books and his files. It smelt slightly musty. He looked at the paper residue of the last project he'd been working on. The Ofsted inspection had taken place just before Sheila's collapse, thank goodness, but it had left him thinking about how much effort it took to present St Mungo's in such a positive light.

He had been worried even then about Brenda Hodgson. She was a dull teacher, whose air of mild unhappiness tainted the rest of the school. He knew she was desperate to retire and that she was just waiting for her pension. Liz Rudder seemed a more forceful character, but she, too, had lost interest in actually teaching. But whereas Brenda was just fading, Liz maintained her negative drive through territorial plots. Installing her as deputy head had been a mistake, but he hadn't had much choice once Sheila was ill.

He could still see Sheila pottering happily when his mobile rang. When he saw the digits on the screen he felt a sudden pressure harden behind his eyes. It was a number he hadn't seen for a long time, but he knew at once who it was. He watched Sheila trundle the wheelbarrow towards the shed. He thought – maybe I can answer the phone now and get rid of the call, while Sheila's still out there?

'Hello, Callie.'

'Oh, so you've picked up, have you? Good. I thought you wouldn't want me to leave a message.'

'It's Sunday, Callie.'

'So? Some of us with kids have got to work seven days a week. I've been thinking. I've told Jonty I want him to go in for the Dodsworth exam and I want you to see to it that he's one of the lucky ones.'

'But Callie, that's ridiculous.'

'Why?'

'I can't swing it for favoured children. And anyway, there's no way Jonty would get into Dodsworth. He's not interested in schoolwork.'

'Whose fault it that? You know he's bright enough.'

'Well, he's certainly not stupid—'

'Stupid? Jonty? How could he be? You know I've been trying to speak to you for a few days now. I've got something to say to you, Ray. And it's pretty serious. You'd better take a deep breath ...'

On the morning of the May Bank Holiday, Robert woke early after a restless night, with Suzy tossing and turning beside him. What should have been a pleasant evening by themselves – with Jake out playing saxophone in his band – had turned out to be fraught with barbecue preparations. Suzy had slid into restless sleep before he had even undressed. In the dawn light he crept downstairs. He tried to find the metal colander but it was nowhere he could see, so he washed the salad leaf by leaf and left it to dry on a tea towel. Then he washed and pricked the potatoes for baking and put them in the oven. He went into the garden to set up the barbecue, lining the basin with silver foil, and collecting the charcoal in the bottom.

And then he sat on the bench looking across the lawn to the wall where his dead wife had managed to grow one of the few wisterias in this part of Cumbria.

He thought of her fleetingly. It all seemed so long ago; so much had happened. He was a different person now, with a family. Of course I love them, he thought; I've lived with their ups and downs for nearly five years. But as Suzy said, he wasn't their dad. And for the first time, he turned the question on its head: in what way did they love him? In the end, how would they feel when he married their mother? He had tried hard not to get between the children and Suzy. He had always played it as just 'Robert, a nice guy to have around'. But how would it be when he was their mum's husband, the one she chose to love and cherish. Would the kids be jealous? Resentful even?

There was a noise behind him.

'Morning, Robert.'

'Morning, Jake.'

'This is going to be a bit of a crazy day, isn't it?' Jake said. He perched his neat bottom on the arm of the bench.

'There are a lot of people coming,' Robert said. 'I don't know if your mum is very happy that I've invited the Dixons, but Molly will be delighted to see Becky.'

'Robert,' said Jake thoughtfully, 'can I ask you something?'

'Yes, of course,' Robert said, warily.

'It's actually about Becky.' Jake screwed up his eyes as the first real sunlight came over the treetops to the east. 'But I can't really explain, not quickly. Can we talk later, when everyone's gone?'

'Sure,' Robert answered. He felt a rush of pleasure. Jake genuinely wanted his advice. Things must be all right, mustn't they? But then again, what was it he wanted to say about Becky?

For Ro, the arrival at anyone else's unfamiliar house was always a nightmare. There were the practical problems like steps and furniture and loose rugs. And there were the emotional problems. How would people behave? How would Ben react?

She parked outside The Briars, in the lane.

'Hey, I can smell cooking,' Ben said excitedly. 'Smoke! The barbie's on.' He started his hurried, swaying walk.

'Be careful, Ben,' Ro called out. The unmetalled track to the house had ridges and potholes, but with a sixth sense Ben seemed to avoid them. He opened the gate and lurched up the path.

Suzy had heard the car and stood to welcome them at the front door.

She saw Ro anxiously following her son, far enough behind to be unnoticed by Ben in his hurry, near enough to be there if he fell. Her stance, standing behind the swaying boy, leaning slightly forward with her arms out, reminded Suzy of when the children had been toddlers learning to walk. Ro was still on patrol, Suzy thought, and she had been on guard for twelve years. It must be tough.

'Hi! Go through to the back garden,' Suzy said. 'Jake will look out for you, Ben.'

But for how long? Ro thought anxiously. Other kids were often kind to Ben until they got bored or irritated. Her eyes flashed to the kitchen window. But Ben was already outside, hooting with laughter, and Jake was holding sausages up with a long pair of barbecue tongs. A pleasant-looking man Ro assumed was Robert Clark was putting out garden chairs.

'I'm sorry we're early,' she said to Suzy. 'Sometimes it takes us ages to get out. Sometimes it all goes smoothly. It's difficult to get it right.'

'You're not early,' Suzy said. 'The others are late.' She was surprised at how tense Ro seemed to be. 'Have a drink?'

Ro accepted an orange juice, and then turned to see two new visitors. Phil and Becky Dixon: grandfather and granddaughter, hovering at the door.

Phil followed Becky in and smiled at Ro, but she felt too uncertain to smile back. Did he remember her as the PCSO from the school-window incident? Would that make things awkward? And what about yesterday? Had Becky told him about having to defend Ben from bullies?

'Nice to meet you again,' Phil said to Ro. 'You look better without the broken glass.' But she doesn't, he thought. She looks as if she's swallowed it. He followed her eyes to the window and to the boy with the thick spectacles and the uneven walk.

'My son,' Ro said.

So that was it, Phil thought. No wonder Ro looked constantly worried. Phil said, 'Judith's sorry she couldn't come. She'd already planned to go over to the Metro Centre with some friends from the WI. Where's Molly?'

Suzy explained that Molly's dad would be dropping her off shortly, and Phil ambled outside, leaving Suzy and Ro alone. Maybe I'm not the only one on edge, Ro thought.

'Are you OK?' she asked Suzy.

'I was going to ask you the same, Ro.'

'Well, it's easy to see what's wrong with me. Disabled child, new place, new people. We don't do this sort of thing very often. But that's me. What about you?'

'Nigel is about to turn up any minute. You remember Nigel from uni, don't you? He's balding now.' Suzy smiled. 'But this isn't going to be easy. Robert has hardly spoken to him in five years, and I can't imagine us all standing around sipping red wine and making conversation. It's going to be awkward. I don't know how I'm going to get through this, Ro.'

'Try the red wine. You're not driving.'

'Good thinking,' Suzy took a gulp from her glass, and Ro started to feel better. This wasn't a competition and Suzy was as nervous as she was. Tentatively Ro put her hand on Suzy's arm. It felt warm and smooth. Ro realized how infrequently she actually touched anyone else besides Ben. For a moment she wondered if she had done something out of order, but Suzy rolled her eyes at her over the rim of her glass and for a nanosecond Ro thought they were both going to giggle.

But there was no time. There was the sound of another car coming down the lane. 'Better pour me another,' Suzy grimaced. 'That's bound to be Nigel.'

It would be different if it were good red wine, Faye Armistead thought. A strong gin and tonic at noon had given her a slight headache, and now her husband was opening another bottle of white wine.

'If Toby has taken off for the day we might as well enjoy it,' her husband Roger said.

Faye raised her eyebrow. Roger had always said that letting Toby hang around with the local kids was a bad strategy, but this weekend he seemed to have changed his tune. Faye had prepared a salad for lunch, using what was left after the au pair had raided the fridge. Somehow, rocket drenched in dressing left over from Saturday supper, supermarket garlic bread and some very tired cheese didn't look appetizing.

'Are you happy about Toby going off-piste like this?' she asked, her voice sharper than the usual combination of drawl and staccato which she adopted in company. 'Do you know who he's with?'

'As a matter of fact I do,' Roger said. He was actually quite flushed. His nose was a deeper shade than the rest of his rosy face. Faye couldn't help the corners of her mouth turning down in disgust. He poured himself a very large glass of warm white plonk. 'The au pair told me. He's gone off to the shore with that McFadden boy again.'

Faye pretended to be shocked. 'But the McFaddens live on the Pelliter Valley estate. I know the mother. She's a teaching assistant at the school.'

'Yes. Rather a hippy type. Big bust, lots of hair. But actually, the boy seems rather a strong character. I think it might do Toby good to team up with someone like that.'

'But if Toby is going to Dodsworth, surely there isn't any point in letting him hang around with the local riff-raff?' she asked.

'Ah well,' Roger smiled knowingly. 'There you're wrong. Toby told me last night that the McFadden boy might be going to Dodsworth too. His mother wants him to sit the scholarship and apparently some shadowy benevolent figure could be willing to stump up the rest of the money.'

'Good heavens! Jonty McFadden at Dodsworth? Callie never breathed a word of this!'

'Talk to her a lot, do you?'

Roger smiled rather viciously. Faye said nothing, but she didn't like the feeling of being excluded by Callie and wrong-footed by her husband. Still, she had her own secret satisfaction. She looked at Roger. His hair was thinning a bit and he had a little pot belly on the end of spindly legs, crossed one over the other so that his trousers rode up and revealed unattractive flaky shins above cream-coloured socks. He was still handsome but in a rather worn way. She had seen the way the au pair looked at him, fancying her chances. He was still an asset. For a start, he was her husband, and he was an Armistead of Pelliter Farm.

But the gentry needed to strengthen the stock now and then with an injection of more resilient genes. Was that what Roger was thinking of when he admired the au pair's robust curves? I may have beaten you to it, Faye thought. She recalled Toby's stocky little body and dark curly hair, and a rather superior smile returned to her lips. He didn't look a bit like Roger, did he?

For Alison MacDonald, the weekend had been a failure. She had enjoyed working on the mural with Becky for a couple of hours on Saturday morning, but they had both missed Molly's sharp direction. The girls were bright kids, Alison thought. She felt some satisfaction that her plan was working.

Nothing more had been said about the window incident, though Jonty swaggered more confidently around the school these days. Sometimes, all the different things which had happened in Pelliter lately made a stew in Ali's head: the man in the playground, the body at the chapel, the broken window, the Dodsworth exam, even meeting Ro and the aggressive young constable who had been so unpleasant. And the Marsh Murder, of course. Mark had continued to be fascinated by what had happened to Miss Hodgson. It was the only thing he had ever asked about. They'd talked about it on the phone and on MSN all week, and Mark had said several times how much he was looking forward to seeing her for more insider gen.

But it hadn't worked out quite like that. On Saturday afternoon, the motorway traffic had been bumper to bumper and Alison hadn't arrived at the flat until three o'clock. They'd had a rocky start, with Alison unprepared to jump into bed immediately, and Mark wanting to have a disco nap for a few hours followed by a really late steamy session.

'It's the weekend, what's left of it,' he had moaned. 'The time for having a few drinks, lots of nookie, and getting out on the town. If we go to bed now we can keep rockin' all night long.'

'And tomorrow?'

'We've got all day, babe. Let's get up at noon and take the motor into the Peak district. And on Bank Holiday Monday we'll go to Altrincham and look in estate agents' windows and have brunch. Bingo – great weekend.'

Alison had hated the frowsy feeling of lying in bed on Sunday, waiting for Mark to surface after a night drinking and dancing. She lay watching the sunlight speckle the white walls. When he finally roused himself, he had been crabby and overtired. The trip to Derbyshire had not been a great success. They had both been hot, the car-parks were full, and Mark had not wanted to walk far. He couldn't drink, as he was driving; Alison wasn't insured to drive his car, something which made her cross in turn. In the evening they had ordered a take-away supper which wasn't very appetizing, and Mark had gone to sleep watching a DVD. Then he had woken and spent most of the night on his computer while Alison slept fretfully. For someone who worked hard all week, Mark played hard at weekends too, and Alison had forgotten what it was like to be with him for more than twenty-four hours.

She sometimes wondered what Mark might be taking, to keep him going at the clubs and bars and internet games. The sales culture depended on drive and energy; many of his mates got their boost artificially. Alison knew that many of her friends took recreational drugs. But there were several reasons why she didn't. She worried about how it might affect her work with kids and she hated the whole sneaky, hole-in-corner criminal thing which excited some of her mates as much as the illegal substances. She didn't need it. She couldn't afford it anyway.

But what about Mark? He earned twice as much as she did. He was in that sort of culture. Did he take stuff? Possibly. But his frantic lifestyle would stop when they had their house to pay for and kids to bring up. When they had first got engaged, Alison had lain in Mark's arms and imagined the children they might have. Redheads like her, perhaps, or blonds like him. But lately, it was as if the children were at the other end of a long country lane, walking away from her.

On Bank Holiday Monday she and Mark went out for the inevitable brunch. Talking about the house they might have, and the things they might do, was getting a bit repetitive. As they sat at the pavement café, two young men walked past, wearing shades and loose, short-sleeved shirts over faded, torn jeans. They had shaved heads; they swaggered.

'Markie!' one said, and slapped his hand down on the little metal table. 'Howya doin'?'

Mark had been absorbed in yesterday's Sunday paper. He looked up, and Alison saw at once that he was embarrassed.

'Archie my friend!' he said. The other man just smiled and nodded.

'This is my fiancée,' Mark added.

Alison said 'Hi' without much enthusiasm.

'Fiancée, eh? Well, well. Who'd've thought it. We're off into town now,' the one called Archie said. He leered mischievously and Mark squirmed under his long, slow smile. 'Will we be seein' ya tonight, Markie? Or is your fiancée goin' to be around?'

'Maybe,' Mark said. He attempted a dismissive wave as he went back to his paper. The other man banged the flat of his hand on the little metal table so hard it shook.

'What about later, today Markie?' he said in a thick, slow, emphatic sort of voice. 'We'll call you later.'

Mark looked up quickly. 'Yeah, yeah, OK, Dazza. Speak later.'

The two men slunk away. 'Who were they?' Alison asked.

'Five-a-side footballers,' Mark said without looking up. Alison watched the heavy men swagger down the street. They didn't really look the five-a-side type, but then how would she know? She hardly knew any of Mark's friends these days. For a moment she felt worried, as well as guilty.

Chapter Seventeen

'… yet the dogs eat of the crumbs which fall from their masters' table.' Then Jesus answered and said unto her 'O woman great is thy faith:'

Matthew 15:27 and 28. Folio 164r. **Les Très Riches Heures du Duc de Berry**

At the same time, the barbecue at The Briars was in full swing. Nigel had been pleasant enough when he arrived with Molly, and meeting Ro again had taken the strain off his coming to The Briars. Suzy had watched gratefully as Ro greeted him enthusiastically and got him talking. Robert had actually asked Nigel to stay for lunch and he'd agreed, much to Suzie's amazement. His girlfriend was a nurse, he explained, working until mid afternoon at the Freeman Hospital. She sounded a far cry from the glamorous PA he'd left Suzy for.

Phil and Becky helped the atmosphere too. Phil was easy to talk to and seemed genuinely interested in Ro's PCSO work. There had been lots of laughter around the table, especially when Robert had nearly dropped a Cumberland sausage into the ashes and Jake had rescued it with reflexes that astonished himself as well as everyone else.

When the serious eating was over, the young people sat drinking cans of Coke at the bottom of the garden. Surprisingly, they were still outside rather than hooked up to various electronic games, though Jake told Suzy that Ben was known, school-wide, as a wizard at Intergalactic Warrior. Suzy served tea and coffee, and the conversation turned inevitably to the murder at Pelliter.

When they'd exhausted the topic, Nigel said, 'Wasn't there another body in suspicious circumstances around here recently? I heard something on the regional TV news. A body found by a weird chapel? How spooky is that?'

'The chapel is Phil's place. It was on Phil's land,' Ro said quickly, to spare him embarrassment. I'm saying too much, Ro thought, but Phil raised his eyebrows and nodded at her ever so slightly in gratitude. Ro felt herself colour up again. It was the first time she had blushed since she had fallen out with Jed Jackson, but it was once too often. It must be my age, she thought.

'Yes,' Phil said. 'The mystery man. We know nothing about him except he had a Canadian coin in his pocket.'

'But something else has cropped up too,' Ro said. 'One of the teachers at St Mungo's says she saw someone who sounds a bit like the mystery man in the school playground the same Friday. I've tried to get her to talk to the CID but she won't …' For a second Ro thought about Jed, and her face clouded.

But Suzy was turning to face her. 'Hey, I think I saw him, too. I was at St Mungo's because Molly's teacher wanted to talk to me. I saw a smart young chap getting into a black cab. You don't see many black cabs round here. He must have driven from somewhere else. He had black curly hair and glasses.'

'Maybe he had flown over from Canada?' Robert suggested. 'That would explain the coin.'

'And got a cab from Newcastle airport …' Suzy said helpfully.

Ro shook her head. 'Not very likely, I suppose.' But the thought stayed with her.

'And then there's the drawing,' Robert Clark was saying. 'I met a girl who was on work experience with the local free newspaper. She said the dead man had a doodle. Or a tracing, she called it. It was too faded and pale to photograph well. But it looked like this.'

Robert was wearing his jeans again for the barbecue and the picture Poppy had drawn was in his pocket. He spread it out and put it on the table.

Ro stared at it. 'That looks familiar,' she said.

'It looks a bit like a medieval picture to me,' Suzy added. 'Maybe it's something to do with the St Trallen *Book*.'

'I thought that,' Robert said. 'But it's not quite right. It looks very like the sort of art in the *Book*, but at the same time it isn't. It reminds me of something in my book on Ontario.'

'I know why,' Ro said. Her head was spinning. Was it the drink, or this very odd coincidence?

She took a deep breath. 'This is a picture of something called Fraktur Art. It's a sort of artwork done in North America, especially Canada. It's derived from medieval manuscript art. It was done by religious groups for a long time, and it's becoming very sought after now.'

'How do you know all this?' Suzy asked. 'It sounds fascinating.'

'I know,' Ro said, 'because I own one. It's on the wall in my cottage.'

Alison backed her Mini out of the drive outside Mark's flat and turned towards the North.

Mark had collapsed into bed when they'd got back after the brunch. She had been left looking at sheaves of house details, while he snored off whatever it was he needed to get out of his system. At three o'clock she had tried shaking him but he was so deeply asleep that all he did was mumble and turn over.

She had thought about the children's work she had to mark, and the test preparation, and the programme for the concert which she needed to draw up. It was a waste of time lying here listening to Mark's snoring. When he woke up he might try making love again, and get aggressive and irritable if it didn't work.

I don't actually want to be here, she'd thought. For some reason, Ro Watson's cottage with the view of the fells came into her mind. She had liked Ro, her son with the sense of humour, the calm of Burnside. Alison thought about the wind on the shore at Pelliter, and felt a burst of homesickness. On Bank Holiday Monday lots of people went to Briggs' ice-cream place. But even if everyone was there, there was still masses of space. You could walk along the low grassy dunes and see the ponies. Or walk out on the long flat shore with silvery ribbons of silt running down to the endless sea which lapped round the Isle of Man and Ireland on its way to America.

Mark had snuffled, coughed, and sunk into a deeper sleep. I'm sneaking off and going home, Alison had thought.

At The Briars, Ro heard herself saying, 'Why don't you come and see my picture, if you're interested? Come tomorrow evening.'

'I'd love to!' Suzy said. 'Molly's getting very interested in art. Could we all come?'

Phil said, 'I'd be interested too. I could bring Becky.'

'Yeeesss!' said Ben. Some new shouting and running game had started and he was in there with the others. It really has been a remarkable afternoon, Ro thought.

'You're very welcome. Come anytime around seven,' she said. She thought of Alison McDonald's remark that her house would be lovely for a party. Now, it seemed, she was having one. She took another sip of her red wine. In the distance Ben, Becky and Molly were being chased by Jake with the barbecue tongs. Jonty McFadden and his bullying seemed light years away.

Liz Rudder was spending a very dreary May Bank Holiday. John's carers weren't the usual team. Instead the agency sent two brisk new ladies whom she didn't know. They weren't local and they weren't interested in chatting about the murder. Nor did they offer to do any little extras for Liz as a Pelliter celebrity. Worse, they could only do the morning session, which meant Liz needed to put John to bed, something she had only done once or twice before and which she hated.

By and large, though, Liz felt better. She had got over the shock of seeing

Sheila Findley smiling at her in the garden centre on Saturday. It had strengthened her resolve. There was no way she was going to let the Findleys get back on track. Liz's little one-to-one chat with Callie McFadden had been very useful. She was well aware of Callie's hold over the head teacher, and suggesting that Jonty be entered for Dodsworth was her own stroke of tactical genius, really pushing up the pressure! Liz smiled to herself. She knew exactly what had gone on between Callie and Ray Findley – and Jonty's birth nine months later had been a useful little bit of information she had been nursing for some time. Along with the murder, the stress of assessment tests, and Miss MacDonald's problems with the parents, this new bombshell would mean the head teacher would have no chance to think about disrupting her comfortable life.

Liz tried some more of the Spanish language CD, but on hitting a difficult bit abandoned it for the time being. Later on, bored, she planted out the remaining begonias and tidied the front of the house. It needed painting, she thought. Would it be worth waiting until John died? Or should she get it done now, and risk having to do it again in a few years? Really, living with a disabled husband was very difficult to pace. She had read about these places where people went to commit suicide in Switzerland. She would have been prepared to take John if she could have squeezed agreement out of him. People might even think her rather noble. She couldn't see the point in sick or inadequate people living half a life. Even someone like Brenda had been only half alive. Once Liz had grown away from her, there was really no other emotional outlet for Brenda. Poor virginal Pasty Podgy!

Liz looked down at her own body as she took a shower after doing the garden. It was interesting how the pink flesh of her stomach, buttocks and thighs still looked firm while her face had become wrinkled. Even her breasts weren't bad. Pity no one but John had ever seen them. Maybe Peter Hodgson would have liked to, really, under his sanctimonious exterior. And he probably wasn't the only one. But Liz had been faithful to John. Most of the time she had treated his infidelity with disgust, confiding in Brenda with laughing contempt each time John strayed during that awful patch about twelve years ago when he had gone off the rails.

Until that terrible time when John had really fallen for someone else. Someone twenty years younger than him, and he had thought it really was love!

Liz scrubbed hard at her thighs. Eventually she had managed to get things back on track so no one knew, except herself and John. And Brenda, of course. After that John had been different. For the last ten years of their marriage he'd been like a man who wasn't really there. But that never bothered Liz. As long as they had a marriage in the eyes of the outside world she really needed nothing more. Sex had stopped – which had been a pity because she wouldn't have minded having John back in bed, but he had totally lost interest. But that didn't matter as long as the holidays, the neighbourhood gatherings and the upkeep of the house had gone on as before.

And then, out of the blue, John had seemed to wake up. Suddenly he'd started to make those horrible plans to change everything. Then he'd had his stroke. In a way, it had been a stroke of luck! She giggled naughtily as she soaped her body.

And really, things had worked out very well, as long as John didn't go on as a creaking gate forever. She congratulated herself on having no children. They would have been in their twenties or thirties now, wanting money for a university education, or to set up their own homes. She might even have had grandchildren demanding school fees at Dodsworth, like Kevin's brood.

She put her hands on her own stomach. Her hands were tiny, white and almost completely smooth. Like a child's. I'll still be in reasonable shape in a few years, she thought. With luck, everything would come together. John would pass away. She could retire from St Mungo's. She would be on full pension. The recession would be over and she could sell the house for a decent price. And then she would be off to Spain and the sunshine.

She practised her Spanish to herself as she dried herself on the pink fluffy towels in the new en-suite bathroom she'd installed. Then she wrapped herself in her lovely pink, downy dressing-gown and, wafting sweetly of shower gel, went through to the bedroom and sank on to her bed. She picked up her phone.

'Father Peter!' she said. 'I am so glad to have caught you. It's Liz Rudder here. We haven't spoken since this terrible thing happened to poor Brenda. But I've been thinking of you every day. I have been too devastated to do anything for a week.'

There was some noncommittal grunting at the other end of the phone.

'It would be so good to talk. I know Brenda was very concerned about St Trallen's Chapel and I'm sure you want to keep up the good work. As a senior teacher in a Church of England school I might have some influence myself! The problem is my husband John, who has had a terrible stroke as you know. I can't leave him. Could you come round and see us here at High Pelliter? This evening? For a drink perhaps and some canapés?'

Peter Hodgson thought about the ham sandwiches and trifle from the corner shop which he had planned to have for supper. Since his sister's murder, he hadn't been able to face eating out. One good thing about Brenda had been the way she had cooked for him on Sundays. He enjoyed his food, but cooking was something he had really never mastered. It was hardly the preserve of a priest, and in the past he'd had a housekeeper. He really longed for someone to make his meals again. His reservations about Liz Rudder began to dissolve.

'I dare say I could come if I make some rearrangements,' he muttered.

'That's marvellous, Peter. I'll see you in an hour.'

There was absolutely nothing wrong in having a plan B, was there? Liz thought.

Alison had driven in a sort of frenzy, mad keen to get back to Cumbria, but after about twenty-five minutes she was reconsidering. She pulled into a petrol station, where there was a queue. Think clearly, she told herself. What were the problems, and why had they blown up now? Firstly, Mark's idea of how to relax was becoming increasingly different from hers. Manic clubbing and living life at breakneck speed was not what she wanted, and she was pretty sure there was an issue of 'recreational substances'. Secondly, she was worried about the way he spent money but expected her to save. It didn't seem fair. Thirdly, he seemed to have a parallel life which excluded her. He didn't spend every night playing five-a-side, and what about the repulsive Archie and Dazza? Who were they? Fourthly, it was annoying that he was so insensitive about the everyday problems at St Mungo's, but managed to take a prurient interest in Brenda Hodgson's murder.

They'd been through another bad patch a few years earlier. Mark had gone out for a stag night while Alison had stayed in at her flat, working. The following lunchtime he'd turned up, obviously the worse for wear. Alison had finally wrenched out of him that he had been to a lap-dancing club and stayed out all night. It wasn't a question of him tagging on in embarrassment with the crowd. He had really enjoyed his evening, and defended himself with an air of injury. He was truculent, as if her wringing the truth out of him made it her fault. But I'm the injured party, Alison had wanted to say. She felt betrayed and disgusted; no amount of 'boys will be boys' and 'everyone does it' and 'it's only once or twice in a lifetime' made her feel better.

But rather than running away like this, back to Cumbria on a Bank Holiday Monday, wouldn't it be better to confront the problems? She and Mark were hoping to marry in just over a year. Her mum was already making pointed remarks about a venue and a budget for bridal wear. If she went back now, she could tell Mark that she had just popped out while he was asleep, to get some petrol and pick up a newspaper. He might even still be in bed. The crisis would have passed and they could try and talk about it.

She shunted her car towards the pump, jumped out, and filled up with petrol. The pungent smell seemed to energize her and she felt new resolution. She would turn around, go back, and tackle Mark that evening – about the money, about what he really wanted, and about her own future.

Alison paid in the shop and came back with a newspaper and jumbo packet of crisps. Mark loved Roast Chicken flavour. She dumped them on the front seat, drove out of the garage and made a u-turn. Then she drove back the way she had come, singing along with Jamie Cullum.

An hour later, Liz Rudder opened her front door.

'Father Peter, do come in.' Liz ushered the priest into the luxurious lounge of the High Pelliter villa. Brenda's brother looked paler but even plumper then before. White rolls of flesh curved over his collar.

Liz had made an effort, even though she knew it was probably wasted. She wore a tight-fitting beige cashmere pullover, and deep brown trousers which emphasized her small waist. She had dried her hair into a shiny chrysanthemum and used straighteners to primp the ends. There was just a touch of make-up and small gold ear-rings. Tasteful, but rather feminine, she thought.

'Sherry? Or G&T?' she asked.

Father Peter opted for sweet sherry. Before she had returned from the drinks cabinet, he had started scooping up nuts and raisins from a little cut glass dish on the occasional table.

'And how are you?' Liz asked in her light, sympathetic, professional voice.

'I think I'm coping,' Father Peter said. 'Of course, there is always less support at these terrible times than one would hope for. My own vicar has only been to see me three or four times, and I'm sorry to say the bishop has merely called once.'

'Dreadful. You've been through such a lot. But Peter, I would very much appreciate your advice on how to deal with a matter which is worrying me. I know you believe that it's so terribly important to keep up standards....'

'I cannot think of anything which matters more.'

'I'm glad we agree. More sherry?'

For a moment when she stood up, her round bottom bouncing away from him towards the drinks cabinet, Father Peter had a rather repulsive reminder of how Liz Rudder had once made advances to him. But that had been over forty years ago. She seemed like an exemplary matron now. He glanced round her home with approval. It was immaculate. Warm, clean, not cluttered with ornaments like Brenda's little front room, or smelling of damp like his own. It did occur to him that he had no idea where her husband might be; but as he had never considered visiting the sick to be one of his talents, he put it out of his mind.

'You see, Peter, now Brenda is no longer with us, I fear we are slipping a little bit at St Mungo's school.'

Peter Hodgson couldn't for the life of him imagine Brenda having the slightest influence on standards at St Mungo's, but he nodded gravely.

'The problem,' Liz went on, 'is the new teacher of the top class. It's a very sensitive time in a child's life, Year Six. It's a time when hormones are just starting to play up, and when there's a great deal of anxiety about tests and secondary school. You know how important it is for the right children to go to the right school.'

'Absolutely,' Peter Hodgson breathed.

'Sadly we have a new teacher for Year Six. She's very excited about a sort of concert she's putting on. She sees it as a lowest common denominator, with everyone joining in. It's based on that awful TV talent show and they are going to video it. I personally feel it's encouraging the children to act in what I can only call a precociously sexual way. What's more, she has encouraged people from outside to get involved, without the agreement of senior members of staff.'

'Not a good idea,' Father Peter said roundly.

'And worst of all, from your point of view, the scenery features a sort of pastiche of our lovely St Trallen's Chapel. I really don't feel it's appropriate to have girls in mini skirts gyrating around the nearest thing we have to a sacred monument.'

'Good heavens, it sounds most tasteless.'

'But you see, in my position I really don't want to be seen to be stepping on anyone's toes. Mr Findley, the head teacher, is really rather taken with this young woman and, as you may have heard, his wife is an invalid. It's a very difficult situation.'

'I can see that it is!' Peter Hodgson sat back in his chair and sipped some more Bristol Cream. 'Would you like me perhaps to have a little word?'

'Do you know, I think that would be most apt! Now, do come into the dining area. I've got some really delicious little smoked salmon nibbles, and those tiny profiteroles for afters. And we can talk about St Trallen's. One of the last things Brenda said was how interested you were in the chapel. More sherry?'

Chapter Eighteen

'The wicked walk on every side.'

Psalm 12:8. Folio 61r. **Les Très Riches Heures du Duc de Berry**

In the little room which used to be his office, where Liz had wheeled and dumped him, John Rudder decided to take a risk. He no longer had Brenda's help and Liz was being more vigilant these days. His grasp on reality seemed to be slipping. Sometimes he was in a complete daze. There were whole weeks when he felt he had never really woken up. How many chances would he have left?

He managed to lever the wheelchair towards the desk and heave his way towards his old office chair. It took him several minutes to lower himself down into a seating position. He had to be careful to make sure there were no signs that the desk had been touched, in case Liz found out. Not that she was on the look-out – it would never occur to her that he could do this by himself. As far as she was concerned he was the living dead; attempts to improve his condition were pointless. She wanted to see the back of him. On Bank Holidays for example, when his carers didn't always come, Liz often failed to give him all of his pills, though she knew that he needed to stay medicated enough to get through his routine blood tests and check-ups. It would never do for anyone to think she was less than devoted.

John could move his right arm pretty well these days. Kevin and Brenda's routine had helped a lot. He knew it was Brenda who had found out more about the exercises, going to the library to look up physiotherapy guides and using the school computer.

'If only I had a computer myself,' she had said, 'but I've no idea how to go about it. And they're so expensive. My brother would be horrified.'

And John, although he couldn't speak properly, had coughed and nodded and pointed with his head until she had seen the keyboard and screen on his old desk.

'Oh, John,' she had said. 'Of course! We can use yours.'

When the time had come for her to go home, he had been able to distract her by coughing and spluttering and lurching in his chair so that she had left the computer on. The hard drive was under his desk. Liz would never notice. She didn't do cleaning in John's room. If he could get to it he could use it. That, more than anything, had motivated him. That, and the fact he intuitively knew that Brenda would help him. He was not the only person to be neglected by Liz in the new scheme of things.

'Oh, John,' Brenda had simpered, fluttering her eyelashes at him when he had managed to point at what he had written on the screen with one aching finger. 'You want me to print it? And witness it? Good heavens! And who's it for?'

But she had done it, gasping in genuine shock, and rolling her eyes and 'oohing' and 'aahing' at the contents. Then she had giggled softly and rather viciously. 'Well, well,' was all she had said.

'We'd better delete it,' she had whispered when the printing was over. 'I don't think you want Liz to see this just yet, do you? It's a very, very big secret. But we must keep it that way, mustn't we?'

His sense of time was confused and he thought that had only been a few weeks ago. But now Brenda was dead. How long had it been since he had seen the news on the television, parked in front of it by his wife? He wondered if he was the only person really to mourn Brenda. He had never liked her before, but she had been there each Wednesday like clockwork to help Kevin with the exercises, turning up the moment Liz was out of the door. He had wondered what Brenda's motive might be – until it had occurred to him that what she really wanted was to have the edge over Liz for the first time in forty years. And that had given him the idea that she might help him with what really mattered. First she had one little secret from Liz, and then, when John had managed to communicate, a much bigger one. He wondered if the delight of that secret superiority had given Brenda the taste for more. And secret power was dangerous. Perhaps Brenda had bitten off more than she could chew.

John hoped he hadn't done the same. He only had the use of one arm. But he could lean forward and switch on the screen. He could feel his heart beating faster now, and he knew he was tense and perspiring. It wasn't good for him. But he never knew when the opportunity might come again.

The problem would be getting to the printer. He needed to have a printed hard copy, with a signature, for what he was writing to be legally binding. He had no idea where the last document had gone. Brenda had said she would take care of it for him. But now she was dead and he had no idea where she had hidden it. He knew the police had searched her house. But if they had found it, wouldn't they have returned it to him?

He heard Liz talking to that horrible priest fellow in the hall, Brenda's creepy brother. He shut down the screen and levered himself back into his wheelchair, breathing heavily. He heard the front door close, and Liz walk on the thick soft carpet back into the lounge.

But she didn't come near John, although he never knew when she might patter across the hall for the pleasure of taunting him. Feeling sick with the effort and the frustration, he slumped back into his wheelchair and the long lonely wait until bedtime.

It took Alison over an hour to get to Mark's flat. She hadn't bargained for the Bank Holiday traffic back to Manchester after the day out. Stuck at the wheel, chugging along, she couldn't phone him either. He would be awake now, for sure, and would know that she had gone. So, in return for his agreeing to talk the whole situation over, she would offer to stay another night, and drive back very early in the morning. That would please him. She would insist that they had a real heart-to-heart.

She let herself in at the main door and pattered up the stairs carrying the crisps and the newspaper. She tucked the paper under her arm. The key to Mark's flat went into the lock smoothly so that the door swung open without any warning.

'Hiya!' she called 'I'm back.'

Mark was sitting at his computer with his back to her, but he wasn't alone. She took in Dazza's gloating, sweating expression.

She could see over Mark's shoulder quite clearly. The picture on the screen was moving slowly with grunting and panting noises. What happened next seemed to be in slow motion to Alison. Mark turned, saw her, and fumbled with the mouse to exit the screen. But he wasn't quick enough. She could see quite clearly that the caption said *Babes in Chains*; the two naked women on the screen, one black, one Chinese, were wrapped around each other.

'Ali,' Mark said in a throaty sort of gasp. 'I thought you'd gone. We were just …'

Just what? She wanted to say. Just being boys? Just doing what everyone does? If she had caught Mark looking at porn by himself it would have been awful, but not nearly as awful as being with this crude, leering man, in some sort of disgusting duo.

'Not five-a-side is it?' she said. 'Or do the other three turn up later?'

She threw the crisps at him with such force that the bag hit his chest and burst; the horrible smell of chemical roast chicken made her want to gag.

'Ali, wait …'

But she turned and hurtled down the stairs before she had time to think. If it had just been Mark maybe she would have stayed to talk; but Dazza's thick, throaty laugh echoed down the stairwell.

In the garden of The Briars, Robert was clearing up after the barbecue when Jake came over to him.

'I'll take that bag of rubbish down to the bin.'

'Thanks, Jake. Did you have a good time?'

'Yeah, actually. The kids were fun. Ben's famous at school for being an Intergalactic Warrior, but I didn't know he could be such a laugh.'

'You were very good with them. Maybe you should think about being a teacher.' Jake would be going into his final year at Norbridge High in September. He was wondering about what to read at university.

'I don't think they'd let me run round schools with barbecue utensils.'

'Maybe you should suggest it.'

They both laughed.

'You wanted to speak to me about Becky?' Robert asked.

Jake looked away, down the garden. 'Yes I did. It's difficult to explain. She was so good with Ben. And she and Molly are a great double act. Molly was in a really bad state at Easter, you know. Her friends at school had all dumped her because she had spots and only liked reading or painting. But the real problem was that she was so grumpy. And she cried a lot.'

'I didn't realize it was so bad.'

'She didn't do it in front of you and Mum so much. Anyway, she's been much better since she teamed up with Becky.'

Robert thought about it. He hadn't really analysed the events of the day. He was still enjoying the feeling of it having been special – remarkable, really. It was the sort of social triumph you don't get very often, which would bind them all together as friends – even Nigel, who had been surprisingly pleasant once he had stopped being defensive.

Robert had watched Molly running around the garden. It was interesting to see her with her father. She was going to be a large dark-haired woman, the opposite of her mother. But Nigel was tall and big-boned, and his thinning hair was still very brown. Her face had been flushed and her eyes bright. There's an attractive person in there, Robert thought. Just not the one we expected our petite little girl to become.

Jake was patiently stacking plates.

'I thought you wanted to talk about Becky?' Robert asked again.

Jake sat on the table and squirmed a bit, swinging his legs. 'Yeah. It's nothing horrible. Except it is really.'

Robert waited.

'You realize, don't you, Robert, that things go missing when Becky's around. Metal things. The colander, the potato peeler, the Le Creuset pan.'

Robert's first reaction was to ask, really? Are you sure? But Jake looked worried.

'Are you suggesting that Becky is nicking things?'

Jake looked at him as if he was mad. 'No, of course not. Well, not deliberately anyway.'

'So what *are* you saying, Jake?'

'You mustn't think I'm being silly or childish. I've thought about this and been on the net about it.'

His soon-to-be stepson looked back at him. For the first time Robert thought, I'm dealing with a man. This isn't a kid's concern. Jake was deadly serious, and also scared.

'I think she's got a poltergeist,' he said.

When they got home from the barbecue, Ro Watson sat with her coffee at her kitchen window looking at the beauty of Burnside Valley. The sun was sinking in a red ball over the distant fells.

Ro had stopped to look at her picture for even longer that evening when they had come in. It had been given to her by one of her mother's brothers who had emigrated to Canada in the sixties. For decades, thousands of Liverpudlians had looked west to America, rather than south to London. Ro knew she had a whole branch of the family living in Ontario. Her mother's brother had made his money in house clearances, and he had given Ro the amazing piece of Fraktur Art which he had found in a deserted home on the shores of a northern lake. Ro had loved it on sight. For a long time she had wanted to study art. It was an ambition she would be unlikely to fulfil in the short term, but whenever she felt desperate, she would stare at the picture. At least she had one beautiful, original artefact in her own house.

But now she was in the kitchen; the beauty she looked out at was natural. Life was in danger of feeling good. It would all probably come to nothing, but it had been a really special day. Ro stared into her cup. Since she and Ben had moved from Liverpool, she knew she had kept herself a little too much to herself. She had told herself it was because of sensitivity over Ben's condition, but it was also because of sensitivity about her own. For the first time in ages, she let herself think about their life when Ben was little, after she and her husband had parted through sheer weariness and apathy. She had tried working part-time, and met the great love of her life at an office party. Her new lover had seemed to accept everything, welcome it even, and she and Ben had moved in with him. But within months it had deteriorated into a nightmare. Part of it had been caused by Ben's problems, but most of it had been her own misjudgement. Since then, she had lost faith in her ability to make relationships. Only now, slowly, through her work in the Community Police, was her confidence creeping back.

But then she had made that mistake about Jed Jackson. What an idiot she had been about him! Was that another example of having hopeless judgement about the male sex?

She thought about the men at the barbecue. Were they what they seemed? Surely Robert wasn't an old fart at all, as Suzy had affectionately described him, but a considerate and gentle person who seemed really to care. Nigel Spencer she remembered well, once they had got talking. Just as he had been in his early twenties, Nigel in his forties was silly and pretentious rather than wicked. He had confided that he had now met 'someone special' but she guessed he was a serial romancer. And Phil? Ro sorted out the fruit in the bowl on the table. Phil had been kind, and had laughed with her, and watched her when she talked. In the kitchen, helping her wash up for Robert and Suzy, he had said, 'You're doing a good job with your son.'

There was nothing specific. But when Ro thought about Phil, she felt a little warmer. Was that another mistake?

Sitting in the peace and warmth of the kitchen, as darkness fell, Ro thought about the dark marks on her fingers after using the marker pen at the school. They were still there, faintly. She felt a strange affinity with the young man at the chapel because of the tracing of Fraktur Art he had carried. Now looking at her hands, she wondered if he also had held a marker pen. Could he be a teacher too, like Brenda Hodgson?

Slowly, without being too intent or focused – because this really wasn't her job – Ro started to write out on her shopping list pad all the things they had learnt about the young man who had died at the chapel. Perhaps this was one teacher whose death had been forgotten in all the drama of Brenda Hodgson's murder.

So what did they know? The young man had a Canadian coin. He had been interested in Fraktur Art. He had been smartly dressed. If he was the same man who had visited St Mungo's School, then he had problems with his eyesight.

So start from the other side, Ro thought. Who might want to attack a young man at St Trallen's and obliterate his eyes? An angry lover or partner? A homophobe, perhaps? Someone who had found him trespassing? Or who had connections with the school? Or both … Could Phil Dixon be implicated? It was his land, his granddaughter was at St Mungo's, and often too many coincidences hinted at an explanation.

Ro felt uncomfortable. Had she stepped in just a little bit too smartly at the barbecue, to try and deflect curiosity from Phil when Nigel raised the question of the chapel? She hoped not. But the question was lurking there in her own peripheral vision – could Phil be implicated? Again, she hoped not.

And what about Jed Jackson? He had been out alone in the squad car and was the first copper at the scene. It was odd that he had been so close by. His views on drugs were conservative to the point of intolerance. Had he seen what he thought was a dealer, out there on the headland, and had he lost his rag, like he had done with her on the Sunday night a week later?

There were endless possibilities. But she could do one thing: she could speak to her sergeant and ask if they could find out about black cabs, and who could have driven the young man to Pelliter. She could research it herself without wasting anyone else's time. Tomorrow, Ro thought, when I'm back at work, I'm going to talk to Sergeant Liddle about this, and I'm going to make sure we make that enquiry.

But what if it meant working with Jed Jackson? Ro grimaced. Not under any circumstances. It would be easier to go it alone.

Chapter Nineteen

'Wherewithal shall a young man cleanse his way? by taking heed thereto according to thy word.'

Psalm 119:9. Folio 48v. **Les Très Riches Heures du Duc de Berry**

Jed had had a bad weekend. His early morning trip to the shore on Sunday had left him feeling spiritually abandoned. Going to church had made it worse. He felt no peace during the prayers, and the visiting speaker had preached in a banal way. Lunch with his parents had been pleasant but dull; he felt tired and unsettled. His brother, home from college for the weekend, was a far more 'normal' character, texting his mates and arranging to go drinking.

'Come with us, Jed. You're really boring these days.'

But Jed had refused. He trudged round the garden or attempted to read.

On Monday he finally agreed to go into Norbridge with his brother for a drink at lunchtime. But later, the others wanted to go on to the fairground or drive to the shore and Briggs' ice-cream shop. Jed wasn't interested.

Instead he found himself wandering around the shopping centre in Norbridge, wondering whether he could justify his aimlessness by buying a birthday present for his mother. But her birthday was weeks away. He walked up to Norbridge Abbey, set just a few yards back from a busy road and flanked by two attractive pubs. It was a place he had known all his life but he had never been to see it as a tourist.

It was half an hour before Evensong and there was time to look around. It wasn't as impressive as Carlisle Cathedral or Hexham Abbey, but it was dramatic in its own way. There was a rose window to the west and the fragmented light, like the shards in a kaleidoscope, speckled the stone floor. By the north door, where he had come in, there was a small shop which had not been there at the time of his schoolboy visit. It sold rather flimsy guides and gave out free diagrams of the building, and there was a poster outlining the points of historical interest – a piece of St Cuthbert's coffin (oh yeah, Jed thought), the tomb of the one of the earlier members of the local gentry, some silver and gold communion vessels, and the page of the *Book of St Trallen*.

'You don't make much of the *Book*,' Jed said to the pleasant elderly lady minding the stall.

'Well, no.' She leant forward confidentially. 'It isn't much to look at. And between you and me, the dean thinks it might not be quite what we think.'

'You mean a fake?'

'Good heavens no. Just, well, perhaps a copy. A very early copy, of course. Or a draft of some sort. But do go and have a look for yourself. It's in the crypt. Next to the monument to the Fellside Pals in World War One.'

'Thanks.' Jed knew where the crypt was; he turned away from the little shop and walked to where the door led to some bumpy steps. He was trying not to think about Ro Watson, but Ro had asked him about the *Book* when they had been working together outside St Trallen's Chapel. He thought about the dead man too, still unidentified in the morgue at Cumbria Coast Hospital.

The page from the *Book* was framed in a large gilt Victorian wooden frame which detracted from what was already a slight piece of work. The frame must have weighed a ton and the paper inside looked very fragile. It was obviously paper, not vellum, which he knew meant it could be no earlier than the early sixteenth century. Not really medieval, then. The style was cruder than he remembered from seeing it as a child, but it made a compelling impression. It showed a huge illustrated spelling of the word 'Trallen'. Then, in a pointed Gothic script, there were the Latin words which a helpful, if tired and curly, sticker on the wall underneath identified as from the Lamentations in the Bible.

> *She weepeth sore in the night, and her tears are on her cheeks*
> *Among all her lovers she hath none to comfort her*
> *All her friends have dealt treacherously with her, they are become her*
> *   enemies.*

Underneath the writing was a picture of a beautiful young woman with something dripping from her eyes. Jed moved closer and squinted at it. Was it tears or blood? As schoolkids they had debated the point.

But what struck him this time around was the youthfulness of the saint. She had the slightest of female figures and a rather mysterious smile. He decided that when he got home he would Google her and find out more. There had been a much bigger shrine to St Tribuna at Restalrig in Edinburgh, he knew that. But the Cumbrian connection seemed to focus on her as a girl, rather than the esteemed matron she became. It was odd to think of this beautiful creature growing stout and jolly, running an abbey.

Jed didn't know much about women – as opposed to girls, and he knew as much about them as most young men. But Ro Watson was the first older woman he had ever really talked to, besides his mother. He had only one aunt, but they had lost touch after a family row. He had no sisters and he had only had one serious girlfriend, whom he'd met within days of arriving at university. Most young people clung to these early pairings with the desperation of survivors in an emotional lifeboat. Jed and his girlfriend only split up when she went to London to take an MA course and met someone else who was 'more fun'. Since then Jed had been out with one or two people – another friend from college, and a police cadet he had met during his training. But nothing seemed right. Maybe he had been too preoccupied with starting his career to get seriously involved.

And, in a way, he had been too preoccupied with something else. It had been a hidden soundtrack beating through his adult life, causing all sorts of problems. When he was sixteen, his older female cousin, who had been beautiful, exciting and the subject of a serious crush on his part, had died. It had looked like a suicide from a drugs overdose and it had affected Jed deeply. While he had been at university it had been parked for a while in his subconscious. But later, after he had decided to join the police, her death had come back to haunt him and to appear as a sort of *ex post facto* reason for his unusual decision.

He had been bitterly angry with her for dying – not just because he would miss her, but because she had let the side down in some unexpressed way that he felt tarnished them all. Despite everything, he knew she had been a lovely person. She had lived in Pelliter with his grandparents; that was how he had become so friendly with her. She hadn't minded an adolescent boy tagging along with her and her glamorous friends from the art college. But she had gone away, about six months before she died so suddenly. The teenage Jed had felt abandoned.

He had pushed it to the back of his mind and settled down to work for his A levels. But that couldn't isolate him from the family row that erupted after her death.

'Phil's in a terrible state,' Jed's mum had said. 'Of course he's to blame, he let her go wild. He's been far too soft with Samantha all her life. But I can't bear to hear Judith berating him like that. I'm afraid I gave her a piece of my mind. We've had a serious falling out.'

So the two sides of the family had never met again, even though the Jacksons heard on the grapevine that the Dixons had recently come back to Pelliter to live. And Jed had been left with the residual impression that being soft on people led to tragedy.

Jed looked at St Trallen. There was something about the slight figure and the cryptic smile which reminded him of Sam. She had been no saint, but she'd had that air of mystery and ethereal beauty which might have entranced a pagan prince. In fact, she must have entranced someone, because he had heard later that Sam had had a child and his Aunty Judith had adopted her.

'That will suit Judith down to the ground,' Jed's mother had said nastily. 'A baby to mould to her satisfaction. She'll get her own back on Samantha now.'

Jed went up into the abbey, where Evensong was beginning, and sat at the back. He prayed for Sam and Sam's baby whom he had never met. And he prayed for his mother, and for the first time in years he prayed for his Uncle Phil and Aunt Judith.

And now, Jed felt the service call to him in a way none of his other attempts at prayer had done. Every time he had tried to relate to God that weekend it had been all about him, Jed Jackson. But this time, when he was least expecting it, the message sneaked under his radar and left him breathless, because it was about someone else. The clergyman read from St Matthew '*Judge not, that ye be not judged....*'

And then he found himself praying for Ro Watson and the brave way she cared for her son. He had been very wrong, he realized, to be so rude to Ro the evening they had been to interview Alison MacDonald. He had found the young teacher almost unbearably attractive, and the slight love bite he had spotted on her pale neck had given him confusing sensations. She had reminded him of Sam. So much about her had been so good – her dedication to her job, her intentness as she tried to answer the questions, the confusion on her face as she decided not to trust him. The idea that she had been clubbing in Manchester with some moron, probably taking drugs and ruining herself like Samantha, had given him a sense of panic.

But he had been very wrong to behave as he did. He flicked back in the Prayer Book and read the Magnificat.

He hath scattered the proud in the imagination of their hearts.

He thought, I've been such an arrogant idiot. I'm proud, and my unhappiness this weekend has been because I behaved really badly. The verses at the beginning of Evening Prayer said:

The sacrifices of God are a broken spirit: a broken and a contrite heart,
   O God, thou wilt not despise.

I have been so wrong, he thought.

But that meant it was time to apologize. And Jed Jackson would find that very hard. That would be his punishment.

Sheila Findley lay in bed on the evening of Bank Holiday Monday. She thought about the day with some sort of satisfaction. Beside her, her husband was sleeping silently and peacefully. It occurred to her that for months she hadn't been aware of him doing anything independently of her. That was the trouble with depression – it really was very selfish. Or self-centred anyway. She could understand how it infuriated others, but at the time she couldn't have cared less about how others felt. Even Ray.

But it was different now. She'd actually become fed up with her own misery.

She'd known it was tough on him, too. But then, he wasn't the one who was depressed. She also knew, all the time, that a massive misunderstanding was at the root of their problems. He wasn't to blame for her crisis, but she hadn't the energy to explain. Circumstances had come together in a way which had left him thinking it was his entire fault. But it wasn't. What he had done wasn't so very terrible, and if she hadn't started her miscarriage when she did, she would have had the strength to help him. But after losing the baby she had been too fed up, exhausted and miserable to bother.

Things had been a bit better lately. Life had been improving, thanks to her medication, but without anything really being said. They had been tiptoeing around the issue still, but smiling as they did so. But it couldn't go on. It needed dealing with.

Bank Holiday Sunday had been great. She had planted about three-dozen bedding plants and the garden had looked abundant in a sort of super-bright, suburban way. In the evening, though, Ray had been white and terribly quiet. With her renewed perception she had noticed his over-attentiveness, a sure sign he was worried.

'What's wrong with you?' she had said, eating a supper which he had cooked with silent concentration.

He had looked at her. 'What's wrong with me?' he'd said.

'Yes. I know I've spent the last six months completely insensitive to your feelings, but my empathy is coming back. A bit like getting the sensation back in numb feet.'

He had played with the broccoli on his plate.

'Oh come on, Ray. I'm not going to stab myself with the bread knife, or put my head in the dishwasher. What's the problem? Have you remortgaged the house or pranged the car?'

Her husband had said with forced brightness: 'Really, Sheila, there's nothing wrong.'

Sheila looked back at him intently. 'It's that wretched woman, isn't it? You'd tell me about anything else. What's been going on with her?'

'Nothing's going on with her. Nothing ever did go on with her. I made one mistake after a party and she's made me pay ever since. You know that. Why are you bringing it up now?'

'Because I know you, Ray. There's something new.'

He'd pushed his plate away. Every so often, since her breakdown, Ray had watched Sheila revisit the shock of her discovery. It was one of the few facts that penetrated her depression and made her react, but each time it had been horrible because of the erupting row which flared and died, seeming to push her further into her lonely hell. He waited for the routine storm of contempt and disgust to break over him and wash away, leaving her marooned on an island he couldn't reach.

But this time was different. Sheila had got up and came round to his side of the table.

'Ray, I'm sorry.'

'What?'

'I'm really sorry.' She'd paused. 'I let you think that your misguided moment with Callie, years before we got together, really mattered to me. But it didn't. It was just a symptom, an excuse for me to rage on at you.'

'But the day you found out, you lost our baby ...'

'Yes, but why should finding out about something so petty cause me to miscarry? It was bad – but not that bad. To be honest, I hadn't felt well all day; that's why I was stupid enough to lose my rag with Jonty McFadden and after that the pains started. It was all a hideous coincidence, and what happened to me was so wretched we both got cause and effect muddled up. And afterwards I was so mad at the world, I let you think it was all your fault.'

I did believe it was all my fault, Ray had thought. He'd known what had happened because Sheila had told him, sobbing in the front of the car, clutching her stomach as he drove through the evening traffic to Cumbria Coast Hospital. Until that afternoon, Sheila had been four months pregnant and life had been rosy. But then she had come across Liz Rudder and Callie McFadden in the staff-room when everyone else had gone home.

Liz had said, 'I think you should tell her, Callie. After all, now she's having a baby she ought to know.' Then she had sidled away with her funny, sideways glance, leaving Callie red-faced and aggressive, standing in front of Sheila.

'What you've said about my lad isn't right,' Callie had snarled.

Sheila had tackled Jonty McFadden earlier that day about his bullying. She had mentioned in the staff-room, in front of Liz Rudder, that she thought the boy was causing real problems. She had wondered aloud if Jonty needed help, some sort of counselling. She could see now how Liz Rudder could report her words, to provoke Callie to a tantrum of self-justification.

Before Sheila could explain any further, Callie had started screaming.

'You've picked on him, you cow. You've got it in for my son. Maybe that's 'cos you want your own back on us. Just because me and Ray ...'

Callie had got redder and redder, her mouth moving like a dying fish. She had worked herself up into an immense rage. Sheila had felt strangely detached watching her, thinking more about the strange sensation which was starting in the pit of her stomach. Callie had started to scream and spit, and in the middle of the tirade Sheila had heard the unbelievable.

'What?' Sheila had said.

'Your wimp of a husband. You ask him what happened in the car park of the Crossed Foxes that Christmas! He was with me in the back of his car. And he's been under my thumb ever since.'

Sheila had left the staff-room, with Callie roaring in triumph after her. But it wasn't Callie's words which had sent her away. She had felt the stomach cramps worsening.

Ray had been working in the little bedroom-cum-office back at their house, and by the time Sheila had driven home, braced over the steering wheel, she was seriously ill. That evening she was admitted to Cumbria Coast Hospital.

Now she'd said, 'We should talk about it, Ray. I've been thinking about it all the time, deep down, almost without knowing I was doing it. What Callie said didn't cause the miscarriage.'

'But she told you—'

'Told me what? That something went on between you in the back of your car after the Christmas party.'

Ray had put his head in his hands. 'But that's the trouble, Sheila. I genuinely can't remember. I'd have sworn nothing happened. But if she says it did ...'

Sheila had pulled her chair up to his and put her arms around him. 'I'm to blame for a lot of this, Ray. I didn't listen to you. I was wrapped up in my own pain. Look, I can't believe for one moment that you actually seduced her, or even the other way round, in the back of your car.'

'But she says I did.'

'Not in so many words. Instead of all this guilt and obfuscation you need to try and remember exactly what happened. You were tipsy, and that was downright stupid for someone in your job. But somehow I don't think that you would get so drunk you would forget years of discretion and profession-alism. Do you know what? I think at most you probably had a harmless snog and then passed out.'

Ray's head had snapped up and his chin jutted forward. 'Well, that's what I always thought. She had a flask and offered me more in the car. I told you I couldn't remember and it's true, I can't. But now ...' Ray had suddenly put his head in his hands again. His back heaved.

'Now, what?'

He'd looked up, his face yellow with strain. 'She says Jonty could be my son.'

To his amazement, his wife started to laugh.

'Oh, don't you see, Ray? She's gone too far this time. Jonty? Your son? For goodness' sake, if there was any likelihood of that, a woman like Callie McFadden would have taken you to the cleaners long ago. She's enjoyed your embarrassment for ten years, and she's made petty little advances as a result. But this? It's ludicrous! For some reason she's decided to put the screws on tighter, but this time she's gone too far and made a fool of herself.'

Ray had said nothing, and she'd had the sense to leave him to think. She had gone out of the kitchen, over to the cupboard in the dining room to fetch a bottle of good red wine. She'd poured him a glass and then sat back and waited.

Eventually she heard the whole story for the first time. Ray had had a few drinks at the Christmas party and Callie had bumped into him several times as they all staggered out of the pub. Ray was facing another lonely Christmas: the usual bleak stay with his ageing parents, with his father making snide remarks about his lack of a wife. Callie was warm and soft and seemed undemanding. He had offered her a lift home. In the car she had taken out a hip flask and offered him another. The next thing Ray knew, he was waking up on the back seat, dry-mouthed and headachy. Callie had gone, and he was in no state to drive. He'd called a cab from the Crossed Foxes bar and gone home to sleep it off. It was only when Callie made sheep's eyes at him back at school that he wondered what had really happened. And he had cursed himself for his stupid behaviour.

'Why didn't you tell me when we got together?' Sheila had asked.

'Shame, I think,' Ray had said. 'And denial. Callie was emerging as a monster and Jonty was already spoilt and disruptive. One of the things which attracted me to you, as soon as you joined the school, was the way you took no nonsense from her. So how could I tell you I had fallen into her trap like that? And I always felt that somehow I owed her support.'

'For what?' Sheila had said again, snuggling into him. 'Call her bluff, Ray. We'll deal with this together.'

And on Bank Holiday Monday they had gone to the garden centre and bought a gnome, and laughed a lot. In the night, Sheila put her arm round her sleeping husband and fell peacefully asleep herself. Together they would see off Callie McFadden and her stupid threats, Sheila thought. And the threats *were* stupid, really stupid. She wondered, fleetingly as she drifted into sleep, what had made Callie overplay her hand.

Chapter Twenty

'I am weary with my groaning;'

Psalm 6:6. Folio 65v. **Les Très Riches Heures du Duc de Berry**

The Tuesday after the Bank Holiday was day ten of the Marsh Murder enquiry. The school computer had yielded nothing unusual except a great deal of information about physiotherapy, and job searches which left some people looking a little sheepish. Brenda's house had been unnaturally clean and tidy, with all her ornaments dusted and her paperwork filed. The local sociopaths all had alibis.

Jed Jackson had planned a quiet day at the station for the first day back at work after the Bank Holiday. He had been involved in house-to-house enquiries in Pelliter the previous week, trying to find anyone who had seen Brenda Hodgson on her last walk. It had been pretty fruitless. Six o'clock on a spring Saturday in Pelliter saw most people sitting in front of the telly or in the back gardens.

'Come on, lad, get a move on,' Sergeant Liddle had said, passing Jed's desk. The community team had an open-plan office, but Sergeant Liddle had artfully arranged a noticeboard screen to cordon off his bit of the territory.

Jed was watching for Ro. She would be coming in to the station at some point. He hadn't liked to enquire too deeply into her schedule for the day, but he knew she was on shift.

She finally arrived at about eleven after a couple of hours on the usual foot patrols. All had been quiet. Ro's younger colleague was bemoaning the fact and Ro was laughing. Jed's face jerked up to see her. His first thought was that she looked better. She's caught the sun, he thought. Her scar showed up as badly as ever, but the suntan suited her. And the laugh was easier too.

But when the other PCSO went to report back to Sergeant Liddle, and Jed caught Ro's eye, he saw the old anxiety tightening in her face. I should remember, he thought; she's had to face a lot of people being rude and insensitive over the years. I'm just another one. Ro ignored him and sat at the PCSOs' hot desk. He saw her glance round almost furtively as she picked up the phone.

'Hello, is that the Manchester hackney cabs office?' he heard her say.

She had begun this personal investigation; it was as if she was on a roll and had to go through with it. Newcastle cabs weren't black, and in Glasgow they had no one who had travelled as far as Cumbria that Friday. But when she had emailed Manchester she had been in luck. A cabbie from the airport rank had told 'control' that all his birthdays had come at once – a fare had asked him to drive over a hundred miles to West Cumbria. The cabbie had picked up a chap who he said he had flown in from Toronto. The bloke had enough money to pay for a cab, and said he needed to go by car because he had problems with his eyesight. The cabbie had taken him to a school in Pelliter, then dropped him on the shore road. He'd said he was going to be picked up later by a local.

Bingo. That had to be the man Alison and Suzy Spencer had seen. But was he the dead man? Or was he still alive and well, back in Toronto perhaps, or travelling around the Lake District? If they could find out more about him they could at least eliminate him.

The next step was to speak to Air Canada. The cabbie was pretty sure his fare had travelled with them; he remembered the red and white luggage labels.

The Air Canada customer services adviser put her through to operations and Ro explained what she needed. As she had expected, it wasn't straightforward, but she was neatly passed from department to department with no chance to back out. She would need to fill in a data protection form and send a written request for the passenger list detailing any men between the ages of twenty and forty, travelling alone on the flight which had landed in time for the young man to pick up his cab at around lunchtime. The form needed to be signed by a police officer. But would that mean a PCSO? Hardly. But Ro wasn't stopping now.

'Thanks,' she said. 'I'll get on to it.'

As she sat thinking, Jed took his chance and walked over.

'Coffee?' he said to her with his most winning smile.

'No thanks,' Ro said curtly, and turned away to her computer screen.

Jed had half expected Ro to blush and launch into a conversation, but he had been too optimistic. He lolloped out, towards the canteen. Over his cooling coffee, he thought, why should she forgive him? His behaviour had been unforgivable. He had to do more than just casually apologize.

When he came back into the office ten minutes later, there was some sort of muted but heavy discussion going on behind Sergeant Liddle's screen, and Ro was not at the desk.

'I really don't know what you thought you were doing,' Sergeant Liddle was saying loudly. 'You've been enquiring about a plane passenger. What's this about?'

'I'm sorry,' Ro said. 'I didn't realize it would be such a sensitive issue.'

'Of course it's a sensitive issue. You can't just get passenger lists and start ringing people up. The airline called back to verify who and what you were. It put me in a very difficult spot. You're just a PCSO. It's not your job to make enquiries.'

'But if it turns out that this man has disappeared, it could have been him at the chapel.'

'And how do you think we're going find out? Fly you over first class to Toronto to make enquiries, since you're such a budding detective? Look, CID has got enough on their plates with the Marsh Murder. The man in the morgue can wait. And you should wait for instructions. You're lucky to be here anyway.'

'What do you mean, lucky? Are you saying I've only got my job because I've got a disabled son?'

Sergeant Liddle looked at her, frowned and shook his head. 'What? I mean that you're lucky to be making enquiries. You're just a PCSO. You got the job because you were smart and committed, but now I think you might be too smart by half.'

'Sorry.' Ro blushed. Over the years, she thought she had learnt not to over-react to her situation. It was embarrassing to find herself in the wrong. It was because of Jed Jackson, she thought. It was Jed who had fuelled her fear that her job was just the result of some wretched diversity policy.

Sergeant Liddle was saying patiently, 'I've spoken to the airline. They're going to send the information over as soon as they get the data protection form. But it needs a proper police officer to do that and I've no one to spare.'

'Sarge.' Jed Jackson put his head around the screen. 'I've just overheard. Could I be of any help on this one?'

'Well, you've nowt to do at the moment, have you, so I suppose you might. You and PCSO Watson can get back on to Air Canada – with the proper procedure – and see if there's anything in this. If there's one thing that annoys me more than the public wasting police time, it's the police wasting police time. So you'd better come up with something pretty damned quick!'

Ro stood up. She had no option but to walk away with Jed, watched by the sergeant.

At St Mungo's School, Alison MacDonald felt the atmosphere in the class was better, which was just as well because she felt dreadful herself. She had left Mark's flat the day before and driven blindly up the motorway. At Tebay services she had stopped, parked at the back of the car-park, and cried for about half an hour, a miserable anguished wailing in the privacy of her car. When her mobile phone rang and showed Mark's number she didn't answer.

She knew that if she spoke to him he would try to talk her round. And put her on the defensive. He would argue that it had all been a one-off, something Dazza had thought of; or something they'd just come across. And anyway, he would say, everyone did a bit of porn now and then. She must know that. It was a massive internet industry. And it was human nature – well, men's nature anyway.

'It doesn't mean I don't love you. Or fancy the pants off you,' he would say. 'It's just that men are different.'

But how would Mark feel if she got sexual pleasure from other men, even in pictures? It was a double standard of the most insidious kind because by and large women didn't lust after pictures of perfect men. There were reasons for that, she supposed – less economic power, social conditioning, 'time and place' pressures, and a more realistic approach to sex. Women weren't schooled to expect perfect creatures to perform for them. So it was an unfair comparison.

'Watch the stuff with me,' Mark might say, though she felt that the feral male mob thing was part of his turn-on. Could she get to like stuff like that? No. Porn of any sort would have been bad. But this wasn't even straightforward voyeurism. Something really nasty had been happening in *Babes in Chains*, and she felt sick thinking of it.

Father Peter Hodgson woke up on Tuesday morning feeling pleasantly contented. He had slept astonishingly well after three sherries the evening before. Well, four actually, because he had found a bottle in the cupboard. It had been crystallized and sticky round the top through lack of use. He suspected his mother had bought it for the odd occasion when the Hodgsons had visitors. He had finished it off. The only disappointment was that he hadn't been able to bring home the last scrumptious little profiteroles from Liz Rudder's.

He wondered how on earth she had made them. Although, they could have been from a supermarket – they had been extremely regular and consistently shaped. If those little profiteroles could be bought, maybe he could try to get some himself. He hated the thought of braving the stores. Brenda had done his shopping for him since he came to Pelliter, and she had usually cooked his Sunday lunch. Previously a helpful lady parishioner had often obliged (until she started to get ideas!). But perhaps he could risk a trip to the supermarket. With luck, people would avoid him. If he looked suitably devastated by his sister's death, no one would have the gall to come up to him for a chat. Mmm. Perhaps that would be a good idea.

He pulled the bedclothes up to his nose. Even though it was May, the bedroom at the back of the big old house was chilly. But not for long, Father Peter thought. He would put Brenda's house up for sale as soon as it was decent to do so and he would get rid of it, whatever it took – a house would always sell if the price was low enough. There would be enough money from the sale to put new heating in at the family home, decorate the place and do the kitchen. The more he thought about it, the more he realized Brenda's death had been even more of a windfall than he'd expected.

That made him think about Liz Rudder's strange assertion that standards at St Mungo's were declining since his sister's murder. It was hard to see how things could have changed in such a short time. But he could see Mrs Rudder's point. It did seem inappropriate to have children cavorting in front of a picture of St Trallen. And surely a concert of this nature was most insensitive when a teacher had been brutally murdered.

An idea which had been brewing for a long time in Father Peter's brain began to bubble. His sister had felt very strongly about St Trallen's being 'off limits' to the plebs of Pelliter. He glossed over his row with her the night she had died – no one else knew that she had ever advocated closing the chapel. And no one had said anything, as yet, about a memorial to Brenda. There had been mutterings about special services, and plaques in the church, or gifts to the school in her name. There had been the vague suggestion of money being donated. Nothing had seemed right.

But a plea from her distressed but dignified brother for the chapel to become a working church in memory of Brenda might have the sympathy vote! The chapel could have its own chaplain, for a small but reasonable stipend. There would be a congregation of none – the perfect place for someone with a vocation like Father Peter's.

The first step would be to put his marker down on the legitimacy of the chapel by insisting this indecent concert at the school was stopped. Thank goodness Liz Rudder had alerted him to it.

It's turned chilly again, Robert Clark thought, as he drove towards Norbridge Community College on Tuesday morning. That evening they were due to go to Ro's to see her picture. He was interested in it and, despite the change in the weather, looking forward to seeing her cottage in the remote Burnside valley. He watched the thick grey clouds blow in from the west. But the memory of the barbecue had been overshadowed by anxiety.

Robert had spent a great deal of time thinking about what Jake had said the evening before. Robert had Googled 'poltergeist' and 'kinetic energy' himself late on Monday night, with interesting results. The information on the web seemed to be quite categorical. Young women, usually around puberty, could cause manifestations of strange things. There were endless anecdotal accounts of furniture moving, or utensils flying through the air. The girls seemed to have other power too, the ability to make things happen.

But nothing seemed to have been proved, despite the confident tone of the articles.

Robert went over everything Jake had itemized. The first time had been on Becky's initial visit when Suzy had lost the casserole dish. Since then there had been several disappearances. But were they really significant? Robert couldn't actually remember seeing Becky in the kitchen, in a position to move things. But he had no evidence that she couldn't have done it either. So it could be a form of theft, or it could just be a coincidence. The most convincing thing for Robert had been Jake's intuition. The boy asserted that he had been disturbed by Becky's presence.

'It's not all the time,' Jake had said. 'I don't want you to think I'm nuts, Robert, but sometimes she can have a really funny effect when she stares at you. She can be very intense.'

'What do you mean?'

'She looks at you with those eyes as if she knows exactly what you're thinking. And during the barbecue—' He'd stopped.

'Go on,' Robert had said.

'It was as if she could keep Ben upright just by willpower. And there's also the way she's calmed Molly down. It was unbelievable really. Molly's like a different person now.'

'So this power you think Becky has – is it good or bad?'

Jake had said slowly, 'Good. But it's also scary.'

Robert had put his hand on Jake's shoulder. 'Then if it's good, there's no need to worry.'

But he wasn't so sure himself. Instead of going to work, Robert found he was driving towards Uplands where Neil Clifford's rectory was. He and Neil had been friends for years, which was just as well if he was going to ask the rector's advice about something which might sound utterly barmy. He pulled over and called Neil from his mobile.

'Can I come and see you?' he asked. 'There's something that's bothering me.'

In the police canteen, Ro pushed her spoon around in the saucer and waited.

Jed had been all smiles in front of Sergeant Liddle, but now, opposite her across the table, his face had set into the harder, more reflective expression, which reminded Ro of the evening when he had blown up at her. Jed Jackson had two personalities, she thought: the happy-go-lucky bright boy at the station, whom everyone liked, and someone with a darker side which perhaps only she had seen.

She wasn't going to help him. He had deliberately insinuated himself into her discussion with Sergeant Liddle. He must have a reason. He clearly wanted to be friends again, but there was no way she was going to let him gloss over what he had said to her about Ben.

'This airline enquiry …' he said.

'It needs a proper police officer to follow it up. Here are the details.' Ro slid a piece of paper across to him. 'I'll get back to spying on shoplifters and tracking down litterbugs. Plastic police work.' She started to get up.

'Ro, sit down. Please. I've wanted to speak to you all day.'

Again, she waited.

'Look, there's no excuse for what I did and said the Sunday before last. It was so wrong. It was rude and insensitive and unkind.'

'Yes, and unchristian too.'

'That's below the belt, Ro.'

'No, it's not. You're the churchgoer with the high principles. Does that make it OK to lash out at everyone you think morally beneath you? Which, by the way, I'm not. I'm not a bleeding heart and I don't think Miss MacDonald does drugs. To be honest, you owe us both an apology.'

'I know. I'll apologize to her too.'

Ro felt slightly surprised. She was cynical enough to see the advantage for Jed in saying sorry to a colleague. But there could be no advantage in apologizing to Alison MacDonald, a woman he might never see again. She listened to him less sceptically.

'Ro, we had a tragedy in our family when I was in my teens. My cousin died of a drug overdose. She was just like that teacher, pretty and talented, and she wasted her life with clubs and drugs. It caused a huge rift between my mother and her brother. I think that's the real reason I'm in the police force. I should have said that when you asked me.'

Ro nodded. 'That's interesting.' Then she leant forward. 'But it shouldn't lead to you being so intolerant. Perhaps if you'd studied psychology instead of theology you'd have a better understanding.'

'No, Ro, that's not true. Understanding the human need for God tells you more about people than it can possibly do about God, by definition. It was me that was limited, not my subject.'

'You may be right there. I've never understood religion. The usual cliché – why does God let bad things happen? It always puts me off.'

'I'm not surprised, in your situation. No one can answer that. It's one of the mysteries of faith. But I want to say something else …' Jed reddened. 'I think it's great how you cope with Ben. I'd like to meet him. Maybe I can help you with him, sometimes, you know, lifting or carrying. Or just being a bloke….'

This was all starting to get embarrassing. 'Don't worry, Jed, we manage. But it was a kind thought. Maybe I'll take you up on it sometime.'

For moment Jed looked rebuffed, and she felt sorry for him. It must have cost him a lot of effort to make this approach, however ham-fisted it sounded. Jed was a confusing mix. But then so was she. That was probably why they got on with each other, despite all the differences. And it was much simpler now she no longer blushed each time he spoke to her. Suddenly he looked to her like a kid who had been rude and overbearing, rather than an attractive young man. That's all he was, really. A bigger, less easy-going version of Ben. And she and Jed did have things in common. She remembered the first time they had chatted, about art, outside the old chapel.

She said, 'Actually, if you really want to meet Ben, and this isn't just talk, come over to my house this evening. I've got some friends coming and I can show you something which might really interest you.' Even as she heard herself talk, she thought how odd it sounded to say she had 'friends coming'.

Jed smiled. 'I'd like that. And Ro, please believe me, I've learnt a lesson. I really am sorry.'

'OK, I think you mean it. No worries. Except about this airline passenger. We'd better get the paperwork faxed over as soon as we can. You're the religious one. Start praying that we're on to something useful.'

Robert Clark and the rector, Neil Clifford, were sitting in Neil's study. Robert had refused a coffee and felt slightly embarrassed. But he knew he could trust Neil Clifford completely. He had outlined Jake's claims, feeling silly. But Neil had been mildly surprised rather than horrified or amused, and had listened intently.

'It's OK, Robert. Just talk.'

'I've been looking up all this poltergeist stuff on the Internet and I don't know what to think. What's the Church's view?'

'I'm not sure we have one,' Neil said. 'People do still come to us for exorcisms and I know a few clergymen who've done them. But I also know of one priest who went to exorcise a house where the owners had been hearing a gruff voice coming out of the walls. It turned out to be a battery toy jammed down the back of the bookcase.'

Robert laughed. 'But I can't deny that the things have disappeared. And Jake is a very down-to-earth kid. He's convinced this girl has some sort of power.'

'And what do you think, Robert?'

'Well, I'd heard of poltergeists before. In fact, looking back, I remember some friend of my sister alleging that furniture moved around in her bedroom. But I've always written this sort of thing off as hysteria, to be honest.'

'Yes,' Neil said thoughtfully. 'We do tend to do that when women get hard to handle, don't we?'

'You don't think I'm being male and dismissive, and that there really is something in it?'

'I don't think *you're* male and dismissive, Robert. But society is. You can't deny that over the centuries, particularly before industrialization, it was accepted that there were some people amongst us who had powers we couldn't explain. Maybe that was what led to the witch hunts. Misguided religious fervour certainly. But also a cull of women who challenged the theory of a totally material world. Witch hunts didn't really get going until the seventeenth century when trade and industry began to prosper and those outside the system had to go.'

'So are you saying you believe in it? And that Becky Dixon might have some sort of paranormal quality? Not a witch, surely?'

'No, of course not. But who knows about the supernatural – or the spiritual, as I would call it? We belong to a church which believes in paranormal experiences, much as we tend to forget it. The biggest mistake in religion is to fight elements you don't understand. Don't think witches, think saints.'

'So you're saying Becky Dixon is a saint? That's absurd.'

'Well, the word has quite an extensive meaning. In medieval times there were smaller saints who did a few miraculous things and then settled into being good, solid church organizers. Like St Trallen, who was nearly a martyr, but ended up as a first-class manager. Jake certainly feels this girl has some sort of power.'

'Yes he does. His intuition is the most compelling evidence.'

'In many of the cases, the young women emanate some sort of abnormal power when they're young, but it passes. It seems to be to do with hormones, if it has any basis in reality at all. My advice is to let whatever is going on between Becky and God run its course. And in two or three years, or even two or three months, you may well look back at the missing kitchenware and write it off as one of those things.'

'So the jury is out?'

'Rob, who knows? It could be a coincidence. It could be mild kleptomania, or sleepwalking, or whatever. But it's doing nothing but good, from what you've said. Tell Jake that these things sometimes happen, and that Becky is special, but not some sort of alien. And let it go. I can't say more than that.'

Robert felt himself relax. 'OK. Actually, that's been very helpful.'

The two men walked to the door and Neil saw Robert out into the blustery morning. The grey clouds had descended and spiky rain was coming in from the west. Even in Uplands, Robert had the sense of the sea only a few miles away.

'Thanks again,' he said as he pulled up the collar of his jacket.

'Good to see you,' Neil said. 'And, Robert, never forget. Great are the mysteries of faith!'

*

Goodness, it was four o'clock already, Peter Hodgson thought. Where had the day gone? He had meant to telephone St Mungo's School, but time had raced by. He'd had a very satisfying visit to the supermarket. He had to admit he'd had no idea that such a high-class food store was within reach of dear old Pelliter. Whenever he had come home to visit, his mother had served up her usual staples of tough roast beef or fried fish, and Brenda had kept up the tradition. But Liz Rudder had purchased the very dainty profiteroles (and who could blame her – delicious!) from a bakery counter which rivalled anything he had seen in the South. It made him realize how much he had missed out on, by spending so much time eating at Brenda's house, which was hardly dinner at High Table. Liz Rudder's smoked salmon vol-au-vents had been outstanding.

His brain was really working well. It must be the fish. He tittered. But another idea had been slowly forming and had bubbled up when he had been in the wine department choosing a sweet sherry and rather nice claret. It was more of a vision than an idea, to be honest. He suddenly saw himself and Mrs Rudder ambling contentedly around the supermarket, selecting interesting ingredients which could be turned into the sort of mouth-watering Sunday lunch Brenda had never achieved. These days, he thought, Liz Rudder would be beyond the stage of wanting any sort of physical contact with a man. Very usefully, she had a husband, so any harpy ideas would be out of the question. It could be a mutually beneficial partnership, he thought.

It had been late afternoon when he had returned home, having treated himself to tea and a fresh cream scone in the supermarket café. Now, though, he was back, and rather grateful that he'd had the day to think about things.

Whom should he talk to about this dreadful concert at the school? The headmaster perhaps? Liz Rudder had made it clear that there was something distasteful about this man. '*Mr Findley, the head teacher, is really rather taken with this young woman and, as you might have heard, his wife is an invalid. It's a very difficult situation....*'

Peter Hodgson congratulated himself on being a man of the world, like many celibates. It seemed quite clear to him that Liz Rudder was implying an unhealthy attraction between Findley and the new teacher. And the chap had an invalid wife! It sounded an unwholesome situation. It was too late now to telephone the school. He would certainly do so tomorrow, in the morning, first thing. But now it was tea time. He spent a long time trying to decide whether to go for salmon-en-croute, luxury moussaka, or chicken Kiev ready meals.

Chapter Twenty-one

'Why art thou cast down O my soul? and why art thou disquieted within me?'

Psalm 43:5. Folio 61v. **Les Très Riches Heures du Duc de Berry**

R o looked round her cottage with a sense of panic. It was six o'clock and she had invited people for seven. She'd left work later than she should have done, hovering around the fax machine and constantly checking emails, but there had been nothing from the airline, even though their London office was still working after six. Then, on the way home, there had been a traffic diversion around Pelliter Marshes which had delayed her. The CID was planning a reconstruction of Brenda Hodgson's last walk and the usual gawpers had turned up to watch.

She raced around the house, tidying up, putting white wine in the fridge far too late in the day, and shovelling crisps and nuts into bowls on the kitchen table.

What have I done? she thought.

They had never had a party before, but this wasn't a party, she told herself. This was just a little gathering of people interested in her picture, who would breeze in and then breeze home for supper. But even so she regretted the impulse. She should have given people time to wind down after the barbecue, to rethink, and refuse her invitation nicely. She couldn't believe they really wanted to come to Burnside, and the idea that they might turn up out of sympathy for her and Ben made her feel sick.

She snapped the light on over her picture and instantly the atmosphere changed. The Fraktur, a huge coloured painting showing birds and animals and illuminated text in Gothic German, lit up the room. It was a *Taufschein*, or baptism certificate, and the name of the child was Rosemary, with the word hooked into roses of all sorts. That was why her uncle had saved it especially for her, and Ro had been touched – as well as astonished when she discovered the picture's potential value. There was no signature or identification, except for the tulips which were so common on the Fraktur pieces. The Fraktur artists had proliferated in North America from the early eighteenth to the mid nineteenth century, and their roots came directly from the world of medieval illuminated pictures. Like the *Book of St Trallen*, which Ro had yet to see.

Now the room was looking welcoming.

'Ben!' she called. 'Have you changed yet?'

An incoherent grunt from upstairs indicated that Ben was still trying on different shirts. He had also insisted on wearing mega-baggy jeans with the crotch round his knees which was doubly dangerous given his wobbly walk, but Ro didn't care. Ben was growing up.

There was a knock on the door. She glanced at the clock: half past six. Really too early.

'Hurry up, Ben!' she yelled, and went to open the door. Standing there was Alison MacDonald.

'I hope you don't mind,' Alison said. 'I would have phoned, but I didn't really think it through. I was driving home. There was a diversion around the Marshes and I found the car pointing this way, so I just kept driving till I got to the turn-off to Burnside. I wanted to talk to you.'

'About St Mungo's?'

'Yes, and not just that.' To Ro's alarm, Ali's face started to melt, the way children's faces do when they start to cry. 'Oh, Ro, it's so awful. Mrs Rudder is back at school. She wants to cancel the end of term concert. I was really upset. I lost my temper. It was awful.'

Alison had already plumped herself down on the sofa, with a clump of tissues in her hand.

'I was so upset. I'm having a bad time anyway. My boyfriend and I have split up. But that's not what this is about. Mrs Rudder didn't say openly that she thought the concert should be cancelled. She just said that some local people thought it was disrespectful, and that I should talk to Mr Findley about it. But she looked so—'

'Smug?' Ro suggested.

'Yes! That's it exactly. She was pleased. I've really been putting everything into this concert, with the mural and everything. Now Mark and I have broken up, it's all I've got.'

'So what did you say to her?'

'I said that I thought she had no right to interfere with my class. I told her she had been trying to keep me down since I arrived at St Mungo's, but I wasn't having it any more.'

'Good for you!'

'And that she and Callie McFadden teamed up together to bully everyone else; and that I thought she was trying to cover up for Jonty because he had

broken the window and he was Callie's son. And, like an idiot, I told her I had
seen the hammer. And that I had told you.'

'Ah. What did she say?'

'She didn't say anything at first. She just went paler. And then she said
'What hammer?' and I said the hammer that I had seen, and that Becky Dixon
saw. Then she said, 'You aren't a very reliable witness and Becky Dixon is a
weirdo. I doubt anyone would believe either of you'. I had to go back to my
class then. But at home-time, I was so upset I just got in the car and came here
instead.'

'I'm glad you did,' Ro said. 'Look, I believe you about Jonty. You know
that. But I think that now you've said these things to Mrs Rudder, you need
to tell a police officer. I can help. But I'm only a PCSO.'

'But remember the way that awful police officer treated me? I can't go to
someone like that.'

'You won't have to,' Ro said. She looked out of the window by the front
door. Jed Jackson's car was bumping down the lane. 'I think he's coming to
you.'

How had it all happened? Looking back at the evening, from the warmth and
quiet of her own bed, Ro had been astonished by the way things had
unfolded. Jed and Alison meeting each other was odd enough, but then within
minutes Phil and Becky Dixon had arrived, without Judith. She was at
another of her local activities.

There had been a most peculiar atmosphere, a sort of huge corporate
intake of breath, which left Ro looking at Alison and then at Jed and Phil.

Jed had said, 'Hello, Uncle Phil. It's been a long time.'

Phil had looked astonished and his eyes had flickered to Ro, who was
flinching. I had no idea, she'd wanted to say; I'm so sorry if you're embarrassed. Instead she'd said, 'I'll get the drinks. They're downstairs in the
kitchen.' As she'd left to go to the fridge, Becky had been busy quizzing Alison
about the picture, kneeling on the sofa, her face alive with excitement as if she
knew something significant was happening. Glancing back, Ro had seen Jed
hold out his hand, and Phil take it, and then suddenly and with real affection,
they'd hugged.

When Ro had come back upstairs with the wine, Phil was smiling.

'Ro,' Phil had said, 'this is my sister's son. I had no idea he was in the police
force. I'm so glad to have met him here. We haven't spoken since he was a
teenager.'

Becky Dixon had been looking at Jed with that intense expression. 'So you
knew my mum. You were her cousin.'

'That's right.'

'Am I like her?'

'Your grandad can tell you that.'

'I want a second opinion.'

'Well, you don't really look like her,' Jed had said. 'But you're clever, like she was.'

'Tell my teacher.' And then Becky had laughed. 'You're all here,' she had said, with an air of satisfaction. For a fraction of a second Ro had felt the hairs stand up on her neck as she looked at the girl. There was something about Becky. As if she had brought them all together ... Then Ben crashed down the stairs in his new jeans and shouted, 'Hey, it's a party.'

So that's what it had become, the first party they had ever given. When everyone had drinks and nibbles, Ro had made them gather around, and had talked them through the picture. Alison had been particularly fascinated. But it was Jed who had grabbed everyone's attention.

'I went to see the *Book of St Trallen* on Monday at Norbridge Abbey. It looks remarkably like this sort of art. Of course the text of the St Trallen picture is in Latin not German. And to be frank the *Book* isn't nearly as beautiful as this. But the look of it is similar.'

The party had broken up into little groups. Ro noticed that Jed and Alison were talking animatedly. Thank goodness, she thought. She'd found herself with Suzy, who said, 'Well, you secret party animal!'

'Suzy, that's not true. I have no idea how this happened.'

'Well, this picture has got everyone going. We mustn't forget that the mystery man had a Fraktur template in his pocket. And he was found at St Trallen's.'

'It's not my job to investigate,' Ro had smiled. 'My sergeant would be very annoyed with you for leading me on.'

'No, but you've got Mr Gorgeous Plod over there on the case, haven't you? You're a dark horse, Rosemary Lloyd.'

Now in bed, still unable to sleep, Ro thought about it all. Phil and Becky hadn't left until after nine o'clock and Becky had wanted to stay later, though Phil had said, 'Come on, love. Gran will want you in bed. It's late and you've got that exam on Saturday.'

'Dodsworth House,' Becky had said to Ben, and pulled a face.

'Good luck.' Ben had shaken her by the hand.

And then they had all gone. The house had been empty and there was nothing left to do. Robert and Suzy had already washed up for her. It had been a remarkable evening – even more remarkable than the day before. It had consolidated the friendships of the barbecue, reintroduced Jed to his uncle and brought Jed and Alison together.

Ro sat up in bed. She was overexcited by this sudden social success. She should calm down and do her job. Tomorrow would be vital, when she was allowed to be a real police officer for a day. If the information from the airline came through, she would need all her wits about her. Sleep!

I must keep on the ball, Liz Rudder thought to herself on Tuesday evening as she lay in bed. She opened her bedside table to check that the hammer was still there. So far, the hammer had been very useful for nudging Callie into doing what Liz wanted. But if Alison MacDonald had told the PCSO about it, that could cause difficulties. Still, no one took PCSOs seriously, and Alison MacDonald was widely regarded as a flake. She had certainly behaved like one recently. She had looked dreadful, on the verge of tears all day. Maybe she was cracking up at last.

Wriggling down under her pink duvet, Liz did an audit of her own situation. On the good side, she was still in her job, comfortably trudging through routine things with the pre-pubescent Year Five. John wouldn't last long now. She had noticed him weakening over the last few days, and she had managed to lose his pill supply after telling his carers she would administer them herself. When John died she would own the whole house. Its sale would fund a high-end apartment in Spain, and her pension would keep her in relative luxury. Brenda, the dependent friend, was out of the way – so no one could ever accuse Liz of dumping her. And anything damaging which Brenda knew about the Rudders' less than perfect relationship had died with her. As far as Pelliter was concerned Liz was an exemplary teacher, who was universally respected and known to be a good, if martyred, wife.

And that was how she saw herself, too. She would float off to Spain on a cloud of goodwill and enjoy herself. If she was lucky and John popped his clogs quickly, then it wouldn't really matter if Ray Findley had it in for her. And if John lingered, she could maintain her position, teaching Year Five and then collect her full pension – as long as Ray Findley was preoccupied. And she had both Callie and Father Peter working on that.

So all was well. Eventually Liz could put two fingers up to St Mungo's and take the plane to Andalusia to scout out condos, while Kevin sold the house for her. Poor Kevin. He would miss her and the little treats she provided for him, his droopy wife and his family of cloth-headed boys. But she couldn't take care of everyone.

Tomorrow was Wednesday, her Spanish class and the best day of the week.

She hoped Peter Hodgson was fretting about the insult to his sister implicit in Miss MacDonald's concert. A nice political row at the school would bring the Findleys to heel again, even if Callie McFadden somehow failed. Liz sighed happily, turned on her side and waited for sleep to take her to Spain.

*

Alison woke on Wednesday morning with a sense that the world was still upside down, but not quite the nightmare mess it had been the day before. Being without a boyfriend at twenty-five years old was a scary prospect. But she was also surprised by her sense of relief. This morning, she felt more able to face the other issues in her life without the drag of worrying about how bored Mark would be by her problems. She took off her engagement ring and put it in its box on her bedside table. She would send it back. Mark might find that the money came in useful for a new computer.

When she opened the curtains it was a beautiful day. Her parents' house had a view of fields, which she had taken for granted since childhood, but today they looked fresh and new, while the blossom freckled the hedges like soapsuds.

She needed to think about school. First, the concert must go ahead. Most primary schools held celebratory displays at the end of Year Six. It would be as inappropriate to cancel it in memory of a teacher as to ignore her life and work. A suitable speech about Brenda, maybe even a few minutes' silence, would be enough. And then the show should go on.

Secondly, the Dodsworth exam would be happening in three days' time, on Saturday morning. Alison expected that the atmosphere in the class was going to be increasingly charged. She would need to keep the children's agitation under control and the parents calm too. It wasn't her job, but she would offer to hold a class after school on Friday night to go through some of the possible questions, and to prepare the children both academically and psychologically. She would try and give those who might fail a sense that it wasn't the only thing that mattered in the world.

Thirdly, and more long term, there was Liz Rudder. It was obvious now that the deputy head was hostile to her. But at Ro's house the evening before, Alison had confided to Jed Jackson that she was sure Jonty McFadden was the window vandal. This time Jed had listened to her, his brown eyes watching her, encouraging her. At one point he had glanced at her engagement ring and to her own surprise she'd covered her left hand with her right. It seemed to burn on her finger and she knew then she wanted to take it off.

Jed had said, 'Thank you for telling me all this. I was rude to you last time we spoke, I know.'

'Yes, you were.'

'I'd like to explain but it's complicated,' he'd said. 'It's my personal neurosis and I shouldn't have landed it on you. Maybe I could talk to you sometime about what happened to Becky's mum.'

Alison had smiled. 'I don't think anyone can really understand Becky,' she'd said. 'But I'd be interested to talk to you.'

'Thank you,' he'd said. 'And I'm truly sorry for the way I spoke to you.' She thought that he probably meant it. It had occurred to her that Mark would never say sorry.

Ro opened the curtains before the alarm clock went off because the sun was reflecting off the fells opposite and the room seemed full of a softer light. Ben's transport was picking him up at 8.15, and she always waited to see him into the taxi to make sure he was all right. But today she wanted to get started earlier. Lying there, she realized that for the first time she could leave him to cope. He had grown up just that bit more over the weekend. She crept around getting ready for work, and then tiptoed downstairs. She put his breakfast out for him, fed the cat, wrote him a note and checklist, and then called him awake.

When she put her head around his door, he stirred on the pillow, his face like a little boy's at first glance. But when she came close, the few spots and the new muscularity of his features hinted at the teenager he would be in a few months' time. He looked and smelt older. She realized with a shiver of pleasure in the crisp morning air that this would be his first really independent morning, when he would get ready alone, without having her within shouting distance. But she knew he could do it.

'I'm going to work early,' she whispered. 'Everything is out for you downstairs. The school taxi will be here in three-quarters of an hour. Don't go back to sleep.'

He woke and stared at her with his half-seeing eyes. By the autumn, his sight would be improved if the cataract operation went ahead, and that would bring its own problems. Ro touched the scar on her cheek. It had been days since she'd thought of it. In the mirror in the living-room, her face looked different. She was tanned, and her hair was longer than usual. She cut it herself, in between occasional visits to the hairdresser in Norbridge. But she hadn't had time this weekend and, anyway, the longer look seemed softer. She smiled at herself, and was astonished at the difference it made.

The drive into Norbridge took her through one of the prettiest valleys in this part of the world, and the town itself was sparkling in the early sunshine. When she parked at the station, Jed was already in the car-park.

'Morning, Ro. Isn't it a superb day?'

'Morning, Jed. You look like you had a good night's sleep.'

'I did. Thanks so much for inviting me last night. It was great for me to meet Uncle Phil again. It was so lucky. Though, if Aunty Judith had been there, it might not have been so easy.'

Ro stopped herself asking about Mrs Dixon. 'And you apologized to Alison MacDonald?'

He was the one who blushed. 'Yeah.'

'She's nice, isn't she? Not a daughter of evil. And I understand she's ditched her boyfriend.'

'Really?' Jed took the steps up to the station a little faster. 'Anyway, let's see if we have anything from Air Canada. And in the meantime, I'm going to find out more about Fraktur Art and the famous, or not so famous, *Book of St Trallen*, patron saint of eye specialists.'

Two hours later the phone rang in Ray Findley's office at St Mungo's. He had just settled the supply teacher into Year Four. She would be with them until the end of term, but Sheila had said she wanted to be back at work in September. He really believed that she would be better by then. There would be difficult decisions to take in the future. Tackling Callie wasn't going to be easy, either personally or professionally, and he was still unsure what to do about Liz Rudder. In a way, she was a more difficult problem. There was nothing she had actually done wrong. It was more her insidious negativity. Yet there would have to be a confrontation and he dreaded that more than the inevitable battle with Callie.

He took the phone call. The confident tones of Peter Hodgson brought him back to earth.

'Father Peter Hodgson here. My sister taught at your school until her untimely death.'

'Oh yes, of course. My sincere condolences. I hope you received my letter of sympathy. I know the Chairman of our Governors, the Reverend Neil Clifford, has mentioned to you that we should do something in Brenda's memory.'

'It's exactly that matter which I wish to discuss. I hear you are thinking of putting on an end-of-term concert. A pop concert! I have to say that idea is deeply offensive to me personally.'

Fifteen minutes later Ray Findley put the phone down and rested his head in his hands. It was such an unnecessary fuss. He was sorry for Father Peter's loss, but he was sure Liz Rudder had alerted this self-important man to Alison MacDonald's plans. The confrontation was going to come sooner than he'd been expecting.

He put his head around the office door. The school secretary's birdlike face looked up at him, bright with excitement at this latest disruption. She had put Peter Hodgson's call through and had doubtless caught his tone. Ray had never been quite sure whose side the secretary was on. But there would be no more taking sides at St Mungo's.

'Could you ask Miss MacDonald to see me at lunchtime? And then ask Mrs Rudder to come at the end of the day. Thanks.'

Chapter Twenty-two

'For all the gods of the nations are idols'

Psalm 96:5. Folio 34v. **Les Très Riches Heures du Duc de Berry**

It was midday when Jed got the call from Air Canada. Amazingly there had only been half-a-dozen men of that age on the daytime flight from Toronto. As it was a police request the airline would provide him with their names.

'OK,' he said. 'Thanks. But what about billing addresses if possible? ... Yes, I know that would take time, but we'd be grateful for it. Thanks ... Yes, I'll pick up the fax personally and ensure that no one unauthorized gets the information. And I'll keep you posted.'

Ro raised an eyebrow.

'The info is coming by fax. Old-fashioned, but more secure than email. They aren't very happy about the billing address, but they can see we need that too. Once we have it, we can start making enquiries.'

Ro's stomach was tight with nerves, which was silly. It was only a minor lead. It might be no help at all. The fax machine wheezed and buzzed like the tired creature it was. Jed sauntered over to it.

'Oh,' he said. He was looking at the fax. He sounded surprised. She went to stand by him at the machine. He pointed at the details on the print-out. There was a list of names which were hard to read. But one stood out.

'Richard Rudder. It might mean nothing, but it's not that common a name,' Ro said. 'So, say he was the man coming to Pelliter? But the Rudders have never reported someone going missing. Maybe they didn't know he was coming? Or maybe he's nothing to do with them? Or maybe he did come, and then he went away again, innocently. What about the Toronto end?'

'We need to call police in Canada I suppose, and see if they can spare someone to go and see if Richard Rudder is at home. That'll take time. And it's pointless going to see the Rudders here before five o'clock, because we know she'll be at work. It looks like we have a wait on our hands, which is a nuisance. But the least we can do is ask the Rudders if they knew this man.'

Faye Armistead was furious. Toby had spent the May Bank Holiday hanging around with his mates, and he had pleaded a tummy ache on Tuesday and refused to go to school. At this rate, he would certainly fail the Dodsworth exam. He hadn't taken the usual earlier entrance exam. Despite their elegant farm, the credit crunch meant money was tight at the Armisteads'. But this time round he would have a real chance of a scholarship, as long as there was no competition from inappropriate families like the Dixons. But to succeed, Toby needed to work. On Wednesday, Toby still stayed at home, looking list-less in his pyjamas and doing nothing more than play on his computer when he should have been doing online exam preparation.

At lunchtime, Faye gave in to her curiosity and called Callie McFadden on her mobile at the school.

'Callie? It's Faye.'

Callie thought that Faye's voice sounded even further up her bum on the phone. 'Hi, Faye, whatya after?'

'I'm after you. I'm rather surprised, actually, Callie.'

'What at?'

'I've heard that you're putting Jonty in for Dodsworth. You never mentioned it.'

'I never thought of it till this weekend, that's why. Anyway, what's it to you?'

'Well, it lessens everyone else's chances, doesn't it? I mean Jonty is hardly an intellectual, but the more children who enter, the harder it gets for the others.'

'For your Toby, you mean? Tough. My boy's as good as yours. The only thing that stopped me before was the money. Parents still have to pay some-thing even if the kid gets the scholarship. I haven't got that sort of dosh.'

'So where are you getting money from? If he passes.'

'Oooh, that's got you wondering, hasn't it?'

'Callie? Tell me.'

'It's nowt to do with you.'

'Are you somehow getting the money from Jonty's father? This isn't fair. I just don't see how it's possible....'

You're right there, Callie thought. Threatening Ray Findley with the possibility of being Jonty's father had never seemed very realistic to her. She was getting fed up with Liz Rudder pulling her strings and forcing her into an impossible position. She sighed a bit theatrically. 'Look, maybe we could have a chat. I don't want to fall out with you over this, Faye. If we play our cards right, perhaps both lads can end up at Dodsworth. Let's talk.'

'All right. When?'

'Tonight. Why don't I come over to the farm? It's busy at my place....'

I bet it is, Faye thought, shuddering at the idea of Callie's children lounging over the shabby furniture, scattering cans and take-away food cartons through the tiny kitchen-cum-diner-cum-living room. But she couldn't invite Callie to the farm that evening. Roger was at home on Wednesdays. On Thursdays, though, he went to the auction mart.

'Tomorrow would be preferable. Come to the farm after school. Four thirty. I'll make afternoon tea.'

'Oh, jolly nice of you,' mimicked Callie nastily. 'I'll see you then.'

In Norbridge Police Station, Jed Jackson said to Ro, 'Let's go. Liz Rudder will be home from school soon.'

It took twenty minutes to drive to High Pelliter and park in the Rudders' drive, a gravel sweep outside their imposing home.

Ro said, 'What did John Rudder do for a living?'

'I'm not sure. Something to do with personal finance. I think he organized a pension, or maybe an endowment mortgage, for my dad. He was obviously successful.'

'When did he have his stroke?'

'I can't say. Maybe a year ago? He was in business with Liz's brother, Kevin. You know how it is round here, family's everything. Unless you're feuding, of course.'

Jed rang the Rudders' doorbell. There was a long wait, and then a man answered and looked at them in surprise. He had floppy hair, and his face opened with a smile.

'Yes?' he asked.

'Is Mrs Rudder at home?' Jed asked. 'It's a police enquiry.'

'Liz? She's my sister. I'm Kevin. Liz isn't here.'

'When will she be back?'

'Not till much later. She's delayed at school, and going straight from St Mungo's to her Spanish class in Norbridge. I'm sitting with my brother-in-law. It's our Wednesday evening ritual. But do come in. I'm sure I can help. This must be about Brenda, mustn't it?'

'Not exactly,' said Jed, and followed him into the house.

At St Mungo's School Liz Rudder was sitting in front of Ray Findley's desk, her head characteristically on one side, her face creased with a smile.

The head teacher said, 'All I'm asking, Liz, is what you think about Miss MacDonald's concert project? After all, you were Miss Hodgson's closest colleague.'

'But there's no need to put me on the spot like this!'

'Your opinion is vital to my decision. As you know I have the greatest respect for your views on matters of diplomacy.'

Liz Rudder squirmed. Sarcasm was not what she had expected. Nor was a direct approach from Ray Findley, virtually accusing her of provoking Peter Hodgson. In her plan, the demoralized Ray Findley would have capitulated at once in the face of Father Peter's pressure. Instead he went on, 'Have you talked to Brenda's brother by any chance? You must know him too.'

'Well, yes, of course.' Her credibility as Brenda's closest friend was in question if she denied it.

'I thought so,' Ray Findley said. 'So really, I'd like to hear what you think, as a long-standing family friend of the Hodgsons. I personally feel Alison's concert idea is a marvellous way of bonding Year Six together. Surely it could be a tribute to Brenda too, after all the problems of this year?'

'Really?'

He smiled. 'You know, Liz, with your closeness to the family, maybe you could talk to Peter Hodgson and explain to him that the class will be paying tribute to Brenda at the show. Maybe we could start by singing her favourite song or something like that. I can rely on you to help, can't I?'

Disputes were not Liz Rudder's thing. That was Callie's preserve, and she wasn't here. The deputy head was never anything less than perfectly professional and completely respectful. No one could ever say otherwise. She squirmed.

'Of course you can rely on me, Ray. You've done it a great deal over the last few months. I'll talk to you about my views tomorrow when I've thought about it. And now, if you excuse me, I must leave. I always go into Norbridge on a Wednesday evening for my Spanish class. It's my personal career development. One mustn't get stale in teaching, as you so often tell us.'

'No indeed,' said Ray Findley. '*Buenos tardes!*'

In the smoking area of the car-park at the Crossed Foxes, Callie McFadden looked at her watch. Ray Findley had kept her waiting half an hour. At first she had thought he was bottling out of meeting her, but the longer she waited, the more she wondered if he were doing it deliberately, to make her sweat. It wasn't characteristic. Ray had previously been terrified of anyone finding out about his indiscretion, and once Sheila had come on the scene he'd been doubly malleable.

It had been really funny, because to be honest there had been nothing to it. Callie had been pretty drunk on the night in question too, though she could remember everything quite clearly. It had meant nothing to Callie except a bit of a laugh. She'd enjoyed Ray's obvious embarrassment afterwards and the whole thing had been a bit of a joke. Of course nothing had happened. They'd chatted a bit. She'd offered him some gin from her hip flask and he'd gone out like a light, slumped in the back seat, snoring. Poor bugger. He'd had a pretty hectic first term and he'd relaxed just a bit too much at the Christmas party.

But Liz Rudder had seen them get into Ray's car together, and noticed that the car was still there, with steamed-up windows, when her own husband came to pick her up fifteen minutes later. At that moment, Callie had got out of Ray's car, and had caught John Rudder looking at her. She'd adjusted her blouse ostentatiously. No one else had really been aware of it. Still, afterwards there had been useful mileage in Ray's guilt and confusion.

But now, thanks to Liz, she was embroiled in this stupid scheme and she knew she had overplayed her hand. She didn't give a toss about Jonty going to Dodsworth House, and she was pretty sure that ultimately Ray Findley would brazen it out. Liz's idea that Jonty might be Ray Findley's son was all too far fetched. Callie knew very well who Jonty's real father was. She shifted uncomfortably on the bench. What had started as a bit of teasing fun, putting the head teacher on the hop occasionally, now seemed disconcertingly out of hand. Callie was good at bullying and putting on the pressure. But real black-mail was a much bigger ball game.

Ray Findley's car drew into the car-park. He got out and gave her a jaunty wave.

'No, Callie, don't move,' he said cheerily. 'I'm not worried about who sees us. Have another smoke. It's a nice evening. You've still got some lager left, I see. This won't take long.' He dropped on to the bench opposite her.

Callie's mouth swung open, and to cover her surprise she stuffed another fag in it. Ray made no attempt to produce a light for her. He went on brightly, 'So you want Jonty to sit for the Dodsworth exam, do you? Well, on reflec-tion why not? He's a bright boy in a "native wit" kind of way.'

Callie started to cough. 'But what about the rest of the fees?' she rasped.

Ray leant forward. 'Look, Callie, I've discussed this with Sheila. If Jonty's my son, we'll gladly pay the fees. It isn't necessarily what I'd want, but you're his mother and you know best.'

Callie began to feel the ground slipping from under her.

Ray said, 'Although you've never given me the chance to know him, have you?'

Callie gaped at him. 'You want to *know* Jonty?'

'If he's my son, isn't that reasonable? And I'm happy to go for a paternity test any time you want.'

'You are? But then everyone will know that we—'

'Yes. They will, won't they? But what exactly *did* we do, Callie? I should never have offered you a lift – I wasn't fit to drive. But we never left the car-park. You say I acted unprofessionally, for ten minutes twelve years ago when I was new to the school, lonely and under pressure. But we've only got your word for it.'

Callie narrowed her eyes. She was never speechless for long. 'She's put you up to this, hasn't she? Your bloody wife—'

Ray got up. 'I'm leaving now, Callie. I'll deny any assertion you make about us having a sexual relationship, and if necessary I'll take a DNA test. How will that make you look? You might just have to come clean about who Jonty's father really was. It's laughable to think it might be me, and you know it. I'm happy to support any child in my school who wants to sit the entrance exam for Dodsworth, but I'm not paying for Jonty. Think about it and tell me tomorrow what you want to do. Now, can I offer you a lift? Or after last time, would you prefer to walk?'

Ro and Jed were back in the car. They had just left the Rudders' house.

'Isn't that Ray Findley driving past?'

'Looks like he's just been in the Crossed Foxes. Let me pull away out of the village,' Jed said. 'I'll park down the road and we can have a talk.'

He accelerated past the Crossed Foxes and parked a few hundred yards away, in the lay by, where the High Pelliter Road dropped down to the Marshes.

'So what did you make of that with Kevin?' Ro asked.

'Well, we didn't get anywhere, did we?'

Kevin had ushered them into the overheated living-room where he had been sitting with John Rudder in his wheelchair, watching TV. He had offered them coffee, which they'd accepted, and they had sat in a friendly circle. Kevin had gone out of his way to make sure John was included, turning his wheelchair so he was illuminated by a soft pink lamp. It was a kind gesture to help a man who couldn't communicate.

Jed had handled the situation well, Ro thought. He had explained that a Canadian visitor to Pelliter had been identified as a Mr Richard Rudder. Did Kevin know if the man was any relation to his sister's husband? John Rudder had become agitated and attempted to talk, but Kevin had calmed him.

'It's all right, old chap. I'll tell them. John hasn't had much contact with his family for a long time so he's understandably upset that you're asking. John's mother died when he was a boy. John's from Newcastle, though Rudder is a Cheshire name, I think. Is that true old man?'

John had spluttered and bobbed his head.

'Yes, I thought it was,' Kevin had said. 'But I don't know anything about any other Rudders around here. There's really no reason for any Rudder to come and see us, at least not to our knowledge. Liz and John certainly weren't expecting anyone, or she'd have told me.'

'Could this have been an unexpected enquiry? To do with family history?' Ro suggested.

'Hardly! Maybe there are other Rudders in Cumbria,' Kevin suggested. 'Have you thought of checking churchyards, registers, that sort of thing?'

'Thanks. We'll move on to that,' Jed said in a neutral voice. This was proving to be a dead end. Literally.

Kevin smiled and shrugged. 'I'll ask Liz when she comes home, in case it's something I've missed. She knows everyone in Pelliter, and who their grand-parents were. *And* what they're up to now!'

Including attacking people with hammers through windows, Ro thought. But Kevin probably knew nothing about that. He was a very different person from his sister, she thought. She had only met Liz Rudder once, but she could see a physical resemblance in their small but muscular build, which wasn't replicated in their manner. Kevin was much more approachable.

He smiled. 'I'll ask her to call you tomorrow. She may well be able to come up with something.'

He had actually looked rather eager, as if he wanted to dredge up a Canadian connection just to help them. But then John Rudder had lashed out with his arm in an arbitrary jerk, and knocked over the lamp which had been giving out a soft light in the corner, despite the evening sunshine still coming through the window. The disturbance had seemed a signal for them to go.

In the car, Ro said: 'Funny how they had the light on in the living-room, with the sun streaming through the windows.'

'Yes. But maybe John's stroke affected his eyes. Talking of which, how are the plans for Ben's operation?'

'Oh, going well. He's scheduled to have it after they break up from school. It's a risk of course.' She tailed off. Suddenly the outlook seemed less prom-ising, as the sun went down and grey dusk turned everything into a shadow.

Jed had reached the turn-off for Burnside. He said 'Look, don't be too upset, Ro. Police work is like this all the time. It's only on the telly you get instant results.'

'Shall we still ask the Canadian police to check on Rudder's address in Toronto?'

'Yep. It'll take time, but if Rudder's gone missing he could well be the dead guy. If that's the case you'll have been really helpful.'

'But we'll never know why he came here, and what really happened, so what's the point? Thanks for encouraging me, Jed. But I feel it's been a dead duck. I'll leave this stuff to the real police in future.'

'Goodnight, Ro. Don't worry. Sleep well.' But she knew she wouldn't.

*

It was just after nine o'clock when Ro went in. Ben was perfectly happy on the computer, and still delighted with himself for being so independent that morning. Mrs Carruthers exchanged pleasantries and left. Ben settled into another game, though on school nights he was supposed to be in bed by ten. Ro was too tired to argue. But she was restless, too. Something was nagging in her mind.

She wasn't hungry. She seemed to have spent most of the afternoon snacking in the canteen. And there had been more coffee and biscuits at the Rudders'. Kevin had been very co-operative and friendly. But he hadn't been able to help. Then again, how much would he know anyway? He was only Liz's brother. He wasn't a Rudder himself.

Ro mooched down to the kitchen and impulsively picked up the local phone directory from its place on the kitchen shelf. She looked up the name Rudder. Only one entry for the area was listed, John Rudder, High Pelliter, as Jed had thought. The phone number leapt out of the page at Ro. Would it do any harm to call Liz Rudder now, when she would be back from her Spanish class? Tomorrow Liz would be at school all day and doubtless Ro would be patrolling the streets of Norbridge looking for litter louts and stray dogs. It wasn't late. Ro punched in the number.

'Hi,' she said. 'Mrs Rudder? I'm sorry to bother you. It's Ro Watson, PCSO. I'm sure your brother will have mentioned that we called to see you this evening.'

'Yes, he did.' Liz Rudder's voice sounded like a high-pitched version of Kevin's. 'What is it now? I've only just got in from my evening class and it's rather late.'

'It's about a man who was visiting Pelliter. A Mr Richard Rudder.'

'But I thought Kevin told you everything. This Richard Rudder is nothing to do with us. Rudder is not an uncommon name.'

'I realize that. But Richard Rudder was a Canadian and they're often very interested in genealogy. Family history.'

'I know what genealogy is,' Liz Rudder said in a prickly voice. 'But I can assure you, as my brother did, that the likelihood of anyone coming to Pelliter to seek out John for family history reasons is virtually nil. John cannot communicate with people. And he's had no contact with his family since we married. They weren't the sort of people with whom we associated.'

'And there are no other Rudders you know of?'

Liz Rudder was getting crosser now. 'Look, my brother has been very helpful to you tonight, and you have already upset my husband. I came home to find he had knocked over the lamp in the living-room and scattered his

belongings everywhere. It's very inconvenient. My husband has night blindness on top of everything else and he relies on that light at twilight.'

'I'm sorry.'

'You should be. We've really been quite disturbed by your call. I cannot
think of any way in which we can help you and I'd be grateful if you'd let us
get some peace this evening. In fact, I may well have a word with the proper
police tomorrow about this.'

'I'm so sorry, Mrs Rudder. Please forgive me. It was just a follow-up call
and it will save any trouble in the morning.'

'But enough's enough. I've now got a mess to clean up in my lounge. Good
night.'

'Good night, Mrs Rudder. And thank you.'

Ro went thoughtfully back upstairs to the living-room. Ben was still
playing on the computer.

'Budge over,' she said. 'I want to use this now.' She nudged him with her
hips so that eventually he had to relinquish the seat.

'Mum, this isn't fair.'

'Yes it is. Go to bed. There's something I want to look up.'

Ben made irritated noises but he left her to it. She heard him bumping up
the stairs. Ro wasn't sure why she was doing it, but something about John
Rudder and the twilight had intrigued her. She clicked on to Google and
entered 'night blindness'.

Chapter Twenty-three

Aries, Leo, and Sagittarius are hot and dry, choleric.

Commentary on Folio 14v Anatomical Man (illustration)
Les Très Riches Heures du Duc de Berry

Liz Rudder had put the phone down on Ro Watson. She was feeling distinctly out of sorts. She sat in her lounge with a nightcap glass of Rioja. John had been more animated after the visit from the police; his skin had looked pink and healthier. He'd only been grunting at her, but she didn't like the fact that he seemed to have livened up. She'd been hoping he was in decline.

She hadn't even enjoyed her Spanish class as much as usual. And her interview with Ray Findley after school had been quite disturbing. Clearly Father Peter Hodgson had failed to derail the head teacher. Liz held her hand out to the phone to call Brenda Hodgson for a good old moan, but it was a reflex action. Brenda was dead. For a moment Liz almost felt sorry.

But what about Callie? Callie was still onside. What had happened there? Callie had said that she was going to have a face-to-face meeting with Ray Findley that evening. Surely the head teacher would be a bit less chipper, now that Callie had given him her ultimatum in person?

Not so smart when it comes to keeping it in your trousers, are you, Ray, Liz thought. She knew Ray had been deeply ashamed of his dalliance with Callie in the Crossed Foxes car-park. Liz had watched him avoid Callie afterwards at school. He had obviously been relieved when Callie had gone off on maternity leave. But that had made Liz think. Liz knew that Callie's husband had already absconded a good few weeks before that crucial Christmas party, because she had suggested that Callie ask John for some financial advice! So someone other than the disappearing Mr McFadden had to be Jonty's father.

Liz remembered that Callie had been rather nervous of her when she came back to school to show off her baby boy, but Liz had cooed over the buggy like everyone else. Then, when the others had gone, Liz had said, as if it were just coincidental, 'You know, the baby's got rather a clever look, hasn't he? A bit like Mr Findley!'

She had watched the light and the relief dawn on Callie's face.

'Don't worry.' Liz had leant forward. 'Your secret is safe with me. By the way, have you heard about these new teaching assistant posts? Why don't you apply?'

From then on, Callie had been Liz's secret weapon. With Callie as a teaching assistant and Brenda under her thumb, Liz's position at St Mungo's had been unassailable, culminating in the new deputy headship. The collapse of Sheila Findley had helped, of course. And with luck, and some effort from Callie, things would stay that way until John died. Liz just wished he would hurry up and go.

The phone rang out again, its trill bouncing around the room.

'Hello?'

'Ah, Mrs Rudder. Or, Liz, if I may be so bold.' The fruity voice of Peter Hodgson boomed in her ear.

Good heavens, Liz thought. He sounded a little bit tiddly. 'Father Peter. I gather you spoke to Ray Findley today about the concert?' And a fat lot of good it did, she thought.

'I most certainly did, but he was hardly sympathetic, I am sorry to say. I will though make my feelings known to Neil Clifford and to the bishop if necessary. But I don't want to alienate the local clergy if what we really want is for St Trallen's Chapel to be re-consecrated as a memorial to dear Brenda.'

'Is that what we want?' Liz said sharply.

'Didn't we both agree?' I don't remember agreeing anything of the sort, Liz thought. But Peter Hodgson was in full inebriated flow.

'And, dear lady, we agree on so much! I must say I thoroughly enjoyed your outstanding hospitality on Monday evening. I wondered if you might consider joining me for lunch this coming Sunday?'

Liz had a vision of Peter Hodgson stuffing his fat face with roast meat at the Crossed Foxes Carvery – and grimaced. He had been about as useful to her as a chocolate teapot.

'But I have to look after my husband, as you know....'

'Ah, of course.' Peter Hodgson's voice grew even more enthusiastic. 'So, if I may be so bold, why don't I come and see you at your home for Sunday lunch? I could bring a bottle of sherry and perhaps contribute a dessert? Those delicious little profiteroles, for example.'

Liz felt nauseous. Frankly, Peter Hodgson was actually rather gross – and politically he had been worse than useless to her. His intervention with Ray Findley had gone nowhere: in fact, it had caused her greater embarrassment. He was just a nuisance.

'Are you propositioning me,' she snapped, 'while my husband is in a wheel-chair?'

'That's an outrageous suggestion! I was merely suggesting a pleasant social encounter. I can't believe you could interpret my invitation in this way.'

'What invitation?' Liz Rudder was yapping. 'You invited yourself. Now if you don't mind, it's late. And next time you call a woman at ten o'clock at night, I suggest you don't go at the sherry first.'

Liz slammed down the phone. The conversation had left her seething but stimulated. She gulped her own drink, and then banged Callie's number into the phone.

'Callie? Liz Rudder here. How did you get on with Ray this evening? ... What?' She listened in growing anger as Callie described Ray Findley's treatment of her at the pub.

'Callie, that is quite dreadful. You must expose this man for the cheat and cheapskate he is. It's too late to talk now. You need to think about what to do. Should we meet tomorrow after school? ... What? ... You're going to Faye Armistead's? Well, after that then. I'll make arrangements with you tomorrow.'

She slapped the phone down.

Ro had a bad night. As ever, sleeping was one of her problems.

When she finally woke from drowsing on Thursday morning, she lay in bed wondering why it all felt so different. The excitement had gone. The urge to bounce out to the police station was exhausted. Anyway, she couldn't dash off and leave Ben again. Once was fine, but he still needed a lot of help. She had noticed that his bedroom, always untidy, was even more of a tip because she hadn't been able to go around after him on Wednesday morning.

'This room looks like the recycling dump!' she had yelled at him, a little unfairly.

'I'm going to be teenager in a few months!' Ben had yelled back. 'That's what teenagers are like. I'm just like everyone else, Mum.'

His words had silenced her. It was a daunting thought. Sex and drugs and rock'n roll. The concept made her think of Jed Jackson, who was just the opposite. But if Jed was so judgemental about the things that made other young people tick, what rocked his boat? Self-righteousness? Religious fervour?

But then, she thought, there were plenty of fierce, moral young men about. It was just that you expected them to be in the Taliban, not Norbridge Police Station.

You are way out of order, she told herself. Something was causing these melodramatic thoughts. She got out of bed and opened the curtains. Across the valley, thick grey clouds looped over the fells like oily ropes and she heard the wind ripping through the woods on the other side of the burn. The weather had worsened. It was odd, as if the blustery wind was coming from the east, off the fells, when she had been so used to the spring breeze coming from the sea. This was a drier, colder, more biting wind, like winter all over again. She shuddered.

The radio alarm clock came on with the local news. There had been a development in the Marsh Murder investigation after the reconstruction. The police had received a tip-off from the public after the event the CID had held the previous evening. They were looking for two young cyclists, a girl and boy, seen in the vicinity the night Brenda had died.

I didn't know about that new information, Ro thought. So much for being police support. She and Jed had been out of the station, *chez* Rudder, and had missed the developments that really mattered. I've been out of my depth trying to solve anything, Ro thought. I'm a PCSO and it's a fine job. I'm not a detective. Being a PCSO is what I do well and the other stuff is for a different kind of person.

Uncharacteristically, she scuttled back into bed and pulled up the covers for another ten minutes. Outside, the wind dribbled among the tree tops.

At The Briars everyone was getting ready for the day ahead when the local radio bulletin cut through the breakfast clutter with an item which made them all stop. A breakthrough in the Marsh Murder investigation. Jake held his toast and marmalade halfway to his mouth, and Robert stopped drinking his tea.

'I often wonder what makes people suddenly come forward with this information,' Suzy said. 'I mean, they talk about people's memories being jogged, but half the time people make stuff up which they think they remember.'

'But someone must have seen something,' Jake said reasonably. 'I mean, six o'clock on a Saturday night in Pelliter is hardly midnight at the oasis, is it?'

'What do you know about oases?' Suzy said playfully.

'Not much now,' Jake said. 'But there's always my gap year.'

Suzy stopped dead, even more stunned by this, than by the news. 'Gap year? You mean before going to university? Some half-baked battening on to the Third World? Or indulgent backpacking round the fleshpots of the Far East, pretending to broaden the mind?'

'That's right,' said Jake, grinning and biting into his toast again.

Suzy and Robert started talking at once and Jake pointedly ignored them, gathering his books and laptop, DVDs and sports kit. No one noticed that Molly was pale and quiet, sitting waiting on the stairs in the hall. Her fingers and thumbs were going over her phone keys like a musical instrument. She was texting Becky.

'U heard news on Radio C?' she asked anxiously.

Later, at St Mungo's, Miss MacDonald was teaching Year Six. She was taking a break from tests and scholarships, and trying some old-fashioned personal inspiration.

'Who has heard of *The Darling Buds of May*? Anyone? It was a television series years ago, based on a famous book by a novelist, H.E. Bates. Look out of the window. See how cold it's gone. The wind is shaking the blossom out of the trees, isn't it? Yet at the beginning of this week it was all warm and summery and lovely. This is the beginning of May and May is a changeable month. One minute it's summer and the next it's not. The title of the book is actually a quote from Shakespeare. Who was William Shakespeare?'

'Was he a Viking?' shouted Toby Armistead.

'No,' Alison said. 'He wasn't a Viking. But he is our greatest playwright ever. He died in 1616, that's nearly four hundred years ago. He wrote poems too, called sonnets. One went like this. *Shall I compare thee to a summer's day?* And it has the line in it *Rough winds shall shake the darling buds of May.*'

Jonty McFadden made a loud farting noise at the back of the class.

'Not that sort of rough wind,' Alison said sharply. 'Let me read you the sonnet.' It would be hard to get this class to concentrate for fourteen lines but she would give it a go. It went reasonably well except for Jonty making rude noises and obscene gestures and whispering at the back. But as Alison read, she looked up and noticed that, for once, Becky Dixon wasn't listening. She was staring out of the window, an expression of anxiety on her face. Across the aisle Molly Spencer was white and distracted too. What is bothering them? Alison thought.

'Becky, you weren't concentrating, were you?' she said.

'Miss, she's upset 'cos she's lost her phone,' Lily Smith said.

'Is that true, Becky?'

'Yes, Miss MacDonald.'

'I'm sure we'll find it. I'll help you look at playtime. In the meantime, what was that poem about?' Becky looked even colder than the rest of the class. She was wearing her bulky pea jacket, the collar turned up and pockets bulging.

Becky turned from the window with an agonized look.

'It's about dying young and being remembered,' she said.

Alison thought, I hadn't seen it quite like that. But Becky's right.

Liz Rudder found the day dragged. She was dealing with arithmetic in the same way she had done for years and she was as bored as the children.

But she was also angry. She had woken up slightly hung over, still furious about Ray Findley, disgusted about Peter Hodgson, and affected by the grey, depressing weather. It certainly wasn't like Spain. How many more years of this would she have to stand before John did the decent thing and died?

And added to all that, she had the oddest sensation that Callie McFadden had been avoiding her. When Liz had arrived at school that morning, bustling in from the car-park, she had seen the edge of Callie's flared patchwork skirt whirling out of the door. At lunchtime, Callie had come into the staff-room as usual, but she had been summoned to see Mr Findley and had disappeared. Liz had eaten her neat packed lunch at the staff-room table, and made conversation with the Year Four supply teacher before making a tour of the playground. Usually Callie would disappear down the road for a quick smoke at lunchtime, and Liz would find her in the playground on the way back, which would give them a chance to chat. But Callie did not reappear from Mr Findley's room until the lunch break was nearly over. She had a more flexible timetable than Liz and was dashing off, her skirt and shapeless brown cardigan flapping in the nasty sniping wind, when Liz managed to intercept her.

'Has Findley caved in?' Liz snapped.

'Not exactly. I don't know what he's doing.' Callie's little eyes flickered in unusual nervousness.

'So why did he want to see you this lunchtime?'

'He's told me Alison MacDonald is holding a special class tomorrow for the Dodsworth exam, and Jonty should go. He's repeated that I've got to decide whether I want him to do a DNA test to see if Jonty is his son.'

Liz frowned. There was something about this which didn't make sense. 'What do you mean, *if*?' she said, but Callie was scurrying away, already lighting up. 'Callie!' Liz called in her most imperious voice. But the wind snatched the words away and Callie disappeared around the corner.

All afternoon, Liz fretted about what Callie had meant. And about why Ray Findley was suddenly being so forceful. At home time, the head teacher popped his head round her classroom door.

'Can I have a word, Liz?'

'Certainly, Mr Findley,' Liz said pointedly. She was a stickler for formality in the classroom. She followed him into his office.

'Liz, take a seat. I've been thinking about making a few changes as Sheila will be coming back in September. I'll have to consult with the authorities – it's always worth having a second opinion especially where a husband and wife are involved, but I wanted to ask you to do me a favour.'

'Yes, of course.' Liz smiled smoothly, belying the panic she felt.

'Good. You've taught Year Five for several years, haven't you?'

'Since the year you came to work at St Mungo's, Ray. Twelve years ago.'

'So how about a change? I'd like you to let Sheila take Year Five next year. It would be a less stressful return to school life for her. And Alison MacDonald has done well with Year Six, but it's a big responsibility. I thought maybe she could have a change next year and take Brenda's old year, Year Four.' He paused. 'So could you take on the big job next year, Liz? Year Six?'

Liz felt winded. Year Six, the worst year in the school. Controversial tests. End of Year celebrations. Issues over secondary schools. This is a ploy by Ray and Sheila Findley to get me out, she thought. He doesn't really want me teaching Year Six. It's a win-win for him. If I say yes, then it means he has forced me out of my rut. If I say no, he has a valid reason for challenging me.

'But that would mean teaching the same children two years running....'

'Not a problem. In fact after the terrible events of this year a little stability might be good for next year's top class.'

'Well, Ray, I'm very surprised. And won't Alison MacDonald be moving down to Manchester? She's getting married, you know.'

'I gather she wishes to stay at St Mungo's.'

Liz swallowed. 'But she's done very well with Year Six. She should stay there. I knew she'd be good when I chose her.'

'Yes, you showed great judgement there.' Ray Findley smiled at her as if he knew exactly why she had picked Alison. 'But she can still teach art across the whole school. And if she does want to stay with Year Six, maybe you'd be interested in some other role? Something a little more challenging? Anyway, all this is just a thought. But I do want you to consider Year Six. Have a think about it yourself, and let me know how you feel. On Monday perhaps?'

Liz had walked out of his office like an automaton. She felt detached, as if she was floating dreamlike through her normal motions, but her mind was reeling. Year Six? They were always terrible to teach. She thought of the little detonators she always planted during her teaching of Year Five – the nudges to parents to make a fuss about secondary school, the tiny remarks she made to the children to destabilize or over-stimulate them, so that there were problems in store for the Year Six teacher. Now she would be inheriting her own time bombs.

What was going on? She had set two people off on missions to keep Ray Findley preoccupied and running scared; neither had worked. Peter Hodgson was a washout. But there had always been plenty of fight in Callie McFadden. And where was Callie? Usually, when there was change afoot, Callie scented it and was to be found lurking, waiting for scraps of gossip. But she had gone home.

Except she wasn't going home, was she? She had said on the phone the night before that she was going to Faye Armistead's. Faye could be a tough cookie in her effete upper-class way, Liz thought. Maybe she could be useful now. If Callie was going to let her down, perhaps Faye might be enlisted? She could be encouraged to set up a petition against the concert, or to issue a formal complaint against Alison MacDonald for favouring Becky Dixon. Faye might be a very useful ally.

Liz marched to her little red car, opened the door, and sat at the wheel. Instead of turning out of the school car park towards High Pelliter, she set off towards the Armisteads'.

Becky and Molly were still at school, working on the mural. Except that they weren't. Miss MacDonald had left them and gone to make a cup of hot coffee. School was cold. The change in the weather seemed to be seeping through to everyone's bones. Becky and Molly were huddled together, sitting on the floor below the picture.

'What should we do about the police?' Molly asked.

'We should do nothing,' Becky said. 'Anyway it was all my fault in the first place. I made you go out on the bike. You were all for staying at home.'

'They don't know it was us, do they?'

'No. They think it was a boy and a girl because you were riding Jake's bike. And don't worry, Molly, no one knows that we saw Jonty at the Marshes and we'll never tell.'

Molly had begun to cry softly. Becky put her arm around her. 'Please don't cry, Molly. I swear I won't let him harm you.'

And I won't, she thought. Whatever she had to go through herself, she wouldn't let Jonty McFadden touch Molly.

Chapter Twenty-four

L iz Rudder drove quickly and efficiently to Pelliter farm, carving up a school bus and a tractor with satisfaction. Her car hissed around on the gravel sweep in front of the gracious Georgian farmhouse, painted a pale dove grey with white facings and decorated with an elegant porch. Callie's old banger was already there. Faye opened the door to Liz with a surprised look which stretched her elegant arched eyebrows even higher.

Liz said, 'Hello, Faye. I know Callie's here. I do hope you don't mind me joining you. I wanted to see Callie, and it might be very convenient for me to speak to you as well. May I come in?' She was already across the threshold and moving towards the farmhouse kitchen with the air of a small, plump terrier.

Callie was sitting at the kitchen table, looking pale. A very pretty china tea-set was in front of her. Even in her annoyance, Liz Rudder noticed how tasteful it all was. The thought calmed her slightly. Faye Armistead might seem a little bit affected, but she did have class. It was surprisingly reassuring.

'I'd love a cup of Earl Grey,' Liz said, although no tea had been offered, and she sank down on to the hard but satisfyingly large kitchen chairs. 'Callie, I've come here because I need to speak to you. Actually it's worked out very well, because Faye might be able to help too. I presume I can speak in front of Faye, even though she may not be quite aware of everything?'

'Oh she's aware all right,' Callie said, and laughed darkly. 'She knows all about Jonty's dad. In fact, she knows the truth.'

'The truth? What on earth do you mean?' Liz said, and for the first time she felt the prickle of panic.

'Liz.' Faye came up behind her and put her beautifully manicured hand on Liz's shoulder. 'Maybe we should all three of us have had this heart-to-heart a long time ago. It really is quite fortuitous that you've turned up.'

Callie growled at Faye from across the table, 'If you tell her, everything is going to be out of the bag.'

'Yes,' Faye purred. 'But really, Callie, that would probably be a good thing. And the fact that we have to come clean is all thanks to Brenda! How odd that we thought we were pulling her strings, but she was pulling ours!'

'Don't trust Brenda, that's what the ouija board said,' Callie muttered.

'For goodness' sake!' Liz Rudder felt as if the classroom was out of control. 'What are you both talking about? What on earth has anything got to do with Brenda any more?'

'Because Brenda knew everything. We're talking about your husband,' Callie hissed. 'John Lover-boy Rudder who couldn't get enough at home.'

Faye sat down gently beside Liz and held her arm, as if to comfort her.

'What do you mean?' Liz said. Her voice sounded astonishingly like a whimper.

'John Rudder, whom Callie and I knew very, very well …' Faye leant forward confidentially, her dark eyes full of mocking sympathy. 'John Rudder was the father of our both our boys. Jonty and Tobias. It must be an awful shock for you. But didn't you always suspect it? That black curly hair…?'

'What?' Liz was white and shaking now. The empty teacup she had imperiously commandeered only minutes before rattled in its saucer. 'But Callie – it was Ray Findley.'

'No,' Callie said. 'Of course it wasn't. Mr Nice Guy Findley was far too respectable to want a shag in the back of his car. I let you think that, though. I was frightened you'd take one look at Jonty and know he was your own husband's boy, but you were so full of your own importance that you couldn't see what was in front of your eyes. You thought, because you'd seen me in the car with Ray Findley, that he was Jonty's dad. Well, you were wrong. It was your own man. You were the one who sent him my way. With financial advice,' she sneered.

Faye laughed her tinkling laugh. 'And he's also Toby's father. Probably. Amazing, isn't it? John was our financial adviser too, at the time. The farm was going to rack and ruin under Roger's management. John came here almost every day. We spent a lot of time together.' Faye laughed brightly. 'John was a sweetie, really. I felt sorry for him. It was a pity his marriage was just a sham.'

Liz put her head in her hands.

'The funny thing is,' Faye said, in rather a musing voice, 'neither Callie nor I had any idea about each other, or that our boys might be half brothers. Until Brenda told us. Fancy that!' Faye laughed again, and the cut glass on the shelf of the dresser vibrated.

'Brenda?' Liz looked up. Her eyes were dazed and her breath came in little rasps. 'How would she know all this?'

'We don't know. But she was right,' Callie growled. 'She got us together and she told us. After that we had to put up with her on a Saturday morning. Why do you think we were so friendly with the old bag? Charity?'

Faye laughed. 'I think Brenda told us John's secrets because she needed friends. You'd dumped her, after all, so she decided to put a wee bit of pressure on us to be her pals and we obliged. Of course, we have no idea how she knew about our little flings with your husband, but she was right.'

Liz was swaying with shock. 'Toby and Jonty. I had no idea. But Brenda should have told me,' she said, almost pleading.

Callie laughed harshly. 'Why should she? After John's stroke you ditched her. She had a grudge against you.'

'But I was always her closest friend!' Liz cried. She yelped like an animal in pain. Then she put her head back on the chair and closed her eyes. The other two women exchanged glances and waited until Liz Rudder opened them wide again.

'Now,' Faye said managerially, 'I'm sure you don't want the Child Support Agency, or anything like that, involved, Liz, and neither do we. I think all this could be resolved very happily if you agree to pay school fees for both boys. At some point you will have to sell your big house and buy a little flat in Norbridge. If you get one that's small enough, you should have enough money left for a basic nursing home for John, and school fees for his sons as well.'

Liz Rudder's eyes were glassy. She got up from the table and knocked the bone china cup on the floor, where it cracked. Then she turned and walked out. The other two women heard her feet on the parquet, then the front door of the farmhouse opening and, after a few seconds, the sound of a car screeching away.

'We just need to give her time to think, and then I'm sure things will turn out very well.' Faye Armistead smiled like a cat. 'More tea, Callie?'

John Rudder's carers had left for the evening. It had been a day of unusual clarity for him, so this was probably his final chance to write the document again now Brenda was gone and the original had disappeared. He knew he was weaker, and he could calculate for himself how many of his pills Liz was putting down the toilet. His medication now was virtually nil.

John had been pushed into his little bedroom and undressed, although it was early evening. Liz sometimes let him stay in the lounge, but more often she asked the carers to take him to his room.

'Poor John gets so tired,' she would say, so she could have him bundled out of the way.

If John had ever given Liz the benefit of the doubt before, he knew now how vicious she could be. What an idiot he had been. When he had first suspected she had deceived him over the failure to have kids, he had taken revenge by seducing every woman he could. As a financial adviser he met lots of women and visited them in their homes. Some had useless husbands who had made a mess of the family finances. Others were divorced or separated. But the last one had been different. She had been a student, introduced to him by his arty stepbrother who'd been living in a student house not far away. 'Even Bohemians need financial advice,' he'd joked, and John had gone round prepared to be contemptuous and a bit disgusted by their alternative lifestyle. But instead he had been wowed by the talk and the artwork and the excitement. And he had fallen head over heels in love. It had been so very different from his life with Liz.

He should have left Liz there and then, but he had dragged his feet. And in the end the girl he loved, and his kid brother, had gone away. He suspected he had broken her heart, but young hearts heal quickly and his own smashed life had never been put together again.

Until the emails from his brother had started coming in, and given him the most bittersweet moment of his life. For a few months he had cherished the idea of trying to put things right again. He would leave Liz, and find the only person left who really mattered to him. The daughter he had never seen. But when he had told Liz he was leaving, the rows had led to his stroke.

And here she was now, his torturer and guard. He could hear her car coming up the drive in the sort of fast aggressive spurts he associated with Liz in a bad mood. He would be in for another ghastly evening with nothing accomplished.

Liz Rudder arrived home with no idea of how she had got there. It was only six o'clock. Her husband was supposed to be tucked up in his little bedroom, but when she stormed in there he was sitting at his desk, a horrible parody of what he had been.

'I know it all, John,' Liz said. She went behind the wheelchair and tipped it up. John Rudder smashed forward into the table and crashed on to the floor.

'I'm not going to keep you alive any more. I want you dead before those harpies can prove anything. I've had enough. I know all about your two little bastards.'

John Rudder could hardly speak. He was lying face down on the carpet, his back twisted and in pain and his good arm broken underneath him. But he could still feel some triumph.

'Three!' he managed to shout in his mangled voice. 'Three!' But Liz had no comprehension of what he was trying to say. She was lifting the Anglepoise lamp to bring it down on his head. Then she heard the front door opening and her brother's cheery voice.

'Hi Sis!' Kevin called. 'Just a surprise visit. Oh my goodness, what's happened here?'

Ro woke on Friday to an even worse day. The bedroom felt dark, and when the radio alarm went off she lay in bed, waiting for the weather forecast. It was still unseasonably cold owing to a weather system moving in from the east. She thought of the wind blowing across the steppes, down through Scandinavia and over the North Sea to Cumbria where it met the warmth of the Atlantic, provoking storms to follow. It was tempting to stay in bed, but she was booked in to attend a meeting of Norbridge market-traders complaining about new traffic regulations. She went through the usual routine with Ben, who moaned and groaned a bit more than usual.

'What are we doing this weekend, Mum?'

'I thought we could stay at home after all the recent socializing. I've got washing to do.'

'No friends coming round? No parties?'

'Well, that's not what we normally do, is it? On Sunday we'll probably go to Grandma and Grandad's.'

'What about Becky and Molly, and Jake?'

'I think we've got to be careful of overdoing it with people. Outstaying our welcome.'

'You always say that,' Ben said moodily, picking up his backpack for school. She saw him get into his taxi, and then followed him out of the house.

That morning the market traders' meeting was crabby and aggressive. When they arrived back at the police station, Ro felt an air of unfocused tension.

'PCSO Watson?' Sergeant Liddle said. 'Can you come here?'

Jed was sitting in front of the sergeant's desk, his long legs stuck out in front of him. Unusually, there was another chair waiting. Sergeant Liddle motioned Ro into it.

'This is a difficult one,' Sergeant Liddle was saying as she sat down. 'The lady concerned was absolutely hysterical in the circumstances. But she was vociferous in her complaint when she telephoned me.'

'Sorry?' Ro looked first at the sergeant, then at Jed.

'John Rudder is very ill,' Jed said. 'Liz Rudder went out just for a few hours yesterday evening and when she came back he had fallen out of his chair and hit his head. Liz Rudder is in a terrible state too, apparently. John's in the Coast Hospital.'

'Will he survive?'

'Fifty-fifty.'

Ro started to think more clearly. 'You mentioned a complaint?'

'Yes, I'm afraid Mrs Rudder is going to make an official complaint, about you harassing her and her husband. I know it's probably just displacement activity on her part, but we need to take any complaint seriously.'

'But that's crazy. We played by the book, didn't we, Jed?'

'Yes.' Jed looked at her and then at the sergeant. 'If anyone gets it wrong Sarge, it's me. Ro is always great with people. There's no way she could have upset Mrs Rudder.'

Ro smiled at him gratefully. But Sergeant Liddle said, 'As far as I can see, you played by the book, PC Jackson. But you didn't, did you, Ro? You phoned Mrs Rudder late at night asking more questions. That's not what a PCSO does.'

'I'm sorry, Sergeant. It was just a very mild enquiry, really just like a neighbourly thing to do.'

'That's not how she sees it. And it's not how I see it either. I think you should go home for today, till we find out how this complaint squares up. And, Jed, you leave this Canadian connection alone for the time being. It's causing more trouble than it's worth.'

Ro felt her scar burning and her face was flushed. It was mortifying having to leave the office. It was clear no one wanted to associate with someone in disgrace. Except Jed.

He whispered, 'The sergeant'll get over it, Ro. Mrs Rudder's always been a bit of a cow. She always picked on the weak kids.'

'I'm not weak, Jed.'

'No, you're not. Maybe that's why she's complained about you.'

'Or maybe she's got something to hide?'

'But what? If the dead man was called Rudder it could be a coincidence. Or he could have been here without her knowing. He's not alive to tell us, is he?'

'And don't you think that's odd?'

'Not necessarily. I told you, Ro, things are only neat in TV cop shows.'

Ro drove home cursing herself. Why had she been so stupid? She might have known that Liz Rudder would complain. She had let her curiosity get the better of her, and she should leave detecting alone. Yet at the same time she was sure there was something odd about the Rudders' reaction to the visit from the police. She remembered John Rudder's arm striking out wildly when she had been at the house. Why had he been so agitated? Had they been too tough? But this time, Jed had been a model of sensitive policing.

As she was sitting with the inevitable coffee, looking at the steel grey hills and the dark, rushing river, the phone rang. It took her a moment to recognize Jed's voice again. And his excitement.

'Ro, listen. Never mind what Sergeant Liddle said, I need to talk to you. I've been in touch with the Toronto police and they've got back to me really quickly. A Ricky Rudder's been reported missing by his flatmates. He's a teacher. An art teacher.'

'So what? It doesn't mean he was the man at the chapel. And what would a Canadian art teacher be doing in Pelliter? Especially if he was nothing to do with Liz and John Rudder?'

'But that's just it! I called the flat, it's first thing in the morning there. They told me Richard Rudder was originally from the UK. He emigrated from England to Canada about ten years ago. You can transfer as a teacher relatively easily. You just need your certificate of professional training or something.'

Ro said tersely, 'But *you* told *me* not to start imagining things! This doesn't really mean anything and we're just going to get into serious trouble—'

'Well, get this. He was doing a doctorate on Fraktur Art!'

'You're kidding! Really?'

'Yes. He told his flatmates he was coming over to visit his brother to sort out some really difficult family business. And at the same time he wanted to look at some artwork which he felt proved a link with Fraktur Art and medieval illuminated manuscripts. Something he remembered seeing with a girlfriend years ago. He was quite sentimental about it, his friends said.'

'That sounds like the *Book of St Trallen*.'

'Yeah. But here's the funny bit. He had problems with his sight. That's why he wanted to come over now and see his brother and this artwork at the same time. He feared he was going blind; that's why he got in touch. He had something called retinitis pigmentosa.'

'I know what that is,' Ro said. 'It's commonly called night blindness. It's inherited. And John Rudder had it too. Jed, they *must* be related.'

Chapter Twenty-five

'Except the Lord build the house, they labour in vain that build it.'

Psalm 127:1. Folio 55v. **Les Très Riches Heures du Duc de Berry**

Peter Hodgson had spent all day Thursday stewing. What an awful way Liz Rudder had treated him when had called her with his kind and innocent invitation for a meal! Women! They were all such conniving creatures. Liz Rudder had obviously schemed to get him into her clutches, so she could humiliate him by a rude refusal. They enjoyed such petty power. Even his own sister had been like that, glowing with excitement about her silly little secrets.

'You're the only one I don't have any secrets from, Peter,' she had said more than once over Sunday lunch, flattering him as the senior sibling. And then, when he was half asleep after three helpings of pudding, he would sit in his chair, feeling his eyelids drop, as she burbled on about another of the petty scandals or misdemeanours she had come across.

And hadn't there been something in all that rabbiting about the Rudders? Slowly, Peter Hodgson rooted through those slumbering Sunday afternoons, searching for what it was that Brenda had actually told him which rang a bell now.

'I'm going to make sure the right person gets it,' she had said. 'But in the meantime I've made rather an exciting little plan to hide the will somewhere no one will ever think of. I know Liz used to be my best friend, but I don't feel I owe her any loyalty any more.'

Peter remembered agreeing with Brenda, though he was half asleep, that Liz Rudder had treated her in a way that was somewhat cavalier. And now he, too, felt furious with Liz Rudder. It was one thing for her to insult Brenda but it was quite another when she insulted him! Who did the woman think she was? How appallingly rude and disrespectful she had been. To suggest that he was inebriated when he phoned her! And she'd had the effrontery to think that he would help her scupper the school concert.

In fact, he thought suddenly, the more St Trallen's was seen at the forefront of village life, the more his plan was likely to succeed. The concert might actually be a good thing. He should never have listened to Liz Rudder's silly arguments. She didn't even have a university education. He really ought to put things right with the school. He was more than happy for the concert featuring St Trallen's to go ahead if the school would back his campaign to have the chapel reopened as a church, housing the fragment of the *Book of St Trallen*.

He positively leapt out of his chair to get the phone and call Mr Findley's office in order to backtrack. After all, any inconsistent behaviour on his part could surely be explained by his grief.

The secretary said, 'I'm so sorry, Mr Hodgson. Mr Findley is teaching Year Five. Mrs Rudder's absent. Her husband has been rushed into hospital with another stroke. He's unlikely to live. It's very tragic. It must be all the stress.'

'Oh how dreadful. Thank you for telling me,' Peter Hodgson said. What an interesting development.

Now, what was it Brenda had been chattering on about that Sunday lunchtime? Peter Hodgson sat down in his favourite armchair and treated himself to a few chocolate marshmallows. A will. That was it. Brenda had been going on about John Rudder and a will. Apparently Brenda was helping John Rudder. She had said that Liz was doing nothing to help John regain his movement, while Brenda and Liz's rather dim little brother were giving him exercises to do. Absurd. As if Brenda could really help anyone. But in the middle of all this, John Rudder had somehow communicated something to Brenda about a will.

Oh yes. Peter Hodgson remembered now. Ha! This really would put the cat amongst the Rudder pigeons, especially if Liz thought she was going to come into money. In fact Liz Rudder reminded him of a little fat little pigeon herself: big-chested, bright-eyed and waddling. What impeccable timing, remembering all this today! God really did have a plan, and Father Peter was being repositioned at the centre of it after a very uncomfortable few years.

'Mr Clifford!' Peter Hodgson boomed down the phone a few moments later to Neil Clifford, the rector. 'I've recalled something Brenda told me which could be very important. As you're my vicar, in the circumstances I would like your advice.'

When Peter Hodgson put the phone down five minutes later, he felt he had done a good job. He had offloaded the problem on to Neil, and he was sure that it would percolate down to Liz Rudder and cause her inconvenience at least, and downright damage at most. Serve her right, he thought. Now he could have a small sherry and make plans about something that really mattered – the future of the chapel under his stewardship. Father Peter Clifford, Chaplain of St Trallen's, West Cumbria. It had a very superior ring to it. What a pity that the young man had died outside the building – a death inside would have guaranteed that the place needed reconsecrating – and then there would have to be a priest in charge! What an interesting thought....

At St Mungo's the after-school class for the Dodsworth examinees was about to start.

'Jonty?' Alison McDonald asked. 'Shouldn't you be going home now?'

'Me, miss? Nah. I'm going to do the test as well. Effin' loony, but that's what me mam says.'

'Oh!' Alison was surprised, but it wasn't her business to question or comment which parents were putting their children forward. She knew better than to bring that down on her head. 'OK, everyone, I've got some old exam papers here. I've photocopied them. Let's go through the model answers.'

It was teaching of the most routine sort, but it might give them all some experience of what they would be up against in the Dodsworth House scholarship exams.

Molly Spencer had gone home. Without her, Becky Dixon looked even paler and more stressed than ever. At the end of the class, the parents arrived to pick up the children, except for Jonty, whose bike was parked against the school railings. While the parents waited, Alison made a little speech.

'Good luck, everyone. You've done some good work today. I wish you could all get a place at Dodsworth, but we don't know how many they will choose. But the point is – don't ever think this is it. You have all your lives to grow better and better in, and what you are now isn't necessarily the way you are always going to be. If you get to Dodsworth it will be brilliant, and I hope you'll have great success. But if you don't get to Dodsworth, it could still be brilliant and you can still have great success. See you on Monday.'

As she said it she realized it would be the first weekend for months that she hadn't seen Mark. She actually had no idea where he would be. The thought distracted her. The children and parents were milling around, but she hurried out to her car, not wanting to get involved in good luck wishes that might lead to allegations of favouritism, or cheerleading, which would wind the children up.

Becky stood in the playground as the rest of the crowd dissolved. There was no sign of either Grandad or Grandma. But she had known they wouldn't be here. The Devil would have seen to that. She felt the metal keys in her pocket. She had done as she had been told to do. If she hadn't, then who could know what might happen to Molly?

Becky slunk back against the school wall. Jonty's bike was still there. Perhaps someone will still be inside the school, she thought. Maybe I can put off the evil hour and still escape? She began to creep along the wall in the shadows. No one was hanging around to chat in the cold wind, and the cars were revving up and disappearing.

She smelt the Devil before she felt his arm round her neck.

'Trying to creep away, are you, you little bitch? Well you can't get away from me this time.'

Jonty McFadden twisted her round with his left hand as if she was a doll. The cat-skinner knife was in his right. He flicked his wrist and slit open her jacket. Becky looked mesmerized at the split. He really could do it, she thought.

'Have you got the keys?' Jonty breathed in her ear. 'Yeah, I can feel them in your pocket. Take them out and show me.'

Becky groped in her pocket and pulled out the keys to St Trallen's Chapel.

'Good. Come on.'

'But you said that all you wanted was the keys.'

'Yeah, well, that was what I *said*. But not what I *meant*.' Jonty gave his funny half-man, half-child high-pitched laugh. Like the demon he was, she thought.

They walked together towards the playground exit in a parody of kids in an old-fashioned advertisement, the boy holding her hand and the smaller girl scurrying after. Except that this time she was being pulled against her will. There was a car at the gate, and the front passenger door swung open. Becky felt the point of the knife cut through her coat and into the small of her back; she jumped forward.

'That's OK, Becky, climb in,' a voice said. The driver was wearing a big waxed jacket with the hood up, and was looking out of the driver's window. The door slammed behind her. As Becky turned to the passenger window to shout or signal, she felt a blindfold being pulled over her eyes. The last thing she saw was Jonty grabbing his bike and cycling away, putting two fingers up in the air at her and rearing his bike. The funny smell of the cloth round her eyes and mouth made her feel sick. She gagged, biting the material. And from then on everything seemed to be happening in a strange, woozy dream as she drifted in and out of consciousness.

The rector, Neil Clifford, had worried what to do about Peter Hodgson's strange information. On one level, he could try and locate Liz Rudder, or John Rudder's solicitors, and alert them. But when it came to Brenda's involvement he felt he might be wading into murkier waters. On the face of it, all this spiteful anecdotal chitchat about a will seemed irrelevant. But then again …

Neil had a good relationship with the local police, but he knew they liked straightforward information. This was a lot woollier. A PCSO was supposed to be a bridge between the public and the police, surely? What about calling that woman Robert Clark had told him about? Ro Watson. She had done a good job at the school too. He looked up her number in the phone book and was pleased to catch her at home.

'Hello, Mrs Watson. I'm Neil Clifford, the rector. We have friends in common. Philip Dixon and Robert Clark. I wonder if you could help.'

Ro put the washing basket down and listened to what Neil Clifford had to say. He went on, 'This could be important, or maybe not. Peter Hodgson, Brenda's brother, has been bending my ear. Apparently Brenda spent every Wednesday night trying to give John Rudder special physiotherapy exercises. Liz Rudder didn't do anything in that respect for her husband, but her brother Kevin, and Brenda, used to help him. It was an attempt to get him walking again.'

'Kevin seems that sort of person. Rather sweet.'

'But apparently John Rudder asked Brenda to draw up a will for him.'

'Really? How could he do that? When I met him he couldn't speak.'

'Father Hodgson says he thinks John Rudder managed to type things on the computer.'

'You're kidding! But why didn't his wife help him?'

'I gather there was some sort of issue about her not knowing how he was disposing of his property. It's all rather complicated.' And Neil had heard the malice in Peter Hodgson's voice. He went on, 'Now I gather from Peter Hodgson that John Rudder is very seriously ill. Perhaps the police should be alerted to the fact there might be a controversial will in Brenda's house.'

'Why didn't Peter Hodgson mention this before?'

'He says he only remembered when he heard the news that John Rudder was seriously ill.'

'But why did he tell you and not the police?'

'Peter feels rather hostile towards the police. Apparently they asked him some question he described as impudent, about his sister's death. And I'm on the board of governors for St Mungo's. Like a lot of people, I suppose he felt he'd unburden himself by telling me, and that what to do next was my problem.'

'I think the CID should know if Brenda was involved in anything, even something which seems irrelevant like you say. But I can talk to our community sergeant if you like?'

'Yes, thank you. I'd appreciate that. I think the community people would be much more sensitive about something like this. John Rudder really is very seriously ill so contacting his wife with upsetting news like this might be very tricky....'

Don't I know it, Ro thought. She immediately rang off, took a deep breath, and called Sergeant Liddle. To her surprise, he took her call, but he cut in when she started to tell him what Neil Clifford had said.

'Never mind all that. I thought you were calling me because you'd already heard.'

'Heard what?'

'A kid's gone missing. We got the call minutes ago. Let's hope it's nothing but a hysterical grandmother, but it's on your patch and you've got good antennae. With luck she'll come home soon, or be at one of her friends' houses. They usually are. Do you know where PC Jackson is? He's not answering his phone.'

'No. Why should I know?'

'Because you're big mates. You and your toy boy, they say in the canteen. Look, I know I sent you home, but I need you. Pretty damn quick. Get straight down to the school. Let me know as soon as the kid shows up. This is your chance to redeem yourself with me.'

'OK. Which school and which kid?'

'St Mungo's, Pelliter. And the kid's name is Becky Dixon.'

Ro tried to phone Jed as she hurried out to her car, fumbling with her mobile in the growing cold wind and smattering rain, and she missed him twice. Wherever he was, he would want to be involved in searching for his niece. As she drove towards St Mungo's, she thought of calling Suzy Spencer too. Ro stopped the car and pulled out her phone with Suzy's number in it.

In The Briars' kitchen a white-faced Molly listened to Suzy's end of the conversation and began to cry in great howling sobs.

Suzy said anxiously to Ro at the other end of the phone, 'Judith's already called us, Ro. Becky's definitely not here. Molly left school much earlier than Becky today. Look, Molly's upset. I'll ring you back.' Suzy put the phone down, went over and hugged her daughter. 'Molly, I need to ask you again: do you know where Becky is?'

Molly shook her head. Suzy heard herself shouting in her anxiety. 'But do you know anything about what's going on? It's Ro on the phone. Not the police. Are you scared of the police, Molly?'

Molly started to howl again, the noise filling the room.

A few minutes later, Suzy rang Ro back. 'Molly's in a terrible state. She's told me that one of the boys, Jonty McFadden, has been bullying Becky about something, but I can't get it out of Molly. Becky has been upset all day. Her phone was stolen, apparently.'

'That's odd. My sergeant's just been on the mobile filling me in on the details. Apparently Judith Dixon had a text message from Becky saying the class finished at five thirty when it really finished at five. When Judith turned up, Becky wasn't there and the school was deserted.'

'But if Becky's phone was stolen, then it couldn't have been her who texted her grandma.'

'Exactly.'

This was beginning to sound frighteningly like a planned event. Someone had deliberately given Judith the wrong information about the time the school class finished. And according to Sergeant Liddle, Phil Dixon had told his wife he was going to Carlisle for a meeting with the bishop about the chapel and he'd not been heard from since. It was a crazy possibility, but had Phil abducted his own granddaughter to save her from sitting the Dodsworth exam? Ro suspected that the Dixons' marriage wasn't all it seemed, but Phil would not have to go to such desperate lengths to defy Judith, would he? Ro shook her head vigorously, started the car again and continued driving towards St Mungo's, hunched over the wheel. The rain was heavy now, smashing against the windscreen. It came in odd bursts, stormy and hard, then easing off between each assault.

As she drove, Ro went over the facts. It wasn't just Phil who was out of contact. So was Jed. She hadn't heard from him since his revelation about Richard Rudder. Where was he? There was another crazy possibility. Had Jed met Becky from school? Had he taken her off somewhere, with some mad idea of protecting her from the world, the flesh, and the Devil in one of his self righteous, sin-hating moments?

Ro reached St Mungo's car park, sat in the car and racked her brains for the answer. She was under orders to stay at the school, and this time she was going to do as she was told. So she could do nothing but sit, think, and listen to the rain on the car roof.

The car, with Becky Dixon sitting white-faced, trussed, gagged and blindfolded in the front, bumped up the track which led from the shore road to St Trallen's Chapel. It was unnaturally dark, with a strong wind blowing, and rain sweeping in bursts from the sea. The shore was deserted, and the car had passed an empty Briggs' ice cream shop, with the plastic awning flapping hysterically in the wind.

The vehicle swayed and dipped over the humps in the path; it pulled up just beyond the chapel in a dip. It couldn't be seen from the road or the track. The driver headed right into the gorse and bracken, until it was as high as the car.

Becky knew it was wrong to get into a car with a stranger, and yet with Jonty's knife in her back it had been a reflex action to jump forward into the seat. She could still feel the chapel keys in her pocket. Jonty had told her to bring them to school, and that if she didn't he was going to do something horrible to Molly. 'She's big now and she's got tits. She might even enjoy it,' he had said. But why did he want the chapel keys? Becky had thought that maybe Jonty wanted to vandalize the chapel, or use it to smoke in, or as a love shack, or a place to take Molly. All day long Becky had felt a sense of something awful impending. For hours, her mouth had been dry and her knees weak because something bad was going to happen. And now this was it. And it was worse.

'Get out of the car,' the driver said. The voice was odd, neither squeaky nor gruff. 'Walk through the bracken. It might scratch you, but that's the least of your worries. We're walking to the chapel. Be quick. This is the only worrying bit. If they don't see us now, once we're inside we're safe. The chapel's a wonderful place, isn't it? You think that, don't you? You love it.' There was a tinny little laugh which made bile come into Becky's throat.

The wind was whipping at her hair, and was icy on the bit of her face that was still exposed. She stumbled; she was picked up and pushed forward. Her arm was twisted up her back, and they ploughed through the undergrowth towards St Trallen's. At the door, Becky felt hands fumbling in her pockets, and the keys dragged out. The heavy hinges swung and she heard it creak open. She was pushed inside, and she fell face downwards.

'Ouch!' she said. She heard the laugh again.

'Now,' the voice whispered in her ear, 'do you know what is going to happen to you? It's what happens to an awful lot of neurotic little girls of your age. You're going to commit suicide. You're going to do it now, and quickly. You're worried about the Dodsworth exam and you're going to do it here because this is your special place. It makes a lot of sense, doesn't it?'

'What do you mean?' Becky didn't realize for a moment. Then she understood. 'You want me to kill myself? You can't make me do that.' It seemed so crazy that for a moment she thought it was some sort of joke.

'Yes, I can. And then I'm going to look for what Miss Hodgy Pasty Podgy hid in here. We're going to kill two birds with one stone.'

Becky heard the noise of rustling, as if through the pockets of a heavy waxed coat. Then she could smell the linseed and feel the roughness on her neck. It was a rope.

Chapter Twenty-six

'And he cast down the pieces of silver in the temple, and departed, and went and hanged himself.'

Matthew 27:5. Folio 147v. **Les Très Riches Heures du Duc de Berry**

Ro sat in the car outside St Mungo's. She had the edge of an intuitive feeling that she was on to something, but it wouldn't come. She nagged at it. How often did people die mysteriously in Pelliter? Maybe once every decade? And now there were two in three weeks. Both teachers. Ricky Rudder had come to England to chase up some theory about Fraktur Art and to see his brother about 'serious family business'. He had extreme night blindness. Ro suddenly realized that that was why the dead man's eyes had been slashed.

'So no one would know he had retinitis pigmentosa! Night blindness,' she said to herself. 'That was the only way he could be associated with John Rudder once he was dead.'

So the Rudders had to be involved in this somehow – but she couldn't see why. And if she put the question to Liz Rudder again, she would be in more trouble than ever. But now there was this business of John Rudder's will. She hadn't managed to explain all that to Sergeant Liddle. From what the rector had said, Brenda Hodgson had been secretly helping the kindly Kevin to get his brother-in-law back on his feet. And John Rudder had made a will, unbeknownst to his wife, with Brenda's help. He had given it to Brenda to hide, according to Peter Hodgson. But where could it be? The CID had gone over Brenda's house with a fine-tooth comb and there had been no mention of any will being found. Jed would have known, and surely he would have told Ro. So the will had disappeared – and even if it *did* contain something to upset Liz Rudder, it wouldn't matter now. Brenda was dead and she was the only one who knew where the will was.

Or was that *why* she was dead? Had Brenda been killed because she knew about John Rudder's will? The idea came to Ro like a physical shock. She felt herself shaking inside her jacket. She ought to tell the sergeant. But he would be preoccupied looking for Becky. The issue of the missing will could wait: the missing child was much more important.

But say they were linked in some way? Wasn't it all too much of a coincidence – the Rudders, the Hodgsons, the Dixons? All local. All with personal tragedies. What else did they have in common? Could they be related? Ro had lived in Cumbria long enough to know that if you drilled down far enough most local families were connected. Did Richard Rudder look like John Rudder? Alison had seen him. Perhaps she would know. After all, she had said that the young man reminded her of someone.

On impulse, Ro fumbled with her phone and found Alison's number.

'Alison. It's Ro Watson. Look, I know it might seem irrelevant, but listen to me. The man you saw at St Mungo's that Friday afternoon … Rack your brains Alison. You said he reminded you of someone. Did you know Liz Rudder's husband John? Was it him?'

'I've never met John Rudder. But yes, the man did remind me of someone. I was thinking about Molly and Becky when I saw him. The man's hair was black like Becky's, blowing in the wind. I know it's ridiculous, but that was the connection. He reminded me somehow of Becky….'

'And now Becky's missing …'

Alison cut in 'Missing? I didn't know….'

Ro cursed herself. She'd assumed that Alison had been told. But why would she have been? Ro herself had only heard twenty minutes ago, though it seemed like an age.

Alison was talking frantically. 'She was so upset today at school. She really didn't want to take the Dodsworth exam.'

So maybe that was it. Maybe it was much more straightforward. Maybe Becky had gone to ground by herself to avoid the exam. Ro interrupted. 'You're her teacher, Alison. If she was unhappy about the Dodsworth exam where might she go? Somewhere her grandma couldn't find her perhaps?'

'What about St Trallen's? Her grandma wasn't very keen on it, but Becky told me it was her favourite place.'

'That's sounds a distinct possibility. I'll go there now. But I'm supposed to stay at the school. I need someone else to help and I can't get hold of Jed.'

'That's because he's here, with me. He's listening. He says he'll meet you there. He says sod Sergeant Liddle. You're nearest. Get to the chapel straight away.'

The rope was tied around her arms. Becky felt the whole proceeding with a sort of calm. If I'm going to die I'm going to die, she thought, and her mind seemed to float above her body. Suddenly she felt her head wrenched back.

'Mustn't do this too tight and leave marks,' the funny light voice said. It was almost conversational now. 'I want you to stand on the altar. There's rather a convenient beam above.'

She heard the whishing sound as the rope flew heavily over the beam and plunked down the other side.

'It's going to be easy-peasy, Becky. I lift you on to the altar, prop you up with the noose round your neck then push you off. It'll be just how you would have done it, if you'd thought of it yourself. I'd originally thought we could do something interesting with the bell rope. But that might have made a noise.'

Becky felt herself being lifted bodily and, though she kicked, it made no impression. She knew from the cold feeling that she had been laid on the altar table. She tried to pray. She had called on St Trallen before, and Jonty's knife had fallen on to the path. But had her prayers really been answered? Or had Jonty just had a failure of nerve, or a pain in his wrist? Whatever had happened then, it wasn't happening this time. But though Becky felt apprehensive she felt no abject terror. It all seemed ludicrous. And then, like a wave of sweat breaking out over her, she realized that she really was going to die. It was as if her mind came to the surface and told her it was going to hurt. To her horror, part of the wave seemed to be moist and warm. She had wet herself in fear. She screamed soundlessly and then felt herself drifting away again. The last thing she heard was the strange voice saying fussily, 'Oh dear, I hadn't bargained on that.'

She faded for a moment, and when she came round she drummed her feet on the altar table, but they hardly made a noise. I'm floating away, she thought. I've got to concentrate, to think of something to get help.

She heard the boom and crack of the storm hurling itself at the chapel door. It seemed to have stopped the person doing anything, as if the weather was a warning.

And then the bell at St Trallen's began to ring for the first time in decades, the noise crashing out in the tiny chapel. The chiming went on and on, more and more frantically. It's me. Becky thought. It's the power. I have to keep concentrating, making the bell ring. But it is so exhausting. I really am going to faint now, she thought.

Then she heard her name being called from outside and the bell was more hectic than ever. The tinny little voice was some way away now, making a strange laughing sound. Becky waggled her head, banging it up and down on the altar, until the blindfold slipped.

She saw the hands holding the noose. They were small white hands, like a child's.

Ro's phone rang as she drove and she answered, holding the mobile to her ear and trying to see through the rain. It was Jed, also phoning as he drove. But he would be organized and legal, with a hands-free set, Ro thought. Jed, always right and proper until the moment his niece went missing and he was off-piste himself.

'Why didn't you answer the phone, Jed? Everyone else is on the case.'

'So why didn't anyone else think of St Trallen's?'

'Why should they? Phil Dixon has gone to Carlisle apparently and it isn't Judith Dixon's sort of place.'

'I'll see you there in five minutes.'

He must be driving like a lunatic, Ro thought. What had made him go to see Alison MacDonald and not answer a call from the sergeant? There must be a hell of an attraction there, Ro thought. That would explain Jed's nervy rudeness to Alison from the start.

The clouds made the night unnaturally dark. Big splodges of rain were appearing on the windscreen. On the coast road it was even more uncanny. The wind seemed to buffet the car, and when Ro reached the bend before St Trallen's Head the waves from the usually placid Solway were crashing over the road. At Briggs', the shop owner was fighting to get the racks of goods and the awning inside. Once Briggs' store was behind her, the road was dark and completely empty.

Ro swung the car up the bumpy track towards the chapel and parked outside. It was deserted. She walked round the building and checked the door: it was locked. She heard Jed's car coming up the track, and screech into the dip in front of her, scattering sand and gravel. She called out over the wind, 'I've been shouting her name. There's no sign of her. It's locked.'

Ro turned back towards her own car, and a blast of wind caught her on the side of the face, making her scar sting with pain. And that was when the bell started to ring. The noise was sudden, loud and powerful, a clanging, screaming sound that seemed much greater than any one tiny bell could make. It seemed to shake the ground under them.

'It's the wind!' Jed yelled. 'It's a freaky wind.'

Ro shouted though he could hardly hear her. 'No. It's not blowy enough for that. It could be Becky ringing the bell in there. She could be trapped. The wind might have blown the door shut.' It was a crazy idea but Ro felt that somehow she was right. The bell was telling her …

Jed shouted, 'OK, there's a little round window at the back. I'll lift you. Break it and look in.'

The bell was clanging wildly now. Ro felt the full blast of the wind on her face as she turned around. It seemed to be coming from everywhere. They scrambled through the gorse to the back of the chapel. And for a moment there was calm.

'Becky!' Ro screamed. 'Becky, are you there?'

Jed shouted too, 'Becky! Becky can you hear us?'

Jed lifted Ro up to the little stained-glass window of the saint. She clenched her fist and punched it through, feeling the shards on her skin. Jed heaved her further and she could see inside.

'Becky!' she screamed. The girl lay on the altar. Then a figure leapt up beside her with a rope, placed the noose round its own neck and launched itself off the table.

Swinging there, his neck broken by the force of his leap, Liz Rudder's brother Kevin stared back at Ro.

Jed forced his car through the gorse to the back of the chapel and stood on the roof to break in through the window and climb inside, while Ro phoned the Dixons and assured a sobbing Judith that Becky was safe. Then she called Sergeant Liddle. Most of the Norbridge Force was despatched to the chapel, along with scene of crime officers and paramedics.

Judith Dixon explained how Phil had been summoned to Carlisle for a meeting with the Bishop about the chapel. But when he had arrived at five o'clock, there was no meeting in the bishop's diary. He was driving home now as fast as he could. The police came to take statements and Sergeant Liddle arrived in his own car.

Ro walked out into the garden, turning up her collar against the wind, which had dwindled to a mere whisper. She didn't want to wait with Judith and Jed, who were family after all, however awkwardly they were talking to each other in the big farmhouse kitchen. Ro stood in the sheltered garden of the farmhouse, set in a dip in the rolling foothills of the fells. The wind was dropping now, as if its job was done, and the heavy clouds had started to lift, so that the evening sunshine was filtering softly through. There were still odd streaks of gold and ruby in the sky.

'Well done,' Sergeant Liddle said to Ro when he came outside to find her. 'You've redeemed yourself all right. You'll have to cope with the CID now. It's a dog's breakfast, isn't it? But it'll come clear in the end.'

'I think I understand a lot of it. John Rudder is Becky's father, isn't he? I think he must have left his property to her in his will, the one I was trying to tell you about, Sergeant, when you told me Becky was missing. I think Kevin must have known she was going to inherit his brother's property so he wanted to try and kill her, but when he heard us outside ...' Or when he heard the bell ring, Ro thought, and shuddered. That was the weirdest thing. She shook her head and said, 'So was Richard Rudder from Canada John Rudder's brother?'

'If you say so. You seem to be the only person who knows what's been going on. But what you don't know is that John Rudder died this afternoon.'

'That must have been the catalyst....'

Jed had strolled out after the sergeant. He looked at the two of them. 'I don't really understand any of this.'

'No doubt she'll explain everything to you,' Sergeant Liddle said drily, nodding towards Ro.

Not everything, Ro though. No one could ever explain the bell, ringing like that just when they were about to go away from the chapel.

Then Phil Dixon's car came rolling into the farmyard and Ro had this terrible urge to run up to him and tell him it was all right. But Judith got there first.

That night, Ro slept for six hours without waking. She had seen and heard horrible things which should have guaranteed her nightmares, but instead she slept as she hadn't slept for years. When she woke, she had to pull herself out of a deeper world almost by willpower. Her waking dream was a strange mix of images – medieval artwork of glorious colours and her own Fraktur painting coming to life. It was a happy dream, which made her awakening odd and dislocated. Something terrible had happened, but she sensed it was all right now. Things were slipping into focus. She took in the calm world around her: the sunlight on the curtains, the warmth of the duvet.

She saw Ben off to school in a daze, but he had only been out of the house a few minutes when the phone rang. Not surprisingly it was Jed. He was already at work at the police station.

'CID is going through Kevin Rudder's office. They reckon they'll have an idea of what was going on by the end of the day. Can I come over and see you later?'

'Please do. Fill me in on it all,' Ro said. 'I'm not leaving Burnside today.'

At St Trallen's farm at the same time, Phil Dixon was in the kitchen with a crime squad officer and Sergeant Liddle. Becky had woken with a headache and very confused memories of the night before. She was in her bedroom with her grandma anxiously in attendance. A police doctor and their own GP had been and gone.

'I think it might have been Rohypnol, the date rape drug, on the scarf he used to gag her,' the doctor had said. 'Everything that happened will be either forgotten or seem unreal. In the circumstances that's a good thing.' Apart from the effect of the drug, she was fine.

'You're lucky,' the police doctor had added. 'She didn't feel the real effects of the experience, though being bundled into the car was bad enough. Why on earth did she get in?'

'I don't know,' Judith had said testily. 'She says she's forgotten why. She'd never met this awful man before. I've been on the phone half the night to people who wanted to know what was going on and I know they say he looked like his sister, Mrs Rudder. Big bodies, small hands and feet. But why Becky would get in a car with either of them beats me.'

In the kitchen, Phil Dixon slowly tried to come to terms with what he was being told. John Rudder had died the afternoon before, after another massive stroke. Liz Rudder was under sedation, having been told that her brother had died too. A husband and brother in one day, Phil thought. However awful Kevin had been, it was a dreadful situation for Liz Rudder to be in.

'We'll be able to piece it together eventually,' the police officer said. 'But we think Kevin killed John Rudder's younger stepbrother, Richard, and also Brenda Hodgson. Someone will be flying in from Canada to identify him.'

'I'm sorry, I don't really understand.'

'Well, it will take time for us to work it out, but these family things usually boil down to money. Kevin's business seems to have been struggling. He needed John Rudder's money.'

'But then why did he try so hard to keep John Rudder alive?'

'I think we'll find that John Rudder had some sort of pension or health insurance which kept on paying out while he was alive. When he died things would be bad enough for Kevin, but we suspect that Brenda Hodgson hinted to Kevin that John Rudder had made a will leaving the money outside the family. That would have been terrifying for Kevin, so Brenda had to go. And maybe Richard Rudder too.'

'But how did Kevin know that my granddaughter was one of John's children?'

'It's interesting. We've had someone go through all his computer accounts overnight. John Rudder started with email many years ago. An early adopter. Like a lot of people then, he wasn't very adept at setting up accounts. This one was through the business. It probably never occurred to him that Kevin could access it. Maybe Kevin didn't do so, originally. But perhaps when emails started coming in again from Richard, and John couldn't open them because of his stroke, Kevin opened them for him. And then started answering them.'

'So he knew Richard Rudder was coming to Pelliter to see his brother?'

'Exactly. Richard Rudder was the only one who knew that your daughter Samantha had a child by John Rudder. But John couldn't talk, so the only way the story would get out was if Richard came to Pelliter and managed to communicate with John. Samantha was dead, and you clearly had no idea who Becky's father was. So Kevin set Richard Rudder up, once Richard was determined to come to Pelliter. Richard came by taxi, from Manchester Airport. We think Kevin brought him up to the chapel and killed him. Then Brenda dropped her little bombshell about having hidden the will, and she had to go too.'

Phil put his head in his hands. 'So where does this leave my grand-daughter?'

'Well she's potentially quite a wealthy young woman. She may well have inherited half a house in High Pelliter. If we can ever find this will....'

'I don't care about that,' Phil said sharply. 'I just feel angry, because John Rudder and his brother might have been my last chance of finding out what happened to Samantha, my daughter, Becky's mother.'

'Well, there are mounds more emails to go through, Mr Dixon. Maybe there will be something in there that will help us all understand.'

'Yes.' Phil put his head in his hands to hide his tears. Oh Sam, he thought, will we ever know what really happened?

Chapter Twenty-seven

'He shall judge the world with righteousness, and the people with his truth.'

Psalm 96:13. Folio 34r. **Les Très Riches Heures du Duc de Berry**

That evening, Jed sat in Ro's kitchen with Ben. After fifteen minutes or so, Ben's phone pinged with a text message.

'That's Becky,' he said, looking a little bit pink. 'She's fine now.' He had heard the story from Jed and his mother, and they had told him everything, including Kevin's suicide. 'Can we go and see her?'

'Maybe next weekend. She isn't really fine, Ben. She's had an awful experience.'

'But Mum, Becky's special. She'll be all right. Really.'

Ro looked at her son's intent face. He was right. There *was* something special about Becky. She took two glasses out of the cupboard.

'Come on, Jed, relax. A couple of glasses of vino plonko aren't going to turn you into a sociopath. And what's this about you and Alison MacDonald anyway?'

Jed looked uncomfortable. 'I was sick of traipsing around Pelliter again yesterday. When it got to five o'clock I thought I'd go to Ali's house on the way to Norbridge. She'd just got in from school. Her parents were still at work and her sister was out so we sat and talked....'

'And so is Alison going to rehabilitate you to the realms of ordinary fallible mortals?'

'Don't be mean, Ro, even if I deserve it.'

'But I wasn't being mean; I was being fair. But let's stick with the case. John Rudder and your cousin Sam were definitely an item? Seems a bit unlikely.'

'Not necessarily. Sam was looking for a father figure and John Rudder was looking for a bit on the side, but Sam really got to him. Then years later, finding out about Becky precipitated his stroke in some way, before he'd had a chance to sort things out. He must have really struggled to be able to write a will leaving his property to her. At least that's what Peter Hodgson says his sister told him. And did you know about the other children?'

'What other children?'

'Oh, the gossip is already going round the station. Apparently this Callie McFadden woman who works at St Mungo's is already claiming that her son is John Rudder's child and entitled to some of his money. And rumour has it that the Armisteads have got their snouts in the trough as well, although that must be one in the eye for Roger.'

'What a mess!'

'Apparently Peter Hodgson remembered his sister telling him all about it. He'd dismissed it as local tittle-tattle, but now he's telling everyone. It was only when he heard John Rudder was at death's door that he remembered. All the excitement makes him the centre of attention and that's jogged his memory too. And I think there's little love lost between him and Liz Rudder. I had to go and see him this morning.' Jed shuddered. 'He's not a nice man, Ro. He's amazingly blinkered and self-righteous.'

'Although he's a priest?' she said mischievously.

'They're not all good guys. Though Neil Clifford is OK.'

'Yes,' Ro said. It was because Neil called her that she had started to put two and two together. And Neil was Phil's friend. And Ro trusted Phil's judgement.

'So let's go over it all,' she suggested. 'Richard Rudder realized his eyesight was threatened, and decided to come to Britain, to be reunited with his brother and check up on some artwork for his research. He knew about Becky of course, because Samantha had been his friend. He emailed his brother but eventually Kevin intercepted the emails in the office, and pretended to be John. When Richard turned up, Kevin lured him to the chapel and killed him, maybe even by accident.'

'And then mutilated his eyes with a knife so that Richard was unidentified as having retinitis pigmentosa.'

'That's the weird thing,' Ro said. 'I can see the logic in everything else, but the mutilation with a knife seems so gratuitous, as if it was done for thrills. Who would ever have looked at the dead man's eyes? It wasn't really necessary to mutilate him. Kevin seems to me like a one-dimensional person and I think his sister was the same. Deeply selfish but not necessarily evil, until he needed to defend his interests. He took what he thought were practical steps and when the game was up he topped himself. But the knifing doesn't square up. It's a different sort of behaviour. That sort of psychopath wouldn't commit suicide.'

'Are you saying there were two of them? Do you think Liz did the knifing? She's completely in the clear at the moment.'

'She's certainly nasty enough as far as I can see. But how could she get away with it without being seen? She's a local fixture. Someone would have noticed her prowling around the headland.'

'So if it wasn't Liz – who was it?'

'I don't know. But my antennae are twitching. Knife crime for kicks wasn't Kevin. But if it wasn't him, who the hell was it?'

A few evenings later, Jed turned up again at Ro's cottage.

'Can I talk to you about something that's bothering me?' he said.

'Why don't you talk to Alison?'

'She's up to her neck in these assessment tests for Year Six. It's a tense time for her. Anyway ...'

'Anyway what?'

'I value your judgement.'

You wouldn't, if you knew what a mess I'd made of my life in the past, Ro thought. But then again, it *was* the past. 'Let's sit on the patio now the weather has turned again. It's lovely and warm out there.'

They took a pot of tea on to the table by the burn, which was more sluggish now as summer drew nearer. Ro had made some home-made biscuits, the first for weeks. Jed sat opposite her, staring westwards into the setting sun.

'Something else interesting has cropped up in all the emails between Richard Rudder and John. The crime people asked me to look at them. From their point of view it's cut and dried and they don't really care about the details.'

'So you're raking over the correspondence between your niece's father and his brother? Crikey, it could only happen in Cumbria where everyone's related to everyone else.'

'Yes, well, they don't know about my connection.' Jed shifted uncomfortably.

'But you want to know the whole story about your beautiful trendy cousin who went off the rails? The one who turned you into a pillar of moral rectitude?'

'Ro ... All right, I suppose I deserve all this. But, yes, I wanted to know.'

'OK so try it on me.'

'Well, I've gone back over a year in the correspondence, to try and work out when it stopped being John who was replying and started to be Kevin. The date of John's stroke helps, but the emails could have been intercepted earlier.'

Jed narrowed his eyes and, for a minute, the other, puritanical Jed Jackson looked out. 'Sam's death was discussed in some detail between the Rudder brothers on email. Richard didn't make contact with his brother for several years after he went to Toronto. He must have been angry with him. But when he got in touch again, just before John's stroke, he emailed John about Becky's birth.'

'So John didn't know about that till then?'

'No. It was a huge shock to John Rudder, I expect. It must have made him want to change his life, find his daughter maybe. And then he had that stroke. Total stress, I suppose. But what is odd, is that Richard Rudder says in his email to John that an older woman went to see Sam after her child was born and they had a huge argument.'

'Crikey. Do you think it was Liz Rudder? Had she found out?'

'No, I don't think so. Liz knew nothing about Becky's birth. Neither did John, remember?'

He took a remarkably big gulp of hot tea. 'There's nothing I can do about it, nor should I … I can't tell Uncle Phil.'

'Can't tell him what? Jed, tell me instead. You've got a hunch, haven't you? Who was it who had the row with Sam?'

'The row that made her do something stupid, like overdose? I can guess. Can't you?'

'No.'

'I think it was her mother. My Aunty Judith.'

Two weeks later, Judith Dixon welcomed Ben warmly, and Ro perhaps a little less warmly, to St Trallen's Place.

'Becky's in the garden,' she said. 'Let's go out there.' She led the way to where Becky was sitting on a swing seat. Ben immediately plonked himself down next to her.

'I'll go and make some tea,' Judith said, turning back to the house. Phil smiled. 'Thank you, love. That would be great. We'll stay with the kids.' He and Ro watched Judith walk briskly up across the immaculate lawn, a compact woman with greying fair hair that shone in a neat bob, weaving between the burgeoning flower beds.

'Judith loves it here,' Phil said. 'She's a great homemaker and we'd never have been able to afford anywhere else like this. Pelliter was an odd choice for us after what happened to Sam, but it worked out for Judith and Becky. And me too.'

Ro nodded. The May sunshine was warmer now, and stronger. It was another beautiful Bank Holiday weekend. But she could tell Phil was unsettled. He looked at her.

'Jed gave me all the copies of the correspondence between Richard and John Rudder. There seems no doubt John Rudder was Becky's father. You heard about what happened, didn't you?'

'Yes, I did.'

'All of it? Including the woman who rowed with Sam and tipped her over the edge? I'm beginning to think Judith knew more than she ever told me. But I can't face her with it.'

Ro looked up at the house where grandmother and granddaughter were deep in conversation.

'I couldn't disturb that, could I?' Phil said, nodding in the direction of his wife and Becky.

'No,' Ro answered.

There was silence between them for a minute. Then Ro said, 'Callie McFadden – the TA from the school – and Faye Armistead have both been talking to anyone who'll listen. I think John Rudder fathered both their children. Three eleven-year-olds. I wonder what made him do that, a sort of sex spree in a short time. But with your daughter it was love, wasn't it? What do you think Sam and John Rudder had in common? The squatter and the financial adviser? It seems odd.'

'I should think they both liked art, and history. Richard Rudder certainly did, and he and his brother were very alike to look at, and in character too. The draft of Richard's PhD thesis is apparently very knowledgeable.'

'About Fraktur Art?'

'It has some real significance for the *Book of St Trallen*, too. He thinks it may be one of the first pieces of Fraktur Art. Or one of the last medieval illuminated manuscripts. The family that lived here had Canadian connections like so many people in the North-West of England. They could even have commissioned it.'

'In which case it's a fake,' Ro said.

'Well, not a deliberate one. But certainly something quite different from what we thought. Hardly West Cumbria's *Book of Hours*. And what a lot of trouble it's caused,' Phil said. 'St Trallen has a lot to answer for.'

But maybe she helped too, Ro thought. And she remembered the bell ringing crazily, that bitterly cold spring evening at the chapel. Divine intervention? But surely not. This Cumbrian sea air was giving her fantasies, and Ro had always been a realist.

This was why she still thought that someone else had been involved in these crimes. Someone who persuaded Becky to get into the car with Kevin. Someone who had absolutely no scruples about knifing people. Someone evil and totally unsuspected. For a second Ro thought of the horrible boy taunting Ben outside Briggs' ice-cream shop. Jonty McFadden. Allegedly Becky's half-brother.

Don't go there, Ro thought. It does your head in. Think of something else.

Phil was looking at her. 'I've got to keep the family together after all this.'

'Of course,' Ro said.

'But Ro ...'

'Don't say anything, Phil.'

Judith's voice reached them across the lawn. 'Tea coming up. With home-baked scones and home-made jam.'

'Fantastic, Grandma!' Becky shouted back.

Phil put his hand over Ro's. 'I wish things were different,' he said.

'But they're not,' Ro whispered.

The summer suddenly blossomed in Cumbria. The events of April and May seemed years ago. The Dodsworth exams had come and gone; Ray Findley was back at the helm; St Mungo's was back on track. Liz Rudder had been replaced by Sheila Findley who had rallied brilliantly. Liz was recuperating somewhere, but no one seemed to mind where as long as it wasn't Pelliter.

In early July, Ro and Suzy were having coffee in Norbridge. 'Molly's looking really well. We seem to see her most weekends, one way and another. She's lost some weight, hasn't she?' Ro said.

'Yes, thank goodness. And she's getting a proper shape now instead of that awful tubular look, hugely exaggerated by shorts and stripy leggings. Her crazy clothes are now in the bin, you'll be glad to hear.'

'And how's the artwork?' Ro asked.

'Great. The mural looks fantastic. The concert is planned for next Thursday, last day of term. The date should have been in your diary for weeks. I hear that Lily Smith and the Mungo Minxes are unmissable. You and Ben are coming, aren't you?'

'Alison would never forgive me if I didn't,' Ro said. 'She's worked like a Trojan at it. The school has been so busy. She seems to be finding time for Jed, though.'

'Yes.' Suzy started laughing. 'And the rumour is, Sheila Findley might not be back for long, Someone saw her in the clinic at the Cumbria Coast Hospital. Where they do IVF!'

'Well good luck to her.' Ro laughed.

'Anyway, talking of unlikely things, here's another. First Saturday in October. Robert and I are getting married. We're having a big party. We're inviting everyone.'

'Oh, Suzy, I'm so glad for you.'

'It'll be at Harvest Festival, one of my favourites. I usually get roped into doing the flowers for it, so I'm going to do two things at once. It will be about a month after Molly has settled into Norbridge High so I think we'll have got our breath back. Becky's going to be a bridesmaid too. No doubt Judith will hand stitch her dress for her from top to toe, and it will be impeccably embroidered.'

Ro smiled. She often wondered if Suzy had picked up any vibes about the way she felt about Phil, but her friend was rattling on.

'We're sort of having the honeymoon in advance. We're taking the kids to Canada in August. Robert's found some second cousins over there who have a cottage on Sharbot Lake; it sounds wonderful. It'll be our last holiday with Jake I suppose. He's taking his exams next year and then he wants a gap year before going to university. Time really flies – they grow up so soon.'

'Gosh. I expect that will happen with Ben one of these days. When he's had his eye operation.' Ro looked worried for a minute. 'It's confirmed for the end of this month.'

'Oh, Ro! Fingers crossed. But at least when he sees you properly, he'll see you looking good. You're a changed woman now from when I met you at St Mungo's.'

Ro's smile faded and she fingered the scar on the side of her face. Suzy had never asked her about it but this time she leant forward. 'The scar isn't bad, Ro. Not when you get used to it.'

'But Ben hasn't really seen it. I'll have to tell him how it happened.'

'Did someone do it to you?'

Ro sipped her coffee. 'Yes. Someone did it.'

'Who?'

'Ben did it.'

'What?'

'After I split up with Ben's father I had a disastrous affair. There's no need for me to go into details, but it wasn't good. We ricocheted from row to row. He wasn't violent, but he was manipulative. Some people enjoy the vulnerability that goes with disability. He's miles away from here, thank God, and he doesn't know where we are.'

'So what happened?'

'Ben heard us fighting one night. He was much feebler then. He must have been really disturbed to get himself out of his cot. Either that or I was too stressed to put the bars up properly. He tumbled down the stairs and I went to catch him. It was probably that fall which started off the cataracts. They can be caused by trauma in children, you know.'

'I wondered about that. I thought cataracts just happened to old people.'

'No. A bad fall and bang to the head can do it. And, of course, Ben couldn't balance properly. I tried to catch him but I had a wine glass in my hand. I always did in those days. The glass smashed into my face. After they bandaged me up I didn't go back to the flat. We ran away and went to my mother's. I swore after that that I would forget about relationships with men, and look after my son.' Ro felt herself squirm with embarrassment, but for the first time in years the idea of having a good friend – a friend who knew everything – appealed to her. *We mustn't outstay our welcome. We mustn't get dependent on people.* The things she had said to Ben. All that had to change now.

'What a terrible thing to happen,' Suzy said. 'But you know, the scar is much less noticeable now. And it rather fits your image as a cop. Which reminds me, there's another thing I don't understand about that awful murder business. I still think something more was bugging Molly and Becky.'

'That weird poltergeist idea?'

'Well, I never got my potato peeler back. But no, not that. The girls still seem to have a secret. It worries me.

Ro nodded. In the last few weeks she had gone over and over Kevin's death. He had murdered Richard Rudder and Brenda Hodgson in order to retain John Rudder's money and prevent either Becky or John's sons inheriting. That much seemed certain. But, like Suzy, Ro was niggled by something too. 'I agree. It isn't all explained. However I look at it, I can't see that Kevin did this by himself, yet I can't see why Liz would help him. She wanted John to die, but Kevin wanted him to stay alive. They wanted opposite things.'

'So if it wasn't Liz, who was it?'

'I don't know. And anyway, it's not my job to find out. I'm quite happy with angry market-traders and rows over dog mess in the park now. I'm a PCSO and I like it that way.'

But even as she said it, Ro knew that she would always wonder who had also been there at the deaths of Richard Rudder and Brenda Hodgson. However she looked at it, she couldn't imagine Kevin with a cat-skinner knife.

Chapter Twenty-eight

'My times are in thy hand: deliver me from the hand of mine enemies, and from them that persecute me.'

Psalm 31:15. Folio 65v. **Les Très Riches Heures du Duc de Berry**

Becky and Molly were at St Mungo's school putting the finishing touches to the mural, when Becky's face whitened and she grabbed her stomach.

'Yow. That really hurt,' she said.

'Too many chips?' Molly asked solicitously. She had recently given up eating fatty food with remarkable ease, but she knew how tempting it could be.

'No, ouch. I'd better get to the loo. Tell Miss MacDonald I'll be back in a minute.'

Molly went on, carefully colouring in the blue sky above the chapel. Becky had been back at school for only a few weeks, but already it seemed as if the horrible mess of the spring was a long time ago. Becky was much better now, and though she went to most places with Judith in the car, she was nearly back to normal. Miss MacDonald had spent a lot of time with the two girls and they'd discussed everything that had happened. It had helped them both a lot to talk about it all.

With the exception of one thing …

'Molly, that's lovely,' Miss MacDonald said, coming back into the art room. Her eyes flickered towards the window. Molly wondered if her new boyfriend Jed, the good-looking policeman, would be picking her up that evening.

'Oh!' Miss MacDonald said. 'There's Jed's car. I'll just pop out and tell him we'll be another few minutes. Just carry on.'

Molly concentrated hard on the two types of blue she wanted for the sky – clear bright blue, and a sort of grey blue for round the edges. You never got just one colour in a west coast sky. The mural was nearly finished and the concert was to be the next week. Molly was proud of it. When she looked up, Becky was there. Her eyes were as big as Molly had ever seen and she clutched her stomach.

'Moll, I think I've started!'

'Have you? Crikey!'

'Yes. It's just a little bit of blood. But I feel really faint and my tummy was agony in there.'

'Have you got a pad thing in your shoe bag just in case?'

'Yes and I've applied it according to the instructions. It feels like a nappy.'

'Better get used to it. What a bugger. I thought I'd be first because I'm so big.'

'You never can tell.' Becky slid down and Molly slithered over to join her on the art-room floor.

'I'll have to tell Gran,' Becky sighed. 'And she'll make a huge fuss.'

'It had to happen some time. So now you're grown up.'

'I feel just the same, except for the tummy ache. It's not what it's cracked up to be. But I thought it might be coming on. The power's been lessening a lot lately.'

Molly nodded. Becky had told her about the bell ringing at the chapel, which she remembered through a haze, and the way other metal objects had disappeared. In return Molly had confided that Jake thought Becky had a poltergeist.

'But it's not so strong now,' Becky said.

'So what will you do if Jonty comes after you again? It saved you twice.'

'I don't know.' Becky frowned. 'You know, me and Jonty could have the same dad. Grandad wanted to tell me, but Grandma was dead against it. She hates talking about my mum these days. It's funny, 'cos before she was always the one who was banging on about my mum getting in with a bad crowd, etcetera, etcetera. Now she doesn't want to talk about it to me, and they're always discussing it. Sometimes they act as if I can't hear what they're saying, when I'm just in the next room.'

'Mine are like that too. Whispering about getting married, as if it's going to be a surprise, like, duh. But do you ever think that we should have told the police we saw Jonty at the Marshes when Miss Hodgson was killed?'

'He'd have killed us, too. Or got Kevin to kill us.'

'So how did Jonty get to know mad bad Kevin?'

'I think he knew Kevin through Mrs Rudder, or through other boys' activities. Kevin had two sons, you know, in all sorts of clubs. I think Jonty was Kevin's accomplice. Miss Hodgson was cut up, remember? Why would Kevin do that to her? But Jonty would have enjoyed doing it. He'd have done it to us.'

'And what about that night, you-know-when? Should you tell about that?'

'No.' Becky shook her head. 'I'm never going to tell them how he got me into that car. He could still come back. He's evil. We might have the same dad, but he's got Callie for a mum.'

'And now Mrs Rudder is in a hospital somewhere screaming mad.' Molly grimaced. 'Remember Jonty's song.' She chanted softly,

'Mr Findley long and spindly
Takes his pills to keep him friendly
Mrs Rudder what an udder
When she screams it makes you shudder
Fat Miss Hodgy pasty podgy
Cut her up and make her splodgy'

'It all came true, didn't it?' Becky whispered. 'But Callie's moving away and Jonty's going with her. With luck we'll never see him again. And next term we'll be at Norbridge High. It's going to be all right. No one will ever know about Jonty if we don't tell them. And now I'm maturing. All that funny business will be over. It's all right, Molly.'

That night Suzy found the potato peeler at the back of the drawer.

How could I possibly have missed it? she thought. How silly we've all been.

Ro arrived at the Cumbria Coast Hospital at eight in the morning on the day after Ben's operation. He had had a general anaesthetic the afternoon before, as was usual with young people having this operation, and had been dopey when she visited that evening. Though there was no reason to think he would be any more vulnerable than any other twelve year old, she had had another sleepless night. She walked through the ward and saw him sitting up already in his chair.

'Mum!'

'How are you, Ben?'

'I'm great! They've just put my drops in but I can see. It's amazing.'

Ro bent down to kiss him.

'Can you get me a mirror, Mum?'

'OK – what for?'

Ben laughed. 'I'll show you.'

Ro went to the nurses' station where they had an old-fashioned hand-held mirror for patients to use when they brushed their hair in bed. She took it over to her son. He held it in front of his eyes and she saw his face grow pink. She had never realized it, but Ben had never seen his own face without his thick glasses. He stared at it.

'So that's me,' he said softly.

'That's right,' she said. 'Not so ugly, really.'

'Rather cool in fact.'

She said nothing more, but she had the strangest sensation on the side of her face. It was as if the scar was somehow shrinking. Guilt, and responsibility, the fear that one day Ben would blame her for everything, seemed to recede. It had been an accident, that was all. And Ben hadn't even noticed her own damaged skin. Maybe I haven't seen my own face properly either, she thought.

'I need my mobile,' Ben said. 'I want to call Becky. I know she was rooting for me.'

Ro felt a slight shiver of uncertainty. She was aware that Ben had been a lot less worried about the operation in the end. 'That's nice,' she said. 'But you didn't expect Becky to – well – bring you good luck or anything like that? Or have a special influence?' She could still remember the way Becky seemed somehow to have brought them all together at her cottage. And the way the bell had rung at the chapel.

Ben guffawed. 'Come off it, Mum. Becky's great, but she's not weird. She's just smart. She got a load of stuff off the web about this op. It sounded like there was nothing to it. She's clever. And quite pretty.' He went pink again.

Ro felt herself smiling, a huge big grin – a smile she hadn't used much for years, embedding itself in her face. The scar crinkled to nothing when she really smiled. Everything was resettling. The world was shifting back on to its axis. Maybe ordinary family life was finally on its way.

That year there was an Indian summer in Norbridge. After a wet August, and a stormy start to September, suddenly there were clear skies. Every morning started with a fresh mist from the sea, which cleared to become a halcyon day. Ben Watson's eye operation had been a great success – and he also got a quad bike, courtesy of Phil Dixon, much to his mother's embarrassment, but she could hardly give it back once it arrived. She suspected her colleague PC Jackson of tipping off his uncle that a quad bike would transform Ben's mobility. But Jed maintained he'd had far too much to think about, walking hand in hand along the shore with Alison MacDonald, talking about art, history, and of course, religion. And sometimes soft furnishings!

The SATs test results for Year Six at St Mungo's had been good. Molly had done better than anyone expected. She and Becky both started at Norbridge High in September.

'You must be pleased,' Jed said to Alison, as they strolled along, eating the last of Briggs' ice cream one particularly warm Monday evening a week into the autumn term. 'How's it going with this new Year Six?'

'It's much calmer. No more special scholarships, though nearly every child last year who wanted to get into Dodsworth got in. I don't think they'll be doing last-minute discounts again. Even Toby Armistead got a place, but for some reason he made a huge fuss about it. He didn't want to go to Dodsworth, and he's gone to Norbridge High instead.'

'And Callie McFadden and Jonty have definitely left Pelliter?' Jed asked.

'Yes, though they must be somewhere local. Norbridge, maybe? Jonty was a really nasty piece of work, you know. I think he was one of those people you sometimes meet who are just evil.'

'But he and Becky had the same father. And there were times when she seemed like a saint.'

'That's funny, isn't it? Jonty was evil, Toby was a sort of everyman, and Becky had some sort of spiritual force, or so Ro believes. The three of them represent everyone. Saint, sinner and Devil. Very Middle Ages. Gets us back to all that medieval art which was behind all this. I gather Richard Rudder's posthumous thesis was an academic triumph.'

'Well, we both like art, don't we?' Jed said comfortably. 'We do have a lot in common, Alison. My mum was saying so only the other day.' Recently Jed had introduced Alison to his parents and vice-versa.

She nodded. 'How are your mum and dad tonight, after yesterday's Sunday lunch reunion with Phil and Judith?'

'OK. They're beginning to talk about asking them over at Christmas, that sort of thing. It would be good if there was some big sort of family occasion to bring us all together. A wedding, or something like that.'

'Yes, maybe that would be nice. Well, one step at a time,' Alison said, and watched her footprints sink into the sand of the Solway shore.

That autumn, Phil Dixon sat a lot on the bench overlooking the sea, and sometimes Ro joined him. Ben's quad bike was kept permanently at St Trallen's farm, in an outbuilding. It was easier for him to ride over the dunes and the headland than down the tracks near Burnside.

Phil said, 'I'm not going to let it drop, Ro. When we finally get over all of this, I'm going to find out what really happened to Samantha. I still don't believe she took her own life just like that. I know Judith was involved. Something happened between them.'

'And you really want to know? Wouldn't it be better just to try and forget it?' Like me, she thought, living in fear of the past catching up with me.

'No, not now. I know why Judith dissuaded me from trying to find out. I want to know the whole truth, however painful. You know what I mean, don't you? I'm running into a crisis, and you're running away from one. But we have running in common.'

'Yes, that's true.' She shivered.

'And you're scared? You don't seem the scared type.'

'I'm not scared any more. It's different here. The job, the house and the uniform help. And the new friends.'

'But you have unfinished business too, don't you? Don't you want to revisit the past?'

'I'm more terrified of the past revisiting me.'

'Oh, Ro, you're safe now. I'll be there for you. I'll do whatever I can to help. And you know I'd like it to be more....'

'But it's fine, Phil. Really. This is perfect for me, now.'

She squeezed his lean brown hand and then withdrew her own. They sat in silence, both frightened of saying more. She knew that the Dixons had settled into an unhappy, undiscussed truce. Phil had chosen for the time being not to ask Judith whether she had ever gone to confront Samantha. And as always where Judith was concerned, it was easier to deal with practicalities.

'We need to get Becky tested for retinitis pigmentosa,' Judith had said. 'But at least we'll know the worst.' She had jumped at the chance of getting immersed again in dealing with hospitals and authorities and societies. Retinitis pigmentosa wasn't the end of the world; there was so much that could be done.

No will of John Rudder's was ever found. Sometimes at night, Becky thought she remembered something about hidden papers, but the memory fluttered away before she could get hold of it. Anyway, life was exciting and busy. Becky spent the long warm autumn weekends with Molly, getting excited about Suzy and Robert's wedding, or going round on her bike alongside Ben's quad.

By the autumn things were changing elsewhere in Pelliter. Father Peter Hodgson had a crisis of faith which coincided with a major leak in the roof of his decrepit house. To the relief of Neil Clifford he sold the place, and his sister's house, and bought a flat in Oxford, where he decided to take a cookery course.

At Norbridge Abbey, the dean had the *Book of St Trallen* re-examined by art experts from London who confirmed that it was one of the oldest and most interesting examples of Fraktur Art, a piece from Ontario painted in the early eighteenth century. It seemed the Victorian family who had owned the land around the ruin of St Trallen's Chapel had acquired the picture on a trip to Canada, rather than on a Grand Tour of the Continent. They had assumed at once that the weeping woman was St Trallen, with the text from Lamentations and the misleading gothic-style script in Latin, very rare for a Fraktur piece, and a sure sign of its vintage. The big illuminated 'Trallen' in Fraktur style could have stood just as easily for the name of a village or family, or even the word for a warbler or weeper.

She weepeth sore in the night, and her tears are on her cheeks:
Among all her lovers she hath none to comfort her:
All her friends have dealt treacherously with her, they are become her
enemies.

Wishful thinking on behalf of the family, the dean had said when he sold the picture and used the proceeds to refurbish the abbey loos.

At St Mungo's school the autumn term was going well under Ray Findley's renewed enthusiasm. Sheila was expecting a baby the following spring. She said the little gnome in their garden was a fertility god, but Ray gave the credit to the specialists at Cumbria Coast Hospital.

On the first Saturday in October, in Tarnfield, the guests had begun to arrive for Robert and Suzy's marriage. The church glowed with flowers. Suzy had had qualms about being married surrounded by cabbages and tins of beans, so the harvest gifts were stocked in the vestry. But the flowers were great, and it had all been organized so quickly that she'd had no need to think about it too much.

'It's a question of don't look down or you'll fall,' she had said to Ro, who was a sort of matron of honour. Ro seemed to be taller, browner and more relaxed, and her figure looked good in the dark-pink dress Molly and Becky had chosen to match their own pretty outfits.

'Well, darling, this is it,' Robert said to her. They were alone in The Briars. Jake and Ben were ushers, and had gone on ahead to get everyone into their seats. Becky and Molly had been taken off in the car by Ro. Robert and Suzy would travel to the church together.

'The girls look good, don't they?' Suzy said. 'I was amazed. Molly was almost glamorous.'

'But not as glamorous as her mother. You should wear flowers in your hair more often.'

'Rob, I hate it when you're gallant.'

'I'm not gallant, Suzy. It was an accurate observation. You look great. I love you.'

'As much as you love my kids?'

'Even more. Come on, the car is here.'

For a moment, Suzy looked nervous.

'Suzy, you can back out of this if you want to. Seriously. It's not too late.'

'Yes it is,' she said.

Robert smiled and waited for her to fiddle with her hair one more time. He'd started doing some research for another book recently. It was going to be a fictional version of the life of St Trallen, one-time virgin miracle worker and later dynamic matron, who, for whatever reasons, was the patron saint of eye doctors. Only that week he had done some more browsing about her, and he had found that she actually had her own saint's day. He hadn't told Suzy yet. St Trallen's Day was the sixth of October. Their anniversary would be her anniversary too.

Robert thought about Ben's eye operation, and about Becky finding out who her father was, Phil finding some closure about his daughter, Ro coming out of her shell, Jed and Alison's burgeoning romance, even Nigel Spencer and his new girlfriend.

And about he and Suzy being so happy.

He thought about what Neil Clifford had said about saints. Great is the mystery of faith! Thank you St Trallen, he said to himself. But then again, it sounded rather silly. A bit like that odd idea about Becky and the poltergeist, which had come to nothing, of course.

'Come on,' Suzy said. 'Stop daydreaming. It's time we got married.'

A few weeks later, when the weather in England had turned and was a seasonally grey wet soup, Liz Rudder sat on her spacious balcony on the Andalusian coast and watched the waves on the beach. It was October, dry, warm, sunny and – most important – it wasn't Pelliter.

She was expecting visitors for half term. The flat was large, marbled floored, with three bedrooms, en-suite bathrooms and a kitchen-diner with a stunning view. It had only cost her two-thirds of the money she received when she sold the High Pelliter house. Despite a lot of fussing about a will made by John and entrusted to that cow Brenda, nothing had turned up, thank goodness, and it was all quite rightfully hers. Things hadn't turned out too badly after all and the rather unpleasant spell in a clinic in London had ensured she could take early retirement on full sick pay.

Her collapse when John died and her brother committed suicide had meant that no one could possibly ask her to do anything upsetting like attending inquests, and her solicitor had done everything, for a handsome fee. It had made it a lot easier to leave Pelliter with a sympathy vote. And she hardly thought about the place, or Kevin either, these days. Her brother had always been unstable. Their father had known that, when he had bribed John to take him on as a partner. Kevin was about to be sacked at the textile mill when John had bailed him out. Liz had heard from her lawyer that Kevin's wife had taken the children away from West Cumbria. It had been common knowledge in Pelliter that for years Kevin's wife had been having an affair with a local businessman. She was now making it clear the children were his, not Kevin's, which didn't surprise Liz. Those children had big hands and ugly large feet. They weren't delicate, dancing types like Liz and Kevin.

And astonishingly, Brenda Hodgson, the ultimate snake in the grass, had left Liz a small legacy. She had probably never got around to changing her will from the days when they had been such good friends.

What a joke! Friends were only friends. But family … Liz had known at once exactly who she was going to spend her money on. So odd, that the boy she had always felt such affection for had been a favourite of Kevin's as well as a blood relation of John's. There was something about Jonty even as a baby which had struck a chord. The wrong chord as it happened, but the underlying recognition was there. Liz liked strong characters. She had always thought she could spot the sort of child who was going to go far.

The doorbell from the downstairs lobby pealed. 'Do come up,' Liz said into the intercom.

It was exciting having people to stay. And young people could be so stimulating. Liz felt much more enthusiastic about them now she wasn't closeted with them day after day.

She got up rather more laboriously than of old, and hobbled over to open the door.

'Is this it? Has it got wi-fi?' The familiar voice of disgruntled youth, but with a new cut glass accent. He would learn to love his holidays in Spain with Aunt Liz.

'Callie. Wonderful to see you both. Do come in. And Jonty, I've always had a soft spot for you, haven't I? I admire a young man who gets what he wants! And don't you look grown up in your Dodsworth tracksuit!'

The wind danced over Liz Rudder's balcony, and on further north, gathering speed and strength. Over the Bay of Biscay it nearly raged itself out, until it frisked up the west coast of Britain, cutting between Ireland and the North-West of England. As the Isle of Man approached, the wind suddenly headed inland in one of those typical fretful offshore breezes and scooped up sand and litter as it headed over the brow of St Trallen's Hill.

'It's parky, mara,' one of the workman said. They had gutted the chapel because the owner's wife had never liked the place and wanted it turned into holiday cottages. They wanted to get the work done before the weather really turned bad. The workman shivered. They were piling up rubbish at the side of the building. The altar table had woodworm and the benches were creaky and old. The big photocopy of the *Book of St Trallen* had been tipped to one side, and was peeling and flapping in the breeze.

The wind tugged at it. Slowly, a thin piece of A4 copy paper detached itself from the back of the frame where it had been tucked. It flapped for a moment, and then blew towards the workman. He made to snatch at it and missed.

'What was that?' his mate said.

'It looked as if it said Last Will and Testament.'

'Nah, don't be ridiculous.'

The paper danced over the gorse bushes. Then was taken up by the breeze and fluttered out over the calm, still, grey Solway Firth.